For my children,
who never gave up on me and make life worth living.

Acknowledgements

I would like to thank the following people for their help and inspiration, their willingness to impart their expertise and finally, for their unfailing encouragement:

Patty Sepull, Roger Lunde, retired FBI Special Agent, Patricia Lunde, Jackie Hoisington, Wendy Lippert, R.N., Richard Aber, Carolyn Comilla, James Schwartz, Cindy Mead, Veterinary Technician, Joanie Hussar, Dennis Smith, Bryan Mayer, Security Officer at ECMC, and of course, my children.

A special thanks to Marcia Zuhlke, a friend of many years who took on the arduous task of reading the first draft and pointing me in the right direction time and again.

Many, many thanks to my sister, Judith Drezek, who rescued me from the purgatory of punctuation. Any mistakes that remain are strictly my own. My retired English teacher sister tried her best, but with me as her student she was faced with a daunting task.

Heartfelt thanks goes to Laura Schwartz, a talented artist, for her painting of a beautiful Newfoundland head study which now graces the cover of this book.

Many thanks to my canine pals, Spike and Libby, whose exuberant personalities served as guideposts for their fictional counterparts.

Lastly, I would like to recognize Ch. Darbydale's All Rise Pouch Cove or "Josh" as both his friends and the entire dog showing world know him. I had the great pleasure of being present to see him win the 2003 National Specialty in Ellicottville, New York. If ever there was a born showman, he was it and to say I was impressed is an understatement. In February 2004, I was glued to the television as I watched Josh win first, the Working Group and then, Best In Show at the Westminster Kennel Club Dog Show, held at Madison Square Garden in New York City. He put on a show that will be forever etched in fanciers' minds and it is this very special dog that inspired my character, Cole.

Although based on some truths and real places, this story is a work of fiction. The first clue is that the shop depicted within these pages is highly successful!

Prologue

He sat alone on the uppermost deck of his three-story mansion on the Connecticut shoreline, barely registering the sound of waves lapping. With a drink in his hand, he waited patiently for the phone call he knew should be coming soon. The night was dark, the cloud cover so complete it totally obscured the moon and the stars. There was a brisk wind, but he was sheltered in the alcove of the deck coming off the master bedroom. The faint glow of a bedside lamp was the only illumination. The temperature was hovering around sixty degrees; the day had been unseasonably warm so he waited in relative comfort, dressed only in slacks and a lightweight wool sweater. The ice tinkled as he raised the heavy, Baccarat crystal glass to his lips and sipped, savoring the taste of the Macallan, a single highland malt scotch that he favored above all others. The smooth, mahogany-colored liquid was mellow and soothing in his mouth, the warmth spreading as he swallowed. His cell phone rang and he picked it up. "Yes?"

"It's Bill Thornton, Mr. Cappellini."

"Aah, Mr. Thornton. You have good news I hope. Tell me, do I own him?"

"No, sir, I'm afraid you don't."

There was a brief hesitation while he absorbed the news, then he asked, "And why is that, Mr. Thornton?"

"She wouldn't sell."

"Did you take the offer to $10,000?"

"Yes, sir, but she wasn't interested."

"Did you bother to take the offer beyond that amount?"

"No, sir, after she refused the ten grand she said she wasn't interested at any price. He wasn't for sale."

"I see," he said, his hand tightening almost imperceptibly on the phone, his mind already at work considering other options. He murmured then, as if speaking to himself, "We may have to employ other methods."

"Sir?"

Snapping quickly back to the conversation at hand, he answered, "Never mind, Mr. Thornton, it doesn't concern you. Where are they showing next?"

"I overheard them talking about the Alexander show. It's a few weeks away."

"Are we entered?"

"Yes, sir. I have several of the dogs in."

"Good. I want you to approach her again at the show. Raise the offer to $25,000 and if she still refuses to sell, then I want you to give her carte blanche."

"Sir?"

"Carte blanche, Mr. Thornton, carte blanche. She can name her own price."

"Sir, I understand what you're saying, I just don't think it'll do any good."

"Mr. Thornton," he said, a hint of annoyance creeping into his voice, "I don't pay you to think. I pay you to do exactly as I tell you and I'm telling you to make the offer at the next show. Is that understood?"

Thornton, knowing he'd crossed the line and provoked his employer, was quick to correct his mistake. "Yes, sir,

I apologize for questioning your instructions. I'll certainly do as you say. Is that all, sir?"

"Yes, for now. Keep me informed, Mr. Thornton."

"Yes, sir. Good night, Mr. Cappellini."

He turned off his cell phone and took another drink, this time a full mouthful, not a sip, the difference between the two the only outward sign of his agitation. Inwardly, his stomach had clenched and his heart rate had accelerated. Pausing to take several deep breaths to calm himself, he clicked the cell phone back on and punched in the pre-programmed number. The phone on the other end rang only once before it was picked up.

"Jasper here."

"Jasper, it's Mr. Cappellini."

"Yes, sir. What can I do for you?"

"I'm going to need your services right away."

"All right. When would you like to meet?"

"Come to my office tomorrow afternoon at 4:00. I'll give you the specifics then."

"Yes, sir, I'll be there."

He had one more call to make and this one was overseas. He switched to a secure landline, the one he used for high-level business dealings, and again punched in a pre-programmed number. After a few moments he heard the phone ringing in what he knew was a small villa in the south of France sitting on the Mediterranean shore, specifically, in the study of a man whose services he had used on more than one occasion. Cappellini waited impatiently for the phone to be picked up.

"Hello?" the man answered in a voice carrying a heavy German accent.

"Wilhelm, it's Vincent Cappellini."

"Oh, Mr. Cappellini. It is good to hear from you." Wilhelm Schmidt put down the book he'd been reading and focused all his attention on the phone call, his face breaking into a sly smile. "How are you?"

"I'm fine, Wilhelm, couldn't be better. And yourself? I trust you've been well?"

"Very well, thank you. What can I do for you?"

"If you're available, I have a job for you."

"As it so happens, I am free at the moment. What would you like me to do?" Wilhelm settled his great bulk into an oversized wing-backed chair in anticipation of the conversation that was to follow. He was somewhere in his early fifties, still built like a weight lifter and strong as an ox. His hair was cut in a military brush cut, the color a steely gray. His face was craggy and bore the scars of previous battles, his nose large and rather crooked, no doubt from being broken countless times. His eyes were light blue, cold and calculating, somewhat menacing even now as he looked out toward the sea. His unoccupied hand, large with blunt fingers, was resting on his beefy thigh, relaxed at the moment, but capable of exerting tremendous pressure. He possessed a razor-sharp mind and people who underestimated his abilities in the intellect department were soon brought up short. He was a man skillful in many things and his talents had earned him a very comfortable living.

Cappellini, speaking cautiously, continued. Although Wilhelm's phone was also supposed to be secure, he was taking no chances. "I need you to find something for me. The pertinent information and my exact requirements will be sent to you tomorrow morning via FedEx International. The packet should be in your hands no later than two days from now. Your best bet to find what I require is probably in the Netherlands; there are several good places there that should be able to supply what I'm looking for. If for some reason they can't, then there are locations in Portugal and England that are possibilities and I'm sure you must be familiar with some of them."

"Yes, of course. No need for further explanations; I understand completely."

"Good. When you find what I need, take photos, a lot of them. I want every angle possible, Wilhelm, and gather every scrap of information you can get. Then send everything to me using the same service except use their Next Flight plan. That way I'll have the packet in twenty-four hours. I'll get back to you as soon as I've examined it and if I like what I see, I'll give you more instructions at that time."

"You are in a hurry, Mr. Cappellini?"

"Yes, Wilhelm, very much so."

"What about cost?"

"Whatever it takes. I'll leave that in your capable hands. You can expect your usual fee plus a $10,000 bonus if you're able to deliver within two weeks."

"You are most generous, sir. I will start the search as soon as I have your information. I will try my best to meet your deadline."

"I know you will, Wilhelm, and as usual my name is not to be brought into the negotiations, at least for the time being."

"Of course, sir. I deal always with discretion. Until we talk again. Goodbye, Mr. Cappellini."

"Goodbye, Wilhelm, and good hunting."

He ended the connection and rose from his chair, walking over to the railing. He was average in height for a man, around 5'11", and his body was well muscled from endless hours in a gym, but his physique was not bulky. He was instead, slender and rangy like a professional rodeo rider, although he would most probably take exception to being compared to the like. He was in his mid fifties and had but a touch of gray in his thick, wavy, black hair. He had the olive complexion bestowed upon those of his ethnic background and his still handsome face was one of classic Roman good looks. His dark brown eyes were expressive, but contained none of the warmth their rich color hinted at. His full lips were most often pressed into a hard line with not a trace of softness and if he did have occasion to smile, it smacked of cynicism. He carried himself with authority and the aura surrounding him radiated power and money.

He looked out toward the water, unable to distinguish where the sky ended and it began, the darkness absolute. Bracing his hands against the smooth wood, he leaned into it, letting the wind whip around his body in much the same way his thoughts were swirling around in his head. He thought about the dog. He'd *been* thinking about the dog for several months now, ever since Thornton had brought him to his attention. He was a magnificent specimen and he knew he had to possess him. He'd owned many top show dogs over the years, but this one was special, this one was unique. He'd known it the minute he'd laid eyes on him.

He'd gone to the show at Thornton's urging and when he had seen the dog in the ring it had taken every bit of his ironclad willpower not to approach the woman himself right then and there. He'd been so overcome by the sheer beauty and essence of the dog that he'd felt weak in the knees. As he'd watched him move around the ring, he'd been awestruck by the perfection in movement the dog exhibited. It looked like he floated on air, his gait so effortless, but at the same time his strength and power had been evident. When the woman had put him into his stack, the standing pose the dogs struck in the ring, it was as if the dog had become an exquisite statue sculpted by a master's hand. The dog was truly a living, breathing work of art and had consumed his thoughts ever since. He simply had to have him and he would. That was a given. He always got what he wanted no matter what it took to achieve the final result, and to say he very much wanted that one particular dog was an understatement of gigantic proportions.

Chapter One

The early morning sun gently caressed her cheek as she stirred to wakefulness. She drowsily stretched her limbs, luxuriating in the feel of silk sheets against her body. A soft breeze stirred the bedroom curtains and she could hear birds singing in the distance. She slowly opened her sleepy eyes to greet the day and...

"Oooomph, what the hell?! Oh, God, Cole, you've got to stop doing this. You're going to kill me." As Emma struggled to breathe under the weight of her 150-pound Newfoundland, the dream faded and reality broke through. Not in thirty some years had she awakened to sunshine on her face. Cripe, it was always dark at five o'clock in the morning. Not one ray of sunshine had ever broken through at that time of the day. There weren't any birds singing either, they were all smart enough to still be asleep. As for the silk sheets, what the hell were those? The most luxurious sheets Emma had ever had were cotton and an even better type of cotton, flannel! But in spite of the ungodliness of the early hour, she didn't begrudge starting her day at that time. There was simply too much to do and no time to waste lollygagging in bed till seven or eight. Luckily, Emma was one of those fortunate people who only needed five or six

1

hours of sleep to be bright and chipper the next day, or at the very least, functional.

"Okay, big boy, time to roll off before you crush my rib cage. You don't want me to have to breathe through a tube, do you?" Cole looked down at Emma, giving her what would be a doggy smile and proceeded to give her face a thorough licking before rising and jumping off the bed.

"Thanks for the wash, buddy. Now let's get going." Wiping the remains of Cole's affection from her face with the sleeve of her pajamas, Emma quickly discarded her pajama bottoms, threw on her jeans, pulled a sweatshirt on over her head, shoved her bare feet into her sneakers, which were always at the ready by the side of her bed, and took Cole out to his kennel area so he could take care of his bodily needs. She didn't even own a bathrobe or slippers. Why waste money on clothes you'll never wear. When you hit the ground running so to speak, you needed the right gear.

Emma went back into the house and took care of her own business. It's a wonder her bladder hadn't burst when Cole had pounced on her like that. After all, she wasn't exactly a spring chicken anymore and age did tend to weaken the vital organs a bit especially when they were full to overflowing. Emma considered it a positive sign that she'd been able to retain her water, so to speak, after Cole's full body slam and a testimonial to the fact that she still had pretty good control over her not quite so youthful body. She figured her old "bod" could still serve her well, at least for another few days.

At the age of fifty-five, she still maintained a vigorous exercise schedule and while she didn't ignore the aging process, she didn't give in or cater to it either; that would have been a complete waste of energy as far as she was concerned. Emma thanked the good Lord daily for Leslie Sansone and the *Walk Away the Pounds* videos, which kept her to a regiment of between twenty-one and twenty-four miles of exercise a week.

Cole was ready to come back in and let Emma know with a deep bark. He was a beautiful Newfoundland with a magnificent head and a strong, powerful body. His eyes were a deep, dark brown and his coat, a shiny, jet black. He was sixteen months of age and after very limited showing had recently won his show championship.

Cole had won his championship in just five shows with three majors and two Best of Breeds, not an easy accomplishment considering what it took to become a champion with the American Kennel Club (AKC). An AKC show championship was based on points won during conformation competition, the amount of points determined by the number of dogs in each sex competing that day. The dog/point ratio was different for each breed and was regulated yearly by the AKC. The total number of points needed by every dog, no matter what the breed, was fifteen including two major wins of at least three points each awarded under two different judges.

The fact that Cole had attained his championship in just five shows was remarkable in itself, much less that two of his major wins were for four points each. Add to that his winning Best of Breed from the classes not once, but twice, and you've got a super dog in the making. Fanciers were understandably impressed and his performance in the ring indicated to everyone that he would be a forceful presence in future competition. Cole was very intelligent, full of personality, a natural talent in the show ring, and most importantly, completely devoted to Emma.

Now, having been so summoned, Emma brought Cole back into the house and gave him his breakfast, just a quick snack of a couple dog biscuits and water. How's that for a so-called "breakfast of champions"? There wasn't much culinary value to it, but the biscuits were good for his teeth and besides, Cole had to be exercised a little later and couldn't do it on a full stomach.

Emma changed into her workout clothes, pushed the coffee table out of the way, and got under way with her four-mile exercise. Cole picked a spot on the floor that was out of range of Emma's side steps and kicks and lay down to watch with a look of approval. He knew that she knew she'd better be in shape if she wanted to keep up with *him* in the show ring. One hour later, sweaty but invigorated, Emma hit the shower, dressed and ate her breakfast.

She generally ate a light meal, usually cereal and milk, a little juice. She had always thought of breakfast as a meal to get through quickly, so she could get on with the rest of her day. When the children, who were now all grown and on their own, had wanted pancakes for breakfast, Emma had literally cringed as if experiencing a physical blow and had tried to talk them out of it. It had usually been a no-go and she'd had to make the damn things. The kids, interested only in appeasing their appetites and taste buds, had no idea of the havoc they'd been wreaking with Emma's mindset. Cripe, hadn't they realized how much time it took to make the stupid things? She'd wanted to be moving, cleaning, scrubbing, training, or baking; anything, but standing at the stove making breakfast for an hour or more. Lord, the sacrifices a mother has to make for the good of her children. It was a wonder she was still alive to talk about it.

After the breakfast dishes were cleaned up and the house tidied, the morning agenda continued with Cole's exercise, commonly called roading in the dog world. It was designed to keep him in top condition for the show ring. There were several methods used, but the overall objective was to have the dog run at a controlled pace for a number of predetermined miles to build and tone his musculature. Any type of serious roading however, was done only after the dog was at least one year of age.

Emma loaded Cole and her bike into her red Ford Explorer and drove to the county park, which was about two miles down the road. Once there, she parked, unloaded, and took off with Cole trotting next to the bike on a six-mile jaunt. She went out a distance of three miles and then turned around and came back on the same route to make up the other three.

Emma kept Cole in the shoulder of the road while she stayed on the blacktop with the bike. Constantly watching for any debris that might injure the dog, Emma never really relaxed, or more correctly, she tried her damnedest to keep her mind on the here and now. She'd learned from past experience that if she did let her attention wander, it wasn't Cole who was endangered, it was herself. If Cole saw an opening when her thoughts were elsewhere, he'd take full advantage and pull some high jinks, at Emma's expense naturally.

His favorite trick, when he sensed she was daydreaming, was to stop dead in his tracks and pull her off the bike. He would then gaze upon her, oh, so innocently, as she sat in the gravel on the side of the road, her rear end wounded and her pride injured. Emma knew only too well that behind that angelic look and dignified exterior, Cole was really having himself a good belly laugh and if he could have would've shouted, "Gotcha!"

Sometimes it was a literal and figurative pain in the ass to have a dog that was this intelligent. It was times like these when you might think it would be better to have a dog that didn't possess so much gray matter, but then where would the challenge be to prove who was the smarter of the two. Unfortunately for Emma, Cole could usually out maneuver her if given the opportunity, but if nothing else, she was persistent, so she kept right on trying. Today however, mankind had been the victor. The run had gone smoothly and Emma had kept both her butt and her pride safely ensconced on the bike the entire time. Before long, they were back home and unloading.

* * * *

The cottage that Emma and Cole shared was in a clearing in the woods about two hundred yards back in from the road in a very small town called Glenwood, located in the western region of New York State. They lived about twenty miles south of Buffalo in an area that was considered the Snow Belt and to prove it, there was a ski resort named Kissing Bridge about a mile or so from the house. The countryside was beautiful with forests of evergreen and deciduous trees and meandering creeks. The land was rolling with hills and valleys and picturesque panoramas.

On a clear day, when standing atop one of the many hills, you could see the buildings in downtown Buffalo, if you so chose. Fact is, most people didn't. They lived out here to be away from the city so that particular sight didn't exactly thrill them. They were more likely to turn their backs on the Buffalo skyline and go crazy over the view encompassing the area they lived in. Homeowners living on the high hilltops would concede however, that the distant light show the city put on at night was arresting.

The only detriment that Emma saw to the area was the snow, the many, many, many feet of snow that blanketed the region over the course of a winter. How big a detriment for Emma? Huge, gigantic, gargantuan, and then some. She absolutely hated the flaky stuff. If the city of Buffalo was to receive, let's say, seven inches of snow, the outlying areas, especially those to the south of the city, which was where Emma lived, more times than not, would get close to double that or more. In Emma's mind, the copious amount of snow she had to deal with each winter was the price she paid for living in this beautiful countryside and damn, if she didn't have to pay year after year after...

Not that the people and road crews weren't prepared to deal with it. They were and efficiently so. The residents armed themselves with shovels, snow blowers, four-wheel drive vehicles, plows, and tire chains. They kept themselves informed on weather conditions from any number of sources: radio, television, computer web sites, and a telephone weather line. Then they made their plans accordingly and coped with living in "ski country".

The road crews, the first line of defense, were equipped to move tons of snow overnight and did so on a regular basis. It was to Emma's consternation that it was necessary to do so with such regularity. If the damn white stuff would just stop falling once in a while, then everybody could take a break. Even if it was for only one year, Emma thought, it'd be great if the region had, oh, just one or two inches of snow at Christmas and that would be it for the rest of the season. Yeah, right, in your dreams, Emma! Hell, that fantasy had to be a direct result of overindulging in heavy drugs! Get real, old girl. Winter in Glenwood was one freakin' snowflake after another and it wasn't about to change.

Nevertheless, it took blizzard conditions to close roads and then it usually only affected those in exposed areas. Once the roads were cleared, the crews kept them salted, sometimes working non-stop for twenty-four hour periods or longer, depending on how long a storm continued. People in Western New York didn't let a little thing like snow stop them from carrying on their everyday activities and only the severest of conditions closed schools and shut down businesses.

A large percentage of the population actually loved the snow and enjoyed the many winter sports fanatically. Skiing, snowboarding, and snowmobiling were big business in the area. Emma thought they were all out of their ever-loving minds, but she was willing to overlook their depravity.

7

The people who lived in those counties, and that would be all of Western New York, which were affected by "Lake Effect Snow" or the dreaded "LES" as it was commonly referred to, were a hearty group and Emma was happy to count herself among them, not withstanding her belief that the snow was the work of the devil himself. So, would she consider moving from the area? No way in hell. She figured you had to take the good with the bad and being as that the good far outweighed the bad, she would remain in Glenwood for the duration. The duration of what she wasn't quite sure, but she would be there.

* * * *

The cottage, so-called because Emma thought it sounded just so darn cute, was a cozy, two bedroom, one level house sided with shake cedar shingles and trimmed out in cranberry. There was a porch on the front and one side with a deck that continued on from the porch and extended across the back of the house. There was plenty of room for an eating area with a table and chairs and a grill for cooking. Lounge chairs were plentiful and Emma's favorite wicker rocking chair was there too, just in case she had time to make use of it. Late spring through fall, flowers of all kinds adorned the porch and deck with baskets of fuchsia hanging everywhere there was room to attract hummingbirds, Emma's favorite.

The landscaping was informal making use of the pines, maples, and birch that nature had provided. Flowerbeds butted up to the deck and porch and surrounded some of the trees. There was a large square flower garden used for cutting in an open area off to one side that received full sun whenever the sun decided to show its face, which often times was elusive even in the summer months. Emma had made use of the larger rocks that were in the creek that crossed her property and had built a stone wall along one of the tree lines reminiscent of the ones in the New England states. She had birdhouses and feeders scattered about and marveled at the number of different birds, finches, orioles, bluebirds, chickadees, and doves among them, that were attracted to her yard. There was plenty of open space for Cole to romp and a swing hung in one of the large maples for her granddaughter to use.

Inside, the living room and kitchen enjoyed an open floor plan with the walls done in tongue and groove knotty pine. The floors were hardwood throughout the house and stained to a golden hue with brightly colored area rugs placed in strategic spots. There was a large fieldstone fireplace on the outside end wall of the living room, its antique oak mantle covered with candles and family pictures. The front wall that connected both rooms was graced with four double-hung windows that extended almost from floor to ceiling, with the front door sitting exactly in the middle. Emma's antique furniture and over-stuffed sofa and chairs were nestled into any space that could accommodate them and gave the place a slightly jumbled, but cozy atmosphere. There was a built-in bookcase jammed with books of every size and subject matter from cooking, to biographies, to love stories, to antique collecting, and to Emma's favorite, mysteries. There were shelves on the walls to hold even more books, teddy bears and antique pieces that Emma had collected over the years.

Off the kitchen was the mudroom, an absolute necessity when you lived in the woods *and* had a dog the size of a small bear. It had an outside door on the back wall, which opened directly onto the deck. Two windows on the outer wall made it bright and a well-placed sink saved the kitchen from a lot of dirty hands. There was a built-in closet made of planked pine and all the foul weather gear and dog leashes and collars were stored there for easy access. The inside wall had a door to the basement, which accommodated moving a dirty, wet dog from the outside to the inside, saving the rest of the house from muddy paws and head to tail doggy shakes that sent water flying in all directions.

There was a washer and dryer in the basement along with storage space and a grooming area for Cole, which included a bathtub at waist height. Emma had had the contractor build a ramp up to the tub and then a retractable ramp into the tub, so that giving Cole a bath would not be a problem for a 120-pound woman who happened to own a 150-pound dog.

Off the living room-kitchen area were the two bedrooms and the bathroom. The master bedroom, done in blues and purples, was alight with sunshine from the two large windows on the outside walls. When Emma had had the house built she'd put in as many windows as she could to capture every ray of sun when it appeared. In this area of New York, where there were too many gray days to even count, the appearance of that golden orb was reason to celebrate and to soak in as much as you could for as long as you could.

An antique sleigh bed with a colorful, handmade quilt graced the middle of the room and primitive cupboards made of oak served as dressers. There was a flat-topped steamer trunk at the foot of the bed that held extra blankets and linens. An old pressed-back chair that sat in one of the corners served as home for two of Emma's favorite bears. There was an oak commode on the side of the bed with a brass lamp and a pitcher of fresh flowers. The flowers were a constant, year-round fixture, even when Emma had to buy them at the grocery store in the dead of winter. Flowers were one of her many passions and what better way to start the day than to be surrounded with the fragrance given off by the bursting blooms, especially at five o'clock in the morning.

The second bedroom was the guest room and had been done in pinks and purples since Emma's granddaughter was the most frequent visitor and those were her favorite colors. The antique brass bed was covered with a down comforter and lots and lots of pillows that had been known to sail through the air during pillow fights. A cherry cupboard served as a dresser and an old-fashioned coat rack stood in the corner ready to receive the varied offerings the occupant of the room bestowed upon it. There were two shelves on the walls holding treasures past and present with a touch of the whimsical meant to delight a small child. An antique chair made of cherry graced the corner next to the bed and held a collection of stuffed toys that were made to be cuddled and hugged. A large heirloom basket, darkened to almost black with age, stood on the floor at the foot of the bed filled with puzzles and books, and one or two of Cole's squeaky toys that Emma hadn't been able to find since the last time her granddaughter had visited.

The bathroom was.... a bathroom. What more could you say about it other than it was average size and had all the amenities? There was a window, of course, a place to hang towels, a vanity, a double mirror, which at this stage of the game wasn't the blessing it had once been, and as far as Emma was concerned it was still the worst room in the house to clean. She couldn't figure out why the hell anyone would want these gigantic new houses that were being built with three, four, and five bathrooms. Damn, were these women masochists or what? Emma supposed though, that if you could afford a house with five bathrooms, then you could afford to pay someone to clean them. Pity the poor woman hired to do just that. God, she was living Emma's worst nightmare!

Chapter Two

"Morning guys, how you doing?" Joanie called as Emma and Cole entered the shop. It was just after 10:00 when the twosome walked through the door.

"Great! We're in the pink. Everything's coming up roses and all's right with the world."

Joanie gave her friend a measuring look, then rolled her eyes. "Oh, God, you've been watching old movies again, haven't you?"

"Yeah, I watched two last night. How'd you know?"

"Simple, I just listened to what came out of your mouth. You aren't going to break out in song and dance today, are you?"

"I can't promise anything, but I'll try to hold myself back out of respect for you and the customers."

"Well, try real hard 'cause when you dance, wait, let me correct that to… when you *attempt* to dance, you look more like Jim Carrey than Ginger Rogers."

"Hey, at least I have joie de vie!"

"I'll give you joie de vie. Don't dance and I forbid you to sing."

"Don't worry about the singing, I only do that in the shower where nobody can hear me."

"Well, I've heard you. Don't sing!"

"You don't count; you're my friend. I'm supposed to be able to do anything around you."

"Not that, you're god-awful! Don't sing!"

"Can I hum?"

"If you have to. I suppose I could put up with that."

"Great! And don't be surprised if I skip a time or two. I've got all this music playing in my head."

"Just give me fair warning so I can prepare myself. Maybe if I'm quick enough I can turn away in time so I don't have to witness it."

"Sometimes I don't know when I'm going to do it. It just kind of comes over me. Like, boom, it's there. But I'll try to anticipate the feeling and warn you off."

"Thanks, I'd really appreciate it. It's not a pretty thing when you skip."

"It's still better than when *you* dance."

"What do you mean?"

"Joanie, your little dances are beyond ugly. Actually, they defy description and should be banned from the civilized world."

"That's not true, they're just innovative."

"Innovative, my ass."

"All right, so we both suck at dancing. At least I can sing."

"If you say so."

"What do you mean by that?"

"I'm not going there. This discussion is closed, over and out… Let's move on to a safer topic. What's new with you?"

"Same old, same old, except goofy Tank tried to run a groundhog into his burrow this morning and nearly got himself stuck in the damn hole for what's left of his miserable little life." Joanie shook her head, laughing at how ridiculous he had looked. "I had to pull him out. He was wedged in so tight he couldn't move. Crazy-ass dog."

At that moment, Tank, a Parson Russell Terrier, came out from behind the counter not looking any the worse for wear from his morning adventure. He was smooth coated, compact, and very muscularly built for a small dog. He was predominately white with a brown patch around one eye and a spot on one side. He had good head type and a personality to die for, a trait that could sometimes be elusive in this breed if the dogs weren't properly socialized while still puppies. At fourteen months of age, Joanie had put one leg of an obedience title on him and was working on the second.

The achievement of an obedience title with the AKC was easier for some breeds than others. Certain breeds were naturally more inclined to learn quickly and some would do anything to please their trainers. Other breeds were more independent thinkers and resisted being told what to do, while still others were just plain stubborn. At any rate, in order to win an AKC obedience title, the first of which was Companion Dog (CD), the dog had to obtain a qualifying score in three different AKC licensed dog show trials under three different judges. A qualifying score was earned by the dog performing various commands correctly, then being awarded points for each. He had to receive more than 50% of the points available for each exercise with a total score of not less than 170. Each qualifying score achieved toward the title was called a leg.

Being that Tank was a combination of intelligence, stubbornness, and sometimes spawn of the devil, you never knew what was going to happen when he competed. Often times when he was in the ring, he would outsmart not only Joanie, but himself as well. Regardless, he always had a great time, even if Joanie couldn't say the same.

The two dogs greeted each other, then raced to the back of the shop where they chased each other around the table for several minutes before they lay down with Tank getting on top of Cole. They were still for all of two seconds before the tussling and wrestling began. The squeaky toys were soon snatched out of their box and tossed around, the back room quickly impersonating a child's messy playpen.

Joanie Davis was Emma's friend of many years and business partner in their gift shop, The Whistling Thistle. They had met over twenty years ago at a local dog show and had shared their love of dogs and competition ever since. They'd also found they both loved antiques and primitive country art and that they'd each had a dream of owning their own shop. So ten years ago, with the friendship well established, the girls had made their dreams a reality and opened The Whistling Thistle.

The two had settled on that name one night after they'd had a few too many glasses of wine and neither one of them could say it. Hell, sometimes they couldn't say it when they were completely sober. That was a known fact; they'd been practicing answering the phone with it and couldn't get it out about a third of the time. They'd been just drunk enough that night to think it was kind of neat to have a name you couldn't say sometimes and had filled out the business papers to make it official. This turned out to be but one example of the wacky, insane criteria Emma and Joanie followed when making an important business decision and believe it or not, they all somehow worked out. Thankfully for all concerned, they had never had to make a mission statement. Their first problem with such a statement, and there would have been many as anyone who knew the two would have attested to, would have been to figure out what the hell it even was. Anyway, the name stuck and people never did forget it even if they couldn't say it.

The shop was at the bottom of the hill below Emma's house, so all she had to do was walk down everyday, something she really appreciated in the winter months when storms were raging. Emma was a notoriously bad driver in a snowstorm and those who had heard of her many misadventures were thankful when she was off the road at such times. Her lack of winter driving skills was probably one of the main reasons she detested the snow so much, that and the fact she hated to be cold. Joanie lived about a mile down the road, so her commute was almost non-existent and she'd been known to walk the distance occasionally.

The shop was housed in a wooden clapboard building, which was painted dove gray with dark plum trim. A porch ran along the front of the building and was festooned with decorative flags at every support column. Grapevine and tiny white lights encircled the windows and the door was embellished with a seasonal wreath. The walls of the porch were decorated with antiques and primitive artwork and scattered about to complete the tableau were rockers, antique commodes, rusted watering cans, and baskets of all sizes.

Inside, the store was a smorgasbord of wonderful sights and smells. The primitive country flavor was carried throughout, from furniture, to linens, to candles, to pottery, to cookbooks, to, well, everything. The hardwood floors and the cedar walls enhanced the country feeling and made the primitive art a natural to display. The windows were treated with swags in natural colored muslin edged in Irish lace and draped with grapevine. There was an electric candle on each windowsill, which shared space with various collectibles and antiques that were for sale. The store was always fully stocked and the two friends displayed everything perfectly, or at least they thought so and thus far they hadn't had any complaints.

They made all the primitive wood decorations and the finished product showcased their creativity and skill working with tools usually handled by men and outside the normal domain of most women. Emma, as a rule, made up the patterns and traced out the wood, while Joanie did all the cutting. She was a whiz with a band saw. Both girls painted and stained, drilled and screwed.

Between the two of them they'd had only one injury to date and that had been Joanie's. She'd drilled her finger instead of the screw she was sinking into a piece of wood because as usual, she was talking to a customer and not paying attention to what she was doing. Luckily she realized, maybe due to the pain, what had happened before she went completely through her finger. At any rate, she'd healed nicely and still had full use of the digit as demonstrated quite effectively when she occasionally gave Emma "the finger" to drive home a point. Nevertheless, together, they could pound out a lot of work, a blessing when fall and winter rolled around because that was their busiest time of the year.

"Do we have anything special going on today?" Emma asked.

"No, not really," Joanie answered, "but we have to start thinking about getting another display piece from the Antique Barn. That new shipment of candles we ordered will be here in a few weeks and we've got to figure out where everything's going to go."

"Yeah, you're right. Well…we could get Tammy to watch the shop on Saturday and you and I could run down to Great Valley and check out what they have. Maybe after we're done we could stop in at the Hearthmoor and see Sally."

"Sounds good. I think that'll work 'cause Sam and the boys won't be home and I wouldn't have to worry about getting dinner." Joanie cast a quick glance toward the back room when the girls heard a loud thump, which turned out to be Cole sliding sideways into a cabinet while in pursuit of Tank. Sam was Joanie's husband and a recently retired FBI Special Agent. The girls had never had a bad check passed in all the years they'd been in business and figured that was the reason.

"All right then, I'll call Tammy later and set it up…. Oh, hi, Mrs. Foster. How are you today?" Emma asked as she greeted the elderly woman who had just entered the shop.

"Fine, fine, and how is everyone here?" The older woman was impeccably dressed and coiffed and just oozed money and more money.

"We're just great," Emma answered. "Is there anything in particular you're looking for today?"

"No, not especially. I'm just going to stroll around and see what's new. I'll let you know if I need any help."

"Okay, give a shout if you need one of us."

While Mrs. Foster meandered around the shop, Emma and Joanie busied themselves with the various tasks that running a shop involved. An hour later they were deep into inventory on the computer when their customer made her way back to the cash register, her arms loaded with merchandise.

She had a beautiful antiqued basket filled with greeting cards and a small black-framed picture, wind chimes, dishtowels and matching dishcloths, two cookbooks and recipe cards, a spatter-wear bowl loaded with different scented votives and tarts, a teddy bear, and a black, tin crow. The girls were amazed she could carry it all.

"Well, ladies, I think this will do it for now. I really don't know where I'm going to put all these wonderful things, but I love every one of them and I'll just have to find room somewhere. I'm sure if I look hard enough I'll find the perfect spot for everything. I'm not one of these women, and I bet you get a lot of them, who won't buy something simply because they don't know where they'd put it. They must drive you crazy. I've seen it myself when I've been in here. They're practically drooling over a particular piece, but won't buy it because they can't come up with a spot to put it. You can always find room, even if you throw something else out or put something away for a while or rearrange your wall or, or, well, you know what I mean. I don't have to tell you. Variety *is* the spice of life, right? Bunch of old stick in the muds is what they are."

Emma suppressed a giggle and refrained from commenting, but couldn't hide a huge grin as she rang up the sale and asked Mrs. Foster if she'd like some help carrying her bags out to the car.

"That would be lovely, Emma. Is Cole here? I didn't see him."

"Yep, he's in the back with Tank. Just a minute." Emma called Cole and the big dog came lumbering out with Tank following behind.

"Cole, would you help Mrs. Foster with her bags?" On a hand signal from Emma, Cole went over to where Mrs. Foster stood and took the handles of her two bags in his mouth. He picked them up and followed her out of the shop to her car, depositing them in the back seat when she opened the door.

"Cole, you're such a good boy. Here you go, sweetie." She handed him a dog biscuit, which she always carried, and he carefully took it from her. He immediately inhaled the tasty morsel and then walked back with her to the shop. Cole scooted inside when Mrs. Foster opened the door and she shouted out her thanks and goodbyes before she left.

"God, you got to love her," Emma said and went back to straightening out the shelves she had escaped to when the computer had started to make her crazy. She could only work on it for so long before her eyes refused to focus and she got dizzy.

Five or six people entered the shop on the heels of Mrs. Foster's leaving and the girls, recognizing three of them as regular customers, launched into conversation with all of them. In addition, the customers knew each other and a lively discussion resulted with everybody catching up on events in everyone's lives. The three regulars eventually dispersed and one of the other women, who had arrived at the shop at the same time as everyone else, came up to the counter to pay for her purchases. She had a 12 oz. bottle of hand lotion, a new line the girls had just recently added to the shop, which was doing very well, and two packages of gourmet coffee, Cinnamon Hazelnut and Blueberry Crème. While Joanie rang her up and Emma wrapped and bagged, the woman spoke to both of them.

"You have a lovely shop. There are so many beautiful things."

"Thank you," Emma replied. "We try to fill the shop with unique items, things you can't find everywhere else."

"Well, you've certainly done a wonderful job."

"Thanks," Joanie said.

"Oh, look at the dogs! Are they yours?" Cole and Tank had come out from the back room intending to beg a treat from the girls. They stood quietly behind the counter waiting for Emma and Joanie to give them their full attention.

"Yes," Emma answered. "Cole, the Newfie, is mine and Tank belongs to Joanie."

"What breed of dog is Tank? A Parson Russell?"

"Yes, and a very engaging one," Joanie beamed while digging into the crock they used for dog biscuits and giving one to each of the dogs.

"Well, they're both gorgeous. Are they just pets?"

"No, although they are our bosom buddies, we do show them."

"In confirmation, obedience?"

"Cole is shown in the breed ring and Joanie is getting an obedience title on Tank. Do you show?"

"I used to. I haven't been active for several years. Other responsibilities got in the way, but I always enjoyed it as I'm sure you must."

"Very much so. We've been doing it a long time, haven't we, Joanie?"

Joanie nodded her head in agreement and the woman asked, "Do you have a show coming up?"

"Yes, we're going to Alexander next week."

"That's terrific. Well, good luck to both of you. It was nice talking with you and I'm sure I'll be back."

"Nice talking to you too. Enjoy the rest of your day."

"Thank you, I will."

The woman, whose name they hadn't gotten, left the store and the girls, already busy with another customer, remarked in passing what a pleasant person she'd been. They got totally immersed with what was going on in the shop and the woman slipped from their minds.

The rest of the day went by fairly quickly. Business was brisk and the girls were kept on the go. Emma had time to skip only once and thankfully, Joanie missed it. Cole and Tank were witnesses, but they didn't voice an opinion. Instead, they were happy to be pressed into service. There was no idle sitting around for those two. Cole carried quite a few packages, which was hardly an imposition on him. He loved to carry anything and everything. Tank, while he was strong enough, was not quite tall enough to carry anything, so he kept busy entertaining customers with his silly antics. Emma and Joanie thought that half the people who came in did so only to see the dogs, they could've cared less what was in the shop or even if Emma and Joanie were there.

Late in the day Emma phoned Tammy Brochton to set up plans for Saturday. Tammy was in her mid twenties and worked part time for a local pizza parlor, so she was available to work at The Whistling Thistle most of the time she was needed.

"Hey, Tammy. This is Emma down at the shop. How you doin'?"

"Oh, hi, Emma. I'm great. What can I do for ya?"

"Well, if you're available, I need you to work the shop on Saturday. Joanie and I are going to make a run down to Great Valley and need you to cover."

"Sure, I can do that… What day is today?"

"Today's Wednesday, Tammy."

"Yeah? Really? Umm…let me think… well, okay, that should be fine. Regular time?"

"Yep, ten o'clock till six."

"Okay, I'll be there."

"Thanks a lot, Tammy. We'll see you. Bye."

"Bye."

Replacing the receiver, Emma caught Joanie looking at her with one eyebrow quirked. "What?"

"What was the Wednesday thing?" Joanie asked, knowing full well there'd be no logical answer.

"I haven't the foggiest. Lord only knows what goes through that girl's mind. I don't know, maybe it was a point of reference for her. Half the time she's in another dimension. All I know is, that even though she's got a few screws loose and not the brightest bulb in the pack, she never messes up the money."

"Amen to that! At least we have that to console us. Now if only we could figure out what the hell she sells to bring in all that money. Her sales slips are like a detonation devise for inventory."

"I know, but what else do we have to do other than count every card in the place to see which one she sold?" Emma asked sarcastically. Tammy steadfastly refused to use the identifying product number listed on every piece of merchandise in the shop. No matter how many times they told her about it, her sales slips never had even *one* number on them. Could be she had an inherent fear of them or maybe they just didn't fit into her world as she saw it. With Tammy, anything sounded plausible. The end result however, was that her sales slips were a nightmare to decipher.

Joanie grimaced and then declared it was late enough in the day to start drinking. Hell, it was 4:45. She went back to the small, well-stocked kitchen and poured two glasses of wine and brought them up to where Emma was.

"Here you go, nectar of the gods," Joanie said. "We deserve it. Just knowing the disaster that awaits me in inventory requires that I start to get fortified now."

"Saturday's three days away, Joanie."

"Yeah, I know. Like I said, I need to start getting fortified right now."

The girls sipped their wine, slipping it under the counter if a customer came in. Truth be told, if the customer was a regular, the drinking duo would ask if they wanted to join them. Most did and they sold a heck of a lot of merchandise that way.

Chapter Three

After closing the shop for the day, Emma and Cole walked up the hill to their house. It was early May and the trees were just starting to bud out with vibrant, light green foliage; the forsythia and tulips were blooming, their colors bright against the still greening vegetation of the woods. The air was alive with birdsong and squirrels were darting around at a frantic pace. Cole paid them no heed as they were quite beneath him and, setting his head at a jaunty angle, he surveyed every aspect of his little kingdom, content to do it at Emma's side. He could have ventured out if he'd wanted to, he was off lead and not under command to heel, but he freely chose to stay with Emma. This was simply where he preferred to be, next to his mistress, the place where he was happiest, close to the one he loved and would protect with his life.

Once they reached the house and went inside, Emma gave Cole half of his supper and saved the rest for later. She fed him a high grade, dry dog food and livened it up with a little gravy and leftover chuck roast. She put some cold water in another bowl and set both in his elevated dining stand. Cole ate with enthusiasm and belched afterward as if to signify that he'd enjoyed it. Emma then put Cole in his crate, which was in the mudroom, so he'd relax and digest his food.

Emma took great care when it came to feeding Cole, as she would have with any giant or deep-chested breed. Small amounts of food were preferable to large ones and these types of dogs needed to rest quietly for one to two hours after eating in an effort to avoid gastric bloating and torsion. Dogs of this kind were never to be fed right after vigorous exercise.

Gastric bloating occurs when the dog's stomach fills with gas and cannot be expelled causing the animal's mid section to visibly expand and putting the dog in a great deal of distress. When torsion is involved, the bloated stomach twists around another vital organ, usually the spleen, and the dog is in agonizing pain. It's a life-threatening situation and there is very little time from the moment of onset to try to save the dog. Emma had lost a beloved bloodhound to bloat years before and the experience still haunted her. With Cole, she always chose to err on the side of caution, never wanting to go through that horror again.

While Cole relaxed, Emma went back outside and got her gardening tools from the shed. She reveled in the extra daylight hours after the long winter months and was anxious to get her gardens ready for planting. The actual plantings wouldn't happen until Memorial Day weekend because there was still a threat of frost especially here in the hills. In this area of the state it had been known to snow as late as Mother's Day, hell, it had even snowed in June a few times. There had been many a spring when the crocuses, daffodils, tulips, and hyacinths had all been killed due to freezing weather and several inches of snow.

But with her heart set on getting the job done, Emma got busy and cleaned the winter's debris from the soil. If snow still came, at least the beds would be ready when it melted. It was in gardening that Emma was completely at peace and light in heart. Whether she was planting, digging up soil, or just plain weeding, the outside world slipped away and Emma was in a place of tranquility and ease. All her worries and concerns disappeared and she was as carefree as a five-year-old child.

She finished up, put everything away, and went inside to have her own dinner. Tonight she'd make it quick because she wanted to work Cole a little bit for the show ring. So she pulled out some leftover pasta with roasted vegetables and warmed it up in the microwave. She ate just about as fast as Cole had and finished off with a piece of chocolate cake, telling herself it was necessary for an energy boost and she'd work it off anyway.

After Cole had relaxed for almost two hours, they went outside and Emma put him through his paces. She'd roped off a section of the yard approximate in size to a regulation show ring and used a true to life "stick figure" as the judge. She made it a man by dressing it in pants and a jacket and a woman by switching to a skirt and blouse; occasionally she added a hat. All were meant to familiarize the dog with different ring conditions.

She followed show ring procedure and moved him in a circle, a triangle, and a down and back with Cole moving flawlessly the entire time. It was a veritable thrill when dog and person moved as one; when there was a solid connection along the lead from the human hand holding it at one end to the animal connected at the other. Emma and Cole were such a team and that's what made them so good in the ring.

She stacked or posed him for inspection and walked away. Emma timed him for two minutes and then released him. Cole hadn't moved a muscle; he just stood there majestically with his head up and his bearing regal. The last thing she did was lead him into a free stand, a pose where he had to position himself correctly without help from her, and watched him stick it. He put all four paws down in the correct position simultaneously and stacked himself with his back straight, head up, his attention focused entirely on Emma, and projected an air of complete superiority. He reminded her of an Olympic gymnast coming off the uneven parallel bars in dismount and landing squarely with no wobble. Emma released him and lavished him with praise and cuddling, kissing and hugging. Cole responded with licking and barking, and a love light that shone in his eyes.

The next maneuvers they did were strictly for fun. Using hand signals only, Emma sent Cole out by himself and watched him perform, marveling at his perception and self control even when she threw squeaky toys and balls into his path. They practiced a few more moves and when Emma gave him the signal, Cole went down into a low bow; Emma reciprocated and then rewarded him with a round of applause and a big hug.

Nobody, except for Emma and Cole themselves, would ever know the extent of Cole's training and that was perfectly fine. Public acknowledgement was not the reason Emma taught Cole so many different things. She did it for the challenge and the fun, but mostly to test just how far Cole's intelligence would take him. The most important benefit however, was the bond that had developed between them because of the many hours of training. From the time Emma had first brought him home to now, their connection had grown and strengthened until it had become unbreakable.

Emma had started showing dogs about twenty-five years ago. She had always had a great love of dogs, but hadn't entered the world of show dogs until she attended an AKC event with a newly acquired friend who'd had her Irish Wolfhounds entered. From that day forward, an interest and devotion emerged that was unparalleled in anything she had previously done. Everything about the world of dog showing had captivated her and she had very quickly become totally involved. For Emma, it had been like coming home to something she had never known existed, but at the same time had known that this was where she'd always belonged.

Friends often said that she became a different person once she stepped foot on the grounds of a dog show. She became more alive, more focused, and visibly happier. She supposed it was true because not only was she able to work with her beloved dogs, but also the friends she had made through her participation in the sport were the best she had ever had. Needless to say, Joanie and Sally were at the top of the list, but numerous others formed a type of family that was ready and willing to help whenever the need arose and to offer genuine heartfelt good wishes when circumstances availed it.

During her divorce and afterward, they had supplied a support system that went way beyond anything she had ever imagined. Even people who had been only passing acquaintances had offered help, and Emma personally knew of countless other instances when someone in their world had needed assistance, whether it had been money, a place to live, or simply verbal support, and the dog show family had responded in kind. To be sure, there were some who were cutthroat in their actions and only out for themselves, but on the whole, dog show people were very generous with their time, knowledge, resources, and support. Emma considered herself very fortunate to be a member of such a wonderful family.

When she had been married and a stay-at-home mom, Emma had bred several litters in both Bloodhounds and Bearded Collies. Talk about being at opposite ends of the spectrum as far as breed personalities went! For Emma and her family, living under the same roof with two such dissimilar breeds had certainly been interesting and never boring.

Like most responsible breeders, she had been in attendance at the time of whelping and as luck would have it one year, had helped birth a litter of Beardies in her living room while trying to make Christmas dinner at the same time. Just like babies, puppies sometimes chose the most inopportune time to make their appearance. Characteristically, the dinner took a back seat and after the arrival of the last puppy, there had to be a picture taken with them and their proud mother under the Christmas tree.

The litters and new mothers had taken just about all of her time and attention during the first two weeks of the puppies' lives and Emma had loved every minute of it. Emma in fact had slept on the sofa next to the whelping box during that time period, just in case there had been a problem during the night. By the time the puppies were eight to twelve weeks old, she'd been loathe to part with them, but had found good, responsible homes for those puppies she hadn't been going to keep. However, when the divorce had come and she'd had to get a full time job, she'd no longer been able, in good conscience, to continue breeding since she wouldn't have been there to supervise on a twenty-four hour basis. She'd then had to content herself with training and showing and had been, for the most part, happy with that; if push came to shove though, she would admit that she missed the puppies a lot.

As they were walking back toward the house, Emma heard the phone ringing and hurried to answer it. Cole followed her in and stood near her side as she picked up the receiver. "Hello?"

"Hi, Em. It's Sally."

Sally Higgins was the third member of their friendship triangle and was the oldest of the group by one year. Joanie was the baby by two and never let the girls forget it. Sally, too, had been in dogs forever and had shared in this three-sided relationship for some twenty-one years. Like Emma, she'd been into breeding, but had had to give it up when she was divorced, the responsibility of running the restaurant falling completely on her shoulders. She'd been owner of the Hearthmoor Inn for twenty-five years and during that time her customers had been subjected to the various ins and outs of the dog show world. Heaven help anyone who complained when the TV in the bar was tuned in to the Westminster Kennel Club Dog Show, the crème de la crème of American dog shows held in February for two nights running at Madison Square Garden in New York City. They were likely to be tossed out on their ear.

"Oh, hey, just the person I wanted to talk to. Joanie and I thought we'd drop by on Saturday. Are you going to be there?"

"Yeah, later on. I have to run some errands first thing in the morning and I'll probably be gone into the afternoon, but I should be back between 3:30 and 4:00."

"That'll be perfect 'cause we have to run down to the Antique Barn and we'll be there awhile I'm sure. Plus, we have to make certain that Tammy's okay at the shop before we can even leave."

"Uh-oh. Tammy's working, huh. That means trouble. Did our friend Joanie start drinking yet?"

"Yeah, she started today. I expect she'll be doing so for the next few days. She said she has to get fortified."

"Oh, she'll get fortified all right. She'll probably reinforce here on Saturday. Hey, wait a minute. Did you say you're going to the Antique Barn?"

"Yeah."

"The one in Great Valley?"

"Yeah, is there another one?"

"I thought you two were banned from there."

"Are you kidding? They love us down there. They see us coming and they put out the welcome sign."

"Oh yeah? That's not the way I heard it. Rumor has it that you two get into a bunch of trouble every time you go there and now management wants to lock the door when they see you coming."

"Well, yeah, stuff does seem to happen when we're there, but it's never our fault. I mean, we don't plan anything or do anything to make it happen; it just does. Maybe we're hexed once we enter the place. I don't know. Anyway, we buy so much of their stuff they'd never ban us, no matter what happens when we're there. Cripe, we probably paid for half of their new roof!"

"I'd say it's more like their whole roof."

"Yeah, with the amount of money we've dropped there, especially this year, you're probably right."

"Just try to stay out of trouble this time, okay? I'll see you on Saturday."

"We'll give it our best shot, although I'm not promising anything. See you around 4:00. Bye."

Emma hung up the phone and turned to Cole. "Can you believe Sally's afraid we're going to get into trouble down at the Antique Barn? Hey, don't look at me like that. You don't agree with her, do you?"

Cole was giving her a sideways look that more or less confirmed that he did agree and totally. Emma shook her head in the negative and closed her eyes, pursing her lips. Then she gave a little dip of her head to the left and opened her eyes.

"Oh, all right, Cole. She's probably right. We always do end up in some kind of hot water," Emma sighed. "But we have a hell of a good time while we're getting there!"

Emma turned her attention to cleaning up the dirty dishes from dinner and then fed Cole the rest of his food. After she finished a few other chores, she settled down in her favorite chair to read for a while before bed. Around 11:00 Cole went out for nature's last call and then the two of them adjourned to the bedroom to watch the late news before calling it a day. News over, Emma turned off the television and the light and smiled as she snuggled under the covers, thinking about Saturday and the good time she knew they were going to have. Hmmm, she thought as she drifted off to sleep, sex isn't the only thing that can put a smile on your face.

* * * *

Earlier that same evening, the woman who had visited the shop that day made a phone call to her employer from her hotel room in Springville, a town that was down the road a few miles from Glenwood. The phone had barely rung when it was picked up. "Jasper? It's Connie."

"I've been waiting for your call. Were you able to make contact?"

"Yes, today."

"How'd it go?"

"Fine. I can confirm that they're going to the Alexander show."

"Good. I'll make sure I've got someone in place."

"Don't you want me to go?"

"No, I want you to stay there, learn their habits, find out everything you can about their daily routine. Can they be followed without being spotted?"

"No, I don't think so, the area's too sparsely populated. She'd realize what was going on."

"Okay, just gather information then. I'm sending the rest of the team out tomorrow. Their plane is due to arrive at the Buffalo Niagara International Airport at 4:00. Be there to pick them up. I'll email the specifics to you after we get off the phone. They know what to do once they have the needed information. Keep me apprised of the situation. I have to let our client know what's going on."

"All right, I'll be talking to you soon."

They ended the call and the woman went back to studying the material she already had and thought about how she was going to garner every detail of their subject's life.

Chapter Four

Thursday and Friday passed uneventfully except that Joanie started to drink an hour earlier each day; more shoppers were offered a taste and sales went up as a direct result. Customers were even contributing to the wine bank the girls kept near the register.

Saturday dawned sunny and clear, not a cloud in the sky. Emma knew it was going to be a really great day since a totally clear sky in Western New York was indeed a rare event. She and Cole finished their morning routine and Emma made ready to get down to the shop.

"Okay, big guy, get in your crate. You have to stay home today. Joanie and I have some traveling to do and there's no way you and Tank can go. I know it's a bummer, but that's the way it is. So come on now."

Cole begrudgingly got into his crate and as Emma bent down to put his dish of water inside, he licked her face and gave her a sorrowful look.

"Sorry, bud, it's not going to work. You just can't go this time. Joanie and I get into enough trouble without having you and your sidekick along. Be a good boy and I'll see you later."

Emma scratched behind his ears and closed the crate. Cole lay down and put his head on his front paws, looking up at Emma with mournful, brown eyes. God, he could get an Emmy, maybe an Oscar, for that performance, Emma thought. Dressed in her usual jeans, sweatshirt, and sneakers, Emma headed down to the shop and opened up. She wasn't there five minutes and Joanie sauntered in.

"Hey, Em, you ready to go?"

"Yeah, just waiting for Tammy to get here. I've got everything turned on. Talked to Sally last night and she'll be at the restaurant after four."

"Good," Joanie said. "I don't think I've talked to her in almost a week, if my memory's right. Of course, we all know that's up for grabs. It'll be nice to have a 'girls only' get together, don't you think? Hey, why isn't Tammy here yet? It's almost quarter after."

"I don't know, maybe she's running late or might be the cosmic forces haven't moved her yet."

"Yeah, right, smart-ass. I wonder if she…. hang on, she just blew into the parking lot." Joanie watched out the window as a purple GEO Spectrum streaked across the parking lot to the far corner where the driver slammed it into park and exited the car.

A minute later, Tammy blasted her way into the shop. She was a whirlwind of motion as she opened and closed the door and made her way to the counter. She had a baseball cap on her head, her long, curly, black hair secured in a ponytail, coming out the back. She had big gold hoops dangling from her ears and a bright green tee shirt and jeans on. Footwear of the day was baggy socks and running shoes. God, Emma thought, if only she was as normal as she looked! She was a cute girl with big brown eyes and a few freckles across the bridge of her nose. She had a great figure and a ready smile that showed off perfectly straight, white teeth that she swore no orthodontist had had a hand in.

"Hi guys. I'm here," Tammy announced, huffing a little from her dash into the store.

"So you are, Tammy. Everything okay?" Emma asked.

"Yeah, yeah, just running a little behind. Had my alarm set on Sunday time, skipped right over Saturday."

"Um, what's Sunday time?" Joanie asked reluctantly, giving Emma a knowing look.

"Two hours later than Saturday time. Luckily, I had to go to the bathroom so bad it woke me up or I wouldn't be here. Whew! Thank God, nature called, huh?"

"Yeah, thank God," Emma replied, keeping her tone serious but giving Tammy a sarcastic look when her attention drifted to who knows where. "Let's go over a couple of things, then we're out of here."

While Emma proceeded to give a few instructions, Joanie gave her the old, you've-got-to-be-kidding look, then gathered their things so they could make a hasty exit. Ten minutes later they were in the parking lot headed for Joanie's blue Chevy Silverado truck.

"Who talks like that, Saturday time, Sunday time?" Joanie asked, throwing her arms up in a gesture of frustration.

"Ummm…that would be our Tammy, I do believe."

"Cute, Em. I'm warning you, don't start. Just get in the truck and let's go."

Emma was laughing as the girls piled into the truck and headed south down Route 240. The day was as beautiful as the dawn had promised and the temperature, in the low seventies with low humidity, was above average for this time of year. It was a perfect day! The girls talked about everyday things and enjoyed the countryside. After turning onto Route 242, they were soon in Ellicottville, a picturesque town nestled in the hills of the southern tier.

The village of Ellicottville, located in Cattaraugus County, had beautifully captured the enchantment and allure of the 1800's by preserving and restoring its homes and buildings that boasted an age of one hundred or more years. On streets lined with tall trees that were themselves part of history, private homes sat as a testament to long ago grace and charm, the commercial buildings to architectural artistry. The Historic District had been named to the National Register of Historic Places and small town pride was very much in evidence as you strolled the business district as well as the residential.

In close proximity were two popular ski resorts that brought a flood of tourists each year. Holiday Valley was the most popular ski resort in New York State and HoliMont, the largest private ski area in the United States. In addition to skiing facilities, Holiday Valley prided itself on providing a challenging, eighteen-hole golf course and in the non-snow seasons, the resort allowed mountain bikers and hikers access to its hills. Both the resorts and the various festivals held in the town attracted a multitude of out-of-towners annually and the village of Ellicottville opened its arms in welcome to all.

Another plus to the region was that within a ten-mile radius of this lovely town there were several hundred antique dealers offering all sorts of wonderful antiquities for sale. The girls took Route 219 south out of town and then hit Route 98 south. Within minutes they were at the Antique Barn.

It was a huge place. The building was actually two barns joined by a one-story structure that was sixty feet long and every inch of the place was jammed with merchandise. The barns had three stories each and the connecting hallway, if you want to call it that, had little rooms jutting off of it, some of them with two floors. You could easily get lost in the place and on occasion the girls had forgotten which way was which, although anyone who knew them considered it status quo, them being mixed up, that is.

Pulling into the parking lot, Emma felt chills going up and down her spine and goose bumps broke out on her arms. It happened every time she came here. She couldn't wait to see what treasures they'd find and what fun they'd have searching them out. She was halfway out of the truck before Joanie had put it into park.

"Hell, Emma, hang on! You want to break your leg or what?"

"Just come on, I want to get started," Emma yelled, heading for the door.

Joanie caught up and they pushed their way inside, letting their eyes adjust to the dim interior of the building. While passing the sales desk, Emma called out a greeting to the employee behind the counter.

"Hi, Bernie, we're back."

"Oh, Lordy, not you two again! Damn! I knew the day was going too smoothly. Well, have a care, ladies and don't get into any trouble. Try real hard this time, okay? Watch what you're doing, please."

"We always do," Joanie quipped.

Bernie snorted, gave Joanie a disbelieving look, waved the girls away, then turned her attention back to what she had been doing prior to the two smart alecks arrival.

As Emma and Joanie started down the first aisle, their eyes were darting here, there and everywhere, trying to take in everything at once. Of course, they both knew better than to do that, but they had to get the first rush of adrenalin out of their systems so they could settle down to the serious business at hand. Once they reached the end of the aisle, they turned around and methodically started back up one side. The displays or booths were arranged according to vendor, the wares of each being on a consignment basis. There were wonderful antiques, items that weren't quite antiques, and there was also a lot of junk, but even that was fun to sort through.

Emma found a rug beater, one of the many things she collected, and grabbed it up quickly. She knew from past experience that if you snooze, you lose. Joanie spotted a large wooden bowl with a beautiful satin patina and closed in on it like a hawk pursuing its prey. Holding on to their treasures possessively, they continued until they spotted what had to be the top half of an oak cupboard. It was around six feet long and about four and a half feet high. It had four shelves and, although the doors were missing, would be suitable for display purposes. It was fairly deep and the wood was in good condition, but the best part of the deal was that there was a big sign on it that said it was on sale for seventy-five percent off. Holy shit!

"All right, so what's wrong with it?" Joanie asked, eying the cupboard suspiciously.

"Well, I'm sure there's some flaw, but look, Joanie, this dealer's whole booth is on sale. He must be going out of business. This could be our lucky day."

"Yeah, it could be, but let's find out what's wrong with it first before you go getting all excited."

And so they started going over the piece from top to bottom. They found that the right back corner on the top of the hutch was broken and jagged, but that didn't really concern them. Working their way down, they were forced to get down on their hands and knees so that they could see under the shelves. When they were peering up under the bottom shelf and testing the strength of the supporting wood, they found the problem. The right side was shorter than the left and the piece was wobbly because of it.

"Hey, Em, what do you think?"

"I think we can fix that easily enough. We'll just slide a two by four or something under that side. We can display something in front of it so it doesn't show and nobody'll be any the wiser. Besides, for what it's going to cost us, it's a steal.

If I'm doing my math right, we're going to pay about $75.00 for this. What…what are you laughing at?"

Joanie was laughing so hard she could barely get the words out. "Look…look at us."

"What?" Emma asked, starting to chuckle, infected by Joanie's laugh.

"Look…look at the position we're in."

In trying to examine the underside of the bottom shelf, the girls had laid their forearms on the floor and their butts had risen into the air accordingly. They had stayed in that position while discussing the merits of the purchase and they were now sinking even lower in the front, pushing their rears up higher as they became hysterical with laughter. It just so happened that a group of Mennonite women were passing by at just that moment and with looks of incredibility sketched on their faces, hurried past. A few looked back with definite scowls of disapproval and the girls dissolved into more laughter.

"We have to get up," Emma croaked out.

"I can't… I've got to pee so bad, if I move, I'm going to wet my pants."

"Oh, God…why'd you have to mention that? Now I have to go too. Geez, what a jag…We've got to stop…Stop laughing… Joanie, stop… Joanie…Oh shit."

They started up again, their laughter going silent because they couldn't catch their breath. God, they were killing themselves! Then they heard footsteps coming up behind them.

"Gee, why am I not surprised it's you two causing this little scene?" Bernie asked, a scowl on her face. "Couldn't you at least roll over on your side so your asses were out of the air?"

Emma and Joanie just looked at her, unable to speak; tears were rolling down their cheeks they were so overcome with laughter. At that point, the girls wouldn't have been able to move even if someone had leveled a gun at their heads.

Watching them, Bernie felt the beginning of a smile and turned away so they couldn't see her face. "Do you at least want the piece? Just shake your head if you do."

They both shook their heads and Bernie, after looking back at them quickly, hurried away before she broke into a full giggle. The girls, thankfully, wound down after about five more minutes and composed themselves enough to stand and get themselves to the bathroom. Weak with relief, they started again on their systematic search, only occasionally letting a snicker slip out.

They went back to where they had left off and went through the entire three floors of the first barn, noticing that if they got within range of the Mennonites, the women would skirt around them at a safe distance keeping their eyes averted, although the girls did catch one of the younger women with a small grin on her face.

The three levels of the barn encompassed a huge amount of inventory and the girls were sorely tempted to buy a great deal of it, but they reined themselves in and concentrated on their main purpose for being there, specifically, to find and buy the perfect cupboard for the new candle display. They left the barn and went into the connecting hallway, traversing the length of it. They bypassed the connecting rooms for the moment and devoted their attention to the numerous cupboards that were in the area.

"Man, Joanie, this one's great, isn't it?" Emma asked, leading her partner over to a particularly nice cabinet. "It would look fabulous in the back corner next to the linen display, don't you think?"

"Yeah, it's a nice piece; it would probably look terrific."

"Hmmm...I wonder if it smells."

"What do you mean, you wonder if it smells? Smells like what?"

"You know, that awful musty smell you can never get out."

"Oooh....I don't know."

"Well, I would do it if I could."

"Do what?"

"You know, see if it smells. But my sinuses are all screwed up and I can't smell real well."

"Yeah, I know. You don't smell too good."

"Thanks."

"You know what I mean."

"Yeah. So what do you say, would you put your head in there and see if you can smell anything?"

"Okay." Joanie proceeded to put her head into the cupboard and Emma started to laugh and had to turn away when she heard sniffing noises coming from inside the hutch.

"I don't smell anything, Emma. I think it's okay." When Joanie didn't get any response, she pulled her head out and looked to her friend who had walked away because she was laughing so hard. Narrowing her eyes, she gave Emma an exasperated look. "Very funny."

"I can't believe you did that just because I asked you to." Emma said, again trying to control herself.

"Well, it seemed like a reasonable request since you can't smell for shit. Besides, if it did smell, I wouldn't want it in the shop and some of these pieces definitely look like they could smell really bad. Look at that one over there; it's probably been in the back of a barn for fifty or sixty years. God only knows what's been in it."

"Yeah, well, better He knows than us. I think we should get this one. It's a really nice primitive and the candles will look perfect in it."

"The price is pretty decent too… $385.00. Yeah, let's do it. I'll go tell Bernie we want it."

Joanie went off to inform Bernie what piece they were buying and Emma couldn't help but smile. This day was turning out to be everything she had hoped it would be and it wasn't even half over yet.

When Joanie came back, the two of them continued their hunt, going through all the rooms that shot off the hallway. The girls found another wooden bowl, which would be wonderful to display small items in, and some cowbells they thought they'd hang on the front door of the shop. They found some interesting items in the second barn, but nothing they felt the urge to buy.

Satisfied with the day's spoils, they went back to the sales counter and paid for their purchases. With a final wave to Bernie, they sailed out the door to the parking lot and watched as two burly, young men loaded the furniture into the bed of the truck.

After the two had departed, Joanie climbed up so they could secure their cargo with ropes, tying it down so it wouldn't shift and bang around while they were traveling. Emma stayed on the ground supposedly to help, but she knew Joanie would attempt to do everything herself. That was exactly what happened and Emma ended up being a spectator to her friend's slight miscalculation.

Joanie had secured two ropes, extending from one side of the truck to the other over the two cupboards, and she stood smack in the middle of them up against the side of the truck wall. "Umm…Em?"

"Yeah?"

"I can't move. I… umm… tied myself in."

Emma came over to the side of the truck where Joanie was and looked up at her friend squashed between the cupboard and the truck wall. "Well, damn! How the hell did you do that?" Emma asked, already starting to laugh even though she tried to hide it by lowering her head and covering her mouth with her hand.

"I don't know how I did it. I guess I wasn't paying attention to what I was doing. Now help me."

"I can't," Emma wailed as she collapsed to her knees, holding her mouth with one hand and her stomach with the other, helpless to move as laughter shook her body.

"This isn't funny!"

"Yes...yes...it...is," Emma groaned, her side starting to ache she was laughing so hard. This was just too much for one day!

"You've got to help me."

"Nooo...can't...do...it."

"Emma, stop laughing! You've got to help me get out of here. Loosen one of the ropes so I can climb over the cupboard and get out over the tailgate. Emma, *pleeease!*"

Several minutes went by with Emma just about rolling on the ground and Joanie standing squished in the truck bed, shooting daggers with her eyes at her so-called friend. Finally the howling started to let up and Emma came down off her laughing fit. She wiped her eyes, blew her nose and took a few deep breaths, bringing herself back from the edge of hysteria.

"Well, it took you long enough. Cripe! Are you okay now? Can you function? Can you get me out of here?" Joanie asked, her patience non-existent at this point.

"I can't get up."

"What?"

"I said, 'I can't get up'."

"Well, why the hell not?"

"I'm on the verge of peeing my pants again."

"Oh, for cripes sake, Emma!"

"Hey, I can't help it if my bladder isn't as strong as it used to be."

"Yeah, well, whose is? Just get up and help me."

45

"Is anybody looking?"

"Emma…please. Who the hell cares if anybody's looking? Just get your ass up!"

"Okay, but it isn't going to be pretty." Emma paused for a second, calculated her movements, then taking a deep breath and keeping her legs together from the knees up, struggled to her feet. She hobbled, pigeon-toed, over to where Joanie was and loosened one rope enough to give her legs room to maneuver. Joanie went up and over the cupboard, moved to the tailgate, and down to Mother Earth. Meanwhile, Emma was leaning against the truck, squeezing her legs together and anything else she was capable of squeezing shut so she wouldn't have an accident.

"Thank God," Joanie said, slamming the tailgate into place.

Emma took a deep breath, clenched everything a little tighter and shoved herself away from the truck. She started to move out, walking slowly with tiny, little steps forced from legs that were locked in a knock-kneed position. "I'll be back in a second. Well, it'll probably be more like a few minutes since I can't walk too fast this way."

"At the rate you're going, it'll be more like half an hour," Joanie grumbled, watching Emma's slow progress. She had to stop several times; Joanie figured it was to readjust her clench.

As luck would have it, Emma had to pass the sales counter on the way to the bathrooms.

"Don't bother explaining," Bernie said when she saw Emma approach. "One of the guys saw the whole thing. You'd better get to the bathroom before I have to clean up after you. By the way, that's a very attractive walk you've got there."

Emma didn't respond, just gave a wave of her hand as she passed by, her focus solely on relieving her mutinous bladder.

Chapter Five

On the way back from the Antique Barn, the two magnets for trouble stopped at a convenience store in Ellicottville when they realized they were starving. Not wanting to fill up, knowing they'd be eating at the Hearthmoor shortly, but needing to take the edge off their hunger, they opted for candy bars and soda. Leave it to them to chose a non-nutritious form of energy guaranteed to wire them even more. As though they needed it!

Ever since they'd known each other, going back some twenty-two years, the girls had played off one another and had a natural rhythm between them that some people thought they could turn into an act. They just looked at life the same way- make it fun and laugh, because the alternative was to get bogged down in misery and cry, and who the hell wanted to do that? It was probably this identical outlook on life, even more so than their love of dogs and their interest in the shop, that made them the close friends they were. Anyway, they ate their candy, drank their soda, and laughed about whatever struck their funny bone as they traveled back over the same roads to their friend's restaurant.

The girls arrived at the Hearthmoor a few minutes after four o'clock. When they entered the barroom, Sally was behind the bar, prepping for the night's activity. staurant was located on Route 240, about five miles ...... of the shop, in a converted 120 year-old farmhouse. It sat on about four acres of land that sported a large barn and two out-buildings, and was beautifully landscaped with towering pines, flowering crab trees, and flower beds overflowing with seasonal blooms. A split-rail fence back dropped the gardens and beyond it the lawn rolled over gentle knolls. Sally had created a rock garden that edged the outside patio and had put a goldfish pond next to the stairs to the entrance. Numerous wind chimes tinkled in the spring air and a cast iron bell hung next to the door, ready to call the hungry in to dinner. Bird feeders dangled outside several windows so that customers were able to watch among others, hummingbirds, orioles, chickadees, and finches as they dined.

The entryway was made up of windows on the two outside walls and a side door that led to the patio. It was decorated according to season, so that now it was bedecked in spring flowers, pussy willows, and ceramic bunnies. The fragrance of the flowers filled the space and one couldn't help but draw a deep breath and enjoy. The first signs of spring to Western New Yorkers, bordered on the sacred and they took every opportunity to enjoy them.

The bar area was longer than it was wide with a jukebox and an electronic Pac Man game. There were a few tables, but most patrons preferred to cozy up to the bar. The bar itself was L-shaped, about sixteen feet long with the short leg another six feet in length. The top of the bar was a deep, rich cherry wood polished to a high gloss and there was room for ten stools. The walls throughout the restaurant were paneled with wide plank walnut and tiny lights ran along the top of the walls at ceiling edge. Over the bar, Sally had hung several tree branches into which she had interwoven more mini white lights, and for spring, apple blossoms had been attached. There was a coat rack at one end and beneath it was a large antique trunk with leather straps.

The dining area could seat about eighty people and the tables were draped with cranberry tablecloths to match the upholstered chairs. Fresh flowers were on every table as they were throughout the year, but these spring buds were from Sally's own garden. There were a total of eight windows offering views of the countryside and two columns supported the exposed beam in the middle of the room. A twelve-foot long fieldstone fireplace with a raised hearth dominated the east wall and there was a large, silk, floral centerpiece on the mantle. In the fall and winter months, a cheery fire was regularly in attendance to warm the room and its occupants. There were six small lamps evenly spaced on the walls and candles on each table to softly illuminate the dining room. The atmosphere couldn't help but be warm and relaxing, intimate and friendly.

The waitress's service area was on the west wall and that too reflected the tone of the restaurant. The same lighting extended to here and there was a large, antique hutch made of dark walnut set against the wall in which Sally displayed vintage dishware. The kitchen and storage rooms were located behind the service station.

"Hey, you're here," Sally said, looking up from what she was doing.

"Yeah, we survived another escapade at the infamous Antique Barn," Emma replied.

"Okay, don't keep me in suspense. I know there's a story here, despite the fact I told you to stay out of trouble."

"Yeah, there is, but if you want to hear it, we need to get some liquid refreshment. So please, if you would, Sally, give us what we crave," Joanie urged.

As Sally got their drinks, they both favored white wine, the girls got comfortable on their stools and the story of the day's adventure was reported.

"Jesus, you guys are nuts!"

"Oh, I don't know," Emma said. "Could have happened to anybody."

"Who are you trying to kid?" Sally scoffed. "You two have a talent all your own."

"Yeah, I think Bernie feels the same way," Joanie agreed. "Well, what the hell, we had a good time."

Just then, Kirby, Sally's two-year old Yellow Labrador Retriever, came into the bar from outside, sneaking past a customer when he opened the door. She was a friendly, outgoing dog and had made many a customer her personal friend. Coming from a Canadian kennel, she'd been aptly named due to her habit of "vacuuming up" any fallen tidbit of food and it seemed appropriate that she lived above a restaurant. Kirby had been known to sneak into the dining room and snuggle up to a customer to silently beg with her eyes for what she considered her fair share of the meal, namely the garlic bread. She also had a reputation for relieving a departing diner of their "doggy bag". Although the customers never seemed to mind, Sally sometimes took a dim view of the goings on.

Kirby had a beautiful head and bright, expressive, brown eyes. She had a deep chest and a strong, muscular body. Her movement was smooth and powerful, and Sally had her near to completing her championship in the show ring. She only needed a few single points, having already achieved her majors.

While Kirby enthusiastically greeted two of her oldest friends, the conversation turned to the upcoming dog show in Alexander, New York.

"We haven't decided yet if we're going down Friday night or Saturday morning," Emma said.

"I think we ought to go down Saturday morning," Joanie offered. "Cole's the only one in at 8:30 and there's twenty-five dogs ahead of Newfs, so that'll put him in the ring at about 9:30. If we leave around six, six-thirty, that'll give us plenty of time to set up and get ready."

"Yeah, that sounds about right," Sally said. "That would work better for me anyway, what with the Friday night crowd at the restaurant and all."

"Okay, we'll meet here between six and six-thirty Saturday morning then, but Joanie and I'll come down and load the motor home on Friday night after we close the shop."

"If you do that, it'll save a lot of hassle in the morning. Then all we have to do is load the dogs and take off. I'll have all my gear ready and in the barn so you can throw it in with your stuff. I'll pack all the food in the morning though, and have it ready by the time you get here."

"All right, and everybody remember to pack some warm clothes and a heavy jacket, just in case. You know how at least one day is always so cold and miserable there," Emma warned.

"Oh, God, yes. It wouldn't be Alexander without cold, windy, wet weather," Sally said.

"Well, at least let's *hope* for two days of good weather, even though there isn't a snowball's chance in hell of it happening. With our luck, it'll probably snow."

"Like that isn't a real possibility. Remember that one year it did snow, so bite your tongue, Joanie. Don't jinx us."

"Who needs me to jinx us? We live in Western New York, don't we? That's jinx enough. And if it is nasty, it'll be ten degrees colder in Alexander than it is here."

"Okay, enough talk about the weather. It's too depressing. We'll just be prepared for anything from a heat

51

wave to a foot of snow like we always are, although I refuse to take a shovel."

"Yeah, you're right, Emma. Sally, give us another glass of wine, please. I just remembered what I face tomorrow in inventory."

"Whoops! I was hoping that little detail wouldn't pop into your head today," Emma said. "We'll deal with it, don't worry."

"I'm not worried. I'm just gaining strength. The wine is for purely medicinal purposes."

"Yeah, right."

"So why don't you two move to a table in the dining room and I'll join you. Hank just came in and he can take over the bar. I'll get the drinks and meet you in there."

The girls moved to a corner table and chatted with their waitress, Sharon, while they waited for Sally who joined them presently, bearing their wine and her manhattan. Emma noticed that two tables over, a woman was eating dinner by herself and recognized her as the lady they'd talked to about the dogs in the shop on Wednesday. Emma caught her eye and waved. The woman smiled, waved back, and returned her attention to the open book she had on the table. Emma mentally rejoined her friends, dismissing the woman from her mind as she returned to the conversation flowing around her.

Talk centered around the dinner choices for the day and they quickly decided on what they'd have. They all chose that day's special, Chicken Olivia, one of Emma's favorites. The dish consisted of grilled chicken breast sliced into strips, layed on a bed of linguini, covered with a Parmesan cream sauce, and garnished with bits of real bacon. They each opted for their favorite salad dressing, Emma's being raspberry vinaigrette, Joanie's ranch and Sally's blue cheese. Sharon left to put the order in and conversation again drifted to the dogs.

"Hey, Emma, are you still roading Cole every day?"

"Yep, we're out there every morning."

"She's a fanatic about it," Joanie teased. "Cripe, there's probably a groove cut right into the blacktop on the route she follows up at the park."

"Well, hell, if I'm going to show him, he's got to be in good condition. Besides, he likes it. Keeps me in shape too."

"Is the warmer weather bothering him? I've been taking Kirby out in the back fields earlier in the morning now that it's starting to heat up."

"It hasn't been a problem yet, but then we're usually back home between nine and quarter after."

"Wait a minute. You get up there around eight, right? Hell, you get six miles done in an hour?"

"Yeah, give or take a few minutes. We go at a pretty good clip."

"No wonder you're both in such good shape."

"Well, if we're going to play with the big boys, we'd better have that much in our favor at least."

"Geez, Em, this'll be the first time out for Cole as a Special. Are you nervous about it?" A Special was a dog that had already obtained his AKC championship and was being shown or campaigned to win points toward a national ranking in his breed and group. This however, was not Emma's motivation. She just enjoyed showing and wanted to have a good time with Cole.

"No, not right now, but I haven't really been thinking about it. The day of the show though, could be a whole other story. I always get nervous before I go in the ring anyway. The waiting drives me nuts, but once I'm in and moving, I'm usually okay."

"I bet some of the professional handlers are going to be eying him up. You watch, one of them is going to make a play for him."

"Yeah, I know, but they're not going to get him. We're doing this for fun, nothing more. You guys know I could never campaign a dog. None of us could, we don't have that kind of time or money. They're barking up the wrong tree if they think I can pay a professional handler to exhibit Cole."

Emma figured she'd have to win the lottery before she could afford the time and money it took to campaign a dog, and the likelihood of that happening was nil to zero. The cost of campaigning a dog to a national ranking was exorbitant and involved showing the dog all over the country almost every weekend in shows that totaled well over a hundred for the year. In addition to the cost, a dog that was sent out with a handler to be campaigned, rarely saw his owner since he lived with the handler and unless the owner lived close by or could afford to travel to the shows, owner and dog were apart pretty much for the entire year. That alone nixed the idea of a handler for Emma.

"Hey, what was the name of that handler who wanted to buy Cole at the show where he won his championship?"

"Umm…Thornton, Bill Thornton, I think."

"What'd he offer you…$5,000?"

"Yeah, but when I turned him down, he upped it to $7,000."

"Right, I remember now," Sally said. "He bothered you the rest of the day trying to get you to change your mind."

"He was persistent."

"I forget…was he trying to buy Cole for himself or was he acting as an agent for somebody?"

"I think he said a client of his wanted to buy Cole."

"Did he say who it was?"

"No, I don't think so. I do remember he wasn't too happy with me when I turned him down. In fact, now that I think about it, by the end of the day he'd raised it to $10,000."

"Geez, I didn't know that, Emma. How could you forget that detail?"

"I don't know, I guess 'cause it wasn't important to me. I wasn't going to sell Cole at any price."

"Yeah, but you watch, somebody else is going to throw you a hook, maybe not to buy him, but to handle him for sure," Joanie said.

"Well, let them. It's not going to do them any good. Besides, if I couldn't show Cole, you two are the only ones I'd trust him with." Out of the corner of her eye, Emma watched the woman at the other table put money down on top of her bill, gather her things, and leave the dining room.

"Hey, you hear that, Sally. How'd we get to be so blessed?" Joanie joked.

"By our mere existence, I suppose. We're such good people and besides, nobody but us would put up with Emma, so she had no choice but to name us as her back up."

"Very funny, guys. I try to give you a compliment and look what I get for it."

"Oh, Em, lighten up. We're just fooling around. We know how much Cole means to you and really, we're humbled by the fact that you'd entrust him to us."

"Yeah, well…"

"Hey, Em. You know what you need, don't you? You need to get laid."

"Oh geez, not that again."

"No, really, it would relax you. You're a little tense."

"How long has it been again?" Sally probed.

"Never mind."

"If I remember correctly," Joanie ventured, "I believe she's been dormant for what…fifteen years, Em?"

Sharon had been placing the salads and garlic bread on the table during this exchange, and looked at Emma with disbelief on her face. "Oh, honey, you need to have a good roll in the sack. Let some big, handsome guy send you to heaven. It'll do wonders for you."

"Geez, Emma! It's really been that long? Holy shit! I wonder if you're a virgin again? Maybe that little thingy grew back."

"What little thingy?"

"You know, that virginity thingy. I mean, if the tunnel of love has been closed down this long, would it have grown back?"

"Oh, my God, I feel like I'm talking to Tammy and, no, it didn't grow back, you ass."

"How do you know? You sure as hell haven't tested it."

"I just know that's all. Don't be an idiot. Now can we change the subject?"

"No!"

"Shut up and eat your salads."

Right about then, Tom Ferrelli, Sally's chef, came out of the kitchen and into the dining room, heading for their table. As was his custom, he was checking to make sure everything was okay with the dinner offerings of the day. He liked to keep the girls happy. He'd no sooner reached the table than Joanie peppered him with questions.

"Hey, Tom, what do you think about somebody who hasn't had sex for fifteen years? It'd make them a little tense, don't you think? They'd need to have some, right? Like right away?"

"Whoa! Who are we talking about?" Tom asked, glancing at each of the girls.

"Emma."

"Emma?"

"Yeah."

"Goddamn, Em. Is that true? You haven't had sex in fifteen years?"

"Oh, God." Emma wished she could just disappear, or at least slide gracefully under the table. Maybe she'd take Joanie with her after she popped her one.

"No sex for fifteen years. Shit! Why are you still alive?"

"Spoken like a true man. There *are* other things in life, you know." Sally felt the need to defend her friend if only because now a man was involved in the discussion.

"Yeah, but nothing's better than sex."

"You tell her, Tom." Joanie was psyched; she had a man behind her now.

"Emma, you need emergency sex really fast. You better listen to these two." Tom gave her a wink, knowing she was in for more harassment. He switched gears back to their dinners and said they'd be out shortly and hoped they'd enjoy them. He excused himself and went back to the kitchen after Sharon told him he had more orders.

It took Joanie about two beats to get back to Emma's sex life. "Okay, Em, so listen up. We've got to hook you up with a man, that's all there is to it. Sally, we've got to make it our number one priority."

"I think you're right, Joanie. This woman has been too long without."

"Look guys, thanks for the thought, but I'm going to decline. I'm fine with the way things are. Besides, it's been so long that I don't even know if you do it the same way or if there's new stuff involved."

"Oh, there's definitely new stuff."

"You really think so?"

"Yeah," Joanie said. "Nothing stays the same…I bet there's a whole bunch of new stuff; I just don't know what it is. Sam and I have been married for twenty-eight years, so we're kind of out of the loop. Sally, what about you? You're still kind of in the dating game."

"Well, hell. Richard and I have been together for ten years, so even though we're not married, we're not in the dating game and besides, we still use the same old tried and true forms of sex."

"We're going to have to talk to a young person."

"Like who?"

"Well, we can't talk to our daughters 'cause they think we never had sex. I don't know how they think they got here, but it wasn't by mom and dad doing the deed."

"All right, so they're out. Who's left? What young lady are we on good enough terms with that we can ask her about the latest in sex?"

"I know. How about Tammy?"

"Oh shit, this just keeps getting better and better," Emma moaned.

"Hey, don't worry about it. We'll just pick up a little information to be on the safe side, so you'll be prepared in case you need it. Besides, if we can get you with a guy your age or older, he probably won't know about the new stuff either."

"Yeah, right. Remember we're talking about a guy here."

"Okay, I'll give you that one. I must have wigged out there for a minute. How could I forget that young or old, a guy's a guy? Well, all right, looking on the bright side, if he knows the new stuff, then he can teach you."

"And you won't be going in cold. You'll at least have the knowledge, if not the practical experience, and he can help you with that."

"Damn, and this started out to be such a good day."

"Hey, Em, this is turning out to be a great day. Come hell or high water, you're going to get laid and like it, goddamn it!"

Sharon brought their dinners out and the girls ate in companionable silence, each deep in their own thoughts. Joanie and Sally more or less being of the same mind, plotting ways to get Emma a man, and Emma thinking furtively how she was going to get out of this one.

Chapter Six

After Joanie dropped her off, Emma had a joyous reunion with Cole. She'd been gone for less than nine hours, but to Cole it seemed like forever. He bounded out of his crate and about knocked her over in his enthusiasm to see her.

"Whoa, Cole! Yeah, I'm glad to see you too. Take it easy now, big boy; settle down. You about knocked me down flat. Were you a good boy?"

Cole jiggled and wiggled into her legs and finally just leaned his full weight against her, relishing the feel of Emma's hands rubbing over his head and body. He stood there, soaking up all the attention for several minutes, a sound something akin to a cat's purr rumbling in his chest. They went outside and after Cole relieved himself, the two played a game of "keep away" with a ball. It got Cole running to expend some bottled-up energy and it had Emma chasing so she could work off dinner. It was a pretty good system and they had it down pat with Cole the one in charge and the all-time winner, and Emma, always the loser, but a happy one.

It was only about seven o'clock, so Emma put Cole on lead and headed down to the shop to make sure all was secure. Emma had noticed on the drive up to the house with Joanie that all the flags were down, a very good sign that Tammy had had everything under control. All the main lights seemed to be off, another good omen that she had kept herself mentally rooted in the shop, and the door was even locked. By all outward appearances, it looked like Tammy had come through with the basics once again. Nevertheless, the girls didn't take these simple shut-down procedures for granted with Tammy. You just never knew when her attention would be diverted and she'd be called into that other dimension where only she and her fertile imagination existed.

Emma unlocked the door, stepped over the threshold and turned on the lights. She let Cole off his leash and watched as he purposefully maneuvered down each and every aisle while she stayed where she was near the door. He disappeared into the back of the shop and then came back to Emma, his tail wagging furiously.

"Everything check out okay?"

Cole gave an answering woof and Emma continued into the interior of the store. Ever since Cole had been about nine months old, he'd developed this pattern of behavior whenever they entered the shop after hours. It was as if he sensed that this would be the time when a threat could exist and took measures to protect Emma. The first few times he'd gone on patrol, he'd blocked Emma's way, forcing her to stay where she was until *she* learned what was expected of *her*.

Emma strolled slowly around the entire floor, checking to make sure all the candles were out, all the little display lamps turned off, and the vignettes in some type of order. Walking toward the sales counter, she first checked to make sure the furnace was set at fifty-five. Even though the temperature had gotten into the low seventies that day, the nighttime low was supposed to go to thirty-five as a cold front moved in. Emma made sure the computer was off and the cash register off and locked. The charge machine was closed out and the sound system was off. The day's sales slips were stacked under the counter and it looked like Tammy had had a busy day. Emma glanced at the first few receipts and shook her head. "Damn, everything is pretty near perfect 'til you try to read these things; Joanie's going to be fit to be tied. I ought to call her right now and tell her to drink herself silly tonight.... Nope, on second thought, I'm just going to watch the shit hit the fan tomorrow. Cole, what do you say we call it a day and go home?"

Cole gave her hand a lick in response and the two turned off the lights, locked up, and headed back to the cottage. As Emma walked up the hill, her thoughts turned to the conversation at the Hearthmoor. The dog show was a week away and she mentally tallied up the list of gear and supplies she'd have to get ready. Not a problem really, she'd been doing this for so long it was almost automatic. Some of the dog equipment, in fact, stayed packed since it was only for use at the shows. Her mind drifted over the events at the Antique Barn and she smiled to herself. God, they'd had fun! Then her mind snagged on the man thing and she tried to dismiss it. It wouldn't go away completely, but at least she was successful in putting it on a shelf to be thought about later, hopefully, much, much later.

* * * *

At the same time that Emma was checking out the store, the woman named Connie was doing her own investigating. Having overheard enough of the girls' conversation at the restaurant to know when and where Emma ran Cole everyday, she'd called the additional members of her team and met them at Sprague Brook Park. They were going to see if they could determine what route Emma might follow.

They were happy to find that there were only two roads that branched off the main entranceway and they scouted out both. The road that forked to the left started as a gradual incline, but the gradient increased sharply as they continued to climb for a distance of three miles, the logical one-way distance to be traveled on a six-mile run considering there had to be a turn around. The road to the right was practically level for the distance they needed and it was this one that the team decided must be the route Emma and Cole followed. They got out of their car and, now on foot, went slowly back over the route a second time, then a third, and finally a fourth, learning the curves and dips of the road. Once they were satisfied they were familiar enough with the road, they reconnoitered the entire surrounding area. Then, they made their plans. The weather report for tomorrow, forecasting rain and dense fog, was perfect for what they intended to do.

* * * *

Emma and Cole reached the house and Emma prepared Cole's food. He got dry kibble with slices of chicken today and Cole lapped it up. Emma put a load of laundry in the washer, tidied up the house, and cleaned Cole's crate. She paid a few bills and got them ready to mail in the morning. She still resisted some new technology like paying on-line and email. There was something gratifying in writing out the check, putting it in the envelope, stamping it, and dropping it in the mailbox. It took four steps to obtain the desired result as opposed to one button being pushed. Where was the challenge in that? And then there was the United States Postal Service to contend with. Sometimes that was a real crapshoot. So if the check got to its destination and on time, that was indeed reason to celebrate a victory over one of life's little hassles. Pushing a button was way too easy!

As to the latter, Emma couldn't understand why anyone would rather type out a message and send it through cyberspace instead of picking up the phone and actually talking to another human being. What could possibly take the place of your granddaughter's small voice coming over the line? It was sheer heaven! Why would anyone not want to hear the ring of laughter or the simple sound of someone's voice that you hadn't heard from in years? Call her old-fashioned, but in this regard Emma would gladly stay woefully behind the times.

Emma, shadowed by Cole, went down to the basement and changed the laundry over to the dryer. While the machine ran, she got Cole up on the grooming table and brushed out his heavy coat, an activity that not only relaxed Cole, but Emma as well. She trimmed his toenails, cleaned his ears, and checked his teeth for tarter. When getting him ready for show on Thursday, all she'd have to do is check over what she'd done tonight, bathe and dry him, tidy up his feet and ears, brush him out again, and trim the furnishings on his legs a little. By breaking the grooming regiment into two sessions, she kept both of them happy and neither one got stressed or worn-out.

The dryer buzzed and Emma let Cole get down off the table. She unloaded the laundry into a basket and headed upstairs. While she folded clothes and put them away, Cole played with a favorite toy, a stuffed, green frog, her granddaughter, Sydney had aptly named, "Froggy". Chores done, Emma sank into her favorite chair and picked up the novel she was reading. Cole, lying next to the chair, settled down to take a light snooze. After reading a page three times and still not knowing what she'd read, Emma gave up and let the previously exiled subject take over her mind.

Resting her head on the back of the chair and closing her eyes, Emma let her mind wander as it spun over times past and present. She thought back to the happiest time of her life, when she'd met and fell in love with her husband, or more correctly, her ex-husband. It was a wonderful, magic-filled time that only new love can inspire. The wedding followed about a year later and they had been so happy living together as man and wife in their first home, a small, second floor apartment. Ten months later the first of their children was born and Emma and John had been ecstatic to have a child all their own to love and cherish. Two more children came in the following years and so did the succession of houses as the family grew. Everyday life with its victories and defeats settled in as the years went by, but through it all Emma placed her love and trust in John. They were a team and met life head-on together, strong in their unity, or at least she had thought so.

The children had entered their teen years and any previous childhood problems or squabbles paled in comparison to those now facing them as parents during this critical period. Emma laughed as she remembered getting her first gray hair after an argument with her thirteen-year old daughter. Naturally, more gray hair and arguments were to follow. Teenagers were truly God's punishment and revenge for past sins. But lo and behold, you do survive it and years later can even laugh about it.

Emma quieted and the smile slipped from her face as her thoughts centered on John's leaving the family. After nineteen years of marriage, while the children were still in that turbulent teenage time of life, he decided he didn't want to be married anymore, much less be a father. He was having an affair and wanted out. He wanted a different life, a new lover, and no responsibility. *He* wanted to be happy.

Emma cringed as she recalled those black days. The children had been crushed, their hero gone, and she'd been devastated. It had been almost too much for her mind to wrap itself around. This was the one time in her life that her "make it fun and laugh" outlook on life couldn't sustain her.

In the subsequent months, she had deteriorated physically, and mentally, she'd been in shock. She couldn't grasp that he'd been unfaithful, no longer wanted to be her husband or a real father to his children. This was the man she'd had three babies with, loved with every part of her being and trusted with her life. Guess what, Emma? The joke's on you!

Struggling to keep herself together, she'd had to deal with the children's fears and worries too. She felt she had often failed them during that time, unable to keep up a reassuring front most days. She sometimes thought the children had helped her more than she had helped them. But somehow they got through it and eventually Emma came out of her numbed existence, dug down into her German roots, and came out fighting. She'd hired the best attorney she could afford and safeguarded the children's home and immediate future. John got his freedom, but that's all he got.

As Emma's mind continued to playback, she caught scene after scene behind her closed eyelids of the following years, functioning as a single parent. The crises, the solutions, the tears, and the laughter, all sped by her mind's eye. It all came back as the tears rolled silently down her cheeks, the emotion overwhelming as the losses and mistakes combined with the joys and the victories. They'd all pulled through somehow and managed to make good lives for themselves, despite a devastating blow.

Emma opened her eyes and dried her tears. She hated to look back most times. She hated dredging up the old pain that had never really gone away. She kept it buried, but it was there and it was with her children as well. If only these men realized what they did to the children they left behind, she thought. It's a loss that can never be filled, a void that is forever there. Emma silently, vehemently damned them all to hell.

And now the girls were going to manhunt for her! Oh, Lordy, Lordy, Lordy! The thought was enough to cause her to break out in a cold sweat. It wasn't that she hated men, she didn't. There were many men she greatly admired and she personally knew several husbands who were terrific to their wives, just look at Sam and Joanie. But for herself, well, that should probably just be left alone. Was she lonely sometimes? Yes. Did she miss sharing her life with someone? Yes. Did she miss cuddling or dancing in the arms of a man? Yes. Did she miss sex? Hell, yes. But did she think she could ever love someone so completely again? No. And did she think she could ever place her complete trust in a man again? No, not ever, those days of blind faith were long gone.

Emma stood up and looked around the room, only vaguely seeing what she was looking at. Her mind was racing, going over the answers to her mental questionnaire. With negatives in the two most important categories, she knew that a second marriage was not in her future. But maybe, just maybe, she could allow herself a more casual, laid-back relationship with the right man, if he could ever be found. That, she wouldn't worry about. That was her two friends self-appointed problem. With a slight bounce in her step and a small grin on her face, she led Cole out into the night.

Chapter Seven

The next morning, Cole woke Emma up with a gentle nudge precisely at five o'clock. She loved the gentle nudge, wished it would happen more often, but it was always a tossup, the wakeup method. It could be the nudge, or a face washing, or the infamous full body slam, or a combination of all three. Cole took his wakeup duty very seriously, but he also liked to keep Emma on edge, loved to keep her guessing, and that's what made it so much fun, at least for him. Regardless, Emma had rarely used an alarm clock for about a year now and when she did it was only for backup. Cole had an uncanny sense of time and Emma had learned to trust it almost exclusively. Every once in awhile it might have been nice to get an extra half hour of sleep, but with Cole on the job, it was not to be. She'd learned that if she wanted a little more snooze time she'd better make it a point to place a request with her four-footed wakeup provider.

They went about their daily drill at a more leisurely pace that morning since the shop opened two hours later on Sunday. Normally the girls traded off on weekends, but because they'd taken yesterday off, they were both going in to catch up on things and, of course, they had to decipher what Tammy had sold and get it off inventory. That alone could take up the greater part of the day. Emma wondered if she should bring down an extra bottle of wine or maybe something stronger. From the look of those first few sales slips she'd glimpsed, this could call for 151 Bacardi Rum.

The weather Emma noted, looking out the window, had lived up to predictions and was miserable. The temperature was hovering at thirty-nine and the sky was overcast with dark, low-lying clouds. It was raining lightly and there was a dense fog shrouding the valley. This was the type of weather that went right through you and once chilled, it took forever to warm up. Emma, shivering just thinking about it, dressed warmly and pulled on her rain gear.

She fired up the Explorer and put the defroster on. The windows were fogged up and it was as cold and damp inside the vehicle as outside. After a few minutes, she loaded the bike and Cole into the back, got in, and put the SUV into gear. Lights on and windshield wipers going, she started down the hill to Route 240.

It really was extremely foggy and she was going to have to take her time. Once she turned onto the main road, she kept her eyes moving constantly from the centerline to the white sideline so she could tell where she was. She couldn't see more than ten feet in front of her and felt totally disoriented, having no visual references other than the road markings. Besides that, she had to watch for deer; the area was literally covered with them. If you were unfortunate enough to have one dart out in front of you, you'd better be sharp because more times than not, there were at least one or two more following the first one. It probably would have been smarter to skip Cole's run today, but the park wasn't far and she should be fine if she went slow.

Emma arrived safe and sound ten minutes later, the trip taking twice as long as it normally did. She parked in her usual spot and thankful that no deer had jumped out in front of the car, mumbled that they, lowly creatures that they were, were all smart enough not to be out in this nastiness. They were probably all hunkered down in the woods, sheltered from the rain while she, with the supposed higher intelligence, was out here ready to get soaked. Go figure.

Noticing there were no other vehicles in the parking lot, Emma appeared to be the only person at the park, but that didn't surprise her. She didn't think there were too many other nutty people who would be crazy enough to be out in weather like this. Shrugging her shoulders, used to being the odd man out or more accurately the odd woman out, she unloaded the bike and Cole, and started out on the route they generally followed.

She felt like she was enveloped in a gigantic white cloud as she pedaled down a road that should have been as familiar to her as the back of her hand, but which now looked alien and somewhat forbidding. Cole seemed to be more aware, a little unsettled, sniffing the air, and looking to Emma every few minutes.

"It's okay, big boy, just a little fog, nothing to be worried about. It just looks a little spooky."

Cole turned his attention away from Emma as he trotted alongside the bike. He scanned the area as he moved, his body tensing, his senses on high alert. Emma noticed that he wasn't relaxing and getting into the run as he normally did and she wondered what was making him so uneasy. They had been in fog before, and although this was a bit denser than what they had previously encountered, Cole had never been the least bit bothered by it.

Cole continued to be agitated as they traveled over their route and after another mile or so, Emma decided to cut the run short. She could see no benefit in continuing and would be acting irresponsibly in pushing Cole to go on. Maybe there was a coyote nearby; they were quite common in this part of the state, and perhaps that's what was making Cole so uneasy. Not being able to see more than a few feet out in any direction, Emma was at a clear disadvantage. One coyote would be bad enough, but what if there was a whole pack? She u-turned to the other side of the road and started to make her way back. She strained her ears to hear any sound that might give a clue as to what was out there, but the fog muffled any telltale noise that could have given her a hint.

Cole had increased his pace and was actually pulling ahead of the bike in an effort to make Emma go faster. He was clearly trying to get her back to the car and Emma decided to trust his instincts and increased her speed. Whatever it was, she hoped it would back off when it saw they were leaving.

All of a sudden, Cole stopped dead in his tracks and a deep growl rumbled in his throat. Emma had to work fast not to end up in a pile, taken by surprise at the abruptness of his halt. Cole was staring at a fixed point in the fog, but for the life of her Emma couldn't see a damn thing. They stood there for a few minutes, neither one of them moving. Cole continued a low growl, the hair on the back of his neck standing up. Emma tensed and waited, but for what she didn't know. After a few seconds, she gave it up.

"Geez, Cole. Let's just get the hell out of here. Come on, let's go…now!"

Cole snapped his attention back to Emma and started off as she began to pedal. He was still as diligent, but seemed a bit calmer, not quite so alarmed the closer they got to the car. Once they reached the SUV, Emma made short work of loading up, but instead of lying down like he usually did, Cole remained standing in the back of the vehicle looking out the window in the direction from which they'd come. Emma started the car, put it in gear, and headed out of the park. Cole, satisfied they were safe now, finally lay down; but Emma started to breathe easier only after they were back on Route 240, heading home.

The fog was starting to lift just a little along the road and Emma lowered her foot on the gas pedal, her vision improved enough to warrant picking up some speed. Her only thought as she drove was to get back to the safety of her home. Whatever had been out there had given her enough of a scare that she needed to regroup. The surge of adrenalin that had fueled her fight or flight reflex was dissipating now and making her feel weak, her hand shaking when she lifted it off the steering wheel. She needed to eat something, preferably something full of sugar. She might even need a glass of wine. So what if it was only 10:30 in the morning, this was an emergency! Yeah, wine was exactly what she needed, and maybe a lot of it. Oh, God, she thought, I'm starting to sound and act just like Joanie. But right at that moment, she didn't really care.

* * * *

After they were certain she had left, the four men emerged from where they had been standing, silently watching their prey. They gathered around the vehicle they had parked behind the concession stand, which was located on one of the sidetracks that came off the two main roads. They were not happy and knew their boss wouldn't be either. The dog had known they were out there and had alerted the woman. He must have caught their scent because they sure hadn't made any noise. Once alerted, the woman had known there was a threat, she just hadn't known what kind. But the dog, they knew he recognized it for what it was right away. He'd caught their scent and he knew the threat was human, not animal, and their job had just gotten a whole lot harder.

71

Chapter Eight

One and a half hours and two, not so small, glasses of wine later, Emma and Cole arrived at the shop. Joanie and Sam were already there, unloading the two cupboards. They'd put the $75 bargain in the back room to be dealt with later, and were putting the primitive in the back corner where it would await the incoming candles.

"Hi, Sam. I see Joanie's got you working."

"Yeah, she's good at that. How you doing, Em? Cole, come here, boy. You're looking good."

Cole ambled over to Sam and was rewarded with lots of petting. Tank came out from behind the counter and jumped up to give Cole a doggy kiss of welcome on the face. Cole gave him a lick back and the two went off to amuse themselves.

Joanie, not wasting any time beating around the bush, came over with rags and a cleaning solution in her hand and extended them to Emma. "Fair trade, we got 'em in here, now you can clean 'em. I've got to get started on the sales slips from hell. Besides, you know I hate to clean."

"Yeah, I know, and hello to you too. Fine, no problem, but first I want to tell you what happened to Cole and me today when we took our run up at the park."

"You went out in that fog this morning?" Sam asked.

"Yeah, and I wish I hadn't."

"Christ, Emma! Sometimes you're a little too dedicated."

"It's not a question of dedication, Sam," Joanie laughingly said. "She's just nuts."

As Emma told them about what had taken place at the park, both Joanie and Sam stood quietly and listened, their faces expressing puzzlement, then worry. Joanie's previous lightheartedness was gone.

"I don't know, Em," Sam said. "I guess it could have been a coyote, but they usually don't show themselves during the daytime. Maybe because there was such a dense fog it could have felt camouflaged, but still, unless it was sick or rabid I can't see it being a coyote. They're too skittish to approach Cole like that, much less stalk you for that long."

"I know, Sam, I thought the same thing. But what else could it have been? There haven't been any reports of black bears in the area for a long time, and it sure wasn't any deer."

"No, it wasn't a deer, and I haven't heard anything about bear since the fall."

"Wouldn't you have heard some kind of noise if it was an animal?" asked Joanie. "I mean, wouldn't it have growled or something?"

"You would think so, but I didn't hear a thing and believe me I was trying. I really thought it was just spooky because of the fog at first, but Cole was reacting too strongly for me to ignore it. There was definitely something out there today."

"Well, we'll probably never know now, but at least you and Cole weren't hurt. It was probably a one-time thing. I don't think you have anything more to worry about. Joanie, I'm going to get going; I've got some things to do at the house. I'll come back at five to pick you up."

"Okay, Sam. See you later."

"Bye, Em."

"Bye, Sam."

After Sam left, the girls talked a little more about what had happened and then went back to their chores, Emma to her cleaning and Joanie to figure out Tammy's sales slips. While Emma was scrubbing down the hutch in the back corner, she could hear Joanie ranting and raving. The dogs, she saw, were keeping to the back room, away from the maniac out front. She knew she was in a far better place where she was, but if she didn't go up and help Joanie out, there was a very real possibility that Joanie would self-destruct. Emma could see her face getting red from where she was, and then there were the customers to consider. Emma wanted to still have some at the end of the day. In the mood she was in now, Joanie would probably get out the staple gun and shoot at them if they got too close. God, Emma thought, I have to remember to remove tools like that the day after Tammy works. Emma quickly finished cleaning the cupboard and went up to the counter area.

"Hey, kiddo, you need some help?"

"Son of a bitch, Em." Joanie's hands were full of sales slips and she looked like she was about ready to toss the whole bunch. "These things are impossible. Look at this one: One placemat, $3.50, one card, $2.25. We're going to have to do a count on every single thing we have in here."

"No, now, not really. Let's not exaggerate. We're just going to have to count all placemats that are $3.50 and all cards that are $2.25. That leaves out a whole bunch of placemats and two racks of cards."

"Oh yeah? Well, smart-ass, here's a slip for one placemat at $4.50 and a votive at $1.35. A votive...do you know how many damn votives we have, for cripes sakes? Here's another for...well, looky here, a card for $1.99. So... you were saying what about counting?"

"Shit, looks like I better get busy. But hey, look at this one. Look at the cute drawing she did of a weathervane, probably because she didn't know what it was called. See, we know what that is."

"Yeah? Which one? Rooster, horse, pig, or cow? She didn't write that down, did she? She didn't even draw a damn picture."

"Ummm, I'm going to go over to linens now and start counting. Okey-dokey?"

"Yeah, go. I'm getting a glass of wine. Do you want one?"

"No, thanks, I'm already ahead of you."

"You are?"

"Yeah."

"You're kidding. You never drink in the morning."

"Yeah, well, I did today. I was so shaken up after what happened at the park I had to have some wine to steady my nerves."

"Geez, you must have been really rattled."

"I was, and I found myself reacting like you would have."

"What does that mean?"

"It means I needed to get 'fortified'," Emma laughed, making quotation marks with her fingers.

"Hey, Em, fortify this," Joanie shot back as she flipped Emma the bird. Laughing herself now, Joanie went to the kitchen and got her wine.

The girls worked all afternoon taking merchandise off inventory, counting and sometimes recounting when customers interrupted them. You might know that Tammy'd had a good day, $1500 in sales. A few times Emma had to peruse the shop to see what was gone, the sales slips giving absolutely no clue. Thank God, she had a photographic memory and knew the shop inside out. Joanie kept the wine flowing and at least got mellow.

Finally they made sense of the last receipt, removed the items from the file, and shut down the computer. The last customers had left ten minutes ago and the girls started to close the place down. The dogs, sensing the shift in atmosphere, knew it was safe now; the dragon lady had disappeared. They raced to the front of the store, playing one of their favorite games, a doggy form of tag, up and down the aisles. Tank was almost always the winner. He could scoot into tighter spaces than Cole and used his smaller size to great advantage. Miraculously they'd never tipped over a display or broken anything. Cole knew he couldn't win, but chased after his buddy with good-natured intensity, going full out on the straightaways.

The girls relaxed as they watched the dogs' shenanigans and sat down to enjoy a restful moment. Emma was tired; it had been quite a day. And Joanie, well, she was half in the bag.

"Thank God, Sam's coming to pick you up. I don't think you're in any condition to drive."

"No, I don't think I am either, but all those little glasses of wine m…"

"Little glasses?" Emma interrupted.

"All right, big glasses. They made getting through those damn slips a lot easier. Geez, they were confusing. Let's try not to have Tammy work for awhile, okay?"

"Okay, I know you need some time to recover and get your sweet disposition back."

"You bet your sweet ass I do."

"Hey, look. Sam just pulled in. Your knight in shining armor has arrived to carry you away from all this."

"As long as he carries me home to take-out food. There's no way this little body, or brain for that matter, is capable of fixing dinner tonight. I just want to go home and relax and slowly pass-out."

"I think you'll get your wish."

Sam came in and gathered up Joanie and Tank. With a knowing look at Emma, he grinned and helped his wife out to the truck. When they were gone, Emma turned off the lights, locked up, and headed home with Cole prancing at her side. Thank goodness, the shop was closed on Mondays.

* * * *

Having been informed about what had transpired at the park, Jasper made a phone call to his employer that night. Cappellini was in his study, seated in a wine-colored, leather chair behind an ornately carved cherry wood desk when the call came in. The room was lit by a priceless Tiffany lamp sitting on the left-hand side of the desk, the rest of the surface littered with papers that he'd been studying. Dragging his attention away from the document he held in his hand, he answered the phone. "Yes?"

"It's Jasper, Mr. Cappellini."

"How goes it, Jasper?"

"Well, sir, on the plus side, we're learning everything there is to know about the woman, her habits, her routine, friends, likes, dislikes…"

"What's the problem?" Cappellini cut in.

"The dog."

"What do you mean, the dog?"

"The team set up surveillance today in the park where she takes the dog to run. There was dense fog, visibility almost zero. There's no way the men were seen or heard, they were like statues, but the dog knew they were there and alerted the woman."

"Are you sure no one slipped up?"

"Yes, sir. I have no reason to question my men's performance. They're professionals and act accordingly."

"Aah… then he must have scented them."

"Yeah, that's the conclusion we've come to."

"How many men did you use?"

"Four. They were spaced out along the route the woman and dog use."

"And he scented them all?"

"I think so. From what I was told, the dog was aware almost from the start of the run."

Cappellini smiled, he couldn't help it. "Did the woman know you were there?"

"No. She knew the dog was upset and there was a threat, but she'd have no reason to think there were men watching her. She probably thought it was an animal."

"Well, this makes things a bit more difficult for you."

"Yes, sir, it does."

"For now I want you to back off. Keep gathering information, but don't do anything to spook the dog or the woman."

"Yes, sir."

"I want you to have only one man at the Alexander show, no more. And he's to stay well hidden. Let's see if they pick up on him there."

"All right, sir, we'll proceed in that manner then. I'll keep you posted."

"You do that, Jasper." He broke the connection and looked around the room, ignoring the beautiful things exquisitely displayed. Instead, his gaze locked onto the picture of Cole he'd taken at the show where he'd first seen him. "I knew you were special," he said, speaking to Cole's image, "and you're going to be mine, one way or the other, you will be mine."

Chapter Nine

Monday… a whole day to do whatever she wanted with no time restraints, and Emma still got up at five and got started. She may not have had any commitments for the day, but she had plenty to do. Of primary importance was a trip to the local nursery to buy her hanging fuchsia baskets. The hummingbirds were back. They always reappeared right around Mother's Day and she needed to get her little friends one of their favorite sources of nectar.

Emma sailed through her exercise, having opted for a three-mile workout that morning. She'd recently added ankle weights and for this particular videotape she carried three-pound hand weights. God, was she in shape or what for an old broad?! They wouldn't catch her huffing and puffing in the ring when she put Cole through his paces, no matter how many times the judge had them go around.

After she finished, she made a beeline for the kitchen to get her breakfast. She was so weak from hunger she was afraid her legs might give out. Emma sometimes wondered if she should eat before working out, but was always afraid she'd end up throwing the food right back up. It was really a rather easy decision, to go without eating, that is. Emma absolutely, positively detested tossing her cookies and would do almost anything to avoid it. In fact she hadn't done it in over ten years, most often through sheer determination. How's that for outright bullheadedness?

Once her hunger had been appeased, she went to draw a bath. Baths, to Emma, were considered an almost religious experience and were reserved for Mondays when she had time to relax and enjoy a good soak. Cole had to be kept out of the room however, because without a doubt he would be right in the tub with her. Newfoundlands loved the water and a full bathtub was too much of a temptation to resist. It had taken only one time for Emma to learn to close the door on her furry friend. The cleanup alone had taken forever, not to mention the bruises she had suffered when an enthusiastic Cole had landed on her full force. Emma could testify firsthand that there wasn't an inch of give to a porcelain bathtub.

She allowed herself about fifteen minutes of pure bliss, immersing herself in water that was as hot as she could stand, perfumed with a rich bubble bath. This was heaven, she thought, closing her eyes and enjoying the sensation. She was just starting to drift off when Cole barked from the other side of the door, snapping her back to full alertness.

"I hear you, Cole. Just give me a few more minutes."

The spell broken, Emma shaved her legs and washed. She heard Cole lie down and puff out a big sigh as she drained the tub and toweled off. She stepped over to the vanity to get her body lotion and caught sight of her reflection in that damn double mirror. She was actually in pretty good shape for her age, her body somewhat toned, if not youthful. Her abdomen was pretty flat, that post-menopausal paunch not afflicting her, well, not much anyway. But the thing that she had no control over, the thing that was driving her crazy, was the downward shift of her breasts. Where *were* they going and when would they stop? It wasn't like she had breast-fed, she hadn't, and she had always worn a good supportive bra. So why the *hell* were they sliding down her chest wall? What happened to all those muscles that had always held them up? Was the pull of gravity that great? Well, whatever it was, it sucked! One of Joanie's aunts' breasts were so low she tucked them into her pants, for cripes sake! Well, if hers knew what was good for them, they'd stop right now. They were low enough! And she had no intention of *ever* tucking those babies into her pants! No way, no how, never! She should start a grass roots movement: Surgery to get them up where they belonged, for any woman over the age of fifty, would be compulsory by law for all medical insurance plans. Think of the support she'd have, millions of women storming the capitol, drooping breasts in tow! And once those babies were returned to their rightful place? America, the beautiful!

Emma smoothed on her lotion and got dressed, except for her shirt. She opened the door and Cole sprang to his feet. She still had to wash her hair and went over to the kitchen sink. That was the drawback to taking a bath; washing your hair was a separate deal. Cole tagged along and sat at her side while she got the job done. Pandering to Cole's love of water, she gave the stream running out of the faucet a couple of finger flicks, shooting water in his direction. He tried to catch the drops in his mouth and got most of them, a few landing on his face. Knowing he was happy now, Emma wrapped a towel around her hair, went back to the bathroom and got busy with her makeup.

Never one to stand in front of a mirror for very long, Emma applied a little powder and blush, eye shadow and mascara, and she was good to go. She unwrapped her hair and dried it a little with the hair dryer, then smoothed in some styling gel. She finger combed her short, highlighted to cover the gray, light brown hair and left it to air dry for awhile before she finished drying it with the dryer. She'd never quite gotten the hang of drying with a blower, probably because she was always in a hurry to be doing something else, and if she did it when her hair was too wet, she ended up looking like a haystack with hair going every which way.

It was odd really; she could groom just about any breed of dog to a "T", but couldn't for the life of her duplicate the hair style her beautician had assured her was so easy to do. Luckily, she didn't give a rat's ass about it because she was definitely lacking in the female art of hair grooming, and a lesser woman would have been totally crushed by a deficiency in what some believed should be an inbred talent.

Emma put on her shirt, picked up the house, put the dishes in the dishwasher, and made her grocery list. She ironed a few shirts and when it was safe to continue, finished off her hair with the dryer. She checked in the mirror, pronounced it passable and gave her "do" a quick dusting of hair spray.

It was time to leave for Cole's run and she wouldn't be honest if she didn't admit she felt some trepidation. But, committed as she was, she loaded up and set off for the park. Arriving a few minutes later, she noticed that today there were other cars already parked and she could see people jogging and walking. The sky was blue and the air clear, a totally different atmosphere than yesterday.

She got Cole and the bike out, then started off on their regular route. Everything looked familiar and normal, and Emma relaxed. Cole fell into an easy pace and trotted confidently next to her. He showed no signs of anxiety and appeared loose and steady. They continued on uneventfully, turned at the three-mile mark and started back toward the parking area. Cole watched ahead and exhibited no agitation, content to stay in sync with the tempo that Emma set. When they arrived safely back at the car, Emma gave Cole an extra hug and kiss. She'd been afraid there might be some aftereffects from the previous run and was relieved that Cole had reacted normally to the activity.

Back home, she let Cole romp in the yard for a little bit while she checked the flowerbeds, and couldn't resist pulling a few weeds that had sprung up. Cole trotted over to where she was, sniffing the few remaining daffodils and the abundant, multi-colored tulips, going from one to the next. He loved to smell the flowers, shoving his nose into their centers and inhaling deeply. The end result was he usually had pollen all over his nose and often came up sneezing.

They went into the house and Cole flopped down with his "Froggy", playfully tossing it into the air. Emma gave him a couple of ice cubes to munch on. It was a good way of quenching his thirst without overfilling his stomach with water. She sat down at the table and opened a Diet Pepsi to drink while she got herself organized on whatever else she had to do. Emma decided to get her errands out of the way in what was left of the morning and got ready to go. She called a reluctant Cole back to the mudroom and put him in his crate. She couldn't exactly take him into the grocery store and it was going to be too warm to keep him in the car. The temperature was supposed to rebound up to sixty-five today and a closed vehicle would get way too hot.

"We'll go to the nursery this afternoon, Cole. For now, just sit tight and I'll be back soon."

Emma put several more ice cubes in his dish, then headed out the door. She did her shopping in Springville, a town about twelve miles south of the house. The town had a population of over four thousand, and was easily reached by Routes 219, 39 and 240. There was a blend of town, suburban, and rural life, with the economy based on industrial, commercial, and agricultural businesses. After making the turn from Route 240 onto Route 39, there were beautiful residential homes, which preceded the business district in the center of town. Most of the homes on Route 39, the main road going through the village, were over a hundred years old and charmingly maintained with sweeping lawns that cascaded down from atop the hill where the houses stood. There were eleven churches, a hospital, medical offices, several veterinary practices, VFW posts, five schools, a theater, too many eating establishments to count, bed and breakfast lodgings, a hotel, small town businesses, and major chains.

Next to the fire station and right smack in the middle of everything was Springville's most famous attraction, The Auction. Every Wednesday, without fail, The Auction was in full force. The grounds encompassed several acres, a huge barn, some permanent outside stalls and in non-snow months, aisle after aisle of tables and booths set up by people who came to sell anything and everything. People attended from all over the Western New York area and northwestern Pennsylvania, most coming on a regular basis. The grounds opened at six in the morning and closed at four in the afternoon. The actual auction of livestock took place at noon in the barn and was the highlight of the weekly event. On Wednesdays, traffic was a nightmare to say the least, the number of cars on the road at least tripling what was normal.

Emma had no such problems that day and easily made it to Wal-Mart, where she picked up a few items, like extra socks, that she needed for the show. She drove across the street to Tops, the local supermarket chain, and did her grocery shopping, adding extra snack food and soda for the weekend to her usual order. She finished up at the liquor store, which was just down the road; here she purchased a few bottles of wine. Two were for the shop to replace the bottles that Joanie had gone through this past week trying to bolster her strength for the Tammy/inventory ordeal, and one was for the show.

Emma didn't need to bring more, her other two partners-in-crime were bound to contribute to the liquor supply, of that she was quite certain. When Joanie made out her list for what she needed to bring to a show, booze was placed in the number one spot, and as for Sally, well, her manhattan makings were probably at number three, right behind her dog and her motor home.

Errands complete, she took the back way on old Route 219 and avoided the center of town. Cutting over on Genesee Road, she turned onto Route 240 and went north to get home.

All in all, she'd been gone a little over two hours and was feeling the pangs of hunger as she pulled into the driveway. She parked the SUV and opened up the house, letting Cole out of his crate. He bounded outside with Emma and sniffed around while she unloaded her purchases.

They went inside and after putting the groceries away, Emma made lunch for both of them. Actually, she made a sandwich for herself, ham and Swiss with lettuce, tomato and mayo on thick slices of her homemade beer bread and gave Cole two pieces of ham and cheese, which he ate directly from her fingers. She finished off the meal with an apple for each, cutting Cole's into slices. He loved apples and probably would have eaten the core and seeds if Emma had let him. She cleaned up when they were finished and the two of them headed out to the Explorer.

"Okay, Cole, let's go get those flowers."

Greene's Garden Center was located about a quarter of a mile beyond the Hearthmoor; in fact you could see it from the restaurant. When Emma pulled into the lot, Cole started to spin he was so excited. Emma put the vehicle into park and they both hopped out. Emma put Cole on lead and, even though he was anxious to get into the greenhouse, he stayed at her side never so much as making the leash taunt.

They went inside and as they approached the first flat of flowers, Cole stuck his nose out and gave a sniff. He so loved flowers that this place was like heaven on earth to him; anyone watching could tell they made him happy. His tail was wagging rapidly from side to side as they made their way down the aisle. Emma, stopping at each different kind of flower so Cole could smell the blossoms, enjoyed watching his reaction to the different fragrances. The people that worked at the nursery adored him and several came up to say hello.

Emma spotted the fuchsia she wanted and an employee named Barb retrieved the ones she pointed out with a long hook. The plants were way too high for Emma or anyone else to reach. She got a total of six and then went to look at the annuals and perennials. Barb stayed with her and when Emma decided what she wanted, Barb would put it aside. Emma had to watch herself because she could spend a fortune here and often did.

She needed some red bee balm, another hummingbird favorite, and had Barb grab eight plants. Pansies were one of her favored flowers and had Barb put up two whole flats. She loved their sunny faces and their uncompromising hardiness. They looked ever so delicate, but they were tough little buggers. One winter, they had actually bloomed in the garden during the month of December. You had to love a flower with the audacity to bloom when there was snow on the ground and Christmas was just around the corner.

Emma topped off her selections with a new variety of daisy and putting her hands up to act as blinders, walked back to the cash register. She paid her bill and Barb gave Cole a dog biscuit, which she barely felt him take from her hand. Once it was in his mouth though, all gentlemanly restraint was gone and the biscuit quickly vanished.

Barb came out to the car with Emma and helped her load the plants into the back of the SUV. Cole was going to have to sit in the passenger seat on the way home, his usual space having been completely taken over with flowers. Emma put his seat belt on and off they went. Cole's nostrils were twitching rapidly as he sniffed the fragrant air, an expression on his face that could only be interpreted one way. He was in absolute ecstasy. Emma, glancing over at him, just shook her head and laughed.

Chapter Ten

Tuesday rolled around and Emma was down at the shop a little after ten o'clock. Joanie had arrived earlier and opened up. Tank was lying in wait for Cole and sprang toward him as he entered the store. The two dogs rolled around on the floor and then raced for the back room, where they had their own private playground, the floor already strewn with squeaky toys and rawhide, Frisbees and balls.

"Morning, Em," Joanie called out.

"Morning, Joan," Emma answered, walking stiffly to the counter. "How was your day off? Busy as usual?"

"Yeah, I had a lot of yard work to do, thought I'd better get started on it. The flower gardens were a mess after the winter. I had a lot of dead stuff to dig up. Tank helped. God, he loves to dig. I had to give him a bath afterward though; he was such a mess. What'd you do?"

"Ran errands, went to Greene's and got some flowers. When I got back I planted two flats of pansies and I'm paying for it today. My back is killing me and I'm so stiff I can hardly move. I'm really hoping for a nice, easy, laid-back day."

"Umm, Em...sorry to disappoint you, but we've got an appointment with a sales rep today."

"Oh damn! Really? Who?"

"Our very favorite… George Fleming from Always Perfect Gift."

"Oh, God, not that pompous ass, not today. I just wanted to chill out, have a quiet day. Do we have to do it? Can't we cancel?"

"No, afraid not."

"Damn. Why do we keep dealing with him?"

"Like we have a choice? We like the product, we like the price point, so we deal with him."

"I wish to hell they'd get a different rep for this area."

"Well, take heart in the fact we only have to see him twice a year. He'll be here around 11:30."

Now that her day was completely ruined, Emma went about her work mumbling under her breath about the injustice of it all. All she had wanted was an uncomplicated, normal day and instead she had to deal with the salesman from hell. He was such a totally unpleasant man, neither one of them could stand him. He was even offensive to the customers and to top it off, he had the worst breath in the world. The most atrocious dog breath couldn't hold a candle to this guy. The asshole makes me want to puke, Emma thought, which was saying a lot since she so thoroughly despised that particular bodily function. She took a couple of deep breaths and composed herself, no sense getting all worked up. They'd deal with it and get him out of the shop as quickly as they could.

The minutes ticked by and it was 11:30 before they knew it. As if rehearsed, Fleming pulled into the parking lot right on time. If it was anybody else, they'd have given out points for being punctual, but with him, it was a demerit. The girls moved behind the counter and waited for him to approach. The door opened and in he came.

George Fleming was somewhere in his early sixties, about 5'9" and around 250 pounds. He was balding and had only a few hairs going across the top of his head. His eyes, behind unattractive, black glasses, were small and beady, and he had the nose of a person who indulged in excessive drink. He had a wimpy mustache above thin lips and his ears stuck out from his head. His chest had fallen to his stomach and that hung over his belt. His shoulders were narrow and his hips wide. In other words he was shaped like a pear, an attractive specimen of manhood to be sure. His clothing was unimaginative and cheap, and he reeked of cigarette smoke.

There was a table and chairs on the girl's side of the counter and when sales reps came in, they were always invited to come around and sit. It made for a much more relaxed atmosphere and the reps were thankful to be off their feet. Emma and Joanie generally supplied coffee or a soft drink and, on occasion, one of them would bake a homemade goody, be it muffins, or scones or even a cake, and the reps were always very appreciative. But when they dealt with George, protocol was a little different. They kept him standing on the customer side of the sales desk and offered him absolutely no refreshment.

"Hey, chickies, how you doing?" George asked, already losing points with that anal greeting.

"We're fine. How are you?" Emma answered with about as much enthusiasm as she'd display if she were in the dental chair about to have a tooth extracted.

"Oh, I'm great, just great. Got some good stuff to show you, everyday, fall, and Christmas. It's that time you know, have to get the Christmas orders in."

"Yeah, we know. Let's get started." Joanie grumbled. She'd already fought the urge to retaliate for the "chickies" thing and now just wanted to move things along as fast as she could.

Cole had come out from the back room when he'd heard George's voice and moved to stand between Emma and the salesman. Emma put her hand on his head and softly told him it was okay. He had instinctively moved to protect her, remembering from previous visits her dislike for the man. Cole stayed where he was for a few seconds and then, reassured that Emma was safe, moved a few feet behind her and lay down to watch. Tank followed him over and he too lay down, biding his time in case he should be needed as backup.

George put his books up on the counter and they started to go through them. A lot of the merchandise was not apropos to the shop, designed more for a general gift store, and Emma and Joanie skipped right over it. George tried to slow them down and made several snide comments about the choice and quantity of product they were ordering. The girls let the comments slide until he got a little too insulting.

"You guys don't know shit about what's selling. You've got to order some of this stuff; it's brand new to the market. It'll sell like hot cakes."

"Really? Well, you know what? We don't want any of that stuff, George, it's not right for the shop. And you know what else? If we don't want to, we don't have to order a thing, not one blessed thing," Emma said.

"And if you don't cease with the ever-present comments, we won't," Joanie added, giving George a snide look.

"God, you're such a bitch, Joanie," George fired back.

"Excuse me."

"I think you heard me. Now come on, let's get back to the order. I've got another appointment later this afternoon."

Emma and Joanie exchanged a look and Emma noticed that Cole had risen to his feet during the last bit of conversation. "Joanie, I think we're done here, don't you?"

"Yeah, Em, we're done. George, we wouldn't think of keeping you from your next appointment, so fold up your tent and leave... Oh yeah, we're canceling the order."

"What? What do you mean?"

"I mean we're done dealing with you. We've had it. If we want to order we'll make arrangements in-house or request another rep. That should go over big at headquarters, don't you think?" Joanie had fire in her eyes.

"You can't do that."

"Oh, no? Watch us," Emma answered, her body language screaming, "Come on, try me. I'm ready to get down and dirty."

"You two really are bitches."

The girls looked at each other and then at George. Was he really that dumb or did he just have a death wish? Didn't he realize they were in fighting mode and the level of their hostility was enough to make the air crackle? Maybe he needed it to be spelled out for him.

"George, listen to me," Joanie said in a deceptively calm voice. "Normally we're sweet as pie, but when we're pushed or just plain need to be, for whatever reason, we can be the two biggest, bad-ass bitches you ever saw, so don't push your luck. Now go away, we're done."

Still not completely aware of the bullet he was dodging, George started to gather up his books. Emma, primed for action, motioned Cole over with a nod of her head in the rep's direction. Cole went to the other side of the counter and stood very close to the side of his leg. Emma started to move her head slightly from side to side as Cole watched, and Joanie looked at her like she was crazy.

"What are you doing?" she whispered. "You look like one of those dogs in the rear window of a car with your head wobbling like that."

"Just watch," Emma whispered back.

George, busy getting his catalogs and samples packed, was clueless as to what was going on. While he was bent over loading up his gear, Emma whispered, "Fling it" to Cole who, on cue, shook his head vigorously and spewed drool all over George. Now, Newfoundlands have an unending supply of drool and while sometimes it's a pain in the neck, like when they're groomed for the show ring, it had just proved to be a most valuable asset.

Fleming stood up, his face mottled with rage. He was so angry he was unable to speak, but stared with murderous intent at Cole. Cole held his ground and a low growl started in his throat.

"Mr. Fleming, if I were you, I'd use the brains God gave me and I'd get the hell out of here right now," Emma warned.

He flicked his gaze to Emma, scorn evident in his features, and started walking, not uttering another word. Cole stayed behind him, following him to the door. Tank brought up the rear. The door slammed shut with his departure and the girls let out a resounding whoop. Cole came racing back to Emma who opened her arms and corralled him in, giving him plenty of hugs and kisses. Tank launched himself at Joanie and landed in her arms.

"Hot damn! We finished him off," Joanie said.

"Yeah, I guess we did," Emma replied. "I think I've been wanting to put him in his place since the first day we met him."

"Yeah, I know what you mean. Man, that was a great trick Cole pulled. But when and for what reason did you ever teach him that?"

"I don't know. I guess I taught it to him a few months ago. I was either really bored and needed something to do or just in one of my goofy moods to make use of the natural resources at hand. I mean Cole does have drool in never-ending supply. My clothes will bear witness to that."

"No shit."

"So I guess I thought I'd have some fun with it. See how far I could spread this natural wonder."

"You're not all there, are you?"

"Nope."

"How'd you come up with the command, 'Fling it'?"

"It seemed appropriate to me. Can you think of a better one?"

"Nope, actually it's perfect and it sure came in handy today. But seriously, Em, you've got to get a life. You've got a little too much time on your hands. Anyway, think of all the fun we can have with this little trick."

"Now, Joanie, don't go getting any ideas."

"Are you kidding? This is great. I can think of a few people right off the top of my head we can use it on."

"Joanie…."

"Oh, all right. But it's good to know we have it in our arsenal if we need it. Damn, that was good!"

The girls celebrated by ordering a pizza from the local pizza parlor and Cole and Tank got their share. A few of the regular customers came in and were asked if they wanted to join them. They accepted and an impromptu party ensued, with a bottle of wine making the rounds. The story was told and Cole was hailed as a true hero. Sales were unexpectedly good, undoubtedly due to the magic of alcohol, and the girls ended the day on a definite high note.

Chapter Eleven

Wednesday was duller than dirt and an actual blessing for Emma and Joanie. Customer flow was sluggish and they had plenty of time to get caught up on paperwork. Several deliveries came around noon from both UPS and Fed Ex, and they had the rest of the afternoon to check in the new stock and get it out on the floor. The cartons were filled with Styrofoam peanuts and Tank's little eyes lit up when he saw them. He grabbed one that had fallen on the floor and strode over to Cole and layed it at his feet. Cole took one look, batted it away with his paw and gave a resigned sigh. He knew later on they'd be playing *the game*. Tank, not impressed with Cole's response, picked up the peanut, went over to Joanie, dropped it at her feet, and did a couple of quick spins. Excitement was making his body quiver.

"When we're done, Tank, we'll let you go at it, but not right now. Chill out, bud," Joanie said as Tank continued to watch her expectantly.

"Oh, God, what a mess we're going to have again."

"Yeah, but at least it's confined to the back room."

"Bad enough," Emma groused. "These things get all over the place and they're hell to pick up, they get so full of static electricity."

"Yeah, but he has a ball."

"Yeah, well….it is funny as all get out to watch him."

"He's such a major screwball."

"Takes after his owner."

"Ha-ha. Aren't you the funny one?"

"You betcha sister. Let's get it done so your screwball can play."

Tank, resigned to the fact that nothing was going to happen immediately, lay down to wait although he wasn't at all happy about it. He kept the one peanut he'd grabbed and pushed it around on the floor with his nose from his supine position as a reminder to Joanie that he wasn't about to forget about the promised game.

The girls were just finishing up when a customer, a male customer, came in and walked around the shop, looking a little lost. They had never seen him before and Joanie's antenna had sprung up to full alert. She walked over to him, introduced herself and Emma, and asked if there was anything they could help him with.

"Well, actually, yes. I have to get a birthday present for my seventeen-year old niece and I don't have a clue as what to get."

"Does she have any hobbies, or does she collect anything?"

"I don't know if she collects anything, but she's really into horses. She rides almost everyday."

"Oh, well, we have some fantastic horse things. We've got notepaper and key chains, weathervanes and stuffed horses, sandstone horses and, well, gee, I could go on and on. I'll tell you what…Emma here knows the shop way better than I do and she'd be happy to take you around and point out the various things. Then we'll leave you alone so you can make up your mind about what you want."

"That sounds terrific. Thanks."

Shooting Joanie a look that could, if not kill her, at least do bodily damage, Emma took the man around the shop and showed him what his niece might possibly like. When she was finished, she politely excused herself and went back to what she had been doing. Joanie rolled her eyes in disgust and mentally plotted her next move.

Knowing Joanie was up to no good, Emma kept one eye on her and the other on the customer. She couldn't help but notice that he was very good-looking and tall, well over six feet. He had curly, black hair that was threaded with silver at the temples and a mustache that made Emma wonder immediately what it would feel like against her skin when kissed by those full, sensuous lips. Whoa, holy shit! Where the hell had that come from? Damn that Joanie and all her talk about men and sex! Emma quickly turned away, embarrassed by the turn her thoughts had taken, and made herself busy with whatever was handy.

A few minutes later, the gentleman approached the sales counter and as Joanie rang him up, he asked if his purchases could possibly be gift-wrapped. Emma lunged for the gifts, assuring him that they would love to do it and it was absolutely no problem. She just about ran to the back room, knowing she was taking the coward's way out, but not caring a whole hell of a lot. She had to get away from him and Joanie since there was no telling what Joanie was capable of doing or saying. Of course, there was danger aplenty leaving her alone with the man too. That could also lead to dire consequences. Well, she'd just have to risk it. As she boxed and wrapped, Emma could hear the murmur of voices, but couldn't make out any of the conversation. The job finished, she was forced to go back out front and prayed that Joanie hadn't done or said anything to embarrass her or the gentleman.

They were chatting about the recent weather and the gentleman didn't look like he wanted to strangle Joanie or bolt for the nearest exit, so that was good. Emma put the gifts into a bag and handed them to him. He smiled (oooh, that mustache looked great when he smiled) and thanked her, then took his leave and walked out of the shop. Joanie looked like she was going to burst and she was grinning from ear to ear.

"All right, spill it." Emma knew Joanie well enough to know that she had gathered what she considered fascinating tidbits of information.

"Well, his name is Ben Sie...."

"Ben? Oh, I've always loved that name. Ben, Benjamin. If I'd had another boy, I wanted to name him Ben. It's such a good name; it has such...such character. It's a very strong name, don't you think, Joanie?"

"Yeah, yeah, it's a great name, the best one in the whole damn world. Now shut the hell up, stop interrupting." Joanie chided.

"Okay, I'll be quiet, but it is a great name. It's..." Joanie pierced her with a dirty look. Emma pantomimed zipping her lips. It lasted a total of one second. "Go ahead, tell me. I won't say another word 'til you're done. Promise." Emma held her hand up to reinforce the pledge and Joanie shot her a warning look.

"All right. His name is Ben Sievers and he just moved out here a couple of weeks ago. He's originally from the area, but he's lived in Massachusetts for about seventeen years and before that, he lived in New Jersey. He's taken one of the apartments next door for right now and he's a retired FBI agent, just retired this year. Oh, Sam's going to love that; they can trade war stories. Anyway, he does some carpentry work part time and likes to golf and ski. He's fifty-five and not married and not attached."

Emma's mouth was hanging open and it took her a full minute to close it and get her brain to function. "How...how did you do that? How did you get all that information in so short a time? This has got to be a new record even for you."

"It's a gift."

"More like a curse. But, listen, maybe the guy's gay."

"Get real, Em. I don't think so."

"Could be, not married, not attached."

"Well, you're not married and you're sure as hell not attached and you're not gay."

"Yeah, well, I was clutching at straws."

"This is a gift from God," Joanie announced, a mystical look coming over her face.

"What are you talking about?"

"There's divine intervention at work here."

"Divine intervention? What the hell do you mean by that?"

"Weren't we just talking the other night at Sally's about finding you a man?"

"Yeah."

"Well...."

"Well, what?"

"Don't you get it, Em? God sent Ben to us. This is the guy, this is the one."

"The one for what?"

"The one you're going to sleep with, the one who's going to take you to heaven."

"Oh f...."

"Yes, precisely," Joanie interrupted, giving Emma a knowing look.

"Well, hot damn, Joanie! I don't know this guy from Adam and you've got me in bed with him already. Geez! Don't do this to me. Don't push this guy at me and for God's sake don't go getting weird on me with this divine intervention stuff. And get that stupid look off your face."

"What stupid look?"

"The one that's on there right now. You look like you should be gazing into a crystal ball or something."

Joanie scrubbed her face with her hands. When she took her hands away, she had a big-ass grin lighting up her face and she was waggling her eyebrows. "How's this? Better?"

"Oh, God, no. It's worse, you sicko."

"Want me to try another one?"

"No, stop before I'm tempted to slap your stupid ass."

"All right, all right. But, Em, you have to calm down. You're wired way too tight. Take a chill pill. You'll see; this is going to work out. Besides, I already told him you were single and available."

"You did what?" Emma looked like she was ready to blow a gasket. "Tell me you didn't do that. No way you did that, did you? You're just trying to get a rise out of me, right? Oh, please Joanie, tell me you didn't tell him that."

"Geez! You know what? Maybe you need to take a couple of chill pills. You better relax. I can see the veins popping out on your neck from here and your face is getting all kind of red and blotchy too."

Emma shot her a murderous look. "Joanie!"

"Okay, okay. I didn't tell him. There, that's what you want to hear, isn't it?" Joanie sounded more than a little exasperated. She made motions with her hands implying she was washing her hands of the whole affair. "As of now, I'm out of it, all right? Are you satisfied? Are you happy now?"

"Yes, thank you. You don't know how much. Whew, maybe I can start breathing again. God, you had me going. Whew, okay, I'm better now. Let's go get Tank set up for his jump."

"All right," Joanie replied, acting like she was thoroughly chastised. However when Emma turned away, Joanie had a wicked gleam in her eye and a sly smile on her face. Talking quietly to herself, she confessed, "But I really did tell him, Em, and I could tell he was interested. You're going to thank me when he puts that sparkle back in your eye. God, I can't wait to tell Sally."

Emma was already setting things up by the time Joanie got to the back room. She had one of the big cartons completely full with peanuts and was positioning it at the far end of the room. The carton was about six inches taller than Cole; actually, it was one they saved for these occasions. There was a mark on the floor where Cole was to stand, his side parallel to the box. Joanie cleared all the toys away from the area that served as the runway and got Tank into position. Emma put Cole on his mark, told him to "Stay", and then moved to her position at the side of the box, holding it in place.

"You ready, Em?"

"Ready, Joanie, let him go."

Joanie released Tank and he shot out of her hands, running full speed toward Cole. When he was about three feet away from Cole, Tank jumped into the air, banked off Cole's back and flew into the carton, sending peanuts flying. Emma reached in, got him out, and sent him back to Joanie. The girls were both laughing themselves silly; Emma was covered in peanuts, static making them stick to her clothes, hair, feet, and hands. She poured more into the carton to fill it up again and gave the all-ready signal. Checking first to see that everybody was in position, Joanie let Tank go and he repeated the maneuver. Ten runs later, they called it quits and started to clean up. Tank was happily exhausted and fell asleep on top of Cole, who shot Emma a long-suffering look as the girls struggled to capture the elusive Styrofoam. About forty-five minutes later, they were successful and the place was clean...until next time.

Chapter Twelve

Whatever Thursday brought, the girls didn't care. The place could blow up, terrorists could attack, floodwaters could carry the shop away, and they would still go ahead with what was planned for the day. Hell, there was a dog show to get ready for and nothing on this earth would stand in the way of that! Emma was to open up and work until about two o'clock, and then Joanie would come in and work till closing at six. Joanie was to do all her show prep before she came in, and Emma would do hers after Joanie relieved her.

They'd followed the same routine for many years and had it down to a science, even though over time the breed of dog they were showing had changed occasionally and the grooming techniques and timings had differed from breed to breed. Some breeds needed to be bathed the day before the show, others like Cole, two days. Some breeds didn't get bathed at all when they were showing because they'd blow or shed coat. Other methods were used to clean their fur; one way was to use a solution of water and Listerine, spraying it on and then toweling the coat to remove dirt and odor. Some needed clipping, others stripping, still others scissoring, and some just had to get brushed. Somehow, no matter what the breed or grooming regiment, it had always worked out.

Before Emma went down to the shop, she started to organize the clothing she was going to take. She had to have warm clothes, so that meant jeans, sweaters, sweatshirts, turtlenecks, socks, jacket, rain hat, slicker, waterproof shoes, or maybe her hiking boots. She had to have her ring clothes: skirts, blouses, blazer, the god-awful pantyhose, and shoes. Although the dress code had relaxed somewhat over the years to include pantsuits, most judges still preferred skirts and dresses as proper ring attire for female exhibitors. She needed sleepwear, so she decided on a pair of flannel pajamas because no matter how warm it got during the day, the nights were bound to be cold. She'd double up on the amount of underwear and socks she took, experience having taught her never to be caught short. It had taken only the one time, when she'd been soaked in an unexpected downpour, for Emma to pack prepared for anything. She'd take some lighter clothing too, just in case the weather was good. Well, she could hope, couldn't she? She had everything laid out and ready to put in her suitcase by the time she had to get down to the store.

Her time at the shop flew by with customers coming in at a steady pace. UPS showed up a little early and had four cartons for her. She had worked her way through two of them when Angie Newmann walked in the door and wanted to talk about this, that, and the other thing.

Angie had been a regular customer for a number of years and was a genuinely nice person. The only problem was, she was an unbelievable pain in the ass. She could talk circles around the national debate team and still have something left over. To say she was dense was an understatement and in order to get a point across you had to be ready to go ten rounds with her.

"Hi, Emma. I see you're alone today. Where's Joanie?"

"We split the day up today, Angie. She'll be here later."

"How come? You guys always work together during the week unless one of you is sick. She isn't sick, is she? I mean if she's sick, then you'll get sick because you're always together. And that means that you're carrying the germs right now and could get somebody else sick. You could get me sick. No offense, Emma, but I'm gone step back a bit, okay?"

Emma quirked her left eyebrow, whispered a "whoa" under her breath, and assured the woman that Joanie wasn't ill.

"Then how come she isn't here?"

"Joanie isn't here because we split the day like I said. The reason we split the day is so that we can get ready for the dog show we're going to this weekend," Emma patiently explained.

"Where's the show?"

"Alexander."

"Is that in New York?"

"Yep."

"Where's Alexander?"

"Up near Attica."

"How many days is the show?"

"Two."

"Friday and Saturday?"

"No, Saturday and Sunday."

"Are you taking Cole?"

"Yeah," Emma said, thinking to herself, who the hell else would I be taking?

"Is Joanie taking Tank?"

"Yes, she is."

"Anybody else going that I know?"

"Yeah, Sally from the Hearthmoor."

"Is she taking her dog?"

"Yep."

"What's her dog's name? I can't think of it."

"Kirby."

"That's right. Kirby. Are they all entered in the show or just going to go?"

"They're all entered."

"What do you have to do to enter a dog, Em? I mean, do you do it the day of the show or do you have to do it before? Do the dogs have to pass a test or something? Do they have to be a purebred or can a mutt enter too? I have a purebred Cockapoo, maybe I'll enter her next time there's a show. What do you think?"

Emma could feel her head beginning to throb and her eyes were starting to glaze over. God, but this woman could talk. Now, how do I tell her that her Cockapoo is not purebred, but indeed a mutt, she wondered. "First off, you have to enter the dogs before the day of the show. Entries usually close a couple weeks before the actual show date."

"Oh, yeah? Where do they close?"

"At the show superintendent's office."

"Where's that?"

"Well, there are a few different superintendents, so it depends on who's got the show."

"Do you have to go there in person?"

"No, you enter either by mail or at their web sites."

"Oh, okay."

"And the dogs don't have to take a test before they enter."

"That's good. I can't imagine what kind of the test they would have to take anyway, can you, Emma?"

"No, I can't imagine, Angie."

"Okay, well, so far it seems pretty simple. What else?"

"The dogs have to be purebred for the show ring, Angie." Emma wasn't going to even mention the obedience or agility rings.

"Oh, then I can enter Susie in a show."

"No...no you can't. Sorry."

"Well, why not? You just said the dogs had to be purebred and Susie's a purebred Cockapoo."

"Angie, there's no such purebred breed. Susie's a mixed breed. A Cockapoo puppy results when a Cocker Spaniel and a Poodle are bred together. The name is just a combination of the two different breeds."

"But her mother was a purebred Cocker Spaniel and her father was a purebred Poodle. That makes her purebred."

"No, sorry, that makes her a mutt," Emma blurted as her patience ran out.

Angie looked as though she'd been struck. Her face paled and Emma thought she was going to either faint or burst into tears, maybe both.

"You're, you're just kidding, right? My Susie isn't a mutt, is she?"

Emma knew she'd backed herself into a corner and now had to figure out how to save the situation. She pretended to check the packing slip that had come with the delivery while she searched her brain for a solution. Several seconds passed before it came to her and she knew she'd have to lie, at least for part of it.

"You're right, Angie, I was kidding," Emma said through gritted teeth. "Sorry, I shouldn't have done that, but I really thought you'd know I was only teasing. Your Susie is such a cute thing and so lovable." God, this is downright painful, Emma thought, her stomach roiling with the whopper she'd just told. The simple truth of the matter was that Susie was a total terror and a bitch in every sense of the word. Emma would actually like to dropkick her about twenty yards, and she was a dog lover.

"Oh, Emma, don't ever tease me like that again. My heart almost stopped and what would my Susie do without me? She is adorable, isn't she? She's such a sweetheart."

Emma was ready to gag. "But you know what? If I remember correctly, didn't you have Susie spayed when she was a puppy?"

"Yes, I did. That was the responsible thing to do. We didn't want her to go through the agony of childbirth, or should I say puppy birth?"

"Well, there you have it. Because you were a responsible pet owner, Susie can't be entered in a show."

"Why not?"

"Because the bitches, the female dogs, have to be whole."

"What do you mean whole?"

"They can't be spayed, they have to have all their reproductive parts."

"That doesn't seem fair."

"I know, but that's the rule."

"Who made up that rule?"

"I don't know, Angie."

"Well, it should be changed."

"I don't think it will be. It's been that way since dog showing started."

"I bet a man did it."

Emma's headache was getting worse and she could see that this conversation was going to just keep going on and on. There was no end in sight and she was getting desperate to get this woman out of the shop. She silently prayed for strength and a civil tongue. "You're right, a man definitely made that rule, but dogs have to be whole too."

"Yeah, I know. You just said that. That's why Susie can't enter a show."

"No... a dog is a male."

"What? Not all dogs are males, Emma. That's stupid. You must be getting mixed up. Some dogs are males and some are females, okay? They get together and have puppies and then some of the puppies are boys and some are girls. Do you get it now?"

Emma wanted to scream or better yet, bang her head on the counter and slip into unconsciousness. It was the safest of her three options, because the other one was to kill Angie with her bare hands even though she'd never be prosecuted; it was apparent a certifiable lunatic would have driven her to it.

"Angie... a male is called a dog and a female is called a bitch."

"What are?"

"Dogs!"

"Do you mean that you say B-I-T-C-H every time you talk about a female dog?"

"Yeah, only we say it, we don't spell it."

"But that's swearing."

"No, it's just the name for a female dog."

"Why can't you just say female dog? What's so hard about that?"

"Nothing's hard about it, but that's not what they're called."

"But that other one is not a nice word, Emma. If they had to give the female another name couldn't they have picked a better one."

"Angie...."

"I know a man definitely picked that name. There's no doubt about it. It's so degrading."

Emma could feel what was left of her self-control slipping. She was very close to losing it. "Angie, listen...."

"I don't think I want to talk about this anymore. Let's talk about something else, something less controversial. Really Emma, you always go off on such tangents."

"Hey, Angie."

"Yes."

"Shut the f..."

Emma didn't get to finish. Joanie came barreling up to the counter, talking rather loudly to cover up what was coming out of Emma's mouth. "Hey, Angie, how are you? God, I haven't seen you in I don't know when. Where've you been hiding?"

"Oh, Joanie, good to see you. I was just asking Emma about you. I thought maybe you were sick. I…"

"Sorry to interrupt, but I've got go. Joanie, these two cartons need to be checked in yet. Any problems, call me at the house. Cole, let's go. Move your butt." Without a backward glance Emma flew out the door making good her escape, leaving Joanie to deal with Angie Newmann.

* * * *

That evening, Cappellini was again enjoying a warm spring night on the balcony that extended off his third floor bedroom. The sun was just setting over the water lapping the Connecticut coastline and the site was spectacular. The red glow of the descending sun was reflected in the surrounding sky and shimmered off the top of the water as it sank below the horizon.

Cappellini, sitting in a deck chair, his tanned legs stretched out in front of him, his drink of choice in his hand, was relaxed and in good spirits when the phone rang. It was his secure landline and knowing who it probably was, answered with thinly veiled excitement. "Hello?"

"Mr. Cappellini, it's Wilhelm here."

"Yes, Wilhelm. All is well I hope."

"Yes, sir, very well."

"Would you be calling to tell me the search has been successful?"

"I would have to say, sir, that in my opinion it has been most successful, and when you see the documentation, I think you will agree."

"Splendid. And you accomplished the mission in less than two weeks."

"Yes, sir, that I did. I sent the packet out this morning via the means we had discussed so you should receive it some time tomorrow morning."

"Excellent. If after I examine the contents and agree with your determination, I'll wire your fee and the additional bonus to your account."

"Thank you, sir. That would be most appreciated. Do you want to discuss final negotiations and transport after you read the report?"

"Yes, that would be best, don't you think, Wilhelm? I just might not agree with your findings," Cappellini chuckled.

"I think you will be extremely satisfied with them, sir."

"Let's hope so, Wilhelm. Tell me, where did you find the object of your search?"

"Where you thought would be a good place to look, the Netherlands."

"Aaah, I thought I'd be correct in that. Well, good. Until tomorrow then, Wilhelm."

"Yes, until tomorrow. Good night, Mr. Cappellini."

Cappellini hung up the phone, a pleased smile on his handsome, aristocratic face. He took a drink of the Macallan, holding the spicy, smoky liquid in his mouth. When he swallowed, the eighteen-year-old scotch sent waves of warmth through his body. He was nearly positive that Wilhelm's report would satisfy his needs. From their dealings in the past, which had always been successful, Wilhelm knew better than to waste his time with an unsuitable find. So with the outcome of tomorrow all but assured, Cappellini allowed himself to mentally close down one more step in his quest for that which he desired.

Chapter Thirteen

Friday was a blur of activity, first at everyone's respective homes, and then at the shop and restaurant. In the morning, all three were doing last minute show preparations, checking to make sure they had everything, finishing their packing, and in Emma and Joanie's case, loading their vehicles. Sally was getting all of her pertinent belongings down to the barn.

Emma and Joanie were at the shop at ten o'clock sharp, pumped up and ready to go. They were always psyched the day before a show, anticipation and excitement running high. They absolutely loved everything involved in showing and couldn't wait to get on the road. The dogs sensed the underlying emotions and, having witnessed the elaborate preparations, knew they were going to a show. They were disappointed when they discovered it wasn't going to happen that day.

"Can you believe it? Look at these guys, they're really sulking," Joanie said.

"I know, they're brutal," Emma answered, then directed her comments to the dogs. "Come on, guys, perk up, we'll be going tomorrow."

The two dogs just stared at her with eyes that conveyed their doubt, then turned their backs and loped off to the back room. They lay down side by side, presenting a unified front of pissed-off dog.

"How long do you figure they'll punish us?"

"Cole won't be able to hold out for more than half an hour."

"Tank will go longer," Joanie said. "He's got a vindictive streak. I can see him holding out for two, maybe three hours."

"You're kidding."

"No, he's done it before."

"Well, maybe Cole will have a positive influence on him."

"Don't hold your breath."

Customers started to enter the shop and the girls were soon busy helping them make selections and cashing them out. For whatever reason, this seemed to be a day of indecision. One of their customers couldn't make up her mind about which plaid she preferred for her placemats and napkins, and Emma had to spend almost an hour with her comparing several sets of linens. Another woman couldn't make a decision about which candle burner she liked best, and kept Joanie busy showing her the various types and styles. Another woman, although she didn't require either of the girls' assistance, squeezed different stuffed bears for thirty minutes before she found the one that felt just right. Yet another woman stood at one of the candle displays and sniffed every votive in the line, a total of fifty, went back and did it again, and only then made her choice. She bought two, one vanilla and one cinnamon. Emma thought it hardly seemed worth the effort.

Cole had come up to Emma and given her hand a lick exactly twenty-eight minutes after the rebuff. She'd given him a hug and smiled; he was such a sweetheart. She'd looked over to the back room and there'd been Tank, lying there, staring her down. God, he was a tough nut. Joanie ignored him; she knew nothing she or anyone else did was going to change the way this played out. Tank was Tank and she loved every stubborn inch of him, but right now she wasn't going to let him know that. Besides, it wouldn't do her any good; this was a test of wills. Who the winner was going to be was still up for grabs.

The rest of the morning went quickly with regular customers wishing them luck at the show. Cole carried several bags out to people's cars and earned a biscuit each time. He'd take his prize over to Tank to share, but Tank would have none of it. He just moved away from the offending treat and continued his vigil. Cole finally got fed up with him and didn't bother trying anymore; he just ate his biscuit in front of him.

A little after one o'clock, the girls ordered lunch. They were going to split a turkey sub, and Joanie left ten minutes later to pick it up. Tank stood up and looked to the door where Joanie had gone out.

"Ah-ha! You're not so tough after all, huh?" Emma whispered as she watched Tank.

Tank's gaze never left the door until Joanie returned. Once she was in the shop, he lay down again and averted his eyes.

"He's bluffing," Emma said after she told Joanie what Tank had done when he realized Joanie was gone.

"Yeah, I know. That's why I don't do anything. I like to see how long he'll hold on to the act. It's been what… three hours now? He could be going for a new record."

"He's as crazy as you are."

"Why do you think we're together?"

"Good question."

"We're a perfect team; we counterbalance each other."

"Poor Sam, he doesn't stand a chance."

"No, not at all. But I let him *think* he's in charge and has everything under control. I'm not about to enlighten him and neither are you."

"Far be it for me to interfere. We'll let Sam continue on in his ignorant but blissful state."

"Couldn't agree with you more. Now, is everything all set with Jackie for the weekend? Please, please say 'yes'."

"Everything's all set. No problem."

Jackie McCoy was Emma's cousin and usually watched the shop on weekends the girls had a dog show. She worked at an orthodontic office during the week and had her weekends free. She'd be coming out after work that day and would be staying at Emma's house. She was thoroughly competent, and the girls never gave the shop a second thought when she was there. God, they hoped she never married and had children; they didn't want to lose her, not that they were selfish or anything.

"Thank you, God! If Jackie couldn't make it and we had to have Tammy here, I don't think I'd survive it. It would be too soon. I haven't recovered from the other day yet."

"I know, but we're good. Jackie will be here."

They finished their lunch and went about the day attending to customers, restocking the shelves, answering the phone, and doing paperwork. They were busy, but not frantic and it made the hours slip by.

Tank had decided to call it quits at about two o'clock and made up with Joanie. He'd set a new record and Joanie was almost as proud of it as he was, although she wasn't going to let him know that. The next confrontation, whenever it occurred, and rest assured that it would, could prove to be a real doozy.

It was six o'clock before they knew it and they eagerly shut the place down. Emma had brought the Explorer down in the morning, so immediately after locking up, the girls got in their vehicles and took off for the restaurant. It was just a little after six when they arrived, so the restaurant wasn't too busy yet. The girls, with Cole and Tank tagging along, went into the bar area to let Sally know they were there. Kirby greeted them all like she hadn't seen them in a year and Sally called out greetings.

"We'll take Kirby out with us while we load," Emma said.

"Oh, she'll love that. Hey, did you hear the forecast?" asked Sally.

"No. Do I want to know the forecast?"

"Yes and no."

"What is it?" Joanie asked, already resigned to bad news.

"Tomorrow's supposed to be rainy with strong winds and temperatures in the high forties. Sunday, sunny and in the mid-sixties."

"Don't you just love spring in Western New York? Well, we all knew one day would be bad. At least Sunday should be decent, but it'll probably be muddy as hell after the rain."

"Whatever, let's get started. There isn't anything we can do about it," Emma said, heading for the door.

"Hey, Em, hold on a minute."

"What, Sal?"

"Joanie tells me that there's a new male prospect that just moved into the area."

"What do you…. oh geez."

"From what she said, he's quite a hunk."

Emma didn't say anything, just rolled her eyes. When she turned back to the door, Joanie and Sally shared a conspiratorial wink. Joanie gave Sally a thumbs-up and, along with the dogs, followed Emma out. They walked through the parking lot and went over to the barn alongside which they'd parked their vehicles.

Sally had made a large exercise area coming off the barn and had surrounded it with six-foot chain link fencing. Railroad ties skirted along the fencing to hold the gravel in, which was a good four inches deep. Various toys and balls were littered about and pails of water hung off a few of the posts. Emma put the dogs inside and locked the gate. It took the threesome all of one click of a watch's second hand to start playing; Emma and Joanie went to unload.

They took everything into the barn and found all of Sally's gear ready to go. They opened the motor home and started to find places for everything. The motor home was an older model, a 1984 Cross Country by Coachman, but it served their purposes quite nicely. Sally had removed some of the standard furnishings to accommodate the dog crates, and the six of them were reasonably comfortable during their occupancy.

It took the girls about an hour and a half to get the luggage and equipment stored. They unpacked some of the clothing so that it was at the ready, made the bed up, got the dogs' food and water centralized, and organized the entire interior of the vehicle. Sally had made sure the water tanks were full, the furnace in working order, and all the electrical connections operating. The girls turned the refrigerator on so it would be already cold when they put the food in tomorrow; the motor home, at the moment, was attached to a source of power in the barn. The last thing they did was secure the exercise pens, which were made of lightweight aluminum and could be folded up, to a rack on the back of the camper.

It was past seven-thirty when they exited the barn and went to get the dogs. The parking lot was full. Sally was going to have a busy night. They put Cole and Tank in their respective vehicles and took Kirby with them into the restaurant. The bar was crowded, so Emma kept her hand on Kirby's collar and guided her to the stairway that led to

Sally's three-bedroom apartment above the restaurant. She took her upstairs and got her situated before coming back down.

Sally was flying around behind the bar, so the girls just yelled to her that they'd see her in the morning. She nodded her head, indicating she'd heard, and Emma and Joanie left the restaurant. They said their goodbyes to one another, fired up their vehicles and left, each destined for their own home.

When Emma reached the house, Jackie was already there and making dinner for the two of them. God, that was a welcome sight. Emma was tired and hadn't relished the idea of having to make a meal. Emma got Cole settled in and she relaxed with Jackie over Spaghetti Parmesan, a tossed salad and garlic bread. They cleaned up the kitchen, talked a bit about the shop and the show, and called it an early night. Emma hated to rush in the morning, so she planned on getting up at four o'clock tomorrow morning. She set the alarm as a backup, but knew Cole would wake her up an hour earlier than usual. All she had to do was tell him.

* * * *

When Cappellini called Wilhelm Schmidt that Friday night, he was inordinately pleased and anxious to make the final arrangements. "Wilhelm, I must congratulate you on a fine job. I am extremely happy with your find."

"Thank you, Mr. Cappellini. I had reason to believe you would be satisfied."

"Yes, indeed. Did the wire to your bank come through?"

"Yes, sir, everything is in order. Thank you for being so prompt."

"Not a problem, Wilhelm, especially when you serve me so well. Now I want you to tie everything up there and make preparations for transport. You noticed, I'm sure, that there were extra funds wired into your account."

123

"Yes, sir, I assumed they were to be used for the purchase and transport."

"You assumed correctly. The people you're dealing with have probably surmised that you're acting as an agent for someone and I want you to make sure now that they know who the real owner will be. So after the price is set, bring my name into it. Make sure my name is on the bill of sale and on any accompanying documents. I also want you to act as escort for the cargo. I hope that won't be a problem."

"No, sir, not at all."

"You'll have to purchase the airline tickets in your name however, what with all the safeguards against terrorists they have in place now, but you're officially acting as my agent so documentation on your airfare will be helpful too. Unlike so many of our other projects, I want a paper trail on this transaction, Wilhelm."

"I understand and will do as you wish."

"I want you to fly into Toronto, Canada and then rent a car and drive down to Connecticut. Once you're here, I want you to go directly to the farm in Stafford Springs. There'll be no hassle this way with the cargo coming into the country as long as you have the proper paper work."

"Don't worry about that, everything will be in order. How soon do you want this to happen?"

"As soon as you can make the arrangements."

"All right, sir, consider it done."

"Thank you, Wilhelm. I knew I could count on you."

"It's always a pleasure working with you, Mr. Cappellini."

"Call me when everything is set."

"Yes, sir. I will get back to you as soon as I complete the preparations. Goodbye."

Cappellini stood as if transfixed after the call was ended. They were almost identical in appearance if the pictures were to be believed. Not quite, but close enough that anyone not intimately knowledgeable of the dog wouldn't know the difference. And those who would know, well, he had a way of fixing that so that not even they could question the validity of who the dog was. It really didn't matter anymore if she refused to sell, he was going to own the dog anyway. There had never been any doubt about that from the beginning. The only question that still remained was what to do about her, if she became any more of a problem.

Chapter Fourteen

It was 6:25 in the morning when the girls pulled out of the parking lot at the Hearthmoor. Sally was driving, Emma was in the passenger seat and Joanie was sitting on the couch behind Sally. The dogs, although they would have preferred to travel on the couch or better yet the bed, were in their crates for safety's sake. Cole and Tank had renewed their excitement from yesterday and Kirby was running a close second. Even though they were resting quietly in their crates, their eyes, expressions, and wagging tails betrayed their calm. They were finally on their way and they couldn't wait to show their stuff. Some dogs didn't like to show and did so begrudgingly, but these three thrived on it. The weather was as forecasted and as the rain beat on the windshield, the girls could feel the motor home sway when it was battered with gusts of wind.

"Looks like we're in for a really, really lovely day," Emma announced sarcastically, watching the wipers swipe the rain from the windshield.

"Yeah, as always," Joanie agreed, shivering from the dampness. "God, you could set your clock by this shit."

They traveled over to East Aurora, the town northeast of where they lived, and picked up Route 20A east to Route

98. They went north on 98 and about an hour after they'd started out, they were at the fireman's grove that was the venue for the Alexander show, sponsored that day by the Olean Kennel Club, and on Sunday by the Wyoming Valley Kennel Club.

The show site was laid out in the grassy area adjacent to the graveled parking lot. Vendors had set up booths in the space closest to the lot, selling everything from dog food and vitamins, to squeaky toys and rawhide, to scissors and brushes, to shampoos and conditioners, to doggy sweaters and thermal blankets, to notepaper and pen and ink sketches, to tee shirts and sweatshirts, all dog oriented, to leashes and collars, to finely etched crystal depicting various breeds of dogs. Beyond the booths were the show rings.

There were a total of eight rings for confirmation exhibiting with four to a side. An enormous tent rose over the wide aisle between the two rows and extended a few feet over the rings themselves. The grooming tent, where exhibitors could set up their equipment and keep their dogs during the show if they so chose, was diagonally across from Ring One, which along with Ring Eight was the closest to the upper parking area.

There was a food stand in the immediate vicinity, offering for sale hot dogs and hamburgers, grilled chicken sandwiches, Italian sausage with peppers and onions, potato salad, vegetable soup, potato chips and pretzels, soda, hot chocolate, and coffee. There were also bathrooms in the same general area and Ring Nine, the Obedience Ring, was located behind the food stand. At the far end of the parking lot was the fireman's rec hall. It had hospitably been made available to the exhibitors during the show. There was generous space between the rings, booths, and buildings to allow for heavy foot traffic during the event.

The three friends pulled in through the lower parking lot, then drove up to the higher parking area that was reserved for motor homes. They were on grass and hoped the ground was firm enough that they wouldn't get mired down in mud if the rain continued all day. Sally maneuvered the motor home into position and shut the engine down.

As if choreographed, the girls went into action. First, they rolled out the awning attached to the motor home and secured it. Then they lay down the indoor-outdoor carpeting beneath it and set the grooming tables on top of that. They pulled out the tack boxes that held all their grooming tools and supplies, and put them where they'd be handy. Next came the lawn chairs, but instead of setting them up they leaned them against the motor home. There wasn't much chance they'd be using them today. Not in this weather! They took the exercise pens down from the rack and set them up at the back corner of the motor home. They put the dogs in the ex-pens to relieve themselves and as soon as they were finished, toweled them off and put them back in their crates. It was still raining and the wind was whipping it through the area under the awning, so Joanie got some plastic sheeting and, with Emma's help, attached it vertically to the windward side of the awning. They drove stakes into the ground and tied the bottom corners of the plastic to them to keep it in place. Emma and Sally dragged the generator out and got it ready to use for when they needed power.

It was now close to 8:15 and Emma went down to Ring One to pick up her armband. She passed a few people she knew and exchanged greetings, everyone complaining about the weather. She grabbed her armband and went back up to start getting Cole ready. She got him up on the table and pulled out the hair dryer first. Sally cranked up the generator and presto, Emma was in business. Once Cole was dry, she brushed him out, scissored his coat a little to make sure his feathering was perfect, checked that his eyes were clear, and draped a towel around his neck so he wouldn't get wet from his drool She wouldn't normally put him back in his crate, but the weather was so bad she decided to let him rest there instead of on the table.

Joanie had gone down to the ring to watch the judging and see how it was getting along time-wise. There were several absentees, undoubtedly due to the weather, and that would move the time frame up. They had originally figured 9:30, but it now looked more like 9:15 would be when Newfs were in the ring. Of course, Cole would still have to wait for the class competition to be completed before he went in for Best of Breed, so he didn't need to be at ringside as early as the class dogs and bitches.

Emma had changed into her show clothes by the time Joanie got back and reported on the ring progress. Emma got Cole out of his crate and tidied him up, making sure he looked his best. From their vantage point, they could see that Newfies were starting to arrive at ringside. Joanie said she'd wave them down when it was time and left to take up her post. Emma had put on her winter jacket to stay warm until it was time to go, but she was still freezing with only pantyhose on her legs. Sally was arming herself with brushes, towels, and squeaky toys in case they were needed. Emma had bait in her pocket, but found that she rarely had to use it with Cole. He was always naturally "on" in the ring, but she carried it for emergencies nevertheless.

Joanie gave the signal to come down, Emma whipped off her coat, and they proceeded to do just that. There was no way to avoid Cole arriving at the ring with wet feet since there was absolutely no way Emma could carry him, but at least everyone was in the same boat. Once they got under the tent, Sally and Emma worked feverishly to dry him off as best they could and brush out his hair. Through all the fussing, Cole stood still and cooperated, lifting each paw as he was asked, and Emma was so busy she didn't have time to get nervous.

Class competition was finished and the steward called for the Specials and Winners Dog and Winners Bitch for Best of Breed judging. There were four Specials, all dogs or males, and Cole entered the ring third in line, according to number. The last Special, Winners Dog, and Winners Bitch followed and stacked themselves behind Cole. Two of the Specials were with professional handlers and two with their owners. Winners Dog and Bitch were both with professionals.

A professional handler was just that, a dog handler who made his living showing other people's dogs. It was a full time occupation and they were very accomplished in training and grooming most breeds of dogs, although some chose to specialize in one particular Group. The very successful ones were handsomely paid and they often traveled from show to show with ten or more dogs. Their services were used when the owner had neither the time nor the skill to handle his own dog, but wanted the dog to earn it's championship, or having that, national ranking.

As they lined up under the edge of the tent for the first inspection, Emma lowered her face to Cole, gave him a kiss, and whispered, "Let's give 'em a show, big boy. Show 'em how pretty you are."

She stacked Cole and stood back. He lifted his head into a regal pose and looked straight ahead. The judge, Mrs. Katharine Frost from Columbus, Ohio gave the signal to take the dogs around and they moved out. Cole moved effortlessly at Emma's side, his stride exhibiting powerful reach and drive. The group went back under the tent and relaxed their dogs while the individual inspections began. The first two dogs went through their paces and then it was Cole's turn. Emma moved him out into the ring and stacked him for the judge. She moved back and dropped the lead. Cole stood like a statue. The judge proceeded to examine him and Cole didn't flinch. She came back to his head,

Cole looked her right in the eye, and his whole body exuded presence. Mrs. Frost told Emma to move him down and back and they executed it flawlessly. As they were nearing the judge, she held up her hand for them to come to a stop. Emma swung out to Cole's right and he stopped on a dime, each foot perfectly placed directly in front of the judge. With his head held high, he gazed into Emma's eyes, giving her the expression the judge was looking for. Mrs. Frost told them to go around and they performed the maneuver as one, their movements in complete harmony.

Emma and Cole took their place back in line and waited while the last three dogs went through their machinations. When the last dog was coming back into line, everyone set his or her dog up in a stack for what would probably be the final inspection. Mrs. Frost came down the line, standing in front of each individual dog, doing a mental review of each dogs' attributes. When she got to Cole, she cupped her hand on the underside of his muzzle as she studied his head, and received a lick on her palm when she pulled her hand away. She smiled, gave him a pat on the head, and moved down the line. The judge moved out into the ring and gave the signal to go around. The dogs moved out and as Emma and Cole passed her by, she pointed to them and called out, "Best of Breed," and to the Winners Bitch, she called, "Best of Winners, Best of Opposite."

The Winners Bitch, competing for points toward her championship, could now pick up more points by winning Best of Winners. If the Winners Dog had received more points than the bitch during class competition, then she would get the same number of points he had by defeating him in the Best of Breed competition. For example, if the Winner's Bitch had been awarded one point for her win and the dog, two points for his, then the bitch would now have two points because she had won Best of Winners.

The Best of Breed winner received points toward ranking in his breed, the number dependent on the total number of dogs he defeated in his breed that day. He would now advance to compete in the Group judging, which in Cole's case was the Working Group.

Joanie and Sally were going crazy under the tent, acting like the idiots they were. Emma moved to take her place for the award, being congratulated by the other handlers in the ring as she made her way over to the designated area. She hugged Cole and showered him with kisses while he barked and wagged his tail so fast it was a blur. As Mrs. Frost handed Emma the Best of Breed ribbon, she told her what an outstanding Newfoundland she had and what a fabulous job they'd done in the ring. Emma thanked her and left the ring to be embraced and congratulated by her two friends. They stood and talked a few minutes with exhibitors and bystanders alike, a lot of people asking if Cole was going to be made available for breeding soon. Emma hadn't really thought about it yet, with Cole being only sixteen months old, so didn't commit Cole or herself either way. After pictures were taken, anxious to get dry, Emma and company left the ring area.

They tried to hurry back to the motor home, but had to stop several times as friends and acquaintances came up to compliment her on the win. No sooner had she gotten Cole settled than Emma ripped off the offending pantyhose and got into her jeans, a warm sweater, and bulky socks. She was cold to the bone and accepted a cup of herbal tea from Sally, which under normal circumstances she wouldn't have touched with a ten-foot pole. She hated tea and coffee, but she was so cold she'd suffer through the taste to get warm. Sally had put the furnace on to dispel the permeating dampness and the heat felt like a godsend to Emma. They chatted about the win and then realized that Joanie was due in the Obedience Ring in about half an hour. Kirby wasn't in until the afternoon, so they had plenty of time to get her ready. But right now they had to hustle a bit with Tank.

Joanie put him in one of the ex-pens so he would relieve himself; the last thing she needed was for him to foul the ring. That infraction automatically precipitated a non-qualifying score in the Obedience Ring. After more than enough time, Tank had made no attempt to do the deed so Joanie grabbed him up and put him on the table. She tore a single match from a book of matches and lifting his tail placed the unlit match partially into the area "where the sun don't shine". Tank gave her a disgusted look, but Joanie shrugged her shoulders and said, "You asked for it."

Joanie deposited him back in the ex-pen and sure enough, two minutes later, Tank delivered. In the dog show world, matches, not diamonds, are often a girl's best friend. Put out though he was, the task was completed and Joanie got him on the table, wiped him down, and ran a brush over his coat. She put his collar and leash on, scooped him up, and carried him over to Ring Nine where the Novice B Class was just getting started. Joanie picked up her armband and waited with Sally and Emma for her turn. Competition progressed quickly, before long it was time for Tank to do his thing.

Under the judge's direction, the judge in this case being Miss Betty Walker from Horseheads, New York, Joanie and Tank executed the Heel on Leash and the Figure-8 configuration perfectly.

In the Heel on Leash exercise, the dog must remain on the handler's left side, moving with the handler at different speeds, not tugging on the leash, and staying even with the handler's left leg. During the exercise there are stops, when the dog must sit without delay and starts, when the dog has to move immediately with the handler. There are right and left hand turns and an about-face, which the dog must perform quickly and in tempo with the handler.

The Figure-8 exercise involves moving in, out, and around two people, serving as posts, who stand facing each other about six feet apart. There are again stops and starts, and the dog must be in the heel position, working quickly, not swinging out too wide on the turns or lagging, which means the dog is working behind the handler.

The Stand for Examination is an exercise in which the dog must stand perfectly still, the handler a short distance away, while the judge runs her hand over his head and back. The dog must stay in position until the handler releases him on the judge's signal, and today Tank's went off without a hitch.

The Heel off Leash, the same exercise as before, but without the leash, was almost dead-on.

The Recall, or calling your dog in from a distance, was next. Joanie put Tank in the required sit and told him to "Stay", after Miss Walker had given her the command to "Leave your dog". Joanie walked to her designated place across the ring, which was about thirty-five feet away. She looked at Tank and knew in that instant that he had the devil in him. He had "the look", and she knew he was going to pull something. The judge gave the order to "Call your dog", and Joanie commanded Tank to "Come". He took off like a shot and as he careened toward her, she kept mumbling to herself, her lips barely moving, "Oh shit, oh shit, oh shit…" When Tank got within three to four feet of her, he flew into the air, banked off her chest, did a somersault in the air, and came down in a sit right in front of her, less than six inches from her feet. The gallery erupted with applause and laughter; even Miss Walker had cracked a smile. She gave the order to "Finish", and Joanie, still reeling from the impact, signaled Tank to execute the finishing move, which he did faultlessly. The judge released them and advanced toward Joanie, spoke a few words to her and then turned to get ready for the next competitor. Joanie and Tank left the ring and Sally and Emma rushed over.

"Geez, was he keyed up or what?" Emma shot Tank a reproachful look; he ignored her.

"Hey, Joanie, have you got a chest left or is there a whole punched right through it?" Sally asked.

"I don't know, I'm afraid to look. But come here, guys, I've got to fix my bra. God, he hit me hard."

"Fix your bra?"

"Yeah, he popped the snap when he hit me and I'm kind of hanging loose, if you get my meaning."

"Hey, great shot, Tank."

"Sally, don't be praising him for cripes sake."

"Oh, all right." Sally turned away from Joanie and sneaked Tank a thumbs-up and a wink; he gave her a devilish smirk back.

"Just stand in front of me while I fix it. I don't want people thinking I'm having a good time with myself."

"Okay." Emma and Sally formed a wall while Joanie reached up under her jacket and got things back into place.

"Whew, that's better." Joanie wiggled her torso a little, settling everything back into proper alignment.

"Everything all right now?"

"Yeah, thanks."

"Any time. So what'd the judge say?" Emma asked as she and Sally backed away, dissolving the impromptu wall.

"She said she'd never seen anything like it. That I had myself a real pip."

"Yeah, no kidding."

"If she only knew the half of it," Sally added, giving the Parson Russell a sideways glance.

"He was probably getting even with me for the match, the little bugger." Joanie was rubbing her chest to lessen the sting and to give a final check that everything was back where it belonged. "Listen, if you want to go back to the motor home, go ahead. I have to wait for Sits and Downs."

"No, that's all right, we'll hang in here. It shouldn't be too long."

Thirty minutes later, Joanie and Tank were called back into the ring for the group Long Sit and Down. The competitors filed into the ring and lined up at the far end, their dogs in the heel position. Miss Walker gave the order to "Sit your dogs", and the handlers complied. The judge ordered, "Leave your dogs," and the competitors, after giving the signal to "Stay", crossed to the opposite side of the ring, turned around, and faced their dogs. Miss Walker positioned herself so that she could see all of the dogs and handlers while she timed the exercise for one minute. Tank sat at attention and didn't move, although the dog next to him got up and stood. After the minute had expired, the handlers were commanded to "Return to your dogs". They did so and walked around and in back of their own dog to the heel position. The judge said, "Exercise finished," and the owners released their dogs, praising them lavishly. Tank had done Joanie proud.

Next came the Long Down. Miss Walker asked if the handlers were ready and proceeded in the same manner as the Long Sit except instead of sitting their dogs, the handlers downed them without touching either their dogs or their collars. The length of the exercise was three minutes and for some handlers it was an eternity. Joanie was one of those who died a slow death, waiting for catastrophe to strike.

There were so many things that could distract the dog and make him break from "The Down". Things like, well, the other dogs for instance, and then there was the public address system blaring out its messages at inopportune times, and the smell of those hot dogs grilling in the food stand, a bystander talking loudly at ringside, or a generator starting up. The list was endless and then there was the possibility that the dog might decide he just didn't want to do this today and would get up and leave the ring. Joanie wouldn't put that one past Tank, but on this particular day Tank was satisfied to stay where he was, despite the fact that two places down the dog was howling non-stop for its owner. When the exercise was completed, they left the ring and waited while the judge tallied the points for each contestant. In a few minutes, those who qualified were called back in and given their scores. Tank had qualified; he had the second leg toward his obedience title. Yahooee!

Emma and Sally congratulated Joanie and gave Tank a big hug. People came up and offered their congratulations, then shaking their heads over Tank's earlier antics on the Recall, commiserated with Joanie over the trials faced in the Obedience Ring.

Eventually they made it back to the motor home to warm up and dry out. The girls ate lunch, hurriedly throwing together some sandwiches made of sliced roasted turkey and Muenster cheese on hard rolls. They didn't have time for anything fancy right now. There was only enough time to eat and relax for about half an hour. The dogs, having been given a treat of hot dogs and cheese, adjourned to the bedroom and roughhoused on the bed, squeaky toys making a cacophony of noise.

Kirby was up next and, with time growing short, the girls got started on getting her ready. She was exercised first, which meant she took a bathroom break and then groomed. The whole process took only about twenty minutes because of her short coat. While Emma put the finishing touches on, Sally changed into show clothes. Joanie had run down to Ring Four and came back with Sally's armband. They were due at ringside in five minutes so started to work their way down.

It was crowded under the tent at Ring Four; thirty-five Labs were being shown. The steward called for Puppy Dogs, 6 to 9 months, and the judging began. The girls chatted amicably with other exhibitors and kept their eye on progress in the ring. During the on-going judging, the wind had picked up considerably and was billowing the tent causing it to snap. A few of the dogs were getting apprehensive and their owners were trying to reassure them. The rain was coming down in sheets and, unless it let up, Sally was going to get drenched within seconds of being in it.

Moments later her class, Open Bitch, Yellow was called and Sally and Kirby filed in. The judge, Mr. Ronald Boyd from Silver Springs, Maryland had them immediately go around the ring and by the time they came back under the tent, exhibitors and dogs alike were soaked. The judge did the individual examinations and sent each team out on their down and back. Kirby performed beautifully despite the weather and Mr. Boyd had her move to the head of the line. He went down the line taking a second look at head and expression, and had them move out around the ring one more time. When Sally and Kirby were halfway around, he pointed at them and said, "One," and proceeded to call out which dogs were second, third, and fourth. They went over to the awards area and received their ribbons. Sally stayed in the ring to compete for Winners Bitch against the winners of the other classes.

The judge again had them go around and Sally by now looked like a drowned rat. He had a couple of the dogs do a down and back; then as they went around for the final time, gave Winners Bitch to the Bred by Exhibitor entry. Sally and Kirby stayed in for the Reserve Winners judging and thankfully that was awarded quickly on one go around with Kirby being the recipient.

Sally was shaking with cold when she left the ring and could barely hold onto the lead. Emma grabbed Kirby and hustled everyone up to the motor home. While she took care of Kirby, Sally stripped off her waterlogged clothing and got into a flannel shirt and sweater, jeans and heavy socks. She turned the heat up even higher and boiled water for tea. Emma came in with Kirby and after she put her in her crate, collapsed on the sofa.

"Only an idiot would be here today," Emma groaned.

"Yeah, well, there's three of 'em in this room alone," Joanie answered back.

"God, Sally, I thought you had it. I could've sworn he was looking at Kirby the whole time for Winners," Emma said.

"Yeah, I did too. Kind of surprised me when he gave it to the other bitch. You watch, these last few points are going to take me forever to get."

"Man, I hope not."

"You and me both, but I've got a feeling this isn't going to be quick or easy."

"God, I hope you're wrong about that, Sally. Cripe, you've already got the really hard stuff behind you, you've got the majors."

"Yeah, I know, but you know how it works, everything depends on the judge. Anyway, tomorrow's another show with a different judge and that means another chance. Maybe things will work out better for us tomorrow. At any rate, don't we have to get Cole ready for Group soon?"

"Yeah, I think so, but I don't feel like moving my butt."

"Em, what time is Working Group?" Joanie asked.

"Around three o'clock."

"Well, think really hard about moving your butt then 'cause we better get started real quick," Sally said, looking at her watch. "We've only got about thirty-five minutes."

"Cripes! No need to say more, I'm up and moving." Emma bolted off the couch and made a beeline for Cole.

The girls flew into action like a well-oiled machine and prepared Cole for the Group Ring. Emma changed back into show clothes, different from the morning's ensemble since those were wet, and they headed to the ring.

There were twenty breeds representing the Working Group that day and the ring steward was just starting to call them in as the girls approached. Emma gave Cole's feet a hasty swipe with the towel, followed by a few flicks of the brush and wiped off any trace of drool from his mouth. There was no time to give wet feet any more time or attention this go round. Emma's beforehand jitters were non-existent; there simply wasn't time to get nerved up. It was time to go into the ring. Sally and Joanie wished her luck and gave Cole a kiss before they went in.

Once inside, Emma found her spot and stacked Cole, giving him his pep talk as she bent down to set his feet in place. The judge, Mr. John Taylor from Williamsburg, Virginia looked down the line and then indicated they should move out and go around the ring, which had been expanded to double the size of the ring used for judging the different breeds. Emma waited until the dog ahead of her had gone out far enough and then started to move Cole into his smooth, powerful gait. He caught the judge's eye as he went around, moving effortlessly with his head up. The exhibitors returned to their places under the tent and the individual examinations began.

Emma let Cole relax and played with him while they waited their turn A large crowd had gathered around the outside of the ring and spectators were showing their appreciation with applause as the dogs moved separately. When it was Cole's turn, Emma took him out into the center of the ring and set him up, then dropped the lead and stepped back. Mr. Taylor gave him a thorough look from a distance; then moved in for the exam. Cole stayed steady and didn't move a foot, keeping himself perfectly posed as the judge went over him. The judge stepped aside and signaled for Emma to take him down and back. She moved Cole out and became one with him as he went into motion. When Mr. Taylor indicated that they should stop, Emma again swung out to Cole's right, and he stuck the stand, riveting his attention on Emma. They got the go around sign and off they went, Emma keeping him in stride all the way back to their spot under the tent.

When the individual examinations were finished, the handlers again stacked their dogs and the judge made his cut. He pulled out eight dogs, including Cole, and excused the rest from the ring. He had them go around separately at a pace that wasn't too fast, each dog finishing up back where it had started. The exhibitors once more stacked their dogs and the judge proceeded down the line, mentally reviewing how the dogs measured up against the standard for their breed.

He pulled Cole out and put him at the head of the line. He made his other three choices and shuffled them into place. Emma was barely breathing when the signal came to move the dogs out. She checked with the other handlers to be sure they were ready and led Cole off in perfect stride. Cole turned his head to look at the judge just as the judge pointed at them and said, "One," then continued with, "Two, three, and four," as the other dogs were placed. Emma let out a whoop, her heart pounding wildly, and Cole jumped up barking like a madman. She gave him a big hug and too many kisses to count. The other handlers came over to congratulate her as she walked Cole to the awards area. Emma could hear Joanie and Sally cheering outside the ring and the entire gallery was applauding. Mr. Taylor handed out the awards, congratulating all who had placed. Emma and Cole left the ring and went over to another for a photo with the judge and he again congratulated her and said what a magnificent example of the breed Cole was. Emma thanked him for the win and went over to her two friends.

"Em, I can't believe it! First time out as a Special and he took a Group One! Holy shit!" Joanie screeched.

"I know! I can't believe it either. He was fabulous though, wasn't he?" Emma's face was glowing, her smile a mile wide. She gave Cole another kiss and kept her hand on his head, stroking it gently.

"He was fantastic, Em. He never put a foot wrong and my God, the attitude," Sally chirped in.

"I know! It's unbelievable! When he's in that ring, he just lights up and takes command."

"Oh, my God! We've got to back and let him rest. He's got to go in for Best In Show later," Joanie said as the realization sank in.

"Oh, my God! Best In Show! We've got to do Best In Show yet. Holy Toledo! We're going to Best In Show! Yeah, yeah, let's go back."

They walked slowly back to the motor home, being waylaid numerous times by well-wishers. Emma gave Cole a drink of water and put him in his crate to rest. She was soaked to the skin again; the rain had never let up. So she stripped out of those clothes and right away got into another set of show togs. There was still other Group judging to get through, and it looked like Best In Show would probably be between 4:30 and 5:00. With only an hour or a little more to go, Emma wanted to sit and relax for a while, get her nerves under control and not have to worry about changing clothes yet again.

Her relaxation lasted all of about fifteen minutes. Cole had to get dried and brushed one more time; he was just as wet as Emma had been. The grooming sometimes seemed endless, but the dogs were well used to it.

Puppies destined for the show ring begin their training as early as six to eight weeks of age. Nothing much at first, just getting them up on a table and letting them get used to it, running a brush over their coats, touching their feet, clipping their toenails, opening their mouths, gently brushing their teeth with a finger. It was all done slowly and with a great deal of patience, gradually building to a full grooming session. The end result was a dog that not only put up with grooming, but one who was fully cooperative and even enjoyed it. Once they're up on the table, most show dogs won't try to leave it unless they've been given permission to do so. With the correct training, it's a place where they're comfortable and feel safe and secure.

The girls put Cole up on the table and had two hair dryers going to blow the rain out of his coat. They checked his feet for mud and did a little quick shampooing, toweling the excess water out first and then hitting him again with the dryer. Joanie and Emma began the brushing while Sally worked to finish off the drying. They were just wrapping it up when they heard the announcement for Best In Show. They gathered their gear, got Cole on lead, and quickly headed for the ring.

Chapter Fifteen

There were seven dogs vying for Best In Show, all of them winners of their individual Group. There was Cole, of course, from the Working Group, a beautiful German Shepherd Dog from Herding, a Smooth Fox Terrier from the Terrier Group, a Golden Retriever from Sporting, a striking Standard Poodle from Non-Sporting, an Afghan Hound from the Hound Group, and an adorable Pekingese from the Toy Group.

As of the year 2004, there were 162 breeds and varieties recognized by the AKC and they'd been broken down into seven Groups, according to what they'd been developed to do. The designated Groups were: Working, Herding, Terrier, Sporting, Non-Sporting, Hound, and Toy.

Dogs in the Working Group were created to do many jobs, among them guarding and carting. Those in the Herding Group were bred to work with livestock such as cows and sheep. The Terrier Group members were developed to hunt rats and other vermin. Sporting dogs were bred to work as a team with people who hunted game birds. Dogs in the Non-Sporting Group, a kind of mishmash of breeds that had nothing in common with one another except that they all no longer did what they were originally bred to do, had become excellent companions. The Hounds were bred to hunt by sight and scent, and Toy dogs were developed strictly for companionship.

The dogs entered the ring, the larger ones going in first. Emma, trying to calm her nerves, for she had never been in Best In Show competition before, whispered sweet words to Cole as she stacked him. The other six handlers were doing the same, getting their dogs into position and posing them for the first look by the judge. The judge, Mr. Paul Robertson from Wilmington, Delaware looked down the line and gave the signal to take them around. Off they went, Emma and Cole gliding into a harmonious stride. Once they were back under the tent and individual inspections started, Emma kept Cole in a stack until it was their turn. There was no let down in presentation when competing for Best In Show. Emma did notice however, that she was the only owner-handler in the ring; everyone else was a professional. Talk about being outnumbered!

When it was time, Emma took Cole out into the ring and stacked him, stepping back as the judge approached. Cole remained fixed in place while Mr. Robertson went over him, his entire body emanating majesty. The judge asked for a down and back and the two of them took off, striding down the ring in perfect synch with one another. When the signal was given to stop, Cole again struck a flawless stack, looking expressively and with total concentration at Emma. They gaited around the ring and back to their spot. Emma immediately restacked Cole and he stood unmoving.

The rest of the dogs took their turn and rejoined the line. Mr. Robertson traveled once more down the line-up and went to mark his book. He came back out with the Show Chairman and his ring steward. The judge carried the Best In Show ribbon, the other two, the prizes that were to be awarded the winner. He walked to the center of the ring, turned and faced the dogs and their handlers. After a moment or two of hesitation, building the suspense, he looked at Emma and said, "The Newfoundland."

Bedlam erupted; there were a lot of Emma's friends in the crowd. Emma grabbed Cole in a bear hug and started to cry. After she released him from a death grip, Cole barked and danced at her side. The other competitors gathered around her and offered congratulations, most wanting to shake her hand and give Cole a pat. Sally and Joanie were jumping up and down and doing a little dance that was pretty darn ugly just as Emma knew it would be, but what the hell. The gallery was applauding and shouting a lot of "who-hoos." The judge was finally able to make his way over to Emma and presented her with the award. She thanked him and told him it was Cole's first time out as a Special. He told her that Cole had a great show career ahead of him and felt honored to have had the opportunity to have him in his ring.

The celebration started to die down and after the pictures were taken, Emma left the ring floating on a cloud. Joanie and Sally brought her back to earth as they crashed into her with bone crushing hugs.

"Emma, Emma, I'm so happy for you! Oh, my God, it was fantastic!" Joanie squealed, her voice having raised its pitch to a level that rivaled that of fingernails scraping across a blackboard.

"Thanks, Joanie. I still can't believe it," Emma said as she bent down to give Cole another hug, her ribs aching a bit from her friends onslaught.

"Emma, you two were unbelievable! Everybody was talking about it, they couldn't believe the way you guys move together," Sally reported.

"And when Cole stuck that stack on the down and back, they went crazy!" Joanie added, her voice gradually coming down to normal modulation. She knew that Emma was oblivious to anything outside the ring when she was showing, and so was unaware of the reaction their performance had generated.

"He was just so good," Emma said. "I couldn't have asked for anything more. He gave me everything he had. I just can't believe it."

"Well, get used to it, sweetie, 'cause I think this is the first of many for you guys," Joanie crowed.

"I think she's right-on with that prediction, Em." Sally gave her friend another hug, missing Emma's wince. The hug was followed by a high-five.

"I don't know about that, but this sure as hell feels great. Whew, I think I need a glass of wine, I've got the shakes."

"Okaaay! Let's go up and celebrate," Joanie said, buying right into that idea.

"Somehow I knew we wouldn't have to twist your arm, Joanie," Sally grinned, giving Joanie a playful shove.

Just as they were starting to leave the ring area, Bill Thornton, who had handled the German Shepherd, came up and spoke to Emma. "Emma, let me congratulate you again on your win. Cole was fantastic today."

"Thank you, Bill. He was right on the money, wasn't he?"

"He sure was. This is his first time out since he won his championship, isn't it?"

"Yep, his first show as a Special."

"Well, he sure started out in fine style. Listen, my client, as you know, is very interested in Cole and still wants to buy him."

"Bill, like I told you last time, I'm not interested in selling."

"But, Emma, he's upped his offer. He'll give you $25,000 for Cole."

Joanie and Sally had taken Cole and had stepped away a short distance but were still close enough to hear the conversation. When they heard the amount of money offered, Joanie gasped and Sally's eyes bugged out. Both of them let loose with a whispered, "Holy shit!"

Emma herself was a little taken back by the amount, but when she spoke there was no hesitation. "I'm sorry, Bill, but I'm not interested. I'm very flattered by the offer, but Cole isn't for sale at any price. I believe I've already told you this, so I wish you'd convey it to your client, whoever he is."

"Are you sure? I mean, he would probably go even higher."

"I'm sure, so tell him not to bother with any more offers. It won't do any good."

"Well, to tell you the truth, he told me to offer you carte blanche."

"What do you mean?"

"You can name your own price. He'll pay whatever figure you decide on."

Strangling noises could be heard from the area where Joanie and Sally were standing as they choked in disbelief at what they were overhearing.

"You're kidding. You can't possibly be serious."

"Oh, but I am. He wants Cole and he can afford to pay any amount you want."

"This is crazy."

"Not to him it isn't."

"Well, crazy or not, the answer is still the same. Cole is not for sale. I don't care if he offered me everything he owns."

"Are you sure?"

"Yes, Bill, I'm sure. In fact, I'm positive."

"All right, if that's your final word," Thornton said, struggling to keep a pleasant expression on his face.

"It is, but good luck with the Shepherd. He's a beautiful dog."

"Thanks. I'm sure we'll be seeing each other in the ring again." When Thornton turned away, the anger and frustration he'd been trying to conceal surfaced in the long, angry strides he took and in the vicious tug he gave the leash attached to the German Shepherd.

Joanie and Sally rejoined Emma, and Cole, placing himself in front of Emma now, watched along with the girls as Thornton angrily strode away.

"I think he's pissed," Joanie remarked.

"Yeah, he tried to hide it, but yeah, he's pissed. I hope he doesn't take it out on the dog," Emma said.

"$25,000, Em," Sally whispered, looking in amazement at her friend. "That in itself is a hell of a lot of money, but when he offered to let you set your own price I thought I was going to faint."

"I know, I could hardly believe my ears, but I hope he finally got the message. Cole is not for sale, end of story.... Sooo, what do you say we go have that drink."

"Good idea, let's go," her two friends chorused with Joanie thinking they needed it more than ever now.

The girls started back, people congratulating Emma and Cole all the way up to the motor home. Some stayed around talking about the win while Emma took care of Cole and got him settled. Finally, due in a large part to the weather, they drifted away and the girls were left alone. They cracked open a bottle of wine and after pouring each a glass, toasted the successes of the day.

Emma dumped her show clothes and snuggled into a sweatshirt and pants, pulling her bulky socks over her feet. She layed out her three changes of ring clothes wherever she could find room so they'd hopefully dry out by morning. She dried her hair, giving it a quick shot of hot air from the dryer and then turned her attention to Cole.

She toweled him off and, for what she hoped was the final time that day, washed his feet. After putting him back in his crate, she turned on the heavy-duty dog dryer and directed the flow of air toward Cole. Between that and the furnace it would get deliciously warm in the motor home within minutes.

"God, it feels good to sit down," Emma said, plunking down on the couch. "I'm absolutely beat. I think I could go to sleep right now."

"Don't you dare. We've got a lot of celebrating to do," Joanie shot back.

"I don't know if I'm up to it. Between this wonderful heat and the wine, I feel like I could go out like a light."

"Oh, no, you don't. I brought stuffed shrimp for dinner. I've got stuff for a big salad, plus rice pilaf, and for dessert, crème puffs," Sally countered.

"All right, all right, for that I'll force myself to stay awake, but let's get started before I get too comfortable."

Dinner was prepared in less than half an hour, the activity reinvigorating Emma. As the girls ate and, of course, drank more wine with Sally switching over to manhattans, they went over the events of the day again. Talk then gravitated to the next day's schedule, the judges they were going under, and their plan of attack. Looking out the window, they noticed that it had finally stopped raining and the wind wasn't as strong as it had been. Hopefully the weather forecast would be accurate for tomorrow; it sure hadn't let them down today.

The three friends cleaned up the kitchen area along with the dishes, then got the dogs out. They took them way up in the back beyond all the motor homes and turned them loose so they could play. Emma had grabbed some balls and a Frisbee, and the girls took turns tossing them out. The dogs were quick to do their part, running, chasing, and even catching. The tensions of the day dissolved, due in some part to the booze, but mostly from watching the fun the dogs were having just being dogs. They stayed out there until darkness started to descend and then slowly strolled back to the camper. The dogs had gotten wet from the grass, so they toweled them off and brushed out Cole's coat so it wouldn't mat. The dogs were settled into their crates and after an hour or so had passed, got their dinner.

It was getting near bedtime, so the girls pulled straws to see who would get the bed and who the couch. Joanie pulled the short straw so she got the couch, which was really not a bad deal. She, at least, got to sleep alone. Sally and Emma had to share the bed. In addition, they all had to share with the dogs. Tank went with Joanie on the couch and Kirby and Cole would make themselves comfortable on the bed with Sally and Emma. Joanie definitely got the best deal. It was going to be rather crowded in that double bed with four bodies jostling for position. They took turns in the bathroom, changed into their pajamas, said good night, and tumbled into their beds dead-tired, but oh so elated. It had certainly been an outstanding day.

* * * *

That same night, alone in his motor home, Bill Thornton put through the call on his cell phone he'd been dreading making. Cappellini answered on the first ring. He must have been sitting with it in his damn hand, Thornton thought.

"Well?"

"She won't sell, Mr. Cappellini. I offered her the twenty-five grand, even gave her carte blanche like you said, but she still refused. She said she was flattered, but wanted me to tell you not to bother with any more offers. She won't sell the dog at any price."

There was silence from the other end. Cappellini curled his hand into a fist and brought it down hard on the cherry wood desk, his body visibly shaking with rage. Unable to speak, his fury mounting, silence continued for several minutes.

Finally Thornton, not knowing what was happening, spoke into the phone. "Mr. Cappellini? Are you there? Are you all right?"

"Yes, Mr. Thornton, I'm here," he said through clenched teeth. "So she was flattered, was she? The stupid bitch! We'll see how flattered she is when…." He abruptly cut himself off and took a few deep breaths, trying to regain control over his anger.

"What do you want me to do now?"

"Nothing. Don't do a fucking thing. Just show the damn dogs and keep me up to date on what the Newf does in the ring…. You haven't said, what did he do today?"

"He took Best In Show."

"He did what?"

"He took Best In Show, Mr. Cappellini. He was fantastic! I've never seen a dog so perfect in the ring."

"Son of a bitch! This was his first time out as a Special, wasn't it?"

"Yes, sir, and he was unbelievable! The two of them make quite a team." As soon as the last statement was out of his mouth, he regretted it. Cappellini was quiet again and Thornton could almost feel the deadly chill coming over the phone. After several seconds, Cappellini dismissed him and Thornton breathed a sigh of relief as he disconnected.

* * * *

Cappellini sat down in the leather chair behind his desk after he'd hung up with Thornton. He just sat there, thinking, plotting. He cared little that she wouldn't sell. It was insignificant. The dog was his. It was her attitude that so enraged him. Who the hell did she think she was to turn down that kind of money so off-handedly? She was nothing. She was a nobody who, by some quirk of fate, owned a magnificent animal that she didn't deserve. He was going to see to it that she didn't feel the least bit flattered by the time this was over with.

He opened the cell phone and speed dialed Jasper's number. Of two things he was very sure as he waited for Jasper to pick up. He was going to own the dog in a very short time, and he was going to make life very uncomfortable for Emma Rogers.

Chapter Sixteen

The girls woke the next morning to brilliant sunshine. The winds had played themselves out and all that remained was a gentle breeze. Sally and Emma had been pushed to either edge of the bed, Cole and Kirby having commandeered the center section for themselves. Tank had nestled himself between Joanie and the back of the couch and she was in danger of falling off. It was 6:32; everybody got up and started to move, not that it was a hardship at this point since the girls were none too comfortable where they were anyway.

All of the dogs were showing in the morning. Cole and Kirby were early, at 9:00 and 9:15 respectively, Tank at 11:30. With the dogs constantly underfoot, the girls stepped over and around canine bodies as they rotated time in the bathroom for showers, hair, and makeup. They ate a quick breakfast of orange juice and warmed blueberry muffins slathered with real butter. None of that fake stuff for this crew. Coffee was brewed, but only Sally partook. Emma and Joanie opened cans of Diet Pepsi, preferring to get their caffeine in carbonated form.

The dogs were exercised, given fresh water and biscuits, and Kirby was put on the table to get groomed.

With all three working on her, it took almost no time at all to get her ready. Cole was next and they spent over an hour, spot shampooing, drying and brushing. Emma did a little scissoring on Cole's feet and furnishings; it seemed she could always do that. It was one of those never-ending jobs; there always seemed to be a stray hair somewhere that needed trimming.

Sally and Emma changed out of their grubbies, got into their show clothes, and it was time to go. While they were making the clothing switch, Joanie had run down to their rings and picked up their armbands. The girls put them on, gathered the dogs and all their gear, and off they went. Tank was left behind to guard the fort. Emma was in Ring Four today; Sally was diagonally across the way in Ring Seven. Joanie split her time between the two while they waited to go in.

Emma, nerves jangling while she bided her time, competed first. Cole, "on" as always, repeated his performance of yesterday and took Best of Breed. Joanie shrieked in glee and ran over to tell Sally, who whooped it up at her ring. She got a few strange looks, but that was nothing new. When she *stopped* getting looks that was when she'd start to worry. When and if it happened, it would mean only one thing; she was acting her age and God forbid she should ever do that during her lifetime. The only time she planned on acting her age was when she was placed in her coffin.

One of the professional handlers that Emma had defeated for Best of Breed stopped her as she was leaving ringside. "Mrs. Rogers?"

"Yes."

"Hi, I'm Michael Post. Let me congratulate you on your win."

"Well, thank you."

"He's a magnificent Newfoundland. You should be very proud of him. His performance in the ring was spectacular."

"Thanks again, Michael, and, yes, I am very proud of him."

"Have you had any thoughts about putting him out with a professional?"

"No, not really. We're just doing this for fun."

"You are kidding, right? This dog could be number one in his breed."

"You might be right. In fact, I'll agree with you on that one. I think he's good enough to give any Newf out there a run for the top spot. But that's not why I'm showing him."

"But, Mrs. Rogers, this dog could go all the way. He could probably be number one in the Working Group."

"Well, I'm sure that would be very nice, but I have no interest in going after that particular honor. We're showing simply because we like to do it, Cole and I. And we do it together, as a team. That's the whole point of it."

"But, Mrs. Rogers, if he was with a professional he…"

"Look, Michael, that isn't going to happen, okay? I appreciate your interest in Cole and if I ever change my mind, I'll consider hiring you, all right?"

"I guess it'll have to be, but I think you're making a big mistake. Here, take my card and please, call me if things change."

"All right, thank you."

Emma turned away and went to join Joanie and Sally. Joanie had been watching the exchange and lifted an eyebrow as Emma approached. Sally was just going into the ring, so Emma mouthed, "Later," and gave her attention to the proceedings in front of her. Cole sat at her side and watched his buddy from the sidelines.

Sally and Kirby duplicated yesterday's presentation and won their class. Emma and Joanie crossed their fingers as judging for Winner's Bitch began. Everything was going smoothly until Kirby had to do her down and back. They were fine going down, but when Sally went to make the turn, her foot slipped on the grass that was still wet from yesterday's rain. She went down in a heap, taking Kirby with her. There was a collective gasp from the bystanders at ringside, and Emma and Joanie let out an "Oh damn" simultaneously. Cole jumped up and stood, his eyes locked on Kirby, a small whine telegraphing his distress.

Sally, shaken but unhurt, got up and checked to make sure Kirby wasn't injured. The ring steward came out and asked if they were okay. Sally nodded and the steward asked her to return to the judge. Sally walked Kirby back and the judge, Mrs. Bernice Strickler from Long Island, New York, once she confirmed they were able to continue, had Sally move Kirby along the tent line to loosen her up. When they were ready, the judge had them perform the down and back again and this time there was no problem. Cole however, didn't relax until Kirby was back in line under the tent.

Mrs. Strickler finished examining the other dogs and had them go around the final time. As they were circling the ring, she pointed to Sally and Kirby and called out, "Winner's Bitch." Sally's face broke into a huge smile and she raised her arms in triumph. Emma and Joanie went from hugging each other to giving high-fives, and Cole expressed his pleasure at his friend's win by barking repeatedly until Emma shushed him. Spectators and competitors were clapping, knowing that Kirby had deserved the win in spite of her fall, and murmurs about the fairness of the judge could be heard among the crowd.

Sally came out of the ring after she got her award and Reserve Winners competition came and went. The call for Best of Breed went out, and Sally reentered the ring. The evaluations got under way and each dog performed without mishap. By this time, Sally couldn't have cared less about anything more than what she had already accomplished. She had the point and anything else was pure gravy. As it turned out, when the judging was over, a male Special took the Breed, a bitch Special, Best of Opposite and Winners Dog, Best of Winners. Still, Sally came out of the ring glowing. She had the point and neither one of them had been injured in the fall, that was all she needed. She walked over to her two friends and received their congratulations. Kirby was greeted by Cole and got a huge kiss with a very wet tongue.

"God, Sally, I couldn't believe it when you went down. It looked like you both got hurt the way you landed." Joanie gave Kirby a well-deserved pat on her side.

"Yeah, I know. I thought Kirby was going to come up lame 'cause I landed on her front legs. It was a miracle nothing happened."

"And you got the point!" Emma exclaimed, throwing her arm around Sally's shoulders and giving her a squeeze.

"I know, but didn't I tell you yesterday it wasn't going to be easy."

"Yeah, and you proved it again today. Thank God you had a decent judge."

"You can say that again. She was really nice about it. I'll definitely go under her in the future."

"Won't we all. Make sure she gets in your judges book with a big fat star."

Like most exhibitors, the girls kept notebooks with a list of the judges they'd gone under or had heard about. The judge's likes and dislikes in reference to the breeds were noted and any peculiarities they might have when judging in the ring. Exhibitors also noted when the judge either gave them the win, the loss, or the shaft. Dog show people learned really fast not to go back under a judge who shall we say screwed them over.

Joanie, remembering Emma's conversation with the handler before Sally went in the ring, brought the subject up now. "The guy who was talking to you outside your ring, that was Michael Post, wasn't it? What'd he want, as if I didn't know?"

"Yeah, that was Post. Plain and simple, he wanted to handle Cole."

"What'd you say?"

"Told him I wasn't interested, that we were doing this for fun. I thought he was going to flip out when I said that."

"I bet. What else did he say?"

"Oh, that he thought Cole could go all the way and be number one in the Working Group. But he implied, of course, that he had to be handled right and he was just the man to do it."

"Oh, of course."

"He gave me his card and I let him think I'd call him if I changed my mind."

"Like that's going to happen," Sally snorted.

"Em, it's only just begun. You watch, these guys aren't going to give up trying to get Cole."

"Yeah, well, there's not much I can do about it. Let's get back. Tank'll be going in pretty soon."

They went up to the motor home, stopping several times to talk to people they knew, catching up on news in the dog world and in their personal lives. It was nearing 10:45 and Tank needed to be at ringside by 11:30. Emma put Cole and Kirby in separate ex-pens while she and Sally slipped out of their show clothes.

Meanwhile, Joanie had Tank on the grooming table and was making him pretty while she tried to impart words of wisdom about the day's competition. "Tank, do I have you're attention? Look at me, come on, look at me. I want you to do everything like we practiced at home, just like you did yesterday, except please don't bank off my chest again on the Recall. It won't hold up under another hit. Cripe, I almost fell down yesterday when you hit me. And by the way, that really hurt, you little shithead. So knock it off. No showboating today, just play it straight. Okay? Tank? Hellooo? Are you there? You're not giving me anything here, Tank."

Tank didn't look like he was listening. In fact he looked totally bored. If the look in his eyes was any indication, there was absolutely no productive brain activity going on in that head right now. Not a good sign, Joanie thought, if he could, he'd probably tell me to go suck an egg right about now.

After Emma grabbed Cole and Kirby, Joanie put Tank in one of the now empty ex-pens and dared him not to do his business. Tank took one look at Joanie's set face and came out of his snit long enough to do his duty. He might be stubborn, but he sure as hell wasn't stupid.

Emma took Cole and Kirby up to the back of the field where they'd let the dogs play the night before. She turned them loose and watched them play, running full out just for the pure joy of it. Ten minutes later, she called them in and as the dogs came racing toward her, Emma suddenly felt like she was being watched. She quickly spun around to see who was there, but all she saw was empty space. A chill went up her spine as she scanned the surrounding area. She leashed the dogs and started down, searching the whole time to see if she could see anyone. Cole and Kirby both picked up on her change in demeanor and immediately became more alert. They passed no one on the way to the camper, but Emma couldn't shake the feeling.

"Hurry up, Em, we've got to get to the ring," Joanie called out.

"I'm coming, just give me a minute to get the dogs in." Emma hurried into the motor home and put the dogs in their crates. When she came out, she asked Sally to lock the door.

"How come? We never lock it," Sally asked even as she dug out her keys to comply with Emma's request.

"I'll explain later, let's get to the ring."

Joanie had arrived at ringside ahead of them, had her armband and was getting ready to go in. "We timed it just right. No waiting," Joanie said as the girls came up.

"Good luck, Joanie. Tank, behave."

Joanie's number was called and in they went. Tank worked efficiently, although he seemed to be a bit off. He did the Recall without any dramatics, but his body language shouted nefarious intent and Joanie knew there was a disaster in the making. There was no doubt in her mind that Tank was saving it up for a big finish; she just didn't know when he was going to strike.

Sometimes there was a real downside to knowing your dog so well, especially when you could compare him to the villains in the old black and white silent movies who used to stand there, twirling their mustaches, an evil glint in their eye and needing to say nothing more than, "Heh, heh, heh" to get their dastardly point across. Tank was definitely twirling his moustache, and there wasn't a damn thing Joanie could do about it. They left the ring to wait for the Long Sit and Down.

As they watched the other competitors, Sally asked Emma about the locked door.

"What's the matter, Em? How come you wanted me to lock the door?"

"I know this sounds kind of crazy, but I felt like I was being watched when I had the dogs up in the back of the field."

"Really? Did you see anybody?"

"No, there was nobody there when I turned around to look, but it felt like there was. I could have sworn somebody was nearby watching."

"Did the dogs pick up on it?"

"No, they were running back in when I felt it. Once they reached me though, they got real wary because they knew I was spooked."

"And you didn't see anybody all the way back?"

"Nope."

"Hmmm…well, we better not take any chances. We'll keep the door locked when we're not there. Okay?"

"Okay, thanks."

About twenty minutes later, Joanie and Tank went in for the Long Sit and Down along with the other competitors. Tank was perfect on the Sit and Joanie knew his big finale was coming in the Long Down. As she downed him and told him to "Stay", he gave her "the look". Oh shit, here it comes, she thought as she walked across the ring to take her place. She could almost hear the "Heh, heh, heh". She turned around to face Tank, as the other handlers had done with their dogs, and the judge started to time the three minutes.

The button on the stopwatch had no sooner been pushed than Tank started to crawl, ever so slowly, across the ring. He looked like he was in a training film for the military, demonstrating how to crawl on your belly, keeping your ass down, so it doesn't get shot off by the enemy. It was comical to watch; he acted as though he was invisible and no one could see him moving. Spectators started to laugh and the other handlers struggled to keep straight faces. Joanie wished she could disappear in a puff of smoke.

"Hot damn, that dog," Emma said, starting to giggle.

"Joanie's dying a slow death in there," Sally snickered as they watched Tank's snaillike progress.

It took Tank almost the entire three minutes to crawl across the ring. He stopped at Joanie's feet and then just lay there with his head resting on his front paws, looking up at Joan with devilish, brown eyes. The judge called out, "Return to your dogs," and everyone did. Joanie had the presence of mind to step around Tank and go to the heel position. When the judge shouted, "Exercise finished," everyone released their dog, including Joanie, who finally lost the battle with her emotions and burst out laughing, whispering to Tank, "You are such a little shithead."

Tank, assuming a dignified pose, threw her a look that said she couldn't possibly be talking about him. Acknowledging defeat in more ways than one, Joanie led Tank out of the ring and as they approached Emma and Sally, Joanie announced, "Well, no qualifying score today."

"You think?" Sally giggled. "Come here, Tank." The little dog went over and jumped up, putting his front feet on Sally's legs while she cupped one hand under his muzzle and shook her finger at him. "You are such a bad boy, Tank. You know that don't you?" He conveyed his boredom by shifting his eyes away from Sally. "And you don't give a shit either, do you?" Tank awarded her another look that clearly stated, "Nope".

"Hey, Joanie, remember, according to the judge, he's a pip," Emma laughed.

"More like an asshole, but what the hell, at least he's never boring."

The three friends left, laughing as they walked. This story was sure to make the rounds and Joanie knew she was in for a lot of ribbing. When they got back, they made a wholesome lunch of tuna salad, shredded cheddar cheese, tomatoes and romaine lettuce stuffed into pita pockets. To balance things out, they indulged their sweet tooth with double-chocolate, caramel nut brownies for dessert. The girls made no excuses. There was always a critical need for high levels of sugar to give them the energy they needed to propel themselves around the ring. Sounded good, didn't it? They thought so. While their batteries recharged, the girls relaxed in their lawn chairs, glad to sit for a few minutes, and socialized with friends when they stopped by.

After a while they leashed up the dogs and wandered down to the show rings and watched some of the competitions, enjoying their friends' successes and sympathizing when a few of them lost. It was announced over the public address system that Group judging would begin at 2:00, the order putting Working Group second. It was time to get back to work.

Chapter Seventeen

There were again twenty breeds representing the Working Group. Emma and Cole went in and took their place. The handler in front of them was a professional and waited until Emma had Cole set up before he made his move. He positioned his Bernese Mountain Dog slightly out in front of Cole, crowding him so that Cole was partially hidden. The judge, when he looked down the line from the other side of the ring, wouldn't have a clear view of Cole. It was a subtle move, but effective. Emma, seemingly subdued in her reaction, moved Cole up so that he was even with the Bernese and restacked Cole. The handler looked back and Emma smiled. When the handler started to move again, Emma said in a low voice, "If I have to, I'll chase you all over the damn ring." The handler, looking chagrinned, stayed where he was.

The judging started and Cole again put on a performance that had bystanders whispering among themselves. He was perfectly attuned to Emma not only when they were in motion, but also when he was stacked. When posed, he was a living statue emanating a ring presence that few possess. The judge, Mr. Scott Webber from Baltimore, Maryland made his cut, and the remaining dogs, of which Cole was one, presented themselves for the decisive review.

The judge was quick in his final assessment and signaled the handlers for the last go around. The dogs moved out and as Cole flew by, he got the number one nod. Mr. Webber quickly followed with two, three, and four, but all attention was on Cole. Spectators and exhibitors applauded resoundingly and Joanie and Sally, goofballs that they were, were dancing a jig, although it would never be recognized as one.

Emma and Cole moved from that ring to another for pictures, and when they were finished, joined the girls. Attempting to talk amongst themselves was about impossible; people just kept coming up to offer congratulations. Emma accepted their good wishes graciously, but slowly started to drift away from the ring. She needed to let Cole relax before Best In Show, so she gradually but determinedly moved in the direction of the motor home. The hangers-on fell off and at last the girls were by themselves.

"Guys, I'm having a real hard time even believing this is happening," Emma revealed, sitting down hard in a lawn chair. "I mean I knew he was good, but to get a Best In Show and two Group One's in one weekend. I'm freakin' stunned."

"Em, I hate to tell you this, but you *could* just get another Best In Show today," Joanie said.

"Joanie, hush. Don't jinx her," Sally scolded.

"Well, if that happens, if Cole takes Best In Show today, you better have the EMT's on standby 'cause I don't know if my heart can take anymore."

"This is so friggin' fabulous I can't stand it," Joanie spurted while she did another ridiculous looking dance.

"Hey, Em, nice move you put on that handler when you first went in. Who'd he think he was dealing with, a rank amateur?"

"I guess so, thought he'd squeeze me out."

"Little did he know that beneath that soft façade, when provoked, there's one hard-ass bitch."

"Well, I think he knows it now, even though I was very, very pleasant."

"I bet."

"I was. I killed him with kindness."

"Yeah, well, I've seen that kindness in action before so I doubt he'll mess with you again."

"I don't think he will, but who knows. Besides, he got his due, he didn't even make the cut."

"See, there is justice in the world."

"At least in this case. How much time do we have before Best In Show?"

"About an hour and a half," Sally replied.

"Oh good, more time than we had yesterday. We don't have to rush. I think I'm going to snack on something. I'm kind of hungry. Anybody want anything?"

"Yeah, maybe some chips and soda, a few slices of cheese, crackers. Do we have any pretzels?"

"Joanie?"

"Yeah?"

"Get off your butt and help me. You want a damn banquet."

"Hey, this is hard work, all this cheering and clapping. It builds an appetite."

"Good excuse. Come on."

They prepared their so-called "snack", which turned out to be enough food for ten people, and tried to stay calm while they ate. But as the minutes ticked by, Emma got increasingly antsy and had to make herself busy getting Cole ready. The nervous energy was infectious; Sally and Joanie were soon caught up in Emma's buzz and joined in the preparations. With three charged up women working on him, it didn't take very long at all to have Cole groomed to perfection.

It was getting near to the appointed hour, so they walked down to the ring, Emma trying to steady nerves that were at an all-time high. Once they got there, she took several deep breaths and shook out her hands in an effort to calm down. Cole, sensing her heightened nervousness and trying to help, leaned into Emma's legs and licked her hands once they quieted. Emma smiled when his big, brown eyes met her blue ones. She gave his nose a playful tweak, then bent down and gave him a kiss. "Thanks, bud, I needed that. Now what do you say we go kick some butt!"

Cole gave a short bark. He was ready to go. Thankfully they only had to wait a couple more minutes before they went in.

* * * *

He was going to have to be very careful, he thought as he meandered down to the ring. She'd picked up on him as he'd watched her in the field. Even though he'd been about fifty yards away and hidden behind two rows of motor homes, she had sensed his presence. He couldn't believe it when she'd turned around and looked behind her. She'd known she was being watched and the dog had known the whole time at the park. Damn! When he made his report to Jasper, he wasn't going to be happy. There was no doubt about it; the woman and the dog were both perceptive as hell. It was going to make things really difficult for them. But right now, he had another little test to run. He'd stayed away from the rings when they'd been competing up until now. However, in a few minutes it would be time to see if his presence would be detected in a crowd of people at ringside.

* * * *

The seven competitors for Best In Show entered the ring. Besides Cole, there was the German Shepherd Dog again with Bill Thornton as handler, a Miniature Schnauzer, a Labrador Retriever, the same Standard Poodle from yesterday, a gorgeous Bloodhound that made Emma's heart skip a beat, and a Schipperke. They were lined up once more with the larger dogs in front, and the judge, Mr. William Adamsley from Pittsburgh, Pennsylvania upon entering the ring, took his first look. He gave the signal for the go around and as the dogs circled the ring, he was able to get his first impression of the strength and fluidity of their individual movement.

Emma and Cole were third in line behind the German Shepherd and the Retriever. While waiting her turn for the individual inspection, she murmured softly to Cole keeping him focused in his stack. And then she felt it, that same feeling of being watched. But why shouldn't she, she thought. There were probably a hundred or more people on the outside of the ring, all looking in their general direction to watch the judging. But no, this was different. This was like before when she'd been in the field and a chill went up her spine. As Emma moved Cole up a spot when the Retriever moved to the center of the ring, she felt a sudden tenseness in him. During the time she took to restack him, Cole moved his head slightly to the left, an uncharacteristic move. He surveyed the crowd, his nostrils flaring. Emma knew in an instant that Cole had the same sensation. He'd probably scented whoever it was and had recognized it as a threat.

It was time for them to move to center ring. Leading Cole out, she could feel his coiled tension in the way he moved. She stopped at the center spot and, just before she began to stack him for inspection, Cole scanned the area outside the ring. Emma could feel him relax as her hands moved over his legs and back, getting him into position.

It was when she felt the Newf uncoil that she was certain that whoever had been there watching wasn't any longer.

Emma stepped back and let Cole show himself. The judge drew near and began his examination. Cole stood motionless and projected his presence, alert and confident. Mr. Adamsley signaled a down and back and Emma and Cole didn't miss a beat, moving in rhythmical precision. When the judge indicated they were to stop, Emma swung out and Cole nailed the free stand, his expression saying it all. Then while the crowd gave an appreciative round of applause, they glided around the ring as they went back to their place in line.

Emma stacked Cole and during the time that the other examinations were being done, let him know with her hands and quiet words what a good job he'd done. She'd been afraid the momentary threat would throw him off, that he'd be distracted. But instead, he had responded to her silent wishes as though he could read her mind and had given another fantastic performance. Win or lose, Emma was so proud of him and Cole felt it through her touch and voice.

They were all back in line now, stacked for the last time and the judge was moving down the line, pausing at each dog. He moved back out to the center of the ring and looked, giving nothing away in either his expression or body language. He moved to mark his book and came back out with the ring steward. Holding the Best In Show ribbon and the steward, the prizes, he looked toward the exhibitors and announced, "The Newfoundland."

It took Emma a few seconds for it to sink in, while all around her pandemonium had broken out. Bystanders and dog fanciers alike were applauding, whistling and shouting. The other exhibitors were congratulating her and Joanie and Sally had literally lost their minds. Once she regained her senses, Emma knelt down and hugged her dog. She kept her face buried in his fur, the tears streaming down her face.

Cole laid his head on her shoulder letting her know he was there. He patiently waited for the flood of emotion to pass. When she at last gained control, Emma stood and the judge presented her with the Best In Show awards, congratulating her and Cole on their fine performance. Pictures were taken and Emma left the ring in a dreamlike trance, to be immediately pounced upon by her two friends.

"Hot damn, Emma! You did it again! Congratulations!" Sally cheered as she gave Cole a hug and lightly shook his muzzle. "Cole, you were just perfect."

"Thanks, Sally. He was perfect, wasn't he? I can't believe this is real!"

"It's as real as flies on a cow's ass," Joanie added. "But it's freakin' mind blowing too! Holy shit!" She bent down and gave Cole a pat on his chest, then ruffled his ears.

"Tell me about it."

"Do you realize how many good dogs and pro handlers you've beaten in the last two days?" Sally asked.

"I really haven't thought about it," Emma answered, patting Cole's sides when he jumped up and put his big feet on Emma's shoulders, licking her face.

"Lots. My God, Emma, you've blown them all away."

"It's kind of scary isn't it?" Emma was laughing as Cole continued to lick her face.

"No, it's friggin' fantastic!"

"It's so totally, utterly fantastic, we have to have a party," Joanie stated.

"What, now? Cole, get down. I know you're excited but you're way too heavy. That's a good boy." Cole got all four feet back on the ground and settled down when Emma continued to pet him.

"No, when we get home, you dork. Sally, we could throw a party at the restaurant celebrating the wins, couldn't we?"

"Absolutely. I'll close the restaurant to the public and we'll have a private celebration. How about this Wednesday?"

"Sounds good to me. How about you, Em?"

"Wednesday's fine with me. The dogs are invited, right?"

"Hell, yes! How could they not be? They're the guests of honor."

"Then, yeah! Let's party!"

The girls started to leave the ring area amid the still flowing congratulatory shouts. Walking toward the motor home, Emma tugged on Sally's arm to get her attention.

"I felt it again. In the ring."

"Felt what?"

"Somebody watching me."

"Well, Em, you do know there was over a hundred people watching you."

"Yeah, I know, but this was like before when I was up at the field. Cole felt it too."

"Are you sure?"

"Positive. He sensed it just before we were up for inspection."

"Geez, I wonder what's going on."

"I don't know, but it's giving me the creeps."

"I can imagine. We can't do anything about it now, but maybe we should talk to Sam this week. See what he thinks."

"Sounds like a good idea. Joanie? Do you think Sally and I could come over one day this week and tell Sam what's been going on? You know, get his opinion."

"Sure, I'll see when he's got a night free, okay?"

"Okay." Emma felt better already; just the thought of confiding in Sam eased her mind. "Let's get packed up so we can go home. I'm so tired I can't even think. Winning

Best In Show knocks the hell out of you... not that I'm complaining."

"If you did, we'd probably wring your neck."

"No kidding."

The threesome plunged into the task of breaking "camp" and forty-five minutes later they were on the road heading home, jubilant, exhausted, and slightly worried.

* * * *

He'd already left by the time the girls arrived at the motor home. To say he was frustrated was an understatement. Son of a bitch! Both the dog *and* the woman had known he was watching at ringside. There had been a hundred sets of eyes on them and they'd known he was there. He knew the second they became aware of him and he'd had to back off. He'd left the ring immediately, taking care to keep his movements normal, trying not to draw attention to himself lest they try to spot whoever was watching them. He was going to have to call Jasper right away. How were they ever going to get close to this dog? Well, that was Jasper's problem. He'd have to figure it out.

* * * *

As soon as Thornton got back to his motor home, he broke out his cell phone and made the call to Cappellini. "He took Best In Show again today."

"Unbelievable! I knew this dog was one of a kind the minute I saw him." Cappellini, thinking about what an accomplishment this was for both the woman and the dog, couldn't resist giving Thornton a jab. "Well, looks like all you hot shot pros got the pants beat off you two days in a row. That's got to make you feel good."

"No, sir, not exactly."

"I wouldn't think so. Where are they showing next?"

"I don't know for sure, but probably at the Stockton shows."

"All right, I'll have someone check it out. I presume that we're entered."

"Yes, sir. Is there anything more you want me to do?"

"No, Mr. Thornton, for now I just want you to get the dogs ready for the next show."

"Yes, sir."

Cappellini hung up and swirled the scotch whiskey in his glass, his thoughts focused entirely on the information he had received a moment ago. Two Best In Shows the first two days out as a Special and doing it with an owner-handler! It was truly unbelievable! He wanted this dog so badly it was almost a physical ache. With Jasper's help, he would have him. He was already plotting the final details on how to do it. Everything was coming together nicely including his plans to cause Mrs. Rogers some well-deserved trouble. Cappellini lifted his glass in salute to the picture of Cole and smiling, took a long drink.

Chapter Eighteen

Thank God, Monday was a day off. By the time the girls had arrived back at the Hearthmoor the night before, unloaded the motor home, loaded their vehicles, and traveled the short distance home, it was after nine o'clock. Emma literally stumbled out of the Explorer, taking only Cole with her and left the rest to be unloaded in the morning. After doing only what was absolutely necessary, she fell into bed and slept the sleep of the dead. Cole wasn't much better off. He was out two minutes after he lay down. But before they passed out, Emma told Cole to give her a 6:00 wake-up call. They deserved an extra hour of sleep.

In the morning, Emma moved unhurriedly through her routine. She unloaded the Explorer and stowed all the show gear in its appropriate place. She brushed out Cole's coat and did the laundry. It seemed like a ton of it had accumulated from the show and there was too much of it to wait till later in the week. Cole was moving a little sluggishly so Emma gave them both a day off from roading, figuring a double Best In Show winner deserved a few rewards, not to mention that she could use a break.

The day was sunny and warm and she decided to work in the gardens for a while. It was still too early to plant the other flowers she'd bought at the garden center, but the daffodils had gone by and she needed to cut them back. A few of the tulips were looking like they were on their last leg, so she clipped those off too. The fuchsia had been hung the day they came home, but they needed water and pinching back. The hummingbirds were present and dove in and out as Emma moved from plant to plant. Cole stood back and watched their kamikaze maneuvers, moving his head continuously as his eyes tracked their flight paths.

Emma would phone Jackie later in the day to see how the weekend at the shop had gone, knowing already that everything had been fine by the note she'd left. She'd give her a call just to get the specifics and to thank her for covering for them, and most importantly, to set it up for the next time they'd need her help. The next show they were attending was in three weeks and the girls needed to get her lined up.

Emma had to get to the grocery store, so she put Cole, who didn't seem to mind today, in his crate and made the run to Springville. The store was crowded and several people that Emma knew came up and offered their congratulations on her wins. News traveled fast in a small community and Emma was always amazed at the speed with which information got around.

When she came out of the store and approached her car, she discovered she had a flat tire. Great, just what she needed! She threw the groceries into the back near the front seats and was about to call AAA when a friend showed up and offered to change her tire. He accomplished the task within fifteen minutes and Emma thanked him profusely. He'd saved her a lot of time and trouble. With the flat in the back, she headed straight to the local station and dropped it off to be fixed.

When she got back home, there was a message on the answering machine from Joanie to come over for dinner at

about six. Sam was going to be home and th·
his take on what was going on. She said she'd c·
and she would be there too. Emma called her back, g·
machine, and left a message that she would join them.

It was just coming on to three o'clock, and Emma thought she probably had enough time to make some dessert to take to Joanie's and squeeze in a little nap. She still felt drained from the events of the weekend and wanted to be fresh for the evening. So she got out her cookbooks and thumbed through several before she decided on a blueberry buckle. She got the blueberries out of the freezer and went to work. Soon the buckle was in the oven filling the kitchen with mouth-watering smells of cinnamon, melting butter and simmering blueberries. While she waited, Emma cleaned up the kitchen and read a few chapters in the novel she was currently engrossed in.

About an hour later, the dessert was done and Emma put it on the counter to cool. She had a little time to grab a quick snooze, so she stretched out on the sofa and Cole joined her, perfectly happy to be a couch potato. Approximately sixty minutes later, Cole nudged her awake and they had to hurry to be ready in time to get to the Davises.

* * * *

They made it to Joanie and Sam's a little after six. Sally was already there and sipping her first drink. Kirby was out in the yard with Tank and Cole rushed out to join them. The three dogs exchanged noisy greetings and charged into play. Emma sat down at the table next to Sally and exchanged the dessert for a glass of wine with Sam.

The mixed aromas of pan-frying garlic and chicken filled the kitchen as Joanie busied herself at the stove. Pasta was boiling and cooked broccoli was draining in the sink. Joanie's glass was about empty, so Sam gave her a refill and poured himself a glass. A salad drizzled with balsamic dressing had been made and was sitting on the table ready to be devoured. Warm, crusty Italian bread covered with butter and melted mozzarella cheese was sitting in a basket near where Emma sat, tempting her to dig in. In minutes, the chicken and garlic were done and the pasta was cooked to perfection. Joanie tossed them together along with the broccoli and scooped everything into a large pasta bowl. Placing the dish on the table, she got the remaining coup des grace from the refrigerator, a carton of Romano cheese from a Buffalo Italian deli. She then motioned for everyone to begin. Except for the clattering of silverware against bowls and dishes, silence reigned for several minutes, everybody intent on filling their plates and enjoying their food.

"God, Joanie, this is so good," Emma complimented, reaching for another slice of bread.

"Yeah, kiddo, it's delicious." Sally grabbed the cheese again and sprinkled a little more on her pasta, which was already covered with a liberal coating.

"Thanks, guys. Anybody need anything?"

"No, not right now."

"I'm all set too."

"Sally, would it be safe to say you like pasta with your cheese?" Emma was eyeballing Sally's plate.

"I can't help it. This cheese is the best. I kind of lose control when I'm around it."

"Really? I never would have guessed."

"What? You want me to put some back?"

"Yeah, scoop it right off the top. It hasn't started to melt yet, has it?"

"Emma, quit harassing her. Sally, don't listen to Emma. Just eat and enjoy." For several seconds there was no more conversation or teasing, just the sounds of people enjoying good food.

Sam brought them back to why they were here. "Okay, Em, let's hear it," he said. "Joanie gave me a brief description of what happened, but I want to hear it from you."

In between bites of food, Emma told Sam about what had happened at the show, and how she knew she hadn't imagined it because of the way Cole had picked up on it too.

"I believe you, Em; in fact, now that I've heard about the events at the show, I think what happened the other day in the park could be related."

"Oh, Sam, really? I...I hadn't thought of that, but maybe you're right."

"It's a definite possibility. I myself think the two are connected. Think about how Cole reacted. He knew something was out in that fog and we've pretty much ruled out an animal."

"That's right, Em. It didn't add up to be an animal, but at the time we weren't thinking about a two-legged threat," Joanie added.

"I know, I just never thought it would be a person. But now that we're going over all this, when Cole became aware of us being watched in the ring, he was scenting what had to be the same person from the park. Otherwise, why would he have gotten alerted and so tensed up? Why would anyone be watching Cole and me? It doesn't make any sense."

"I don't know why anyone would be watching you, but the fact that you felt someone watching you here *and* at the show, tells me that someone has definitely zeroed in on the both of you. Taking Cole's reaction into account, it is probably the same person. What's unsettling is that whoever it is knows your schedule, your routine. He, and I'm using 'he' just to simplify things, I mean it could very well be a 'she', but anyway, he knew your route in the park and knew you would be at the show. That couldn't have been a coincidence and it's highly unlikely that there's two unrelated sets of people watching you."

"Oh, Jesus," Joanie breathed.

"Shit," Sally moaned.

Emma turned and looked out the sliding glass doors to see Cole playing tag with Kirby and Tank. Tank was getting the better of both of them as he darted around, under, and in between the two other dogs. Her gaze shifted back to Cole and her heart lurched. She felt the back of her neck prickle and an ice-cold fear crept into her bones.

"What can we do?" Emma asked in a voice barely above a whisper.

"I'm afraid right now, there isn't much we can do. Nothing has happened that you could take to a law enforcement agency. You sense that you're being watched, but you don't have anything concrete. Plus, you don't know who's doing the watching," Sam explained.

"Well, that sucks," Joanie lipped.

"Talk about feeling powerless," Sally complained.

"Look guys, all we can do right now is be very vigilant. Emma, you're going to have to change your daily routine. Don't do things in the same order anymore. Change the times you do things. Do not, and I repeat, do not, go to the park at a time or in conditions when you know that you'll probably be the only one there."

"Sam, that all sounds real good, but I *have* to exercise Cole early in the morning. It's getting too warm now to safely have him run six miles any time other than in early morning."

"All right, then somebody has to go with you. You and Cole can't be alone."

"Em, I'll go with you," Joanie volunteered.

"Geez, Joan, I don't want to impose on you."

"Don't even think about it, besides I could use a little bike action. Sam told me just the other day that my love handles are getting to be more like love barrels."

"I never said that Joanie Davis. Don't go putting words in my mouth."

"No, but I could see it in your eyes, lover boy," Joanie smiled, giving Sam a wink.

"Okay, Joanie, I'll take you up on your offer," Emma laughed; then she gave Sam a nudge. "The other part of it I can do. I can change times and order, that's not a problem."

"Another thing, everybody keep an ear out for anyone asking questions about Emma and Cole. Sally, if what I'm thinking is correct, this person certainly knows who Emma's best friends are. That means he knows about your restaurant. Try to watch out for anyone coming into the bar asking questions, even innocent sounding ones, about our two buddies here."

"What should I do if I notice somebody doing that?"

"Nothing, just try and remember what he looks like and any specifics about what the conversation was. You'll notice right away if it's someone other than a regular customer. Then call Joanie as soon as you can, give her the information and I'll follow up."

"Okay, Sam, I can certainly do that."

"That's it then, that's the plan for now. Emma, you just be really, really careful, okay? Anybody have any questions?"

Three heads shook in the negative and the conversation swung over to the upcoming party while they ate their blueberry buckle a la mode with the vanilla ice cream Joanie had on hand. General details were discussed such as time, menu, people to invite, and cost. After about an hour of hashing it out, the girls cleaned up the kitchen and Emma said her goodbyes and left with Cole. Sally and Joanie had a bit more planning to do, planning they didn't need or want

Emma around for. They had a big surprise in store for her the night of the party and their two sneaky little minds had to go into overdrive to pull it off.

* * * *

Wilhelm Schmidt called Cappellini with the travel arrangements that night. He was to leave France in the early morning on Wednesday of that week and would arrive in Toronto, Canada about 4:00 in the afternoon. He would then rent a car, preferably an SUV, travel toward the border for an hour or so, then get a room in a motel and rest for the remainder of the day. He'd start out early the next morning to cross the border, hoping to avoid the morning rush hour, and then on to the farm in Connecticut. He should arrive in Stafford Springs no later than four or five Thursday afternoon. Cappellini was pleased and asked about the cargo.

"The cargo is good. The final negotiations went according to plan and everything is in order. I have all the documentation you will need."

"Excellent, Wilhelm. I'll look forward to seeing you both on Thursday."

"You will be there, Mr. Cappellini?"

"Oh, yes, I wouldn't miss this for the world."

"Then I will see you Thursday afternoon."

"Again, good work, Wilhelm."

"Thank you, sir. It's been a pleasure."

When Cappellini hung up, it was all he could do not to shout with excitement. Everything was going according to plan. Nothing was going to stop him, least of all that stupid, bothersome woman.

Chapter Nineteen

Tuesday morning rolled around and Emma found Joanie on her doorstep at 8:00, ready to bike herself to good health and a svelte figure. Well, maybe not. Truthfully, her only aspiration was to keep Emma company and that was good enough in her book. Cole, already in the back of the SUV, gave Joanie a welcoming lick as they threw her bike in with Emma's and the three of them took off for the park.

There was only one other car in the parking lot and the girls gave each other a nervous glance. They got out of the car anyway and unloaded the bikes and Cole. While they were climbing aboard their two-wheeled transportation, they saw a man and woman emerge from around a bend, jogging in their direction. The girls stiffened slightly as the couple approached, but they said hello, went on by, and stopped at the other car in the lot. Emma and Joanie started out and Joanie kept checking back to see what was going on behind them. The couple had dried off with towels, and then had gotten into their car, ready to leave. Joanie sighed with relief and focused her attention on the ride. Emma and Cole were a good fifty feet ahead of her and she had to work to catch up. Damn, she thought, she really was going to have to get in shape to keep up with these two.

The run went smoothly other than the fact that Joanie kept crying for mercy, begging Emma to stop and rest. Emma wondered with some amusement what help Joanie could possibly be if there was trouble since she couldn't even keep up. But then, Joanie had a habit of scaring people off with just her mouth, so Emma supposed she was in good hands, even if they weren't physically fit ones.

When they got back to Emma's house, Joanie left to go home and change and Emma did the same. Emma made a quick trip to the gas station and picked up her repaired tire before she went to the shop. When she got there, Joanie was already busy opening up. After talking with Jackie the night before, Emma knew that everything would be in order and there wouldn't be much for them to do except restock and do inventory. One of them would probably have to go to the bank in Holland, the town over the hill east of Glenwood. It was less than a fifteen-minute drive away.

The small town of Holland was located southeast of Buffalo, with a population of about 3600. While the main business district and the village residential area was centered on the main artery of Route 16, the outlying homeowners were scattered over the hills on both sides of the north-south road. The commercial sector had a bank, a hardware store, a pharmacy, a grocery store, a pizzeria, a hotel, a large antique store, and various other small businesses. The town had schools for kindergarten through high school, five churches, a VFW Post, and its main attraction, a NASCAR short track, The Holland Speedway, which pulled in droves of spectators from miles around during the racing season.

To get over to Holland from the shop, you had to go up Holland-Glenwood Road, a steeply pitched track that leveled out at Center Road, a main thoroughfare into the town of East Aurora from this area. Once Center was crossed, Holland-Glenwood stayed at a plateau for only a short distance before starting its gradual descent into Holland.

This stretch of road was home to The Holland Hills Golf Course and offered spectacular vistas of the countryside.

On the top of the hill, along which Center Road ran, the elevation was about 1500 feet above sea level, the highest point in Erie County. Not surprisingly, the local television stations had their broadcast towers in two locations along the road. In the winter months, locals knew that if it wasn't necessary, you stayed off Center Road. The weather conditions up there could be atrocious. While there would be a gentle snowfall in the valleys, the conditions on Center could be a raging storm with howling winds and zero visibility. Snow banks were often twelve to fifteen feet high along the roadway. With Emma's winter driving skills being as bad as they were, this was one trip she never, ever made unless there wasn't a flake in the sky and no chance of one for the entire day.

However, since this was a clear spring day she volunteered to make the bank run. Joanie asked if she'd stop at the hardware store while she was there and pick up some screws and drill bits they were running low on. Joanie offered the use of her truck unaware that Emma's vehicle was in the lot. Emma told her the SUV was parked outside and explained about the tire. She made up the deposit slip and grabbed some money from the register. Emma called Cole and they were out the door in the blink of an eye.

Joanie, figuring she had at least thirty minutes, waited until she saw Emma pull out and then went into action. She had a lot of phone calls to make and had to track down one very important male person to invite to the party. Luckily, the post office was next door and who better to ask for information than Frank Upton, the postmaster. He knew just about everything that went on in the town and was a font of information. Gazing out the window, Joanie was just about to dial his number when she spotted the object of her inquiry walking down the road. She dropped the phone and made a beeline for the front of the shop. She opened the door and rushed out onto the porch, trying hard not to look like she was doing exactly that.

"Hey, Ben," she called, fiddling with an arrangement on one of the rocking chairs, attempting to look busy.

Ben looked over, a surprised expression on his face and after seeing Joanie, strolled over to where she stood. "Well, hi. Nice day, isn't it?"

"Yeah, it's great. Of course, according to Emma, any day it doesn't snow is great."

"What's she doing living in this area then?"

"She doesn't have a choice, all her friends live here."

Ben chuckled, "What can I do for you?"

"Not a thing, really. I wanted to invite you to a party we're having celebrating our wins at the dog show this past weekend."

"Oh, yeah? Who won?"

"Oh, well, Tank, that's my dog, won a leg on his obedience title and Kirby, that's Sally Higgins' dog, she owns the Hearthmoor Inn, won a point toward her show championship and Cole, Emma's dog, Emma's my partner if you remember, won two Groups and two Best In Shows. Like he won big...huge...monstrous!"

"It sounds it," he laughed. "When's the party?"

"Tomorrow night at the Hearthmoor, about 7:30."

"I'll tell you what, I'm not promising, but I think I can make it. I had something else planned, but I should be able to get over there for a little while. Okay?"

"Yeah, that would be great. Any time you can make it will be fine. We'll look forward to seeing you."

"Okay. Bye, Joanie."

"Bye, Ben. Have a good day."

Joanie turned to reenter the shop, a very self-satisfied grin on her face and once the door was closed, she let out a loud "who-hoo" and punched her arm in the air triumphantly. She scurried to the phone and called Sally to report her success.

* * * *

When Emma got back the day progressed unremarkably which was good; the girls welcomed a day devoid of problems or surprises. Sometimes it was rather nice to have a boring, ho-hum sort of day when you could kick back and relax, still accomplishing what you had to, but with no pressure or stress. The dogs were even low key, content to lie around and catch up on some sleep. So they all took it for what it was worth, the girls taking it a step further by breaking out their liquid refreshment a little early. Might as well really enjoy the day! As they were imbibing, discussion swung to the upcoming Memorial Day weekend.

"Em, is Sydney still coming for the weekend?" Joanie asked as she leaned back in her chair and put her feet up on the computer console. Sydney was Emma's two and a half year old grandchild by her daughter, Mandie and her husband, Rob. She was also the apple of Cole's eye.

"As far as I know, she's coming out Saturday morning and staying 'til Monday afternoon."

"You're going to have a ball with her. Cole'll be in seventh heaven; he just adores your granddaughter."

"Yeah, I know. He's so good with her and she just loves him right back. They're inseparable when they're together. It's the only time he doesn't sleep with me. He sticks to her like glue, won't let her out of his sight."

"Bath time should be fun."

"Forget it. He stays on the other side of the door for that. I've got a big enough mess to clean up just from Syd."

"He's not going to like it."

"Don't worry, he'll get over it. This old back of mine can only bend over that tub for so long."

"You going to come up to the house while you have her?"

"Oh, probably. She'll want to see Tank, I'm sure. She gets a big kick out of watching Cole and Tank zip around playing tag."

"If it's warm, maybe we can go in the pool. Sam's going to open it this weekend and the heater will be on."

"She'd love that; she loves the water. You do know though that if she goes in, Cole will too."

"Yeah, kind of figured that. And of course if he goes in, Tank'll be right behind him. Could get a little crowded in there."

"Well, we could invite Sally and Kirby up and make it a real free-for-all. Kirby'll dive in even if she's the only one going in."

"Good idea. Let's make it for Sunday after I close the shop. I'll tell her to bring Richard too. Might as well make it a party."

"Joanie, Queen of the Parties."

"You betcha, Em. You know my motto, have as much fun as you can whenever you can."

"Thank God, you married Sam."

"Yeah, he tends to keep me anchored, but he's no slouch himself in the party department."

"I know, but at least he stays sane and keeps you semi-well behaved. Think about your two children."

"I do, all the time. Why do you think I love my wine? Those two would drive Mother Theresa to drink. You've forgotten what it's like to have teenagers."

"No, I don't think I'll ever forget that," Emma laughed. "But your kids aren't teenagers anymore or did that slip your mind?"

"No, but it's a carry-over thing. They still act like teenagers. Don't you think once kids hit twenty all the crap should just end?"

"Yeah, but it doesn't seem to work that way. I don't think it ends 'til they either move out, get married or near thirty."

"Oh cripe, I don't think my boys are going to be in any hurry to move out or get married. They've got it too good right where they are. I'm probably looking at another ten years of kid stuff. God, I need another glass of wine."

"Looking at it that way, I guess maybe you do."

"Be a good friend and get us a refill, will you? My body isn't responding to stimuli right now, the shock has been too much. Go ahead and pinch me. I bet I don't feel a thing."

"As tempting as the offer is, I think I'll pass. I'll just get the wine."

"Well, hurry it up then. I've got some serious drinking to do if I have to face another ten years with my beloved children."

"Maybe I *should* pinch you, just for the sake of doing it."

"Nah, you had your chance and blew it. Now move your butt and get the wine."

Chapter Twenty

Wednesday was ushered in with heavy rain and temperatures in the mid-fifties. Forecasters were calling for a slight chance of severe weather with thunderstorms accompanied by damaging winds and hail. Joanie was on the phone to Emma as soon as she got out of bed.

"Em, you're not going to the park today, are you?" Joanie said a silent prayer, hoping the answer would be "no".

"Yeah, we're going."

"Are you out of your friggin' mind?"

"Noooo, we're just going to put on our rain gear."

"Oh shit."

"Hurry up, I want to leave by eight."

"You won't be happy 'til I'm dead."

"No, actually I'm quite happy right now."

"You're a masochist."

"I know and I love it. Hurry up."

Emma hung up and turned to Cole, "Aren't we going to have fun with your Aunt Joanie today." Cole barked as if he'd understood every word she'd said. Emma laughed and got her rain jacket and pants ready to go.

Joanie showed up at five minutes to eight with a scowl on her face and her rain gear on. Emma could barely keep a straight face as they loaded up. Joanie's dark mood didn't improve once they got underway, either. She mumbled under her breath for the entire ride, but Emma just ignored her, carrying on a one-sided conversation with Cole.

Nobody was there when they pulled into the parking lot and Joanie gave Emma a worried look. Emma shrugged her shoulders and parked. It was raining steadily so Emma pulled on her baseball cap and got out to unload. Joanie followed, grabbing her bike from Emma.

"You think it's okay?" Joanie asked, scanning the area.

"Yeah, there's no fog today, so we'd be able to see whoever was out there. I don't think they'd risk us seeing them."

"What do you mean, they and them? I thought it was a he or she."

"Joanie, it's just a figure of speech. Don't worry; come on. Let's go."

The girls started pedaling and Emma watched Cole closely for any sign of agitation. He appeared to be fine, steady in his pace, and he had a relaxed fluidity in his movement. They didn't see a soul as they continued on to the three-mile mark and turned around. They were near to the end when a lightening bolt streaked across the sky and thunder rumbled in the distance. Emma picked up her speed a bit and Cole responded. They made it back to the Explorer just as another light show appeared and the thunder boomed, sounding a little closer. Joanie had been further back and was now pedaling for all she was worth to get to the car. Once she arrived, they loaded dog and bikes quickly and jumped into the safety of the vehicle. Cole was soaked and gave a tremendous shake, sending water spraying all over the car.

"This is your idea of fun, huh." Joanie shot Cole a disgusted look and wiped off with a towel

"Yep."

"You're sick. You know that, don't you?"

"Yep."

"Course..." She gave her friend an appraising look. "It got you a Best In Show."

"Yeah... two."

"I guess you're not so sick."

"No shit."

The girls went home and dried off, and Emma put Cole under the big dryer. Joanie made it down to the shop before Emma and opened up. When Emma arrived, the shop was already busy with customers who probably came out due to the rain canceling any outdoor activity that might have been planned.

They spent a bustling morning waiting on shoppers, helping them make selections, and hoping the power wouldn't go out because of the storm. It was a huge pain in the neck when that happened, although the customers actually seemed to like it because the girls would light candles to illuminate the store since they gave it a very old-time atmosphere. It goes without saying the girls would break out their beverage of choice, and its consumption would tend to soothe feelings and add to the tranquility of the situation.

For the girls though, it was maddening as far as cashing people out. With no electricity, the charge machine would be down, so they'd have to run the credit cards manually and the cash register would be out of commission. They could still get the money drawer open but had to use a calculator to tally up the receipts, which they had to struggle to see in the dim light. So as the storm continued, they held their breath that the power would remain on.

The afternoon slid by as customers continued to pour into the shop and more than a few asked for details on the show. Cole was called out from the back room to receive his many accolades and Tank got a mixture of kudos and reprimands. They both took it in stride and went back to playing each time the fuss was over.

Toward the end of the day, when there was still about ten customers in the shop, a man came in and started to browse up and down the aisles. He made a complete circuit of the shop and came to the counter to pay for the small purchase he was making. Emma had never seen him before, but thought nothing of it. They were constantly getting new clientele; today alone there had probably been five or six new people in.

Joanie was ringing up the sale and Emma was wrapping when Cole suddenly appeared and wedged his body in front of her. Emma looked up startled. Cole had knocked her off balance in his attempt to get in position and Emma had to adjust her stance. When she looked up, she locked gazes with the man at the counter, surprised that he was watching her so intently. He continued his scrutiny for a second or two more, then lowered his eyes, paid Joanie, and took his purchase from Emma. He mumbled something and made his way to the door, looking straight ahead and moving with undisguised speed. Emma glanced at Cole. He was attentively watching the man's every movement. Not until the man closed the door behind him did Cole break his concentration. Emma gave him a hug and stifled the urge to shiver.

It wasn't until half an hour later that there was a break in the activity at the sales counter and the shop was cleared of customers. Emma could finally talk to her partner. "Joanie, do you remember the guy who bought the coffee mug with the clipper ship on it?"

"No...Why?"

"I don't think he was ever in here before. He had a black windbreaker on."

"Let me think a minute."

"He was here about thirty minutes ago. You know, when Cole came up to the counter."

"I don't know, maybe. I wasn't really paying attention to people; I was trying to get everybody checked out. Why?"

"'Cause I've got a funny feeling he was here to do more than buy a coffee mug."

"Why do you think that?"

"Because number one, Cole got in between us and watched him like a hawk, and number two, I caught him watching me a little too intensely. After he paid, he made a beeline for the door."

Joanie thought about it for a minute; as Emma's words took on meaning, her eyes got huge and she gasped, "Oh crap! You think he's part of that other stuff?"

"I don't know, but if he is, why would he come into the shop? I mean, I saw him clear as day."

"Beats me, but this is getting really weird. I'll tell Sam a soon as I get home. Okay?"

"Okay… Hey, do you think we can call it a day?" Emma asked, glancing at her watch. "It's close enough, let's do it."

"Fine with me, we've got a party to go to."

The girls made short work of ending the day, locked up, and as they parted in the parking lot made reference to the fact that they'd be seeing each other later. Emma and Cole walked up the hill, Emma consciously checking the surrounding woods for movement. She saw nothing and started to feel a little foolish, thinking she was probably making too much of the man in the shop. Cole, on the other hand, stayed even closer than usual and did his own version of surveying the area, staying very alert until they reached the house.

Once inside, Emma took care of normal activities and gave Cole his dinner. She decided to rest before the party, feeling drained not only from the busy day, but also from the strain of nerves too tightly wound. She lay down on the bed, thinking an hour's rest would go a long way, wondering if she was losing it. She never napped like this, but lately she just felt so tired, like she was zapped of strength. It had to be the strain of what was going on; at least she hoped that was it. Cole joined her on the bed and as Emma stroked his side, they both relaxed and drifted off.

Emma woke to the phone ringing and jumped out of bed to answer it. When she lifted the receiver and said hello, there was nobody there. Replacing the receiver, she grumbled about how lacking in manners some people were and, after checking the time, focused her energies on getting ready for the party.

*   *   *   *

The parking lot at the Hearthmoor was full of cars by the time Emma and Cole arrived. What's going on, she wondered while looking for a spot to park. The list of guests they'd made up had only had eighteen to twenty names on it. Who were all these other people? There had to be thirty-five or forty cars here. Maybe Sally had decided that she didn't want to close to the public after all. Well, she'd find out soon enough, she guessed. She got Cole out of the Explorer and started for the entrance.

When she entered the vestibule, she thought the place was strangely quiet for that many cars, and reached to open the door. As soon as she stepped through the entry, the silence was broken with shouts of surprise. Emma was stunned to see the amount of people who crowded the barroom; there had to be close to eighty people sandwiched in there. Joanie and Sally separated themselves from Sam and Richard, coming forward to greet Emma and swamped her with hugs and kisses.

"What...what is all this?" Emma stammered.

"It's for you, Em. 'Cause of what you did at the show. It's such an accomplishment. Everybody here wanted to celebrate with us," Joanie replied.

"Everybody we invited came, Em. They're all so happy for you." Sally gave her another squeeze.

"I don't know what to say, I'm overwhelmed," Emma gasped.

Joanie, starting to lead her through the crowd toward the bar, told her to just say thank you and enjoy herself. "Just have a good time," she said. "And leave everything to us. We've got everything under control."

"But this party was for you guys too," Emma protested.

"Yeah, well... we just let you think that. This night is for you, Emma. You've accomplished with Cole something that 99% of us will never experience. So, relax and enjoy."

"But..."

"No buts, Em, this is our gift to you. Accept it, please."

"Okay...you guys are the best, you know that, don't you?"

"Yeah, we know, and don't *you* ever forget it," Joanie laughed.

"Don't worry I won't, you'd never let me," Emma joked back, her voice breaking with emotion as her eyes welled with tears.

"All right then, enough of this," Sally sniffed. "Let's have a good time. Em, you want the usual?"

Emma nodded and Sally poured her favorite wine. Emma accepted the glass and, with a shove from Joanie, went into the midst of the crowd accepting everyone's congratulations. Cole had found Tank and Kirby and the three of them were happy to sit and bask in the limelight, numerous people giving them hugs and kisses and pats on the head. Even better were the dog treats that had started in a bowl at the end of the bar, but were now finding their way into the dogs' greedy little mouths compliments of their many fans. Nevertheless, despite all the attention, Cole and friends were aware of everything going on around them and knew where their owners were at any given moment.

People had started to drift between the bar and the dining area, and Emma made her way to the tables where she found her daughter, Mandie and son-in-law, Rob. Surprised, she hugged them both and sat down for a minute to talk. "I can't believe you two came all the way out here tonight." Mandie and Rob lived a little over an hour away in Wheatfield, which was north of the city of Buffalo.

"Oh, Mom, of course we came. We wanted to celebrate with you."

"Yeah, but it's so far to come on a week night."

"I think we can handle it, Mom," Rob grinned. "Besides, we both took the day off tomorrow. We're going to take Syd to the aquarium."

"Oh, she'll love that. Too bad she couldn't have come tonight. But I know, it's too late for her and then she'd be cranky tomorrow for her adventure. I can't wait to hear all about it."

"I'm sure she'll have a lot to tell you, but go on now. You've got a lot of people to see and we don't want to monopolize you. Know how proud of you I am, Mom."

"Thanks, Mandie. Love you."

"Love you too, now get out of here and mingle with your adoring public."

"Okay, sweetie. Thanks for coming."

As Emma rose from her chair and turned to go, a little old lady with pink hair bumped into her. Emma looked and couldn't believe her eyes. It was her Aunt Agnes and behind her, Uncle Lou. Aunt Agnes was about four foot ten inches tall and round as a butterball. Her pink flyaway hair framed a face wrinkled with age but still alive with impish mischief.

She was covered in jewelry, as was her style, wearing every piece she owned. Her arms held no less than six watches each and every finger was adorned with at least one ring. There had to be a minimum of twenty necklaces hanging from her neck and her ears were studded with six earrings apiece. She had a jeweled headband in her hair and her skirt was bedecked with pins of every size and shape. Emma hoped that Aunt Agnes had kept her embellishing to the front of the garment, or Lord help her when she sat down. The rims of her glasses sparkled with rhinestones and when Emma looked down, she saw that every toe on her sandaled feet sported a toe ring. She was a vision of sparkling gold and silver, only not the kind you'd have in a beautiful dream. This was more like possessed jewelry running amok. It kind of looked like Aunt Agnes was a magnet and every piece of gold or silver she passed was pulled to her and clamped itself onto her body. To top everything off, she wore garish blue eye shadow, had bright pink rouged cheeks, and deep red lipstick. A picture of subtlety she was not.

Then, there was Uncle Lou. You were never quite sure if he was among the living or not. He was the direct opposite of Aunt Agnes, tall, over six feet and very thin, almost cadaverous. He was as pale as she was rouged and as plain as she was adorned. Emma had only ever seen him clothed in a black suit, white shirt, black socks and shoes. The sole variance on his costume was a tie or no tie. Tonight, there was a tie, must be for the celebratory significance of the occasion. Of course, it was black.

They were both in their late seventies, retired, free to come and go as they pleased. Emma had always thought it best not to know where they came and went, could be a little bit too much information with those two. She also thought it prudent that she didn't know where all that jewelry came from either, especially when pieces of it, on occasion, still had the price tags attached They were however, two of her favorite people and she was very glad to see them.

"Aunt Agnes, Uncle Lou, how good to see you."

"Emma, Emma, come here and give us a hug," Aunt Agnes trilled as Emma bent to embrace her aunt. Uncle Lou stood stoically by until it was his turn and then enfolded Emma with his spindly arms.

"Emma, you look wonderful," Uncle Lou boomed in his deep voice. "Congratulations on all this dog stuff. I don't know exactly what it all means, but I understand you did good."

"Thanks, Uncle Lou. It's really all Cole's doing though, I'm just kind of along for the ride."

"Oh, there she goes again. She always was so modest, wasn't she, Lou?"

"Yes, she was. But you can't fool us, Emma. We know the truth. We had a little chat with your friends, Sally and Joanie, and they told us about the show. We're very proud of you and you should be proud of yourself, but I know that's asking too much. You'd never give yourself the credit you deserve."

"Uncle Lou, if it wasn't for Cole, I wouldn't have won. I never would have even been in the competition. So you see, all the credit really does go to him."

"Em, I'm not going to argue with you about it. You did yourself proud, end of discussion. Now, tell us where we can get a drink and then we'll say hello to Cole."

Emma directed them to the bar and after they left, she stopped to talk with several other people who had come over to offer their good wishes. Emma spotted Tammy and worked her way through the crowd to where she stood. "Hi, Tammy. Glad you could make it."

"Oh, Emma, me too. This is a really cool party. I guess I should congratulate you on your wins or whatever you did."

"Thanks, Tammy," Emma laughed.

"Oh, no problem. Hope you keep doing whatever it is you do, Cole too."

"Thanks again. Enjoy yourself."

"Oh, for sure. You have a good party."

"I will," Emma smiled as she walked to the bar. A small number of the shop's customers, Mrs. Foster included, were congregated at the far end and Emma stopped to speak with them. They chatted about the show and Cole and Mrs. Foster procured from her rather large handbag, a full box of Cole's favorite dog biscuits.

"This is for that wonderful dog of yours, Emma. He is truly one of the sweetest animals I've ever known and now to think, he's a star."

"That's very kind of you, Mrs. Foster. I know he'll really appreciate these biscuits. And just so you know, you're one of his favorite people, too."

"Oh, isn't that lovely. Well, you let him know that I'll be in to see him real soon."

"If you want, you can tell him yourself. He's right over there with Tank and Kirby," Emma said, pointing to where the three canines were laying.

"I'll do just that and perhaps give him a biscuit?"

"Sure, but you'll probably have to give one to his two buddies too."

"Oh, of course. I'm certain that Cole wouldn't mind sharing."

"Not a bit. I'll talk to you later."

Emma moved on from group to group and somewhere in the process, Joanie exchanged her empty glass for a full one. She had just finished speaking with some dog fanciers she knew from Springville, when she spotted a tall, black-haired man going to the bar. He turned her way as he spoke to Sally and Emma's heart dropped to her feet. It was Ben Sievers. What was he doing here? Emma's eyes searched for Joanie and when they found her, her friend had what you could only call a shit-eating grin on her face. Emma looked over to Sally and saw the same incriminating smirk on her face. Emma quickly looked back to Joanie and saw her mouth, "Surprise!" Emma could feel her blood pooling in her feet and knew she'd gone completely white, so much so that Joanie came over and asked if she was okay.

"Oh, God, Joanie, why did you do this?"

"Because we care about you, Em, and want you to be happy."

"I am happy," Emma stated, draining the remainder of her glass of wine.

"No, not entirely and you know it. You need somebody and Ben is a good prospect to fill the position."

"Damn, Joanie! Does he know this is a set-up?"

"No, I just invited him to share in the celebration."

"Okay, that's good. But I'm not initiating anything. If he wants to talk to me, then he can make the first move, all right?"

"All right."

"Promise me, you or Sally won't push him at me. Joanie? Promise me."

"Okay, okay. I promise."

"All right, I'm going to…"

Just then, someone came up behind Emma and lightly tapped her on the shoulder. She knew instinctively, without having to look, who it was. It was him. It was Ben Sievers. Damn! She composed herself as best she could and turned to face him.

"Hi, Emma. I understand big, no, make that huge, congratulations are in order."

"Thank you, Mr. Sievers. That's very nice of you to say."

"Well, your very welcome and make that Ben, okay?"

"Okay… Ben."

"There, that's much better, don't you think? Would you care for a refill on your drink?"

"Yes, that would be very nice," Emma murmured.

Joanie looked at Sally and Sally looked at Joanie, flabbergasted that Emma was having a third drink when she had driven there by herself. With her lack of driving skills being what they were, Emma never had more than two drinks when she was going to be behind the wheel. Well, she was either going to spend the night upstairs in Sally's apartment or somebody was going to have to drive her home. Gee, now who could that be, they both wondered, shifting their eyes to Ben. The two friends communicated their observations silently but accurately, having had many years of practice.

Ben had appropriated their drinks and led Emma over to a table in the barroom. They sat across from one another and Ben adroitly steered Emma into a discussion about the show. Joanie and Sally, beaming with pleasure, made their way through the crowd stopping to talk to various women, proceeding with phase two of "The Big Plan".

* * * *

Emma was amazed to find herself relaxing as she sat across the table from Ben, relating the details of the show. Of course, she'd already downed the contents of two glasses of wine, but let's not nit pick. She continued to sip occasionally from her third glass and watched Ben's face as she mentally recorded the interest expressed in his beautiful, brown eyes as he listened attentively to what she was saying. She was actually quite shy when meeting someone new and would have been tongue-tied if the subject at hand hadn't been about dogs. When her discourse was finished however, there was a conspicuous silence that threatened to go on and on. Embarrassed now, Emma rose from her chair, looking to make her getaway. "Umm, I really should go and mingle with the other guests," Emma said as she looked everywhere except at Ben.

"I understand. I enjoyed hearing about the show, though. I hope I didn't keep you too long. I apologize if I did," Ben replied as he too left his chair.

"No, not at all. It was nice seeing you again. Thank you for coming."

As Emma turned to go, Ben touched her arm, swinging her attention back to him. "I'm sorry, Emma, I'm not handling this very well."

Emma, very aware that his hand was still on her arm, feeling the warmth of his fingers on her skin, could barely breathe. "What do you mean?" she managed to ask.

"Well, I'd like to get to know you better. I'd like to take you out."

"Take me out?"

"Yeah, you know, on a date?"

"A date?"

"Yeah, like when I pick you up and we go somewhere together and have a good time," Ben laughed.

"Oh."

"Do I take that for a yes or a no?"

"Umm…"

"Emma, please say yes. I'd really like it if we could get together," Ben smiled.

"Ye…yes, if you're sure."

"I'm sure. I'll call you tomorrow at the shop and we can work out the details, okay?"

"Okay. I…I have to go now," Emma said breathlessly, as Ben's fingers slipped from her arm and she turned to go into the dining room, the spot on her arm where his fingers had been now feeling cold without his touch. How she managed to walk under her own power was a mystery to her, but Emma succeeded in propelling her body into the dining area, barely aware of her surroundings.

Joanie happened to see her and raced over, hungry for details. "Em…Em…" Joanie waved a hand in front of Emma's face. "Helloooo, earth to Emma."

"Oh, Joanie, hi," Emma said as she shook her head slightly to dislodge the mental cobwebs.

"What happened with Ben?" Joanie asked, coming straight to the point.

"He asked me out."

"Yahooo!" Joanie cheered.

"Keep your voice down, everybody will wonder what's going on."

"Hell, I think we ought to announce it to the whole damn world!"

"Don't you dare, Joanie Davis."

"Okay, okay. So what's the scoop? Where are you going and when?"

"I don't know the details yet, he's going to call me tomorrow at the shop."

"Holy shit! This is great! I gotta go tell Sally," Joanie called over her shoulder as she darted off to find the other conspirator.

Emma continued making the rounds, trying to focus on the conversations she was involved in, but more often than not, she found her thoughts wandering back to a replay of the discussion she'd had with Ben. God, he was gorgeous, she thought, all that silky black hair touched with just the right amount of gray, and those big, brown eyes that were limpid pools of seduc… Whoa, wait a minute, enough of that! Get your mind back to the business at hand, Emma, old girl.

She busied herself at the buffet table where a sumptuous feast had been laid out and filled her plate to heaping; suddenly she was ravenous. Sally and Tom had outdone themselves this time. There was shrimp cocktail, crab-stuffed mushrooms, chicken wings done mild, medium or hot, a vegetable platter with a creamy dill dip, a garden salad with assorted choices of dressing, an antipasto, paper-thin sliced roast beef warming in jus and kummelweck rolls for sandwiches with condiments of horseradish, mustard and mayonnaise.

Kummelweck rolls were taken for granted in Western New York, but were in reality, indigenous only to this area. The rolls are German kaisers whose tops have been coated with coarse salt and caraway seeds. When making the traditional sandwich, the undersides of the top of the rolls are dipped in the jus; the bottom of the roll is piled high with roast beef slices and served with horseradish so tangy it will clear your sinuses.

There were new, red potatoes with butter and parsley, mini penne with Madera sauce and melted Parmesan and mozzarella cheese, homemade macaroni and cheese, and a juicy, tender baked ham. The desserts were a large chocolate raspberry-filled sheet cake, slices of apple pie and, Emma's favorite, rice pudding with whipped cream.

Emma sat with her daughter and made small talk while she ate, keeping her upcoming date a secret she didn't yet want to share. It could after all, turn out to be a disaster, so the fewer people who knew about it the better. If Mandie knew, then her son, Mack and her other daughter, Tracy, who both lived in Connecticut, would know and all the explanations would have to start. If it went badly, then another whole round of accounting would have to be given and so forth and so on. Better to keep quiet, Emma thought, until there was something definite to send through the family grapevine. Besides, her son was so protective of her, he'd probably want to cross-examine Ben before he gave him permission to take her out.

God knows her two daughters had had enough trouble trying to meet new boys when they'd been dating. Whenever they'd gone out together, let's say to a bar, Mack and his friends would form a circle around whichever of his sisters was there that night and no male person was allowed to cross the barrier. The girls had to resort to diversionary tactics to meet someone, much less date them. It took a stalwart man to hold up under the intense scrutiny Mack put them through. No, Emma resolved, I'll just play this one real close to the vest.

It was getting to be close to 10:00 and people were staring to leave, tomorrow being a workday. Aunt Agnes and Uncle Lou sauntered over to the table and said their goodbyes, closely followed by Tammy and Mrs. Foster. More people followed until there was a line of people snaking through the dining room, waiting to do their leave-taking. Ben had left earlier, soon after he had talked with Emma. Everyone was gone within fifteen minutes, except for the five friends and Mandie and Rob, who were presently getting their things together. Two minutes later Mandie and Rob were saying goodbye to Emma, and as they were going out the door, her daughter promised to call on Friday morning with all the fascinating details of the aquarium adventure.

The five remaining people moved to the bar and pulled up stools, the dogs congregating around them. Cole slipped his head beneath Emma's hand and she stroked him as he sat and watched her. Tank jumped into Joanie's lap and Kirby edged close to Sally's legs where she found a reassuring hand petting her side.

"Well, I think the party was a resounding success," Sally said as she sipped her manhattan.

"Absolutely! Everybody seemed to have a great time," Joanie chimed in.

"I can't thank you two enough," Emma said. "I'll never forget the effort you made tonight to give me such a wonderful party."

"We loved doing it, Em."

There was a brief pause in the conversation as they all reflected on the party and the events that had brought it to pass, including the friendships that spanned some twenty plus years.

"About this afternoon," Sam brought up, hating to break the mood, but knowing the subject had to be broached.

"Joanie told you about the man in the shop?" Emma asked.

"Yeah, and I'm a little unsettled with this development. If this guy is part of what's been going on, then it's an awfully bold step, not caring that you saw him and could identify him later. But again, there's nothing criminal about coming into a store and buying something. It really comes off as more like an intimidation ploy. But why? That's what I don't get."

"I don't know either, but if their object is to spook me, it's starting to work."

"When's the next show?"

"In about three weeks, Stockton," Joanie answered.

"Okay, until then I guess we'll just have to keep doing what we're already doing, but be even more careful, Emma. If anything, and I do mean anything, happens out of the ordinary I want to know about it. Okay?"

"Okay."

"Guess we better break this up, guys. We all have to work tomorrow. Em, I'll drive you and Cole home in the Explorer and Sam can follow us in the truck."

"All right," Emma agreed, knowing she'd had one drink too many to drive. No false pride here. "Sally, you want any help cleaning the place up?"

"No, but thanks for offering. The cleaning crew will be here in the morning; they can take care of it. I'm going to get myself to bed too, I'm kind of bushed."

"Okay, good night then and thanks again."

"Your welcome, it was our pleasure. Now go home. Bye, Cole."

Goodbyes were said all around and Sam scooted the girls, Tank, and Cole out the door. The girls were approaching Emma's Explorer when Sam noticed the SUV had a flat tire.

"What? Again?" Emma couldn't believe it.

"What do you mean, again?"

"This is the second time this week I've had a flat."

"What are you doing, Em, aiming for the nails?"

"Funny, Joan. Cripe! Well, at least it's not the same one."

Sam was already heading back to the restaurant. "Don't worry, I'll grab Richard and we'll have it changed in no time."

It took only minutes and the girls were on their way. Joanie got Emma and Cole safely deposited at home and then hopped into the truck with her husband for the short trip to their house. As Joanie snuggled up to Sam, her worried thoughts stayed with Emma. She didn't understand what was going on, but she hoped they'd all be able to keep their friend protected from the threat that seemed to be following her.

Chapter Twenty-One

Everything went off without a hitch Thursday morning. The weather even cooperated. The skies were sunny and the temperature was in the low sixties; so on that score, Joanie had nothing to complain about during their run at the park. She was improving; able to keep up with Emma and Cole at least part of the time, and Emma actually caught her looking like she might be enjoying herself. Not that Joanie would ever admit to such a thing, but Emma stored the information away.

Emma dropped the flat tire off at the station on the way back and had to put up with the mechanics razzing her along the same lines that Joanie had the night before. Everybody knew that Emma wasn't what would be considered an A+ driver; she was more along the lines of a C-, sliding into a D. Well, crap, she couldn't be good at everything!

When they got down to the shop and opened up, they had customers in the store almost immediately. It was non-stop action for two hours during which time UPS came and delivered the new line of candles they'd been expecting. As soon as they were able, they started to unpack the six cartons, checking the contents for damage and accuracy against what they had ordered. The girls inventoried and priced each piece and then started to arrange the display in the new cupboard waiting in the back corner of the store. Just as they had imagined, the candles and cabinet worked great together. The display was very eye-catching. The time-aged wood of the cabinet enhanced the primitive look of the candles, which were housed in glass jars with antiqued tin lids. Hot damn, they'd done it again!

When they were finished, they realized it was already two o'clock. No wonder their stomachs were growling! Joanie went back to the kitchen and made big salads for their lunch. Both the girls loved good food, so the kitchen in the shop was as well stocked as the ones in their homes. Today's fare was a salad made with cottage cheese, cucumbers, tomatoes, carrots, green and black olives, and fresh broccoli. The choice of dressing was Italian, French, or ranch. They added a few dinner rolls and butter and voila, they had a feast. One thing was certain, if they were ever stranded at the shop during a snowstorm, they'd never starve.

Emma was halfway through her lunch when the phone rang and she went to answer it. "Good afternoon, the Whistling Thistle."

"Hi, is this Emma?"

"Yes, may I ask who's calling?"

"It's Ben, Emma."

"Oh…hi," Emma said haltingly as her breath caught in her throat. Thank God she'd swallowed what she'd had in her mouth or she probably would have choked to death.

"How are you today?"

"I'm fine, and you?"

"I'm great. Did you get home from the party all right?"

"Yes…Joanie drove me."

"Good. Sorry I couldn't stay longer, but I'd already had a previous obligation for that night."

"Oh, that's all right."

"Listen, are we still on for our date?"

"I...I guess so."

"Terrific. What would you like to do?"

"I don't know...I haven't done this in a very long time."

"Well, it's been a while for me too. Tell you what, why don't I take charge?"

"Okay."

"How does dinner and dancing at the Red House Bar sound?"

"That sounds nice."

"Would Friday night be all right?"

"Tomorrow, Friday?"

"Yes."

"Umm...I think so."

"Would 7:30 be a good time for you? I know you're at the shop 'til six. Does that give you enough time?"

"Yes, it shouldn't be a problem."

"Good, I'll pick you up at 7:30 then. You live up the hill in back of the shop, right?"

"Yes."

"Okay, I'll see you then. Bye, Emma."

"Bye, Ben."

Emma replaced the receiver, a dazed look on her face. When she glanced over at Joanie, she saw that her friend was practically bouncing out of her chair, her meal long forgotten. She pounced on Emma immediately, demanding to know the details of the phone conversation. Emma replayed the salient points.

"What am I going to wear?" Emma asked, knowing she was short on dress-up clothing.

"Don't worry about it; we'll get you dressed to the nines."

"I don't have any shoes," Emma persisted.

"Em, between you, me, and Sally, we'll get you outfitted. Stop worrying."

"All I really have are show clothes. They're not dressy enough for a date."

"Emma, Emma, listen to me...we'll get you dressed. Sally and I have a lot of dress-up clothes and we're all about the same size, so we'll find you something. You and I wear the same shoe size, so that's not a problem either."

The enormity of what she had just agreed to, struck Emma like a ton of bricks.

"Joanie, I haven't been on a date in...oh, Lord...thirty-four years."

"Whoa...that *is* a long time, Em."

"Oh geez, thirty-four years, Joanie."

"Well then, I guess it's past time you went on one."

"I don't think I can do this."

"Sure you can; you're going to have a great time."

"I don't know."

"Well, I do and everything's going to be fine."

"Really? You think so?"

"I know so. Besides, Sally and I will be there for moral support before Ben gets there."

"How can Sally be there, she's got a restaurant to run?"

"We've got it covered, Em. I'm telling you, we've got all our little ducks in a row."

"Ducks in a row, huh. Well, you better figure out how you're going to plunk this big chicken right smack in the middle of 'em."

"We've got a Plan, and if Plan A doesn't work, then we'll go to Plan B, if that fails, there's always Plan C and if..."

"Stop, I don't want to know. It's probably better if I don't. Tell me though, when are we going to find this outfit?"

"Tonight, after we close. We'll go to my house first and see what we can put together. If we come up empty, we'll go to Sally's."

"I don't stand a chance of getting out of this, do I?"

"No, not a one. Accept it...you're going on a date, and Sally and I are keeping our feet in your ass to make sure you don't back out."

Emma sighed, resigned to her fate. There was no way she could fight her two friends turned trolls if they were united against her. Separately, she could probably have weaseled her way around one of them, but if they both ganged up on her, it was useless. They'd have both the front *and* back doors covered, literally and figuratively. There was no doubt now, she would be going on her first date in thirty-four years. Heaven help her!

* * * *

Sally met them at Joanie's house a few minutes after six. They went right up to Joanie's bedroom and started to ransack her closet. Emma stood back and watched the two demons at work, wondering if they'd notice if she snuck out. Probably, then they'd hogtie her so she couldn't escape again. Better to stay here and face the music, she thought. It's safer than flirting with rope burns.

After about twenty minutes and much discussion, there were five outfits layed out on the bed the two devil-women thought would be appropriate. Emma finally got to exercise her vote and picked three of the five to try on. She settled on a plum sheath that Sally said complimented her trim figure. Emma didn't know about that, but liked the way the dress felt. It had little cap sleeves and a jewel neckline, the length hitting just above her knee. Joanie agreed it looked good and so moved on to shoes.

Another huge discussion ensued and ten pairs of shoes were flung out of their boxes. Emma discarded the higher

217

heels automatically. She recognized a catastrophe when she saw one. She selected a pair of low, black pumps and slipped them on. They fit perfectly and worked well with the dress. Emma was satisfied and started to remove the dress only to be stopped by Joanie.

"Leave it on Em, now we have to accessorize you."

"Oh shit," Emma said, slumping her shoulders in defeat, her escape thwarted before it even got started.

Her two jailors went into the bottom drawer of Joanie's dresser and pulled out one handbag after the other. They decided everything was a little too large. Sally said she had the perfect bag at home and would bring it to Emma's house tomorrow. Emma looked expectantly from one to the other, hoping they were finished. But no, they still had jewelry to get through.

The debate over gold versus silver began and the contents of Joanie's jewelry box were emptied on top of the dresser. Discussion moved on to necklace versus pin, or a combination of the two, which bracelet and how many, cocktail ring or not. A watch was a given.

Emma, patience gone, jumped in, selected a pin and one bracelet, and called an end to the fashion lesson. She removed the dress and shoes, pulled on her own clothes, shoved the jewelry into her pocket, picked up the shoes, and slung the dress over her arm. She started out of the room, called for Cole, walked through the house, out the door, got into her car, and left for home. Joanie and Sally were left sputtering in her wake. As Emma pulled out of the driveway, the two watched from the upstairs bedroom window with big grins on their faces. They high-fived each other, then began to put Joanie's room back in order.

* * * *

Just about five o'clock that same afternoon, Wilhelm arrived at the farm in Stafford Springs, Connecticut. The farm was located about four miles outside the town on Route 190. It encompassed nearly sixty acres of rolling, rocky land, about half of it wooded. There was a well-kept red barn, which housed the dog kennels, and several out-buildings.

Inside the barn, brilliantly lit by overhead florescent lights, there were twenty runs with ten to a side. The dog runs were made up of stainless steel walls and floors, and had chain link gates. This type of kenneling protected the dog's coat from any kind of breakage, but kept the dogs in a sort of isolation since they were unable to see or interact with the dog on either side. There was a grooming room equipped with all the necessary tools of the trade and an exercise area that included several treadmills, a lap pool, and a Jacuzzi. There was an equipment room, a storage area and a room used by the vet when he was called in.

The house was a restored two-story colonial dating back to the 1820's. It was white with green shutters, a slate roof, a solid plank front door, and had a front porch that just begged for someone to come and wile away the summer hours there. Cappellini never had. His caretakers, who not only took care of the house and grounds but also saw to the everyday needs of the dogs, occupied the house.

The house had four bedrooms, all of them on the second floor. The employees occupied two of the rooms; the others were for guests. Wilhelm would probably be staying in one of them that night. There was a living room, a sitting room, dining room, a modern kitchen, and two updated bathrooms. There was a laundry room and a mudroom, which had undoubtedly been used for different purposes in days gone by, perhaps as a summer kitchen and pantry. The house was furnished in period pieces with oval braided rugs, wing-backed chairs and swag curtains. And although the kitchen held only the best in modern appliances, there were oak hutches and pie safes, along with a claw-footed pedestal table and ladder-back chairs.

The surrounding flower gardens were well tended and boasted varieties of flowers and herbs such as blue indigo, which were propagated in colonial times. The setting was idyllic, the countryside breathtaking, the house, a jewel. Cappellini saw nothing but a means to an end.

Wilhelm pulled the SUV up to the barn and got out. He waited for Cappellini to reach the vehicle and then opened the back of the car. Inside the dog crate that sat on the floor was Cappellini's answer to any problems that might arise. Wilhelm opened the crate and the dog jumped down.

The Newfoundland that stood before him was indeed a very close replica of the dog he desired. He had the same pure black coat, his head was about the same size, and the shape, height and length of his body was almost identical to the dog of his obsession. He looked to be around the same weight. His chest seemed to be near the same width and his eyes were the same dark brown. It was there, however, that the similarities ended. As Cappellini studied the dog, the differences became apparent, at least to him. This dog lacked the vitality of the other. He lacked the bearing and the expression that the other had projected so effortlessly. He'd never possess the presence or the soul of the one he was so fixated on.

He had Wilhelm move the dog down and back and then in a circle in front of the barn. The dog moved efficiently, but didn't have the commanding reach and drive of the other. His gait was smooth, but lacked the fluidity and power that made the other dog seem like he floated on air.

They took the dog into the barn and went into a room that had been set up to be completely operational as a surgical suite for veterinary practice. They put him up on the table, layed him on his side, and lifted his back leg. There on the inside of his right thigh was the spot of pigmentation shaped like a cumulus cloud. Cappellini had Wilhelm take pictures from every angle.

"Roberts," Cappellini called to one of the caretakers, "call Dr. Morton. Tell him to be here in half an hour." As Roberts went to make the call, Cappellini looked through the paperwork, singling out one of the pages. This and what went with it was the dealmaker.

"What do you think?" Wilhelm asked.

"I think this is going to work out rather nicely. He's very close in appearance to the other dog, so the kennel we got him from won't ever question it. Hell, it'll be to their glory. And after we make the necessary adjustments to the other Newf, no one here will have any reason to doubt that he is who we say he is."

When Dr. Morton arrived, he was shown into the room where the dog and the two men waited. Dr. Kenneth Morton no longer had his own veterinary practice; he now worked exclusively for Cappellini. He'd had a somewhat forced retirement when he was found guilty of unethical behavior and had taken to drowning his sorrows in a bottle to assuage his guilty conscience. When he was sober and paid well, he could perform miracles.

"Aaah, Dr. Morton. How are you?" Cappellini asked while raking his eyes over the other man.

"I'm fine, Mr. Cappellini."

"Are you sober?"

"Quite."

"Good. I want you to first study this pigmentation on the inside of the dog's leg. Can you reproduce it?"

Morton bent to examine the dog's leg. After some probing with his fingers, he answered the question. "It shouldn't be difficult to duplicate. I assume you want it to be permanent?"

"Yes, definitely. Are you also prepared to find the chip?"

"Yes, of course. With the equipment I have here, it shouldn't be a problem. You made it clear that was the primary objective."

"All right, good. I'm glad you were sober enough to remember. I want you to prep the dog immediately, find the chip and remove it."

"Remove it?"

"Yes. What did you think I wanted you to do after you found it? Wilhelm will stay here while you perform the surgery and once you've retrieved the chip, he'll take possession of it."

"And then what?"

"What do you mean?"

"What do I do then? What do I do with the dog?"

Cappellini looked at him, a cold glint in his eyes, his face a mask of stone. "Destroy him," he said as he gathered the documents and calmly walked out the door leaving the vet staring after him, his mouth open in shock.

Chapter Twenty-Two

It was Friday. No matter how you looked at it, it wasn't going to change. Today was the day, Emma thought as she came fully awake after receiving Cole's kiss. The kiss was in the form of a face washing, and was the preferred method of waking her up that morning. Oh, Lord, it was really going to happen today, she moaned. She was going on a date. Oh, Lord, Lord, Lord. Maybe she'd luck out and an accident would befall her somehow, something short of death that would make it impossible for her to keep the date. She could only hope.

Going through her usual routine, Emma hoped for something as simple as a charley horse when she exercised, but not even that was in the cards. She didn't slip in the shower. She didn't slice her thumb when she cut up fruit for her cereal. Any other time, she'd be on her way to the emergency room, destined for full traction and reattachment of her thumb. Where was her rotten luck when she needed it?

Joanie arrived at eight and they went to the park. As they biked, Emma told Joanie about a call that was on the answering machine when she got home the previous night. "Guess who left a message on my machine yesterday?"

"I don't know. Who?"

"Remember Nancy Bullis?"

"Nancy Bullis....Nancy Bullis. Yeah, she's a handler, right?"

"Yep, that's the one. We met her at the Buffalo show in January this year."

"Right, she came over to congratulate you when Cole won. She was nice if I remember correctly."

"Yeah, she was real nice. Anyway, she left a message congratulating me on Cole's two Best In Shows and if I was interested, she was offering her services."

"Oh, wow! She's a top handler."

"Yeah, she is."

"Are you tempted, Em?"

"No, there's no way I'd put him out with anybody. He's my buddy. Besides, I just can't afford it."

"I know, but it must make you feel good that somebody the caliber of Nancy Bullis wants to show him."

"Oh, it does. I know it's quite a compliment to Cole, and I'm just amazed that she called me. I know she'll be really good about me not giving him to her too. She even said that whether she gets him or not, she wishes us future success."

"And you'll have that, as sure as I'm struggling to keep up with you. You'll have a lot more big wins with Cole."

"I think so too. You ready to make the three-mile turn?"

"More than ready."

"Then let's do it."

The girls made the change and started back on the remaining three miles. Joanie fell behind a little ways, but Cole and Emma surged onward. They were maybe seventy-five feet ahead of Joanie when Emma felt a prickling on the back of her neck. Her eyes flew to Cole, and saw that he was instantly more alert. His head was higher and his nostrils were flaring, dragging in scent. Emma searched the woods on either side of the road, but could see nothing. Cole kept his gaze to the left, so Emma focused there, trying to discern any shape that didn't seem to belong. She couldn't make out anything, but she knew somebody was out there. She called to Joanie to hurry it up, and slowed her pace so she could catch up. Once Joanie had pulled alongside, she told her to increase her pace and they took off. From the look on Emma's face, Joanie didn't question the order. She just did as she was asked, even though she thought she might not live long enough to make it back to the car due to heart failure from overexertion. Upon reaching the vehicle, they loaded up quickly and took off. Joanie, red-faced and panting, asked Emma what had happened.

"Somebody was in the woods watching us."

"You're kidding." Joanie took one look at Emma's face and knew she wasn't joking. "You're sure?"

"Yes."

"Did you see him?"

"No, but I had that same creepy feeling and Cole knew too."

"I wonder where he was."

"I think he was in the woods on the left hand side of the road. Cole kept his head in that direction; he never turned from it."

"Oh, God, that gives me the creeps, and here I was not even knowing what was going on."

"Yeah, I know."

"What the hell do they want?"

"I don't know, but I don't need this, especially today."

"Yeah, not today. You've got enough on your mind what with the date and all."

"I don't think I can go now. I'm too shook up," Emma announced as she grabbed at what to her was a way out of the impending date.

"Don't you give me any of that horse shit, Emma Rogers. You're going to go on this date even if I have to personally haul your cute little ass into Ben's vehicle. And believe me, it wouldn't be a pretty site. So don't piss me off."

Emma gave Joanie a sideways look and knew she would do exactly that too. Her fate was sealed; she might as well go with it. The rest of the ride home was very quiet.

* * * *

Time at the shop went by very quickly much to Emma's ever growing dismay. There were plenty of customers, a lot of them regulars who had plenty to talk about, so the minutes ticked by rapidly. Fed Ex had a delivery for them and the ten cartons deposited in their back room, containing a new dishware line, had them busy all day. Tank had been watching the Styrofoam spill out during the unloading and he had an expectant gleam in his eye. No doubt they wouldn't be able to leave without letting Tank do his thing.

Mrs. Foster came in and Cole carried her purse as she did her shopping. She'd stop every little while, give him a pat on the head, and then continue on. When she came up to the counter, she remarked on the party and asked whom the gentleman was that she had seen Emma talking with.

"That was Ben Sievers, Mrs. Foster. He's just moved to the area, although he grew up here," Joanie replied.

"Sievers, you said? I think I remember a family by that name maybe, oh, twenty-five, thirty years ago."

"Yeah, well, Emma and Ben have a date tonight."

"Is that right, Emma?" Mrs. Foster asked, turning toward Emma, her smile getting bigger.

"Yes, we're going to the Red House Bar for dinner."

"Well, that's just wonderful, my dear. I hope you have a fabulous time. He's rather handsome, isn't he?"

"Yes, I guess he is."

"There's no guessing about it, sweetie. He's prime beef on the hoof."

"Oh, my God," Emma mumbled, her eyes growing wide as she gaped at her customer.

"I may be old, Emma, but I'm not dead. I still appreciate a good-looking man."

"Good for you, Mrs. Foster." Joanie jumped into the void created by Emma's silence; she was completely speechless. "A woman after my own heart."

"Well, I'll be off now. You have a good time tonight, Emma. Let your hair down and live a little. Put a little bounce back in your step, if you know what I mean." Mrs. Foster, a twinkle in her eye, went out the door.

"Bye, Mrs. Foster," Joanie yelled, giving Emma an elbow in the ribs to break the spell she seemed to be under.

"B-bye, Mrs. Foster," Emma stuttered weakly.

"God, she's great, isn't she?"

"Yeah…great."

"She's rooting for you, Em. I think she hopes you get lucky tonight."

"Yeah, I think so too."

"Hopefully you will."

"Geez, Joanie. This is our first date. What do you think I am?"

"A horny broad who's been without for fifteen years."

"Oh crap, let's not talk about this again."

"Why? You getting hot?"

"Joanie, shut the hell up."

"You're getting all flushed, Em. You thinking about Ben?"

"Shit, I'm outta here. I'm going in the back to set Tank up for his run. Don't come back for a while."

While Emma, in a huff, walked to the back of the shop, Joanie could be heard laughing up front. *I'm never going to live through this,* Emma thought. *Never, never, never!*

Please Lord, she prayed, take me now and end my suffering. Unfortunately, nothing happened. Lightning didn't strike her down nor did the earth open to swallow her whole. Maybe this entire thing was retribution for past offences. Cripe, if that was it, He was certainly getting his money's worth.

When Joanie came back fifteen minutes later, Emma had everything set up for the run. Tank was doing acrobatic spins in excited anticipation and if Cole could have rolled his eyes in disgust he would have. Everyone took his assigned spot; Cole braced himself and gave Emma an I'm-only-doing-this-because-I-love-you look. Joanie released Tank and he flew into action. Styrofoam peanuts were sent flying all over the room and Emma was covered from head to toe. Half an hour later, they called it quits. Tank was tired, but happy; Cole was relieved, and the place looked like a bomb had hit it. The cleanup began.

* * * *

Sally joined the girls at the cottage by quarter after six. She'd left Kirby at home this time and just so there were no distractions, Emma put Cole and Tank in Cole's crate. From there they were both content to watch the proceedings, safely removed from the upcoming flurry of activity. But before she did anything, Emma just wanted to sit and relax, unwind, contemplate, and then prepare herself for battle with the two brutes that disguised themselves as her friends.

"Em, would you like a glass of wine? It would help you to relax," Joanie asked.

"Yeah, that might be a good idea. Sure."

"Stay where you are, I'll get it," Sally said, waving Emma back into her chair when she started to get up.

"Thanks, Sally. I guess some wine would help."

228

Sally came back with three glasses and distributed them; the girls got comfortable. Emma sipped and willed herself to be calm, closing her eyes and picturing the Connecticut shore where her son lived. She just loved it there and could envision the water lapping the sand while seagulls cried overhead. She was just starting to let go when Joanie's voice drilled through her meditative state.

"Time to get rolling, Em. Get in the shower."

Emma opened her eyes and wondered if she'd get life or the chair if she killed Joanie on the spot. Probably life, but it might be worth it to get out of this date. Emma got up, taking her wine with her and went into the bathroom, locking the door behind her. She took a few more sips, turned the shower on, stripped, and got in. The hot water felt wonderful and Emma could have stayed there all day, the tension slowly draining from her body. Reluctantly, she got out when she'd finished rinsing her hair and toweled off. She slipped into fresh underwear and the short, terry robe she had hanging on the back of the door and did her makeup and hair, finishing off her wine as she did so.

She left the bathroom, went to the kitchen, poured herself another glass, and started to drink as she walked down to her room. The two ogres were waiting for her in the bedroom and helped her dress with a minimum of fuss. Sally had brought the handbag, and Emma switched items over from her everyday bag. When she was done, Joanie put the pin on her dress and clasped the bracelet around her right wrist. Emma put her watch on her left arm and changed her earrings. She polished off the rest of her wine and grinned at her two guards, not saying a word; she just stood there and grinned.

"Em, what are you doing?" Joanie asked as she shot a look at Sally.

"Nothin'."

"How come you're smiling at us like that?"

"I don't know… 'Cause."

"Em, are you all right?" Sally asked, a worried expression crossing her face as she shot a look back to Joanie.

"Yeah, I'm just real relaxed."

"How come you're so relaxed? I thought you'd be real nervous."

"I was 'til I had the wine."

"Em, how many glasses did you have?" Joanie asked, comprehension dawning.

"Two."

"Two? When did you have the second one?"

"Just now."

"Just now? What'd you do, chug it?"

"Yeah."

"Why'd you do that?"

"I don't know. It tasted good. Seemed like the thing to do."

"It tasted good. Great."

"Hey! I'm not nervous anymore."

"Good, Em. That's good, real good."

"Oh, my God! She's tipsy!" Sally realized, just a step or two behind Joanie's take on the situation.

"No shit, Sherlock. And Ben's going to be here any minute."

"What are we going to do?"

"What the hell can we do? She doesn't drink coffee; she doesn't even have any in the house."

"Well, how about some Diet Pepsi?"

"Diet Pepsi? Are you smashed too? What's that going to do?"

"I don't know, but at least it's got caffeine in it."

"Yeah, okay, you're right. Let's give it a try, it certainly can't hurt."

Joanie and Sally raced out to the kitchen and poured Emma a glass of Diet Pepsi. She strolled out, not in the least bit hurried, and took the glass when Joanie shoved it in her direction.

"What do you want me to do with this?" Emma looked at the glass like she'd never seen anything like it before.

"Drink it, Emma."

"Drink it? Oh, but I'm not thirsty now. I had my wine."

"Yeah, we know all about the wine, but you need to drink this, even if you aren't thirsty."

"Please, Em, drink it," Sally pleaded, seeing all their hard work going up in smoke.

"Well, all right, if it means that much to you. But geez, you guys are getting weird on me."

Emma tipped the glass, and Sally and Joanie watched intently as Emma swallowed the contents. After she emptied it, she put the glass on the counter and burped. Giggling, she put an arm around each of her friends and all three walked into the living room. The doorbell rang and they stopped mid-stride. Ben was there.

Chapter Twenty-Three

Ben pulled into Emma's driveway and parked behind her Explorer. There was another car there; he assumed it was one of her friend's. He sat there for a few moments, pulled the key from the ignition, and gathered his thoughts. He hadn't dated in awhile; in fact, it had been two years. Even then it hadn't really been dating. He had casually seen women a time or two and left it at that. There had been no chance that anything remotely serious would develop. If he had to be honest, he would admit that all he actually had done was seek out some company every now and again.

His job as an FBI agent probably had a lot to do with it. When he'd been on an assignment, he'd had little time or interest for anything other than his job. It had been a demanding career and he'd very often been totally consumed by it. His ex-wife had also played a major role in how he viewed his personal relationships or lack thereof.

He'd come home one day to find her and the entire contents of their home gone. She'd left only a note detailing her unhappiness, his shortcomings, and her desire for a new life with a man she'd met several months previous to her leaving. Thankfully there hadn't been any children and it had been a long time ago, almost twenty-five years, but the lesson had stayed with him.

He'd hardened his feelings; presenting to the world a man who seemed rigid and distant, his softer side buried so deep that only a few close friends and relatives knew of its existence. He'd ruthlessly closed himself off emotionally rather than risk betrayal and that kind of pain again. He'd lived that way for more years than he cared to remember, shying away from any involvement on a personal level. Now here he was, seeking out the company of a woman he barely knew and, for some reason that hadn't yet made itself clear, longed to know better. It made no sense to him. It had been such a long time since he'd really wanted to know what made a particular woman tick, but this woman from the moment he'd met her had definitely tweaked his interest. So what the hell was going on? He didn't know, but he sure wasn't gong to find out sitting in the car; he might as well get his ass moving. He got out of the vehicle and walked to Emma's front door.

* * * *

It was as if they were frozen; no one seemed to be able to move. The doorbell peeled again and finally Joanie broke free. She went to the door and opened it, glancing back to make sure Emma hadn't made a run for it. She was still at Sally's side, grinning like a fool. Joanie rolled her eyes, swung her attention back to Ben, and invited him in.

"Hi, Joanie, nice to see you again," Ben said as he stepped into the room. "Hello Emma, Sally," he continued, his gaze sweeping to where they were standing.

"Hi, Ben," Emma and Sally said at the same time. Emma took in his appearance in one giant gulp. God, he was gorgeous and big, really big. His shoulders seemed to be about ten feet wide, clothed in a dark blue sport coat under which was a light blue shirt crisply starched; his tie was a deep cranberry. His shoulders tapered down to a narrow waist where gray lightweight wool trousers started and seemed to go on forever covering legs that didn't seem to end. They did finally, his feet shod in black dress loafers.

Ben's eyes remained on Emma, drinking in the site of her. She looked wonderful and very happy. Her smile hadn't faltered once since he'd arrived.

"Emma, are you ready to go?" he asked.

"Yes, I just need to get my purse. Excuse me a minute." Emma turned, a big smile still on her face, and went to her bedroom to retrieve the bag.

While she was gone Joanie confided in Ben. "Umm, Emma got a little nervous and had some wine to relax. Truth is, she had two glasses and chugged the second one. She's a little stewed, but only because it's been so long since she dated. It's not because of you," she hastened to add.

"It's okay," Ben laughed. "I'm a little nervous myself."

"Whew, that's good. Not that you're nervous, but that you understand. It's been thirty-four years for Emma since her last date," Joanie explained.

"Well then, I guess she's got every right in the world to be nervous. Don't worry; I'll take good care of her."

Emma reappeared just then, smile intact. Joanie was starting to wonder if her face was frozen in a permanent grin. Ben ushered her out the door, calling goodbyes to the girls. Joanie and Sally followed them out to the porch and, as Ben and Emma settled themselves into Ben's black Jeep Cherokee, yelled that they'd take care of Cole and lock up when they left. The two girls watched until the Jeep went down the hill and then reentered the house at the same moment the phone began to ring. Joanie crossed the room to answer it and picked up the receiver. "Hello?"

Silence.

"Hello? Is anybody there?"

Silence.

Joanie replaced the receiver and turned to Sally, "There wasn't anybody there, must have been a wrong number."

"Yeah, probably. Let's get Cole situated and then we'll leave."

They let Tank and Cole out to go to the bathroom and replenished Cole's water. While they were waiting for the dogs to finish, they gathered up the wine glasses and put them in the dishwasher. They straightened Emma's bedroom and got Cole back into his crate. As they were locking the door, both their thoughts swung to Emma, hoping she would have a wonderful time and wouldn't drink so much she wouldn't be able to remember it.

* * * *

The ride to the Red House Bar took approximately seven minutes. During that time Ben kept the conversation very light and watched Emma out of the corner of his eye to make sure she was all right. She appeared to be relaxed and was conversing easily. The constant grin had subsided somewhat and she had smiled naturally a few times. Her face was flushed, but that was more than likely from the wine. Ben could see that she intended to keep her head faced forward, not looking in his direction if she could help it. Her hands lay in her lap, the fingers briefly twisting around each other every so often as if they needed something to do.

Once they arrived, Ben parked and came around to Emma's door, opened it, and helped her down from the Jeep. He kept his hand under her elbow as they walked to the restaurant's entrance. Ben opened the door, held Emma close to his side, and led her inside.

The Red House Bar had a bar area and two rooms for dining situated on either side of the barroom. The larger room was spacious enough to accommodate a grand piano and a small dance floor. The walls in both rooms were stuccoed and the floors were wide-planked oak, darkened with age to a russet brown. The ceilings were beamed and the lighting recessed, the overall atmosphere romantic and intimate. The tables were draped with white linen, candles and flowers in crystal bud vases atop each one. The place settings sparkled in the candlelight, china and silverware alike.

Ben guided Emma up to the reservation desk and gave his name. The maitre d' checked his book and signaled them to follow as he led them to a table in the larger room. They were seated at a secluded corner table and the air between them was immediately charged with intimacy and anticipation. Emma could barely breathe, the complacency brought on by the earlier wine faltering under the onslaught of the expectant atmosphere. Ben, sensing her discomfort, led her into a discussion about Tank and Cole while they waited to give their drink order. He'd remembered how easily she'd talked about the show the night of the party and hoped the same type of dialogue would break the ice now. Emma, never at a loss for words where the dogs were concerned, felt herself unwinding a bit as she answered Ben's questions.

The waitress arrived and Emma wisely ordered a sparkling water and Ben, a Jack Daniels. The drinks were delivered and their conversation drifted to other subjects with Emma relaxing more every minute. She found that he was easy to talk to, once her initial nervousness was gone, and he actually seemed to be interested in what she had to say. His dark brown eyes remained intent on her face.

The waitress reappeared to take their dinner order, and they realized they hadn't even looked at the menus that had been placed on the table when they were seated. Ben asked the waitress to give them a few more minutes and, smiling knowingly, she slipped away. Ben and Emma exchanged guilty looks, then started laughing. They dutifully opened the menus to peek at their choices and make their selections. Emma decided on a romaine salad with raspberry vinaigrette dressing, broiled scallops wrapped in prosciutto and asparagus, a baked potato and sautéed Zucchini Parmesan. Ben chose the Prime Rib and bleu cheese dressing, but duplicated Emma's choices for the rest. The waitress returned and they gave their food order, requesting a refill on their drinks.

Their drinks and salads, accompanied by a loaf of warm, crusty bread, arrived in short order and as they began to eat, a comfortable silence settled in. Ben had put her completely at ease and Emma was able to enjoy both his company and her meal. She was genuinely attracted to him, and if she weren't careful would lose herself in those big, brown eyes that radiated such warmth. She loved to watch his mustache as he talked and smiled. She even liked to watch it when he chewed. She couldn't help but wonder again what it would feel like if he kissed her. Would it be soft or scratchy? Would it tickle? She began to hope that she'd find out later that night.

Ben, on the other hand, was becoming totally captivated with Emma. All of his barriers were lowering and he couldn't seem to do a damn thing about it. She was so pretty in the candlelight, appearing almost fragile. Her blue eyes sparkled when she smiled and her ears got red when she was nervous. She wasn't able to conceal her emotions and he liked that. Her initial shyness and timidity were endearing, but he sensed a steel core underneath that would see her through life's problems and uncertainties. She was a survivor, of that he had no doubt. He loved the enthusiasm she showed when speaking about the dogs and her inherent kindness toward them. She had a wicked sense of humor and he found her absolutely adorable.

The main course arrived and the salad plates were cleared. While they were enjoying their meal, the pianist had begun to play what would be called dinner music, adding to the already cozy atmosphere of the dining room. Several couples had left their tables and were dancing near the piano on the polished floor. When they had finished eating, Ben asked Emma if she would like to dance. She hesitated a second or two and then said yes; he led her out onto the floor before she could change her mind.

As Ben took her in his arms, Emma thought she'd died and gone to heaven. She felt completely surrounded by his masculinity and oh, Lord, it felt so good. It had been such a long time since she'd been held in a man's embrace and she took great pleasure in the feeling. As they swayed to the music, her one hand on his shoulder and the other in his large hand, she couldn't help but be aroused by the nearness of him. As he gathered her closer, she all but fainted from the heat coming off his body and she laid her head against his chest. The spot on her back where his hand rested seemed to be on fire and her head swam with the faint scent of his cologne. After living like a nun for fifteen years, her senses were in imminent danger of being completely overloaded and blown clear to hell.

Ben was pretty much dealing with the same thing and was in his own state of blissful upheaval. He was six foot three inches compared to Emma's five foot six, and her head was below his chin, resting on his chest. Her hair smelled like fresh peaches and when he kissed the top of her head he found that her hair was as soft as a feather. He could feel her body against his, her breasts flattened against his chest, her legs brushing against his as they moved to the music. He knew his arousal was becoming apparent and hoped against hope that she couldn't feel it. *Right!*

One song ended and another began, but Ben and Emma were oblivious to the change. They were so wrapped up in the sensations of the moment that they were a world unto themselves, unaware of the goings on in the busy room around them. Time had ceased to exist as they swayed to the music, awareness of their mutual need and attraction the only thing that pierced their enraptured haze.

The spell was abruptly shattered when a busboy dropped a tray of dirty dishes and they clattered to the floor. Ben and Emma hastily broke apart and Emma, blushing, looked away, mortified at what had passed between them in such a public place. She hurriedly made her way back to the table and Ben followed, knowing the moment and all it had implied had been lost at least for now.

Conversation was stilted at first after they took their seats, embarrassment on both their parts straining the air between them. Gradually, with the help of an after-dinner aperitif, they began to relax and were able to resume an easy-going discussion. They exchanged some stories about their lives and what was going on in the present. At one point, Emma's hand had been resting on the table and Ben reached over and took it in his, his thumb making small circles on her palm. The contact was electrifying and Emma found herself returning the gesture with her own thumb. She was becoming mesmerized and wondered how this man could evoke all these sensations so easily and so quickly.

Ben was having his own problems controlling his response to Emma. Just to touch her skin was sending explosive charges through his body and she'd be lucky if he didn't ravish her right there on the table. He released her hand in order to rein in his emotions and was somewhat relieved when she lowered her hand to her lap. Best to remove the temptation until his baser instincts had time to cool down and level out.

It was getting late and they decided to call it a night since Emma had to work the next day. Ben paid the bill and escorted Emma out of the restaurant and over to the car. He opened her door and helped her onto her seat, closing the door after she was settled. As he walked around to his side of the vehicle, he tried to gather his wits and get his body under control. Not much luck there!

At the same time that Ben was struggling with his sexual response, Emma was having problems of her own. Damn, if she didn't feel like having her way with him! It was like she was a mass of quivering hormones just waiting to erupt. God, she sure as hell wasn't dormant now!

The ride home was laced with tension and both their hearts were beating fast. It took everything Ben had to keep his hands on the wheel and not to reach for Emma. It took everything Emma had to stay in her seat and not hurl herself at Ben. Thank God for laws about wearing seatbelts!

When they pulled into Emma's driveway and parked in front of her house, they both remained where they were for a minute, almost afraid to move. Then Ben got out and came around to open Emma's door. She slipped out of the car right into Ben's arms. He pulled her close and Emma's arms went around his neck before she knew what she was doing. Ben lowered his head and his lips brushed against hers. He raised his head and looked into Emma's eyes, then lowered his head again and kissed her. Emma's lips parted and the kiss deepened, Ben's arms crushing her to him. Emma responded and tightened her arms. As their tongues swirled around each other, she sagged against him, her legs having lost their ability to hold her up. The kiss seemed to go forever and they were caught up in a whirlwind of desire and escalating need. Emma finally broke the kiss, her need for oxygen overriding her craving for the man. Ben showered little kisses along her jaw line and then her throat, coming back up to sip at her lips. He suddenly released her from his embrace and brought his hands up to cup her face. Looking into her eyes, he kissed her lightly, fighting for control. My God, he thought, this is our first date! What am I doing?

"I think I'd better be going," he said breathlessly as he stepped back and let his arms fall to his sides.

"Maybe that would be best," Emma agreed, straightening her dress and trying to regain her composure. She reached for her handbag that was on the floor of the car, the door to which was still open. Holy shit, she thought, much more of that and we'd be doing it right there on the ground.

"Let me walk you to your door."

"All right."

As they walked the short distance, neither one of them said anything. When they reached the house, Emma fumbled for her keys and when she finally found them, Ben took them from her and unlocked the door.

"I had a wonderful time tonight," he said, turning toward her.

"So did I, Ben. Thank you so much for asking me," Emma replied, gazing up into his eyes. It was a miracle she could still speak.

"Do you think we can do it again?"

"Yes, I think we can do it again," Emma smiled. Oh, God, *yes*, let's do it again, she thought.

"Good, because I'd really like to."

"Me, too."

"Then I'll call you, okay?"

"Okay."

Ben bent down and gave Emma a quick kiss, whispering as he pulled back, "God help me, Emma, you blow me away."

Ben turned and walked to his car, not giving Emma a chance to respond. He was gone in a flash and Emma, acting purely on instinct because her brain had gone into meltdown, walked into her house and let Cole out of his crate. She shooed him out the door and pretended to watch as he watered a few trees, her mind a million miles away.

Cole came back in and gave Emma a look that clearly asked, "Are you all right?"

Emma hugged him to her and smiling against his fur, told Cole that everything was just wonderful. Talk about being blown away! Ben had not only detonated an explosion, he had scattered her in every direction known to man and then some!

Chapter Twenty-Four

Emma and Cole had to skip their run Saturday morning since Joanie wasn't able to go with them. She'd volunteered to help at her church's rummage sale and had to be there by eight o'clock. Emma had a feeling that the people in charge would probably be wishing she'd go away by about ten o'clock, at the latest. Diplomatically speaking, Joanie had a tendency to take over and though well-intentioned, made a regular nuisance of herself. In words not quite so tactful, she was hell on wheels. Not a good thing for a church event.

This whole arrangement for roading Cole was beginning to be a royal pain in the ass, Emma thought, as she got ready to leave for the shop. She didn't like having to depend on another person to do what she wanted when she wanted to do it, especially when it came to Cole. Not that she blamed Joanie. No, she blamed whoever was making her life more difficult; namely, the people who were watching her for God only knows what reason. Maybe if Joanie was free later, they could go after she closed at six. The temperature was only supposed to be in the low sixties today, so it shouldn't be too warm by the time they could leave for the park.

Emma opened the shop at ten and was busy right from the get-go. Business was good and she didn't have time to do much thinking. That was fine with her because she wasn't capable of it anyway. She'd barely gotten any sleep, tossing and turning so much during the night that Cole had elected to desert the bed and sleep on the floor. Her mind had replayed the events of the evening so many times that she had the permanent equivalent of a DVD inside her head. She wasn't about to lose one second of that evening to memory loss; it would still be there in living color two hundred years from now. Everything else in her life might be erased, but by God, that would be there. To say she was completely shell-shocked over her reaction to Ben and his to her would be the understatement of the century. There were however, only two phases that kept resurfacing in her conscious brain to describe her feelings- Wow! and holy shit!

It was just after three o'clock when things started to calm down that Emma looked up to see Sally and Joanie walk in the door. Forget the calming down thing!

"Hey, Em. We're here for a full report," Joanie called as they strolled up to the counter, expectant looks on both their faces.

"We want all the details, every last one. Don't leave anything out," Sally added.

"I don't think this is a good time, guys. I've still got customers here."

"They won't care. In fact, they're probably as interested as we are. Wait a minute; don't start yet. Let me get the wine. I want you nice and loose so you'll spill your guts," Joanie quickly went back to the kitchen. Her strategy was that Emma always talked more with a little wine under her belt and she didn't want her holding anything back.

She was back in two minutes, loaded down with three glasses and a bottle of wine. The girls arranged themselves around the table and in between customers, Emma told them everything about her date, well, maybe not everything. And damn it all, they knew it too.

"Okay, Em. You gave us the bare bones, now give us the good stuff," Joanie demanded, pouring Emma another glass of wine.

"Yeah, come on, Em. I don't really care what you had to eat or drink, although I think it was real smart of you to switch to sparkling water. Now let's get to the romantic stuff," Sally teased. "Did he kiss you?"

"Yes."

"Did you kiss him back?"

"Yes."

"Jesus, Em! This is like pulling teeth. Tell us what the hell happened," Joanie groused. "Drink some more wine."

"Well, let me put it this way." Emma took another drink. "It was like…"

"What?"

"Yeah, what was it like?" Sally took a big swig of her drink, moving forward to the edge of her chair; afraid she'd miss something if she were sitting back, nice and relaxed like.

"It was like…instantaneous combustion."

"Oh, my God!"

"Holy shit!"

"Yeah, that's what I keep thinking. Holy shit!" Emma laughed.

"Goddamn! You hit the jackpot!" Joanie inhaled and took such a big drink she choked herself.

"Geez, Joanie, don't kill yourself. Are you all right?"

"Yeah, I'm fine. Wait a minute, let me take another sip."

"The moustache, Em. How was the moustache?"

"The moustache, oh Lordy, the moustache! It…felt… wonderful. It was so soft on my mouth, and then when

247

he kissed my jaw and my neck, it was incredible. God..." Emma sighed, her eyes taking on a dreamy look.

"Oooh shit! I'm getting hot just picturing it," Joanie breathed as she slumped in her chair, taking another sip from her glass.

"When we were dancing, it was like there was nobody else in the whole world. He pulled me up against his body and my God, the heat that man generates! I was a goner. Whew! Lordy! It was unbelievable."

"Damn, Em! I'm getting worked up here. I can tell I'm going to have to jump Richard's bones tonight. I'll need relief from all this sexual tension we've got building," Sally said, her face flushed and her body stirring to sensual awareness just hearing about Emma's date.

Joanie groaned, her own thoughts leading to erotic awakenings. "So did you do it? Did you go to bed?"

"No."

"No? What do you mean, no?"

"Cripe, Joanie, it was our first date!"

"So what! You sound like you were on the verge of doing it in the restaurant."

"Yeah, well, I guess you could say we were."

"Holy shit! Really? I just said that to get you going. Oh, my God! They were ready to do it in the restaurant. Son of a bitch!

"Wow!" Sally poured herself some more wine. "Wow! I can see it now, right on top of the table."

"You can see it?" Emma blushed.

"No, no, I can't see it. Can't see it, at least not you and Ben. I mean, I'm not picturing you and Ben. I'm seeing me and ... Well, I can just...just...tell it would be good, on top of the table, that is. Could be I'll have to look into it."

"Sally?"

"Yeah."

"You better stop before you get in any deeper."

"Oh no! I'm going with this one. I'm going to have to approach Richard with this idea. It's too good to let go. Man, my juices are flowing now. Yahooee!"

"Down, girl."

"Just think, I've got a whole damn restaurant to try out. Let me see, I've got how many tables total? I might have to push two together to make it comfortable, but…"

"Enough already, Sally."

"Hell, don't stop me now, I'm on a roll. This could be the most exciting thing to happen to my sex life in years. Thanks, Em."

"Your welcome, I guess," Emma said. "This whole thing's been more than a little mind-blowing."

"Well, why the hell didn't you end up in bed then?" Joanie pressed.

"I guess because we both got ourselves under control. But let me tell you, it was really, really hard."

"Screw that, you should have gone for it."

"God, Joanie, not on the first date. I didn't want him to think I was some kind of…of loose woman."

"You mean a whore?"

"Well, yeah."

"Get real, Em. You couldn't pass for a whore in a million years."

"Thanks, I think."

"Your welcome."

"Does that mean I have no sex appeal?"

"Well, I think you found out the answer to that question last night, didn't you?"

"I think so."

"God, this woman needs help. Pass the bottle, Sally. She's driving me nuts."

"So getting back to it, Em, are you going to be seeing him again?" Sally asked, a big ol' grin on her face.

"Yeah, he's going to call me."

"When?"

"I don't know, he didn't say."

"I bet he'll call today. He won't be able to get you out of his mind."

"Yeah, right. I'm sure he's got stuff to do and other more important things than me in his life."

"Em, you ass, knock it off. I bet you five dollars he calls you today."

"I think you could make that ten and it'd still be a safe bet," Sally put in.

"Well, I guess we'll have to wait and see, won't we," Emma said, hoping they were right, but not counting on it. Changing the subject, she asked Joanie, "Are you busy after six?"

"Not if I go home right now and attack Sam. Hopefully the kids won't be home. Why? What do you need?"

"I want to exercise Cole."

"Damn, I thought I could skate for a day. Okay, I'll meet you at your house about quarter after."

"Thanks, I really appreciate it. I need to keep Cole in tiptop shape for these shows."

"No problem. We're going to get going now though. Sally's got to get to the restaurant and, among other things, count tables for her extracurricular activities; I've got to go home and jump my husband. I'll see you later."

"Bye, Em. Call me if Ben calls you."

"Okay, Sally. Bye."

The two girls left; neither wasting any time getting to where they had to get to for reasons that were running pretty much along the same lines. And Emma, well, she was left to clean up and relive the previous night. There weren't any customers so she got on the computer and took product off inventory, a somewhat mindless job that allowed her thoughts to wander. The last two hours slipped by and at five minutes to six, she was closing up. She walked up the hill with Cole and got ready to go to the park.

Joanie turned up with a lilt in her step, so Emma figured the kids hadn't been home and she'd been able to make good on jumping Sam. They loaded the Explorer and arrived at the park five minutes later. The park was crowded; a lot of people camped there on the weekends. They found a parking spot and started out on the familiar route. There was traffic where in the morning there was none, and Emma had to be more careful and ride at a slower pace. Joanie was in heaven because she could keep up. They reached the three-mile mark and made the turn, Cole giving Emma a look that said, "Come on, already."

The way back was about the same; twice they had to move out into the road to allow walkers to pass. When they reached the car, Emma admitted this hadn't been a great idea and apologized to Joanie for bringing her out.

"Don't worry about it. Now we know. Besides, it didn't take us all that long. I've got the whole rest of the night to spend with Sam."

"Okay, but I am sorry. Let's go and get you home to lover boy."

They loaded up and Joanie was getting into her car at Emma's not even ten minutes later. They waved their goodbyes and Emma went into the house, scrambling for the ringing phone. "Hello?"

"Emma?"

"Yes," Emma answered as she tried to get her breathing back to normal.

"It's Ben. Are you all right? You don't sound right."

"I'm fine, just a little out of breath. I just got back from the park and had to run for the phone."

"Oh, sorry. I've called at a bad time."

"No, no, it's fine."

"Well, I just wanted you to know how much I enjoyed being with you last night."

"I enjoyed your company too." Oh, God, if he only knew how much, Emma thought.

"I'd like to do it again. How would Monday night be?"

"Umm…that would be good. I have the day off."

"Really?"

"Yeah, the shop's closed on Mondays."

"Well, in that case, would you rather do something during the day seeing as how I'm off too?"

"Sure, that sounds like a wonderful idea." Emma was amazed she was able to think and respond rationally.

"Let's both think about what our options are and I'll call you tomorrow to see what we can plan. Okay?"

"Okay. G'bye, Ben." Emma thought she'd better end this before she slipped back into the blithering idiot she knew she could quickly become.

"Bye, Emma."

When Emma hung up, she didn't move an inch until she felt her equilibrium return. Head spins were starting to be the norm. When she felt somewhat grounded, she dialed Joanie and Sally to let them know their bets were safe. Of course, they wanted details and since there were none, the conversations were short. Duty done, Emma made a quick dinner of sliced roast beef and provolone cheese on a hard roll with lettuce, tomato and mayo accompanying. She poured herself a glass of milk, dug out a dill pickle and sat down to eat her feast.

When she was finished, she did a few chores, got Cole fed, and crashed into her favorite chair, too tired to read. She turned on the television and scanned her guide to see what DIRECTV had to offer. Not much. Over a hundred channels and there still wasn't anything worthwhile to watch. She settled on a channel that offered reruns of the old sitcoms and promptly fell sleep ten minutes into the program.

She'd been sleeping for about forty minutes when the phone rang, waking her up. She stumbled over to where it was and picked up the receiver, her mind still foggy with sleep. "Hello?"

Silence.

"Hello?"

Silence.

Emma shrugged and hung up the phone, calling Cole to come outside. She took him out to his kennel and returned to the house, thinking about where she could go with Ben on Monday. Emma could think of a few possibilities right off the top of her head and wondered if he would mind if Cole came along. Well, she'd find out tomorrow.

Emma brought Cole in and got ready for bed. She turned her bed down and got in, still thinking about Ben. She fell asleep remembering every moment of the night before.

Chapter Twenty-Five

They'd decided that because the weather forecast had been for a beautiful day on Monday, they'd go hiking at Letchworth State Park and bring a picnic lunch. Emma was busy making that lunch now. She'd gotten back from Cole's run with Joanie about half an hour ago and was putting together her famous chicken salad as Cole played with his "Froggy" nearby.

She'd parboiled and grilled the seasoned chicken the night before and was now cutting it into bite-size pieces. She added chopped celery, walnuts, garlic salt, mayonnaise, and her secret ingredient, which had been passed on to her children with instructions not to reveal it upon threat of death. After she mixed it together and popped it into the refrigerator, she started on the salad of tomatoes, cucumbers, black olives, and feta cheese dressed with Greek vinaigrette. She shredded lettuce and a partial block of sharp cheddar and put them into containers. She had large soft rolls to make the sandwiches, and although her preference would have been a spinach wrap, she was sure Ben would want something more substantial. She'd also made Jumbo Raisin cookies for dessert on Sunday night and packed a few dozen of them while Cole looked at her beseechingly.

"All right, you can have one," she said, handing Cole half the cookie. He loved sweets, but got them only occasionally. They weren't any more nutritious for dogs than they were for people, but dogs seemed to like them just as much as their human counterparts. After Cole finished with the first half, Emma gave him the second; he happily crunched and swallowed it down.

Ben was supposed to pick them up about 11:00, so Emma had a little time to do some housework and check on her bird feeders. The fuchsia needed watering and as Emma went about it, the hummingbirds danced in flight around her. Cole was never too sure about their crazy maneuvers and ducked down when one came dive-bombing in. Emma, on the other hand, was used to their antics and continued with her ministrations as the airborne circus performers, and she often thought of them in those terms, darted in, out, and around. One little acrobat hovered in mid-air, moving with her from plant to plant, watching as she watered. Cole also watched, fascinated, but preferred to do it at a safe distance. The hummers could sometimes be a little too intense for him.

Ben arrived on time and loaded the cooler and picnic basket that Emma had packed. He had his cooler, filled with iced soft drinks and bottled water, in the back of the Jeep and he placed Emma's things alongside it. Emma came out of the house carrying in one hand a box containing Cole's dish, biscuits, collar and leash, an empty plastic bottle, and a spray bottle filled with water; in the other she had a gallon of water. Ben met her halfway to the Jeep, fleetingly looked into her eyes and relieved her of her burden.

That brief eye contact jolted Emma and unhinged, she hurried back into the house to get the rest of her things. What other things she had to get she didn't know, but by God, she was going to look for them. Lord, he looked good, Emma thought as she scrambled around the house, grabbing a jacket just to grab something so she wouldn't go back out empty-handed and look like a complete idiot.

He had a pale green golf shirt on and faded blue jeans that hugged his hips and long legs. He wore sturdy hiking boots on his feet and looked as comfortable in these clothes as he had in the dressier attire he'd worn the other night. Emma could feel the flush in her cheeks and wondered if she was reacting normally, or if she was overreacting because it had been so long since she'd been with a man. She had barely recovered from the kiss he had given her when he'd arrived and now a simple meeting of the eyes had her completely flustered and tingling all over. No matter, the man definitely did things to her that she'd thought were long dead. He elicited responses from her body just by being in the same general vicinity. Oh, God, she thought, I'm in trouble, big, big trouble.

Ben was in pretty much the same state of upheaval, but his had started when he'd first laid eyes on Emma. When she'd come to the door to let him in, he'd had to swallow hard a couple of times before he'd been capable of speech. She had a lavender tee shirt on that hugged her full breasts and khaki pants that showed off her narrow waist and tight little rear. He couldn't help the smile that caused the lines that bracketed his mouth to deepen as he looked at her.

Emma had watched as his somber expression changed, the smile lighting up his whole face and it caused her to smile back. That was when he'd gently grabbed her arms and pulled her to him, giving her a kiss that melted her bones. Only after setting her away from him had he spoken, and then it had been a simple "Hi". Emma had responded with her own "Hi", quite incapable of saying anything else. Cole had broken it up by nudging Emma's leg and demanding an introduction to this new person in their lives. Emma, blinking away the stupor she'd been put into, did the honors and Cole gave Ben the customary sniff as he crouched down to Cole's level and offered his hand for inspection. Once Cole was satisfied, Ben slowly raised his hand and stroked Cole's head. Cole demonstrated his acceptance by moving closer and giving Ben a wet lick on the face.

Now with everything loaded and emotions somewhat if not barely under control, they were ready to go; Ben helped Cole get into the back of the Jeep. He'd already lowered the back seat so Cole could lay directly behind where Emma would sit in the front. Ben helped Emma in and then took his place behind the wheel.

They turned south on Route 240, then east on Genesee Road; this section of Genesee reminded Emma of a roller coaster. You had to travel over several steep hills to get to Route 16, which was where they were headed, and it was a constant rotation of up one side and down the other of the hills between the two major highways. This was another road that in the winter could be a real challenge and if there was an alternate route to your destination, it was wise to use it instead. The people who actually lived along this section of road were either extremely brave or demented in Emma's opinion, but every one of them was equipped with a four-wheel drive vehicle.

On the corner of Route 16 and Genesee, there was a lovely shop called The Three Oaks Gift Shoppe and Emma and the shop's owner, Peggy McAllister, had been friends for years. Peg's shop, which she had converted from a restaurant and inn, was fashioned toward elegant country appeal, whereas Emma and Joanie's store centered on primitive and rustic charm. Where The Whistling Thistle carried rusted tin, barn-board birdhouses and cast-iron weather vanes, The Three Oaks had fine pewter, delicate lace and glass witches' balls. Rather than compete, they helped each other out and directed customers between the two stores for items one or the other didn't carry.

Heading south on Route 16 a short ways, Ben and Emma made a left on Route 39, going east through the village of Arcade and out to the openness of rolling farmland that straddled the highway. This area was home to large dairy farms and the accompanying barns and silos dominated the landscape. At the village of Castile, they turned down the access road to the park.

Letchworth State Park was originally the private holding of Mr. William Pryor Letchworth, who in 1907 deeded the property to the state of New York. He had begun his 50-year development of the area in 1859 when he purchased a building which would become his home called Glen Iris and the surrounding 1,000 acres.

The Glen Iris, lovingly restored to its original splendor, was now an inn open to the public for lodging and meals during its open season. They served breakfast, lunch, and dinner seven days a week, and could accommodate weddings and corporate events while providing a breathtaking view of the Middle Falls.

The park presently encompassed over 14,000 panoramic acres along the Genesee River. The gorge, nicknamed the "Grand Canyon of the East", was breathtaking in the sheer height of its cliffs, some reaching almost 600 feet. The river itself flowed over three major waterfalls, the highest at a height of over 100 feet.

The surrounding forests were marked with numerous trails and areas were provided for camping with laundry and shower facilities, a store, and a recreation hall. The park also provided camper recreation programs, guided tours, and a lecture series in the summer, while in the winter months, there was snowmobiling, cross-country skiing, tubing, and wonderfully old-fashioned, horse-drawn sleigh rides. Letchworth State Park was one of the most beautifully picturesque natural wonders of New York State.

Ben parked the Jeep in a designated area and together they packed a backpack with what they felt they might need on the hike, including some of those jumbo cookies. When they were finished, Ben slipped the backpack on. Emma put Cole on lead, and they started out on one of the trails, not knowing or caring which one it was. Ben took Emma's hand and held it as if it were the most natural thing in the world. Emma, liking how good it felt, didn't pull away. Cole, observing the two, gave them both one of his doggy smiles as he walked along at Emma's left side.

Emma, though reluctant to let go of Ben's hand, thought it might be smart to know where they were headed after they'd been walking for about fifteen minutes. She needed to study the map that the park had provided, so she grudgingly gave up her hold on his hand and pulled it out. She found they had chosen the Hemlock Trail, which was 3.5 miles long and considered moderate in degree of difficulty. For Emma and Cole, as fit as they were, it was no problem and Ben seemed similarly at ease. The forest they were walking through, with the sun streaming through breaks in the trees, was beautiful and the silence peaceful. Their conversation was limited and, when they did speak, it was in awe of the beauty surrounding them.

Every so often, Emma would look around and behind her; not that she had that eerie sense of being watched, but now it had become a habit, always looking, always checking, always wary. Ben noticed her distraction, but didn't say anything, content for now to observe and learn little things about this woman. As far as Cole was concerned, he was relaxed and enjoying the outing. He was naturally alert, but all his instincts told him they were perfectly safe.

They made it to what they thought was the halfway point and stopped in a small clearing where they found a picnic table. Ben relinquished the backpack and Emma brought out the water, biscuits, and cookies. She spritzed Cole on his underside with the water in the spray bottle to cool him off and while they sat and refueled, Ben asked Emma about her vigilance on the trail. Hesitant at first to burden Ben with her problem, she haltingly explained what had been happening while Ben gently coaxed her on.

When she was finished, he experienced an overwhelming need to protect her from whatever threat was stalking her. The intensity of his feelings completely befuddled him. What the hell was happening here? This wasn't like him. He didn't get involved like this; he kept things casual, friendly, with no attachments. Oh hell, who was he trying to kid? From the minute he'd seen her in the shop that day, something had snapped, the barrier had cracked, and he seemed helpless to do anything about it.

As Ben continued to look at her and not say anything, Emma started to feel uncomfortable and regretted saying anything. "I'm sorry, Ben. I shouldn't have bothered you with this," Emma said as she kept her eyes cast downward, her fingers breaking the cookie in front of her into tiny pieces.

"No, no, I'm glad you did." Ben reached across the table and quieted Emma's nervous hands with his own. "It just upsets me that someone is doing this to you. Please, don't feel you can't confide in me... Emma, look at me." As Emma raised her eyes to his, he smiled. "I want to help you any way I can. I want to figure this thing out. Would it be all right if I talked to Sam? Maybe two former FBI guys can get a handle on this."

"I'm sure Sam wouldn't mind and I...I would appreciate it."

"Is there anything else you can think of? Anything at all?"

Emma concentrated and searched her memory, trying to remember anything odd that had occurred. At her age it was easy to come up with a lot of blanks. She was going to have to work hard at this; short-term memory was not a strong point anymore.

Ben watched as her eyes seemed to widen with recognition, but then closed down as the thought was dismissed. "What is it?" he asked.

"It's nothing."

"No, tell me, no matter how insignificant it might seem to you."

"Well…I've gotten a couple of calls in the last week or so and there's nobody there when I answer the phone. It's probably a wrong number or kids playing a prank. It's nothing."

"Let me be the judge of that, okay? Where are the calls coming in? At the house or the shop?"

"The house."

"Are they at the same time or different times?"

"Different times, I think. I didn't pay much attention. Like I said, I thought it was a wrong number."

"It could be, Emma, but maybe not. Do you have caller ID?"

"No, I never saw the need for it."

"Maybe you should think about getting it now…well, hell, if it is connected to this other business, they could block it anyway…Start to keep a record of these calls, okay?"

"All right."

"And keep your doors locked when you're at home."

"Do you really think that's necessary?"

"To be safe, yes. Is Cole always with you?"

"Yes, pretty much always."

"Would he protect you?"

"For as laid back and gentle as he is, he would protect me with his life if I was ever threatened."

"Good, that makes me feel better. We're going to figure this out, Emma. I promise you that." Ben gave her hands a gentle squeeze to reassure her. "Now are you ready to go back?"

At Emma's nod, they gathered up their things and started back, holding hands, comfortable with each other. When they reached the car, they drove down to the area at the Middle Falls and had their lunch. They enjoyed the raw power of the thunderous water hitting the rocks at the bottom, the breeze blowing the resultant mist occasionally over them. Ben dug in, heartily enjoying the food Emma had prepared and Cole, gentleman that he was, waited patiently for Emma to slip him pieces of chicken salad.

When they had finished, they walked the trail along the gorge but avoided the steep stairs that went to the bottom of the ravine because of Cole. Turning around, they walked back to the Jeep. They'd had enough hiking for the day, so drove through the park to several observation points where they could see different parts of the impressive canyon. For the most part, Cole stayed in the car, content to nap while Emma and Ben viewed the natural wonder. They held each other close, their arms wrapped around one another.

The ride home was quiet, soulful blues playing on the CD player and Emma and Ben holding hands across the console. Cole, stretched out behind Emma, was in a deep sleep and snoring every so often. The Jeep ate up the miles and they were home sooner than Emma wanted to be.

As soon as the car stopped, Cole was awake and attentive, ready for the next adventure. He jumped out when Emma opened the side door and went over to smell his flowers. Ben noticed and Emma had to explain about her flower-loving dog. Ben chuckled as he unloaded Emma's things and carried them into the house after she unlocked and opened the door.

He followed her into the kitchen, his intent to deposit everything there. As Emma turned from the counter where she'd put what she had carried in, she collided with Ben, not realizing he was as close behind as he was. Ben, both hands occupied carrying the cooler, was unable to catch Emma as she staggered backwards off balance. As fast as he could, Ben got rid of the cooler, pushing it off to the side on the floor. Just as Emma was starting to go down, he grabbed her and pulled her up against himself, his arms wrapping around her waist. Emma clutched at his shoulders and found herself staring into his chest. His arms tightened; then he freed one hand to lift her chin. Looking into her eyes, Ben brought his head down and softly kissed her. Emma sighed and Ben deepened the kiss. Emma brought her arms up around his neck and rose on her toes to get closer, giving herself up to all the feelings that Ben stirred up. Ben slanted his mouth one way and then the other, plunging his tongue into Emma's warm mouth and Emma reciprocated with forays of her own. Ben's hands started to wander, moving over her back and brushing the sides of her breasts. His hands settled on her bottom and he pulled her hips into him, his erection hard against her stomach. They were totally involved, the world narrowed down to only them and then... a very loud "woof" shattered their passionate haze. Emma started to laugh first and then Ben. They relaxed their holds, but didn't let go completely as another loud "woof" came through the screen door.

"We've been saved from ourselves by a woof," Ben chuckled, stepping back and letting her go, but not before giving Emma a kiss on her cheek.

"I told you Cole would protect me if I was threatened," Emma laughed. "He could have opened the door if he'd wanted to; he was giving you a break by only barking."

"Yeah, well, he takes this protecting stuff a little too seriously. But then, I guess he know best. I suppose I should get going. I'll call you tomorrow, all right?"

"All right. Goodbye, Ben."

"Bye, Emma. Remember to lock your door after I leave."

"I will."

Ben gave her another quick kiss, this time on her lips as they walked to the door and let Cole in. "And I thought we were friends," Ben said to Cole as they passed each other in the doorway. "Take care, Em, and sleep well tonight."

"I will, Ben, and thanks for a lovely day."

Ben bent his head and stole another kiss. He gave Cole a dirty look, which Cole ignored. Then he turned and whistling softly, walked to his car.

Chapter Twenty-Six

Tuesday was about as nondescript as you could get except for two things. Emma found out about the sex education party scheduled for Wednesday night and Joanie found out that Tammy was going to be working one of the days they were to be at the Stockton dog show. Both kind of reacted the same way- disbelievingly.

"What do you mean, it's all set?" Emma asked as she eased into a chair, afraid her legs were going to give out.

"It's all set. The night of the party we asked some of our friends to help out with your education. You know, get you back in the swing of things."

"I thought we were going to ask Tammy."

"Yeah, well, the more Sally and I thought about it, the more we started to think we might need more than one person's advice on this. So we decided it would be better to have several people who could impart their wisdom to you. You know, if one didn't know, then another one might. So we asked a few people over."

"How many's a few?"

"Well, I don't know for sure."

"Think real hard, Joanie. Count 'em up in your head. How many?" Emma asked, her voice taking on a hard edge.

"Well… umm…let me think…umm…counting us three…thirteen."

"Jesus!…Ten women besides us are going to be there? Why didn't you just take out an ad in the newspaper? Why not let the whole world know my business? Maybe you could get a bullhorn and ride around town telling everybody what's going on."

"Well, if I would of had more time…"

"Stop. I don't want to hear it. This is going to be so embarrassing. I hope to God these people don't show up tomorrow."

"Oh, they're going to show up. They were real excited about it when we talked to 'em. Emma, think about all the neat new stuff you're going to learn about"

"I can hardly wait. Lord help me, I'll be lucky if I can show my face in this town after tomorrow."

"Oh, relax. These people are your friends."

"You did just invite women, didn't you?"

"Well, yeah. What do you think I am?'

"I refuse to answer that question on the basis that I have to work with you every day."

"Hey, you'd be lost without me."

"In your dreams, smart-ass… By the way, I've got a little bit of news for you too."

"Yeah, what?"

"It has to do with the Stockton show."

"What about it?"

"When I talked to Jackie about watching the shop, I gave her the dates, she said she could do it and that was that. Well, then she called me back a few days later and told me she couldn't cover the first day because it was a Friday and she had to work at the orthodontist's. So I checked the calendar and sure enough she was right; the first day of the show is a Friday. So I called Tammy and got her for that day. Neat, huh?"

"I don't believe it."

"No, no, it's true. You can call Tammy and ask her."

"Emma Rogers, you little sneak!"

"Who, me?"

"Yes, you. You've been sitting on this information all this time?"

"Yeah, kind of cool, huh?"

"*Nooo*. I can't believe you didn't tell me about this."

"Why?"

"'Cause you don't do things like this, Sally and I do."

"Guess I must be learning from the two of you. You set such a good example."

"Hey, Em, example this," Joanie said as she flipped her the bird. "Now I'm going to have that mess in the back of my mind the entire time I'm at the show."

"Yeah, and it'll be there the whole time before the show too. Like... right now, huh, Joanie?" Emma laughed.

"You can be a vicious person, Emma."

"You're right, sometimes I can be. Every so often I feel the need to surprise you. Keeps you on your toes."

"Yeah, well, I've only got one more thing to say to you."

"What's that?"

"You better make sure there's a full bottle of wine available to me at all times until after the show."

"I can do that."

"Starting right now."

"Your wish is my command, you lush."

"Sticks and stones, Em. Hey...you better bring a glass for yourself, you've got sex school tomorrow night," Joanie said, a devilish grin on her face.

"Thanks for reminding me," Emma called as she got the wine out of the refrigerator. Hell, she mumbled to herself, I'm the one who needs the whole damn bottle.

* * * *

Late that same afternoon Cappellini, dressed only in the type of scanty bathing suit that would be more at home on the Riviera, was sitting in a lounge chair on his lower deck. His toned body, already bronzed by the sun, was anything but relaxed. He was intently focused on the conversation he was having with Jasper.

On the linen draped table that sat between them, there was a chilled Waterford pitcher full of extra dry martinis and a small Lalique bowl filled with Russian beluga caviar, accompanied by water crackers precisely arranged on a piece of Waterford china.

The sun was still bright overhead, but the breeze out of the north brought some relief from the high temperature. For this Jasper was thankful since he was still in his business suit and could feel beads of perspiration gathering at his hairline. Waves were pounding the shoreline and the ever-present seagulls were crying overhead.

"Our best opportunity will be on the way to the Stockton show. The team has checked out the route they'll probably take and there's a spot that's perfect for what we have in mind," Jasper reported. He took a long drink, savoring the taste of the expensive gin.

"It has to be done at night, in the dark. How are you going to arrange that? It's light until almost nine o'clock now."

"First of all, Connie's going to make sure they're leaving Thursday night. I can't imagine they won't, but we'll make sure. They won't leave 'til after business hours at any rate and then they'll have to load. Even if they load the bulk of it the night before, there will still be a few things they have to do. They'll be under surveillance the whole time and if they leave too early for the conditions we need, then we'll slow them down. Believe me, Mr. Cappellini, they won't be where we want them to be 'til after dark."

"All right, Jasper. I'll trust your judgment on this. Once you have the dog, I want you to bring him to me immediately. I want you to personally see to it. How long will it take you to drive back here?"

"I would say seven, eight hours."

"All right, but I don't want you to let the dog out of the car for any reason. I don't want anyone to see or hear him if you have to stop for gas."

"They won't. My windows are tinted quite darkly and the dog will be tranquilized so he'll be quiet. If I do have to stop, it'll only be once. Don't worry, Mr. Cappellini, I'll get him here just fine."

"I'll take you at your word on that, Jasper. Don't disappoint me. Now enjoy the caviar. I'm going to leave you; I've got some arrangements to make and then I have to go out. Stay as long as you'd like."

"Thanks, Mr. Cappellini."

While Jasper made himself at home with the caviar, Cappellini strode into the house through the French doors. He went straight to his study, his footsteps silenced by the faded Aubusson carpet covering the floor. Upon entering the room, he shut the door and locked it. He went directly to the Renoir painting and pulled it away from the wall exposing the safe behind it. He dialed the combination, opened the heavy door, and reached inside for two envelopes. He opened the first one and emptied it on top of his desk; snapshot after snapshot of Cole rained down, covering the entire surface. There had to be at least fifty pictures and he studied each and every one of them.

Then he moved on to the second envelope and spilled its contents off to the side where he'd made room. There were official-looking papers, several photographs and a small sterile container that held the chip. He compared the photographs with those of Cole and smiled smugly. He reached for the chip and his smile became a venomous sneer. "This is how I'm going to pull this off," he said, holding the container in his hand and gently caressing it. "No one will ever be able to prove it otherwise."

He put the chip down, lifted his gaze to the photograph of Cole he kept on display and walked over to where it sat on the recessed cherry shelves surrounded by expensive objets d'art. He picked up the Galmer sterling silver frame and lightly skimmed his fingers over the photo, his face revealing the full scope of his greed as he admired the object of his obsession. "Soon," he whispered, his voice taking on the seductive tone used when speaking to a beautiful woman. "Very soon, we will be together."

Chapter Twenty-Seven

Much to Emma's annoyance and increasing discomfort, Wednesday flew by. In addition to the shop being busy with customers, and every one of them had seemed to need some sort of assistance, they'd had to deal with a sales rep who came in unexpectantly and was there twice as long as she should have been because of interruptions caused by shoppers. Furthermore, three orders were delivered: one of them greeting cards, another cookbooks, and the last one, clocks. While none of them were very large, they all had to be checked over and inventoried, then put in their proper niche on the sales floor. The only product that gave them any trouble was the clocks. They had to find space on the walls to hang them and that meant rearranging what was already displayed. Customers demanding their attention had hindered their efforts, but that was fine. The customer, after all, took precedence over everything else; it just really slowed them down.

One such customer was a well-dressed gentleman accompanied by his wife who was looking for a house-warming gift for a friend. He was interested in one of the pieces the girls had painted, an antique beaverboard embellished with a winter snow scene, and was trying to barter on the price. The man very obviously had money and here he was, haggling like he was at a flea market. Emma, in no uncertain terms, squelched his attempts at lowering the price and watched as he unceremoniously turned on his heel and left the shop; his embarrassed wife followed close behind. Emma scooted over to a window where she could see the parking lot and watched as they got into a Jaguar XJ8. Unbelievable, she thought as she went back behind the counter and gave Joanie a look that conveyed her thoughts. Joanie had already drawn her own conclusions and they were a bit pithier than Emma's.

Among the customers to visit the premises in the afternoon was Connie, although the girls still didn't know that was her name. She slowly strolled the aisles, nonchalantly selecting what she wanted, listening intently to conversations swirling around her. After some forty-plus minutes, she hadn't picked up anything valuable in the way of information, so went to the check out before her loitering became suspicious. Putting her purchases on the counter, she struck up a conversation with the girls, asking how they'd made out at the Alexander shows. Emma and Joanie retold the events of that weekend and received her congratulations as they cashed her out.

"When's your next show?" Connie asked, taking her parcel from Emma.

"Next week, we're going to Stockton."

"That's somewhere in the southern tier, isn't it?"

"Yeah, it's southeast of Dunkirk."

"I'm not familiar with the area, but I presume you take the Thruway down to Dunkirk?"

"Well, you can do that, but from this area it's easier to take Route 39 out of Springville."

"How do you go that way?"

"You take 39 down through Gowanda, all the way to Fredonia where you pick up Route 20 to Route 60 and then to 58 which takes you though Stockton to the show site."

"Maybe I can make it down. I'd love to see you show. Where exactly are the show grounds?"

"The show's held at the Fireman's Fraternity Grounds just on the other side of the town. It's really easy to find."

"Hopefully I can make it down. Next Saturday and Sunday, right?"

"No, not this time. The show is being held Friday and Saturday."

"Oh, really? I'm glad you told me. It'd be my luck I would've gone down on Sunday and nobody would be there. When do you have to go down? Early Friday morning?"

"No, that's too much of a hassle with Cole being in right at 8:30. We'll be going down on Thursday after work."

"Whew, that makes for a long day on Thursday, doesn't it."

"Yeah, but it's worth it to be all set up and ready to show Friday morning. Everything is just a lot easier and it gives the dogs a chance to settle down before they have to go in the ring."

"Well, if my schedule allows it, I'll see you there, probably on Saturday."

"Great, we'll see you then."

"Bye." Connie waved, then walked to the front of the store and out the door. Her face was lit with a smug smile; she now had all the information she needed.

* * * *

Emma had stalled as long as she could before getting ready to go for her tutoring session at Joanie's. She was changing her clothes when the phone rang. Thinking it was most likely Joanie calling to tell her to get her butt up to the house, Emma started to speak as soon as the receiver was

275

up to her ear. "Yeah, yeah, I'll be there in about ten minutes. Keep your shirt on." She was met with silence. "Hello?"

The silence continued and Emma replaced the receiver, looking over to where Cole lay watching her. "I was going to have you stay at home, Cole, but not now; you're going with me. Come on out to the kennel and do your thing before we go."

Remembering what Ben had said, she quickly jotted the date and time of the call in a small notebook she'd put by the phone. Then Emma took Cole out and stayed with him until he was finished, scanning the woods while she waited. She wasted no time putting the rest of herself together and, with Cole in tow, drove over to Joanie's.

By the number of cars in Joanie's driveway, it looked like she was the last one to arrive. Great, Emma thought, just what I wanted to do, make a grand entrance. Tank met them as soon as they stepped through the doorway and threw himself at his large friend, slamming into his side in an invitation to play "chase". Cole took about one second to debate whether he was going to take the bait or not, then lunged after his small buddy; they both streaked through the house.

Joanie, hearing the commotion before she saw it, knew the signs and anticipating their next move, quickly opened the sliding glass doors in the kitchen as they hurtled toward them. Once outside, they ran full out; Tank was gaining ground as Cole chased behind him. There was no way Cole was going to catch him, but he gave it his best effort. The game continued for several minutes with the dogs racing across the lawn, dodging chairs, tables, and whatever other obstacles were in their way before they both jumped into the pool and swam down its length to the stairs at the opposite end. Climbing out, both dogs shook the water from their coats. Winded from their exertion, the dogs lay down side by side on the cement walkway that encircled the pool. Cole laid his big paw over Tank's back and gave him a lick on the face.

"Not that I mind," Joanie said as she watched the two of them, "but how come you brought Cole? I thought you were going to leave him home."

"I changed my mind after I got one of my phone calls," Emma replied, moving over to where her friend was standing.

"What phone calls? What are you talking about?" Sally asked as she joined the two.

"I've been getting these phone calls that when I answer, there's nobody there."

"Really? When did this start?"

"About a week, week and a half ago. The first one was the night of the party at the Hearthmoor."

"How many have you had?"

"Three, I think. I thought they were wrong numbers, but Ben thought they might be something else and told me to start keeping track of them. This is the first one since I talked to him."

"Umm...I think you've had four calls, not three," Joanie said, remembering. "The night you went out with Ben, and Sally and I closed up the house, a call like that came in after you left."

"Yeah, you're right," Sally agreed. "The phone rang just as we were coming back in and there was nobody on the line. We thought it was a wrong number."

"I bet that was another one then. Cripe, I wish this would all just go away. I can't figure it out. I don't know why anybody would be doing this." Emma sighed, her frustration showing in the way she kept pushing her fingers through her hair.

"Don't let it get you down, Em. Ben was over talking to Sam yesterday and I'm sure the two of them can get to the bottom of it."

"I just hope it's soon. I'm starting to feel on edge all the time. It's getting hard to relax anymore."

"Well, I've got just the thing you need, as always. Here, take this glass of wine and drink up. Let's join the others in the living room."

As they walked to the living room, the noisy chatter of ten ladies, their ages ranging from early twenties to late seventies, met their ears. It was a large room with a cathedral ceiling and a wall of windows that extended from the floor to the peak of the roof. The view was spectacular and the room was extended to the outdoors by a large deck that surrounded two sides of the house. The walls were covered in tongue and groove pine stained a deep, brown umber that matched the exposed beams in the ceiling. In between the beams, the ceiling had been stuccoed in a soft white hue. The fieldstone fireplace took up almost the entirety of one wall and the floor was covered with a thickly piled wall-to-wall carpet that your feet sank into when you walked across it.

Joanie's couch and chairs were large and overstuffed, promising snuggly comfort amidst the many pillows heaped willy-nilly upon them. The end tables and coffee table, a dark walnut in color, were large and sturdily built in keeping with the size of the room. Joanie's uncle had been the craftsman. Right now they were overflowing with an abundance of finger food ready to be devoured by hungry women, whose appetite for food and sexual knowledge was running pretty much even.

There were chicken wings, the staple of any gathering in the Western New York area, cheese and pepperoni pizza cut into bite-size pieces, artichoke dip and assorted crackers, parmesan and garlic cheese spread, potato chips with French onion and horseradish-bacon dips, pretzels with hot mustard, a vegetable platter with spinach dip, and salami with bleu cheese roll-ups. The ladies had their choice of wine, beer, a mixed drink, soft drinks, or iced tea, but every one of them had chosen some form of alcohol. Perhaps their choice was to make themselves more at ease with the subject matter, or maybe because they just liked their booze.

When Emma looked around the room to see who had come, her mouth fell open in astonishment at the presence of two of the women. Right there, smack in the middle of everything, was Mrs. Foster and her Aunt Agnes.

"Oh…my…God," Emma whispered as she continued to stare at the pair.

Aunt Agnes, bedecked in all her glory with enough jewelry on to sink a small boat, drew herself up to her full height, of which there wasn't much, and announced to her niece. "You're never too old to learn, Emma. Your Uncle Lou wouldn't like it if I squandered a chance to gain new knowledge. He likes it when I learn some new little tidbit."

"Oh…my…God," was again the only reply Emma could get out.

"Yes, really dear, you have to keep up with the times," Mrs. Foster added, elegant and sophisticated in her expensive linen pants suit, her delicate gold necklace and bracelet in sharp contrast to Aunt Agnes's tonnage of gold and silver. Remarkably, they seemed to have hit it off with each other.

"Oh, Lord, help me, please," was the silent prayer Emma mumbled as she looked from one to the other.

Joanie shoved Emma down into a chair and told everybody to take a seat. After she made sure that all the ladies had a drink and everybody was eating, she simply announced, "Okay, we all know why we're here, so let's not pussyfoot around. We have to bring Emma up to speed in the sex department and we have to do it fast. So who's going to go first?"

There were a few seconds of total quiet, the ladies looking from one to the other to see who would be the brave one. And wouldn't you know, it was Aunt Agnes! Her hair had been tinted a soft blue for the occasion, and she'd even brought a visual prop. While Emma tried to hide her amazement and sank low in her chair, Aunt Agnes opened the book, turned it around so that all could see, and started to speak like a teacher addressing her students. "This is my very favorite book of Kama Sutra, and ladies, it has served me well for years. It's wonderful, isn't it? It shows so many interesting positions for making love. Look, there's page after page of ways to do it. Now, some of them I can't manage anymore, I mean age does take it's toll, but there are plenty left that someone even as old as I am can do. Emma, dear, shut your mouth, you'll catch a fly. Now I'm going to pass the book around and you can all take a real good look."

As the book made the rounds, the comments coming from the ladies were as entertaining as the pictures seemed to be.

"Well, will you look at that? How the hell would you even get in that position?"

"They're double-jointed, they have to be."

"I could maybe get in that position, but it would take a team of horses to get me out of it."

"You have got to be kidding! How could anybody do that?"

"I'd like to give it a try."

"No human in the world could do that. They have to be fake, rubber mannequins or something."

"I'd split in two if I tried that."

"I don't think that one's legal."

"Holy shit! Look at that one!"

"Hell, I'd need a couple of people to help me get into that position."

"I think I could manage that one, but my husband could never, cripe, he has trouble just sitting in a chair. Let's look for one you could do in a chair."

"I never knew there was so many ways to do it, hell, have I been missing out."

"I wonder if I could do that one; it looks like it could be really interesting."

"You think these two got turned on when they were taking all these pictures?"

"How could you not?"

"I don't know 'cause I'm getting hot just *looking* at this book, much less participating."

"They're used to this stuff, kind of like making a porno flick."

"You think so? God, they sure look involved."

"Nah, it's just a job to them."

"I couldn't do it, you know, pose like that and have pictures taken. Shit, gives me the chills just thinking about it."

"I wonder if they're, you know, locked in, or just pretending."

"I don't know, but I don't think I want to look that closely."

"Hell, I do."

"Oh, man, I hadn't thought of that. Here, let me look too."

The book was examined for almost an hour, but when it was finally put to rest, the ladies had really warmed up to the subject matter. Of course, a second round of drinks had helped too. Tammy, who'd been just as engrossed if not more so than the older ladies in perusing the book, pulled something from her handbag and then stood up to get the others attention. When everyone had focused on her, Tammy opened her hand and let the object dangle from her fingers.

"What the hell is that?" Someone asked.

"It's a thong made up of beads to, you know, get you hot," Tammy said.

"What?"

"To…to stimulate you. You wear it under your clothes or don't wear any clothes, whatever."

"So what? You walk around all day hot to trot?"

"Well, yeah or you wear it a little while before you're with, you know, your boyfriend or husband. Or you wear it when you're making love with your partner and he … umm…you know, moves it."

"Does it work?"

"Umm…yeah, big time."

"That could be an ugly thing…a thong on a fifty-year-old butt."

"Not as bad as one on a seventy-year-old butt."

"It would be almost obscene on mine," Aunt Agnes piped up. "Cripe. I'm almost eighty. Besides, that little thing…it'd get lost on me. I wouldn't be able to find it. Emma, sweetie, you've got to relax, you're going to give yourself a heart attack."

Emma didn't know if she'd ever recover from this. She did know it was going to be difficult to look her Uncle Lou in the eye from now on. There was a little too much personal information flowing here about close relatives and the word pictures were beyond description.

Tammy passed the thong around, the women running their fingers over the beads, and again the comments were enlightening.

"My, they do feel nice, I wonder how they'd feel down under?"

"I wouldn't be able to stand it; I can't stand it if my underwear gets caught in between my cheeks."

"I might have to get one of these."

"It'd make your husband's job a lot easier. Hell, you'd be raring to go before he even touched you."

"Could make it way better for you."

"I wonder how long you'd have to wear it before you got results?"

"Where do you get one of these?"

"I wonder if it works well with KY Jelly?"

Once Tammy had the thong back in her hands, she exchanged it for another string of beads. "I got this from a friend of mine, who...umm...sells...you know...sex toys. It's...umm...never been...umm...used; it's like...a sample. So...it's... you know, clean."

"What is it?"

"It's...umm...anal beads."

"Anal beads?"

"Oh shit."

"Hell, let's not go there."

"I don't think I even want to look at those."

"I'm not interested in that one."

"My butt hurts just thinking about it. Eeuw!"

"Yike, that gives me the creeps, I don't want to know about this one."

"Now wait a minute, ladies," Mrs. Foster said. "We're here to learn, to broaden our horizons, so to speak. Even if we have no desire to use something, we owe it to ourselves to learn about it. Knowledge is power, after all. Go ahead, Tammy. How does it work?"

Emma shook her head in disbelief; she was getting a whole new perspective on these people. Tammy explained how the beads were used, although if you had one scrap of imagination you could figure it out for yourself. After she was finished, Aunt Agnes broke the silence with *her* observation. "Well, geez, this could open up a whole new life for a broken strand of pearls that's sitting in the bottom of my jewelry box, couldn't it? I mean, all I have to do is tie that broken string off and voila, I'm in business. Gives new meaning to the term 'recycle', don't you think?"

Well, that did it; everybody in the room lost it then. The women were shrieking with laughter, some of them reduced to tears. And that's when anybody who had been holding back brought out their goodies and shared their knowledge. A few more sex toys made the rounds in addition to the edible underwear that magically materialized from Mrs. Foster's handbag. Aunt Agnes's book was brought out again and lively discussions erupted as the ladies broke into small groups to talk about whatever held their interest.

Joanie had let the dogs in on one of her many trips to the kitchen to refill someone's drink and they had been content to stay there and lounge at first, but that had been a while ago and Tank was starting to get restless. Cole, not to be left out of anything Tank might be planning, eyed his buddy with a look that clearly asked, "Okay, what do you want to do?" Tank grinned, there was no other word for it, and telegraphed to Cole what his intentions were.

There is definite communication among dogs based on their body language, use of their voice, touch, smell, and natural instinct; these two could practically read each other's minds. The plan? Cole was to cause the diversion and Tank would grab the prize.

Cole lazily strolled into the living room, was greeted warmly by all the ladies, and proceeded to pick up Mrs. Foster's purse and take it out to the kitchen, much to the delight of his newfound audience. He returned for another handbag and carried it too out to the kitchen. He continued in like fashion, gathering all available pocketbooks, making a pile of them. Tank meanwhile, using his patented form of creeping, was slowly moving across the floor and zeroing in on the object that had caught his attention.

While all eyes, well, not quite all eyes, in particular Emma's and Joanie's, were focused on Cole, Tank got close enough to grab what he had set his heart on. It was the crinkly cellophane, not the edible panties inside, that was the prize. Every rustle it had made when the ladies were examining the package's contents had been like a siren's call to Tank. He loved that noise and when he heard it, he made it his mission to seek it out and have it for his own. For what purpose? To tear it apart and crunch the shit out of it, making it crinkle as much as he could.

As soon as he was within range, he moved with the speed of light and grabbed the package. Joanie and Emma, although they knew he was up to something, didn't catch on until a little too late and were unable to intercept his lunge. Tank turned and ran with his prize back out to the kitchen, where Cole waited at the sliding glass doors. Quick as a wink, Cole opened the door. It seemed he was very talented in that particular skill. Tank raced out, leaving Cole to guard his back and bring up the rear. Once they reached the tree line, Tank tore the package apart, discarded the panties, and happily chewed and crunched the cellophane. Cole stood stoically at guard.

"Well, aren't they just so proud of themselves," Joanie said as she stood at the door, watching. "I'm sorry, Mrs. Foster. I'll replace those for you. Umm… where do you buy those things?"

"Oh, Joanie, don't be silly. Actually, I get them through a catalog. I'll give you one if you'd like, but the dogs need to have some fun too. They were actually very clever, weren't they?"

"Yeah, clever. That's the word for it, all right." Emma said, sarcasm rolling off her tongue.

"Oh, Emma. They really are quite wonderful and you know it. They're very smart, those two. They must keep you on your toes every minute, but what fun."

"Yeah, fun. That's another good word, huh, Joanie?"

"Sure is. Should we get into all the other good words?"

"No, I don't think we'd better. We'll leave it at that."

The party started to break up then, the ladies recovering their handbags from the pile, and saying their goodbyes. Aunt Agnes came over to Emma and gave her a hug, telling her what a delightful time she'd had and hoped that she had been of some help in getting her niece back in touch with her sexual self. Emma assured her she had and as Aunt Agnes started to leave, she threw out one more directive to her sister's child. "Emma, I want to be one of the first to know when the drought has ended, if you know what I mean. I expect results from this little gathering. You've got the knowledge, now put it to good use, and for God's sake have fun while you're doing it."

"Yes, Aunt Agnes. I'll...I'll let you know," Emma sputtered, silently bemoaning the turn her life had taken as her aunt walked out the door. After all this, she thought, it had better be worth it. Then she thought of Ben, and knew it just might be.

Chapter Twenty-Eight

Emma scurried around the house Friday morning getting everything ready for Sydney's visit that Memorial Day weekend. Blessedly, Thursday had been completely normal and she had been able to regain her sense of balance before launching herself into preparations for her granddaughter's stay. There had been no more phone calls, no problems at the park, no flat tires, nothing untoward at the shop, no more sex education, and Joanie, her wonderfully predictable friend, had started drinking at three o'clock. Yes, everything had been normal. Thank you, God!

Now however, she was dashing around in the time she had before she had to be at the shop, getting as much done as she could. Cole knew that Syd must be coming by the things Emma was doing, especially when she changed the sheets on the bed in the spare room and put fresh flowers in a pretty vase on top of the cherry cupboard. He went and got his "Froggy" and placed it carefully in the middle of the bed, in its place of honor, to await Syd's arrival. He was as excited as Emma was to have Syd visit and it showed in his restless pacing.

Time grew short, so they hustled down to the shop and opened up. Emma had just gotten everything turned on when the phone rang. "Good morning, The Whist..." Emma answered.

"Em, it's me," Joanie interrupted.

"Oh, hey, Joanie, what's up?"

"I'm going to be late. I've got to get Tank to the vet."

"The vet? What's wrong?" Emma asked, concern immediately apparent in her voice.

"I think he sprained his leg, at least I'm hoping that's all it is. I hope it's not broken. I don't think it is, but I'm not a vet."

"Oh, God. What'd he do?"

"He jumped off the back deck. He saw a damn chipmunk and took off after it, forgetting where he was, I guess. Anyway, he landed wrong and came up lame. I don't know when I'll be back, so if you could handle things at the shop..."

"Don't give it another thought, okay? Take as long as you need. You don't have to come in at all, just take care of Tank. Let me know how you make out."

"Definitely, and thanks. Hopefully I'll see you later."

"Okay. Bye. Good luck."

Cole, who had been standing close to Emma during the phone conversation, looked to her with a worried expression as she hung up the phone. "You know, don't you, big guy," Emma said, leaning down and giving him a hug. "He's going to be all right, you'll see. He may just be a little bit slower for a while. Hey, it'll be your chance to finally beat him in a race." Cole responded to her upbeat tone with a swish of his tail and a lick to her hand.

"Looks like you and me are going to have to hold down the fort today, so I may need your help, okay?" Cole gave her a big woof in response and another tail swish, then sat down near the table, waiting to do her bidding.

Customers were soon in the shop and Emma was kept busy helping them. Cole carried packages and patrolled the aisles, in addition to keeping a steady watch. The phone seemed to be busier than usual, probably due to the holiday weekend coming up.

People would be coming out to the area to camp up at the park and were checking on business hours, making sure the shop would be open. If it turned out to be a rainy weekend, the store would be especially busy with bored campers. Emma would be around part of the time because Sydney loved the store and had a great time playing in Grammy's other "house". Joanie, for the most part though, would handle the shop on the weekend so Emma could have more time with her granddaughter.

Things were going just fine until Emma saw a certain person enter the store. Damn, if it wasn't Angie Newmann and it didn't look like she was going to shop either. She was heading straight for the counter, merely wanting to make idle talk, no doubt. Shit, shit, shit, shit, shit, thought Emma as the woman approached her.

"Hi, Emma."

"Hi, Angie."

"Where's Joanie?"

"She's not here right now."

"Oh? Where is she?"

"She had to take Tank to the vet. He hurt his leg," Emma said, thinking, didn't we do this exact routine a few weeks ago?

"How'd he hurt his leg?"

"He jumped off the deck when he saw a chipmunk and decided to give chase."

"Oh, my. You'd think Joanie would know better."

"What do you mean?" Emma asked, mumbling to herself, "Here we go again."

"To let Tank do that."

"Do what?"

"Jump off the deck."

"I don't think she let him, Angie. He just did it. It's not like he asked her permission."

"Maybe he should have."

"Maybe he should have what?" Emma was already starting to feel the low ebb of her patience.

"Asked her permission."

"And how would he do that?"

"Well, I'm sure *I* don't know. You and Joanie are the trainers."

"No shit," Emma mumbled. "If only we could train certain people to…"

"What did you say, Emma? I couldn't quite hear you."

"It wasn't anything important, Angie."

"Oh. Well, getting back to what we were talking about, Joanie shouldn't let Tank on the deck. It's the least she could do."

"Why shouldn't she let him on the deck?"

"Because this could happen."

"Well, then I guess nobody should be on the deck," Emma declared, starting to turn the tables on her.

"What do you mean?"

"Nobody, no people, no dogs, no cats, nobody should be on the deck."

"Why?"

"They might jump off."

"Well, not people."

"Sure, people. Why, they jump off bridges, don't they?"

"Well, yeah, but not decks."

"Why not?" Emma demanded, really starting to warm up now.

"I don't know why not."

"Well, there has to be a reason."

"Maybe they're not high enough," Angie said, getting a little flustered.

"To do what?"

"Jump."

"But why would they jump, Angie."

"I don't know, Emma. Why are we talking about this?"

"I don't know. You brought it up."

"I did?"

"Yeah."

"Well, let's talk about something else... Where's Joanie?"

Emma stared at Angie, and then closed her eyes in disbelief. Hot damn, Emma thought, I could've sworn I'd won that round. Thankfully there were other people in the shop and Emma needed to turn her attention to them. Excusing herself from Angie, Emma checked out several customers and then had to help a shopper decide which picture to purchase. Angie said she had to be running along and would talk to Emma later, realizing she'd be unable to engage Emma in conversation again in the immediate future. Emma called out her goodbye as Angie headed out the door and then said a big thank you to the Man upstairs.

It wasn't ten minutes later and Joanie showed up, carrying a despondent Tank in her arms. "It's a sprain. A really bad one, but only a sprain, thank God."

"Whew, that's a relief. How you feeling, Tank?" Emma reached out and gently patted his head, then ran her finger down to his nose and back up to scratch between his eyes. Cole came over lickity-split and whimpered for his buddy. Joanie bent down and Cole gave Tank a kiss and nuzzled him with his nose.

"He's kind of out of it. They had to put him out to do the x-ray and he's still feeling the residual effects of the anesthesia. He'll probably be out of it for the rest of the day."

"They did a nice job on the cast. He's going to love that when he's back to his old self."

"Tell me about it. He's going to go nuts with that thing on his leg."

"How long does it have to be on?"

"A couple of weeks, and get this, he's supposed to stay off it as much as possible."

"Yeah, well, good luck with that one."

"I know, it'll never happen."

"Hey, what about the show? I guess you can't compete now."

"No, I don't suppose we can, but we're still going."

"Good, 'cause it wouldn't be the same without you. Why don't you get that poor guy home and don't worry about the shop. I can take care of things here. Will you be able to work the weekend now?"

"Oh, sure, no problem. And I still want you to bring Syd over to the house on Sunday. Okay?"

"Okay. If the weatherman's right, it's supposed to be really nice on Sunday, warm and in the low eighties. Maybe she can go swimming."

"It's going to kill Tank not to be able to go in."

"Oh, well, maybe we shouldn't come then. I don't want to get him upset."

"Are you kidding? It'll be good for him, maybe teach him a lesson."

"I doubt that, but you go ahead and keep on living in your dream world."

Joanie and Tank left and Emma went back to shop business. The day went by fairly quickly. There were enough customers that she was occupied most of the time without being swamped. Before she knew it, the end of the day had snuck up on her. Prior to leaving, Emma made a call to Joanie and discovered that Tank was starting to come around and shades of his old self were flickering through the fog caused by the anesthesia. He'd probably be completely back to normal by late in the evening and then Joanie would undoubtedly have her hands full trying to keep a rambunctious Tank sedate and acting like a lap dog. It would be an impossible task at best.

Emma hurried up the hill to her house, anxious to get Cole fed and settled. She wanted to take a quick shower and change clothes. Ben was coming over and Emma wanted to be ready. They were staying in; Ben was bringing a pizza and they were going to watch a movie. At least that was the plan. Who knew what else was going to happen. Emma could only wonder.

*　*　*　*

Ben arrived a little after seven, bearing a large double cheese, mushroom, and pepperoni pizza. The aroma wafting from the box made Emma's mouth water or was it the site of Ben in a chambray blue striped sport shirt and tan chinos? Whatever it was, saliva was pooling, and Emma's heart was pounding. Ben gave her a lingering kiss once he was inside the door and only the presence of the pizza box between them prevented matters from escalating right then and there.

Emma stepped back, relieved Ben of the pizza, and led the way to the kitchen. Her face was flushed and her hands a trifle unsteady. There's no way we're going to make it through a movie, she thought as she put the box on the counter and busied herself with plates and glasses. The air surrounding the two of them seemed like it was charged with electricity. Emma was so totally aware of Ben hovering behind her that she didn't dare turn around until she had herself under control. Like that was going to happen! The task would be herculean, way beyond Emma's abilities.

"Emma, are you hungry?" Ben asked in a very quiet voice.

Oh, Lord, Lord, Lord, she wailed to herself, how do I answer that one? How do I say this?...I'm not particularly hungry for food, but I'm starving for you? Oh shit, shit, shit! I need some help here, she thought desperately. Aunt Agnes, where the hell are you when I need you?

"Emma?" Ben repeated, placing his big hands gently on her shoulders.

Am I hungry? Emma, her heart pounding, could barely get the words out and what did come, came out as a squeak. "I ...I guess so." Watch, she thought, I'll have a damn heart attack before I make it to the bed!

"Me too," Ben said as her turned her around and pulled her close in a tightening embrace. "I'm hungry for you."

"Oh, Lord," was all Emma managed before Ben was kissing her, gently at first and then with urgency and a burgeoning need. Emma responded, her desperate kisses reflecting her own bottled up fervor and she clung to him, her arms wrapped around his waist. Ben's hands found their way under her blouse and moved along her spine, sending jolts of pleasure to Emma's center as he caressed her bare skin. She shifted her arms up to his neck to offer him easy access to her breasts and when he took her up on the invitation, she went weak in the knees, sensual titillation spiraling downward. She must have moaned, or maybe it was Ben, but whoever did it caused Ben to abandon her breasts and move to cup her bottom with both hands and pull her tight against him, grinding her lower abdomen against his rigid erection. Tearing his mouth away from hers, his breath coming in large gulps, Ben lowered his forehead to Emma's and tried to steady himself before he spoke.

"My God, Emma, I want you. Please, say you want me too."

"Oh, yeah," Emma answered and brazen hussy that she was, took his hand in hers and started to walk toward her bedroom, fervently hoping that she remembered enough not to screw this up. Aunt Agnes, she thought, this is your big chance, so you'd better come through for me.

They reached the bedroom and Emma's nerves got the better of her; she was literally shaking from head to toe. Ben, aware of her uneasiness, brought her back into his arms and kissed her passionately, his hands gently exploring her body until she was once again relaxed and lost to her feelings. He slowly undressed her, continuing to kiss and stroke her as he did. He laid her gently on the bed and kept his gaze locked on hers as he hurriedly took off his clothes and then joined her. He lay next to her and pulled her close, their bodies touching from their lips to their toes. He continued to make love to her until their passion knew no bounds, and together they soared to heaven and back.

* * * *

Sometime much later, their ardor sated, they satisfied their other hunger, which had grown in intensity, with large wedges of the cheesy pizza. Emma, dressed in Ben's shirt, his scent enveloping her, was drinking some wine when the phone rang. She gave Ben a quick look, then got up to answer it. Ben, wearing only his pants, put his beer down and followed Emma to the phone. She picked up the receiver and said, "Hello?"

She was met with silence as Ben motioned for her to put the phone between them so he could listen too. Emma repeated the hello, but the silence continued. At Ben's signal, she placed the receiver back in its cradle.

"Is that how it sounds whenever you get a call like this?" Ben asked, taking her hand and moving her back to the couch where they'd been sitting.

"Yes, it's always just like that," Emma said as she sat down, her leg resting against Ben's.

"There's definitely someone on the line. It's not a hang up. The line isn't dead. Someone's on, they just aren't saying anything. Have they ever called this late?"

"What time is it?" Emma asked, turning to look at the clock. "Oh, my God, it's that late? No, they've never called this late."

"Well, make sure you write this one down on your list, all right?"

"Should I do it now?"

"No, not now. I'm kind of hungry again."

"Oh, let me get you some more pizza. I'll be right back." As Emma started to rise, Ben pulled her back down so she landed in his lap.

"I'm not that kind of hungry."

"No?" Emma asked, her eyes twinkling and her eyebrows wiggling. "And what kind of hungry are you?"

"This kind," Ben said as he buried his mouth in the hollow of her throat where Emma's pulse was beating rapidly.

"Then I guess we better get you fed," Emma said with newfound confidence, sensual stirrings beginning anew. They didn't bother to move to the bedroom; instead they took their journey to the stars and beyond right there on the living room couch.

Chapter Twenty-Nine

Cole awakened Emma the next morning using the gentle nudge method. He must have known that she needed a tender rousing after the goings on of the night before. Always tuned in to her moods and feelings, he now patiently waited at the side of the bed for her to open her eyes. He wanted his morning loving.

"Morning, big boy," Emma said in greeting as she groggily came to wakefulness and rolled onto her side so she could pet his massive head and scratch behind his ears. Cole responded with low moans of appreciation and gave Emma a lick or two in return. Emma's big smile lit up her whole face. She was not only happy with her dog, but with the whole damn world! God, she thought, last night had been absolutely wonderful and Ben, well, he'd been incredible!

"Cole," she said aloud. "Syd's Grammy is a wanton woman and it feels pretty damn good." The big dog gave her a woof and bounced on his front feet. Emma shook off the last remnants of sleep and sat up, shoving her feet into her sneakers before she stood. "Come on Cole, time to get moving. Syd'll be here later this morning and we've got a lot to do." And with that they were off and running.

The weather was warm but rainy, and when Joanie came for their run, she reported that Tank was back to normal and had been raising hell all morning. He didn't care for the cast on his leg at all and was bound and determined to get it off. She'd had no choice but to put a cone around his neck so he couldn't get at it, and now he looked like a walking megaphone. This was not going to be an easy confinement.

When she finished her run-down on Tank's condition, she gave Emma a long look and cocked her head, trying to figure out what was different. Catching the look, Emma started to blush and made herself busy getting her rain gear on with way more concentration than was necessary. Joanie was not to be deterred.

"What's going on?" she asked as Emma adjusted her jacket.

"What do you mean? Nothing's going on."

"Oh, yes there is."

"No, there isn't. I'm just getting ready to go."

"Don't give me that. Something's going on."

"I don't know what you mean."

"Yes, you do," Joanie insisted and then the light bulb went on. "Did you see Ben last night?"

"Yeah."

"That's it! Isn't it? You did it! Didn't you?"

"What are you talking about? Did what?"

"Don't play dumb with me, Emma Rogers. You had sex! Holy shit! Right? Right?"

"I suppose you won't give me any peace until I admit it, so…yes, hallelujah, we had sex!"

"I knew it! Hot damn, I knew it! Yahooeee!"

"Oh, God."

"Was it good? No, you don't have to answer that, I can see from the look on your face it was good."

"Joanie, it was fabulous!"

"Oh damn, this is great! Did he spend the night?"

"No, but he was here 'til around 2:00 in the morning."

"How come he didn't stay?"

"I don't know, I had the feeling he didn't want to push too hard, you know. Besides, I need to take it a little slow; spending the whole night with him is a little too much for me just yet. Makes me feel too vulnerable. Plus, he knew Syd was coming today and I had stuff to do this morning."

"Oh, man, wait 'til Sally hears. You have to call your Aunt Agnes too."

"Yeah, I know, and I should probably let my kids know what's going on soon."

"What? That you had sex?"

"No, you idiot."

"Yeah, they don't need to know about the sex yet."

"They don't need to know about it at all. Cripe, let me have some privacy, will you? They don't need to know *everything*. I meant that I should tell them that I've met someone."

"Oh… all right. Yeah, you probably should. That could be a little sticky though, couldn't it?"

"Nah, they'll be fine with it. But Mack will want to give him the third degree."

"That's for darn sure."

"Hopefully I can head him off at the pass. I am his mother after all, not his sister. He should realize I'm old enough to know what I'm doing. Don't you think?"

"I wouldn't bet on it. Besides, it's more a matter of him wanting to protect you."

"Yeah, I know. He's a good kid."

"He's one of the best, Em…Let's get going. I know you have things to do and I've got to open the shop on time. Okay?"

"Sure, let's load up."

* * * *

By nine-thirty, Emma was back home and in the middle of making strawberry Jell-O with sliced strawberries mixed in. This was strictly a Sydney dish; Emma couldn't abide the fruit herself. When the Jell-O was finished and tucked away in the refrigerator, she started making chocolate chip cookies which she could abide and very much so. There was nothing better than a still-warm chocolate chip cookie, the chips melted and gooey, accompanied by an ice-cold glass of milk. Mmm…Mmm…Mmm.

Emma was just taking the last batch out of the oven when Rob, Mandie, and Syd pulled in. Cole heard them drive up, looked out the screen door, and when he saw who it was, opened the door; Emma had forgotten to lock it again. Cole hurriedly went out to meet their visitors.

He barked a big woof in greeting and dashed over to the SUV, where Rob was getting Syd out of her car seat. Cole couldn't wait and squeezed himself into the car as much as he could to say hello to Syd. He gave her face a big kiss with his tongue and she squealed in delight. Rob managed to get her out, despite being hampered by Cole's bulk being in the way, and set her down on the ground. Cole was at her side in a flash and gently directed her toward the house. Sydney kept her small hand on his back, stopping every few feet to give him a hug.

Emma met them at the door and scooped Syd up in a big hug. "Hi, sweetie."

"Hi, Grammy. Cole gave me a kiss."

"Did he? I bet it was real wet, huh?"

"Yeah, wet," Syd giggled. "I love Cole, Grammy."

"I know you do, honey, and he loves you."

"Whatcha make, Grammy?"

"Chocolate chip cookies. Do you want one?"

"Yeah."

"Okay, just wait a minute 'til Mommy and Daddy get here. They're getting all your stuff out of the car. Why don't you go with Cole and see what's in your room?"

"Okay, c'mon Cole."

Mandie and Rob, loaded down with all of Syd's gear, reached the door and Emma helped them in. They took everything to Syd's room and found her sprawled on the bed with Cole playing with "Froggy", most of the pillows now on the floor. The new *Dora the Explorer* backpack Emma had gotten for her was also on the floor, forgotten. Nothing, not even *Dora*, who Syd loved, could get equal time when Cole was around. For these next few days, they would be inseparable.

"Hey, let's go out to the kitchen and have some cookies," Emma said, her eyes suddenly teary with the picture Cole and her granddaughter made.

"Okay, Grammy. C'mon Cole."

Everybody trooped out to the kitchen and got comfortable at the table while Emma prepared a platter of cookies and poured big glasses of milk. Cole sat at Syd's side and waited for the bits of cookie he knew would be coming. While they ate, Rob told Emma that he'd put the car seat in her vehicle so they were all set if they wanted to go anywhere.

There were enough clothes packed to clothe three kids for any type of weather and every kind of medicine Syd might need. Not that Syd was a sickly child, but Mandie believed in being prepared. All Syd's favorite things were in the suitcase, her Teddy, her *Dora* pillow, her blue blanket, and two books that were currently at the top of her preferred list. All of these things had to go to bed with her, so with Cole and probably "Froggy" joining the mix, it was going to be a very crowded affair.

Rob and Mandie stayed another half hour and then said their goodbyes with all the usual instructions of,

"Be a good girl," "Don't let her stay up too late," "Syd, do what Grammy says," "Mom, call us if there's a problem," and so forth and so on. Once they had gone, Emma got Syd ready to go down to the shop.

It was raining and they were going to walk down; Syd was jumping for joy. Sydney was a beautiful little girl with hazel eyes, sandy brown hair, and an olive complexion than tanned to a golden hue with minimal exposure to the sun. She was tall for her age, her father was 6'7" and that probably accounted for it, but very slender and lithe.

Emma put Sydney's red and green ladybug boots on, her lavender raincoat, and her pink *Dora* hat. What a picture she made! Emma donned her rain jacket and hat and off they went. What could be more fun for a small child than a walk in the rain and jumping in puddles? At two and a half, Syd was the perfect age for this glorious adventure and enjoyed it for all it was worth on the way down, not missing a single puddle between the house and the shop.

When they got to the store, Syd and Cole went running in with Emma trailing behind. Dog and child went straight to the back room, hoping to see Tank. He wasn't there and when they came back out, both were looking a little lost.

"Hey, Cole. Syd, hi," Joanie called, then seeing their woebegone expressions, added, "Sorry guys, Tank's not here." Turning to Emma, who was walking toward her granddaughter, she said, "I thought it would be better to leave him home today. Right now he's hell on wheels with that collar and cast on."

"I can imagine," replied Emma, who then tried to explain to a disappointed Syd why Tank wasn't there. Cole wasn't much better as he scanned the rest of the shop, hoping to see his best friend. But he wasn't to be found and they both stood there in a wide-eyed pout.

"Come on guys, let's find something to do. Syd, let's get you out of those clothes first." Emma took off her boots, jacket and hat and put them in the back. She slipped her *Dora* sneakers on her feet and put a smile back on her face when she gave her some cheddar-flavored crackers and juice. Cole got a couple of dog biscuits and his mood lifted a little, but of the two, he was the tougher by far to bribe into a better mood.

Emma went out to the counter and checked with Joanie about how things were going while Syd and Cole enjoyed their treat. They soon came out, Syd carrying a basket that Emma kept for her shopping expeditions.

"Going shopping, Syd?"

"Yeah, Cole too."

"Okay, have a good time. Get lots of good stuff."

"Okay, c'mon Cole." And with that they started down the aisle in search of treasure. Cole escorted her around the store as she made her choices and carefully put them in her basket. Thankfully she almost always chose items that were unbreakable. Any customer that was around made way for the duo, smiling at the site the two of them made.

"Sally was thrilled to hear your news. She told me to give you a big 'who-hoo'. Said she'll call you later."

"Okay," Emma laughed.

"Have you called your Aunt Agnes yet?"

"No, not yet. I've been a little busy," Emma answered as she checked to see where Syd was.

"Well, don't wait too long, you don't want her getting the news from somebody else."

"Who else would tell her?" Emma asked, looking at Joanie suspiciously.

"I don't know, but you know how word travels."

"Well, word better not travel on this, Joanie Davis. It's a little private if you know what I mean."

"Oh, yeah, sure. You're right, it probably won't travel," Joanie said, looking a tad guilty.

"I'll call her later, I promise. Okay?"

"Yeah, just making sure you do. Can't help it if people are happy for you," Joanie pouted.

"I know," Emma relented. "And I love you for it. Just don't tell the whole damn town, okay?"

"Okay. Look, here comes Syd and she's got a full load."

Syd and Cole walked behind the counter, Syd struggling with her basket, which was brimming with merchandise. Emma sat her up at the table and Syd emptied out the basket, displaying all her treasures and explaining what each and every one was. When everything had been talked about and admired to her satisfaction, Syd put everything back into the basket and returned all the goodies back to their rightful place in the store. For the return trip Emma went with them and supervised.

This adventure was repeated four more times before Syd got tired of it and had to go on to something else. That's when the girls brought out the paint and brushes. They spread out large sheets of paper on the table and let Syd go at it, dressed in a smock that covered her from head to toe. Cole knew from past mishaps to keep his distance or he could end up with a paint streak down his back or worse. He snuck under the table and stayed there the whole time painting class was going on. It kept Sydney occupied for the better part of an hour and when she was finished she had six masterpieces that looked remarkably the same: six big blobs of an indescribable color. There was one for Mommy, one for Daddy, one for Grammy, one for Cole, one for Joanie and one for Tank to make him feel better. Syd was proud as a peacock and the artwork was destined for everybody's refrigerator door.

* * * *

Sydney was busy watching the DVD, *Ice Age*, which she couldn't seem to get enough of, while Emma did a load of laundry that included the clothes her granddaughter had started the day out in. Coming back to the house, she had repeated the puddle- stomping and had ended up on her butt in one of the larger ones. She couldn't wait to tell Mommy, it had been so much fun. Emma hoped Mommy thought so. Anyway, while Syd was occupied, Emma made the requisite phone call to her Aunt Agnes.

"Hello, Aunt Agnes?"

"Yes, this is she."

"Hi, it's Emma."

"Oh, Emma, how nice to hear from you."

"Well, I'm just reporting in about…umm…you know."

"Oh, yes, dear. How goes it?"

"Let's just say that the drought has ended."

"Oh, how marvelous! I'm so pleased and your Uncle Lou will be too."

"Aunt Agnes, don't you dare tell Uncle Lou." Emma could feel her face getting red with embarrassment just at the thought of her uncle knowing.

"Why not, sweetie? He'll be happy for you."

"I know Aunt Agnes, but well, it's embarrassing."

"Nothing embarrassing about it at all, Emma, just a fact of life. Don't worry about a thing. He'll never bring it up with you, but he will be glad to know you've found someone."

"Okay, I guess."

"Tell me, did you have fun?"

"That's one way of putting it."

"Good for you. Now don't wait so long to do it again."

"All right, I won't. Bye, Aunt Agnes."

"Bye, Emma. Don't do anything I wouldn't do."

Well, that leaves it wide-open, Emma thought as she hung up the phone. She went over to sit with Syd who was still totally absorbed in the movie. They spent the rest of the afternoon doing puzzles and reading books; when

305

suppertime came, Emma made hot dogs and French fries with Jell-O and cookies for dessert.

After dinner, they watched another DVD, *Finding Nemo*, which was followed by bath time and an unhappy Cole on the other side of a closed bathroom door. Syd wasn't too happy herself being separated from Cole and as Emma started to wash her, Syd let out a wail of "Coooleeee". Emma tried to reassure her that she'd be seeing Cole real soon, but she continued her sad lament.

With her hands full of a slippery Syd, Emma was helpless to do anything when Cole opened the door and stood there like a conquering hero. It didn't take him long to press his advantage as he half ran, half slid into the room. Emma had barely enough time to scoop Syd out of the way before Cole jumped into the tub. Water was splashed all over Emma, Syd, and the room. Squeals of laughter and happy barking mixed with Emma's shouts of woe. She was drenched and dumbfounded. When the hell had he learned to open the door? He'd been able to open the combination storm-screen door for quite a while, but that had a handle; this was a knob. Where had she been when he was perfecting his technique? The little sneak! The look on Cole's face was pure triumph and all she could do now was acknowledge defeat. Emma let the two of them play for a while; it wasn't like the damage could any worse, well, not much. So she sat back and watched as Syd had fun pouring water over Cole's head. He gave a few good body shakes and whatever hadn't been wet was now soaked.

Emma got Syd out first and toweled her dry, Cole watching from his sitting position in the tub. Then they both watched Cole as Emma let the water out. Cole's attention was fastened on the swirling water as it went down the drain. He cocked his head from side to side, seemingly fascinated by the movement of the receding water. With a word from Emma, Cole and Syd stayed where they were, one in the empty tub and one out while she ran and got the dog towels. She detoured on the way back and grabbed Syd's nightwear from her room.

When she returned to the bathroom Syd had her arms wrapped around Cole's neck, talking to him in a very soft voice. "Cole, you got Grammy all wet. It was funny, huh? You're a good dog. I love you lots." She spread her little arms out straight from her body to show Cole how much "lots" was. "You get in the tub again, okay?"

Over my dead body, Emma thought as she entered the room, catching the tail end of the one-sided conversation. She dried Syd off again and got her dressed, then went to work on Cole. Only after she had the worst of the water sopped up from his coat did she allow him to step out of the tub. Emma then hustled him down to the basement and put him in a crate where she could put the two big hair dryers to work.

Emma persuaded Syd to get into bed and after reading the two books that Syd had brought, tucked her in for the night amongst all her favorite things. Syd was asleep in a matter of minutes and Emma went to tackle the cleanup in the bathroom. It took her almost forty minutes and while Emma put the room to rights, she let loose, albeit quietly, with a few choice words that she'd held back when Syd had been around. Sometimes, she thought, that dog is a little too damn smart. For sure she was going to have to start locking the door now. She only hoped that she'd remember to do it. God, she was going to have to tell anyone who used her bathroom to make sure they locked the door or else they could have an unwelcome visitor. There were bound to be some embarrassing moments because old habits died hard and her memory sure as hell wasn't what it used to be. Damn, this was really going to be a pain in the ass.

By the time she was finished, Cole was dry and he went immediately to Syd's room and climbed up onto the bed, fitting his big body next to her little one. He stayed with her until it was time for him to go out for the last time. As soon as he was done, he went back to her bed and continued to watch over his precious charge for the remainder of the long night.

Chapter Thirty

Sunday was going to be simply perfect for all the outdoor activities Emma had planned. The day was bright with sunshine and the temperature was supposed to be in the low eighties, a bona fide godsend when the majority of Memorial Day weekends in the past had been cold and rainy if not downright snowy. Cole's run in the park was going to be skipped today and tomorrow because of Syd, so after breakfast they went outside to plant the rest of the flowers that had been waiting for this weekend to get here.

Like any other little kid, she loved to play in the dirt, so planting flowers was a natural activity. While Emma and Syd planted the bee balm and daisies, Cole stayed close, but went about his favorite pastime, namely smelling the different flowers. Everything was still pretty wet from the rain the previous day, so they didn't have to water. After they put their gardening tools away in the shed, all three went for a long walk in the woods, bringing a bucket with them for all the valuables they might find.

They saw a couple of rabbits, a lot of squirrels, and even a ground hog. They were too noisy to catch a deer unawares, but they did see where they had been bedding down. Syd found some pinecones and then some wildflowers that she just had to pick. As is the way with all small children, she left about an inch of stem to hang on to. They went down to the creek and found some pretty stones to take back, although Cole made it difficult by constantly pulling Syd back from the water so she wouldn't fall in. Every time she got too close in his estimation, he'd grab the hem of her shirt and try to haul her backwards up the bank. Emma finally had to tell him it was okay and that she was safe; she was holding her hand and wouldn't let her go in the water. He seemed to understand, but nevertheless, kept his eyes glued to her.

When the bucket was pretty full, they decided to start back and along the way Syd added some more flowers and a few sticks that caught her fancy. Once they got back to the house, they went on the deck and sat at the picnic table and examined all their newly acquired riches. Emma got a glass with water in it for the flowers, having to fill it to near full to accommodate the short stems. She put the pinecones and stones in paper bags after much discussion about which was the prettiest. The hummingbirds were flying around and Syd was fascinated with them, laughing at their comical antics while darting from one flower to the next. Cole stayed low, keeping his usual distance from the tiny marauders.

Emma made a lunch of peanut butter and jelly sandwiches, washed down with glasses of cold milk; cookies and Jell-O were dessert again, much to Sydney's continued delight. Afterward Emma got Syd to lie down for a nap, knowing that if she didn't take one, she'd be too tired to go to Joanie's later. While she rested, Emma caught up on the ironing and cleaned up the kitchen. If she was lucky, she might be able to catch a little nap herself before Syd was up and raring to go.

Luck wasn't with her. She'd no sooner lain down on the couch than the patter of little feet, together with the heavy step of four big ones, brought Cole and his energetic charge to her side.

"Grammy," Syd said, patting Emma's arm, "are you sleeping?"

"No, Syd, I just thought I'd rest my eyes a minute."

"Are they rested now?"

"Yep, all rested. What would you like to do?"

"Let's color, Grammy."

"Okay. Move over so I can get up." Emma got the crayons and coloring books and set everything up at the kitchen table, where Syd stayed occupied for near to forty minutes. Then they brushed Cole, took the clean dishes out of the dishwasher, folded the laundry and put it away, read books, did puzzles, took another short walk, went on the swing, and watched *Ice Age* again. Emma was whipped, and they still had to go to Joanie's. And she'd been worried that Syd would be too tired? Forget that. Emma wondered how women in their late forties, early fifties could even think about starting a family at that age. My God, where would they get their patience much less their energy from? They'd have to be better women than she'd ever be or just too damn stupid to know any better.

* * * *

Emma, Syd, and Cole showed up at Joanie's a few minutes after six, giving Joanie a little time to get organized after closing the shop at five. They went through the house and out to the deck where everyone was gathered. Cole and Syd saw Tank at the exact same time and both flew over to where he was sitting, his rear resting on a pillow that Joanie had brought out for him. The cone on his neck not withstanding, Cole and Syd smothered him with hugs and kisses, and Tank reacted with whines and a frenzied high-pitched barking. Emma and Joanie had to go over and settle all of them down before Tank got so excited he'd hurt himself. Kirby came streaking over to place a steadying paw on Tank's back and Emma saw that Sally and Richard were already there.

Sally gave Emma a thumbs-up and a big grin once she got her attention, her eyes flashing a silent message of "Way to go, girl". Emma blushed and grinned back, hoping the guys weren't going to start congratulating her too. She didn't think for a minute that they didn't know, what with Joanie and Sally being their counterparts, she just hoped they wouldn't feel the need to slap her on the back for a job well done.

Once calm was restored, Syd peeled out of her shorts and shirt to reveal a bathing suit underneath and looked at Emma with an expression that unmistakably said, "Well, what are we waiting for? Let's go." Emma dug out her floaties, inflated them, and put them on Syd's arms. She stripped off her own outer clothing to uncover her bathing suit and led the way down to the pool. Cole came right along with them.

When they got to the pool's edge, Cole moved to block the way, but Emma explained in the special way they had of communicating and Cole relaxed, allowing Syd and Emma to go into the water. The pool was heated, the water about 75 degrees, and even though the air temperature was starting to cool just a bit, it was very comfortable. Cole stayed where he was for about two seconds and then decided to join in the fun. He dove into the pool and came up alongside Syd and dog-paddled with her as she moved down the length of the pool.

Not to be left out of the fun, Kirby took a running start and leaped into the water causing a splash that about swamped poor Syd. She came up sputtering, but then giggled and looked like she wanted more of the same. Everybody but Tank joined in then and the pool became a madhouse of splashing, dunking, and laughing. Emma was so intent on Sydney that she didn't realize that Ben was standing next to her until she looked over to see Kirby catch a ball in mid-air that Sally had thrown. She was so startled, she lost her balance and Ben had to catch her before she lost her footing.

"What are you doing here?" were the first words out of her mouth. "I'm sorry, that sounded so rude. I didn't mean it like that. I'm just so surprised to see you."

"Joanie invited me. I just got here and decided to join everybody in the pool. Is it all right that I'm here?"

"Yes, yes, it's fine. I just wasn't expecting you. Joanie didn't tell me you were coming," Emma said, shooting a look at Joanie who was doing her best to avoid eye contact.

"She told me it was a surprise, but you would like it."

"It's fine, Ben, really. I'm glad you're here," Emma reassured him as she mumbled something about giving Joanie a surprise.

"So, this must be Sydney, right?"

"Yep, this is Syd. Sydney, come over here and meet Grammy's friend, Ben." Her granddaughter splashed her way over to where they were standing. Cole, in his role of protector, guided her movements, ready to rescue her if need be. When she was within arm's length, Emma grabbed her and put her on her hip. "Syd, can you say hello to Ben?"

"Hi, Ben."

"Hello, Sydney. It's very nice to meet you."

"This is Cole," she said, laying her hand on his head. "He's my friend."

"Yes, I can see that. You're a very lucky girl to have such a good friend."

"He loves me and I love him. I love my Grammy too."

"I can tell. Are you having fun?"

"Yes, I like to swim. Can I go now, Grammy?"

"Yes, sweetie. Here you go." Emma gave Syd a little push to launch her out away from the wall. Then, although it wasn't necessary, she turned to her dog, "Cole, stay close by now."

"She seems like a great little kid and it looks like Cole simply adores her."

"You're right on both counts and Cole is devoted to her. Do you know everybody here?" Ben nodded in affirmation. "That's right, you met Sally and Richard at the party and I know you've talked to Sam since, so I guess you do."

"This is a nice group of people. I like your friends." Ben lowered his voice, then added, "And I really like you, Mrs. Rogers. By the way, you look terrific in a bathing suit."

Emma blushed all kinds of red and didn't know where to look, but Ben found her hand under the water and gave it a squeeze. Emma squeezed back, and said so softly that Ben barely heard her, "I like you too, very much."

All the exercise in the pool had appetites growing, so Sam put the pork chops on the grill and Joanie went in the house to put finishing touches on the rest of the meal. Everyone else, people and dogs alike, vacated the pool and dried off. Tank, who had gone into a major pout, sat glumly on his pillow, giving everyone the cold shoulder. Cole went over and gave him a nudge, admonishing him in a subtle way. Cole gave him a lick then, and Tank broke down and nuzzled Cole back.

Emma, Syd, and Sally went inside and got changed, then went to the kitchen to help Joanie. Syd did her part by carrying out silverware and paper plates and cups. Emma and Sally brought out the mountains of food that Joanie had prepared. By the time they were done, the picnic table was groaning under the weight of it all.

In addition to the barbequed pork chops, there was coleslaw, baked beans, German potato salad, tuna macaroni salad, a green salad, dinner rolls and butter, and a server of olives, dill pickles, sweet gherkins, marinated mushrooms, and pickled cauliflower. For dessert: strawberry shortcake made with homemade baking powder biscuits, fresh, plump strawberries, and real whipped cream. The adults all had either wine or beer and Syd had a soft drink. Emma probably should have insisted on milk, but it was a party after all and what good was a grandmother's prerogative if she didn't use it?

They all sat, Ben making sure he was next to Emma, and everyone was quiet for the little time it took for them to fill their plates.

"Where are the boys, Joanie? I just realized they're not here," Emma asked as she cut up Syd's pork chop.

"Funny how you didn't notice they weren't here until the food came out. Well, not so funny really, they're like a swarm of locusts around food. Better for us they're not here so we can enjoy a leisurely meal instead of fighting for our share of the food. But to answer your question, they both went to an overnight party on the lake with their friend Nathan."

"They didn't plan on swimming, did they? The lake's still way too cold."

"No, they were going to set up volleyball games and have a bonfire on the beach."

"Sounds like fun," Sally said. "Reminds me of when we were young and the summers we spent on the beach."

"Hey, we're still young, at least in our heads. We'll probably never grow up, thank God, and we sure as hell wouldn't have as much fun if we did," Joanie insisted.

"That's for sure," Emma and Sally said in unison and then started laughing.

"Hey, Emma, anything else happening other than the phone calls?" Sam asked.

"No, everything has been fine except for those."

"Good, maybe whoever's placing these calls is satisfied with this little bit of harassment and doesn't intend to go any further. Could be he's getting tired of playing the game."

"We can only hope," Emma stated.

"Not to change the subject, guys, but we've got to make plans for the show. We're going to have to load up on Wednesday after work, right, Em?"

"Yeah, 'cause we should try and get out of here as soon as we can on Thursday. Sally, when we're finished loading, maybe Joanie and I'll have dinner at the restaurant. You're usually slower on Wednesday, right?"

"Yeah, it's not like on a Friday. That would be good; I could join you if we eat in the barroom. I'd still have to keep an eye on the bar, but I could do it from your table. Would that be okay with you?"

"Sure, sounds great to me," Joanie said. "I don't care where we eat as long as we do. Let's set it up for Wednesday after work then."

"All right, we're on," Emma confirmed. "We'll follow the same plan we had for Alexander."

Everyone had finished their dinner by then, so the girls got up and cleared away the dirty dishes and what was left of the food, although there wasn't much. The dogs, because they weren't dumb, followed the girls into the house to claim what they could in the way of leftovers. And since it was quicker to give it to the dogs rather than put it into smaller bowls, wrap it up and put it away, the canine moochers ended up having their own picnic. Dessert was served with coffee or milk, but when Sydney started to doze off with her mouth full of shortcake, Emma decided to call it a night. Finally, the kid was worn out!

Emma gathered up their things and said her goodbyes. Ben carried Syd out to the car with Cole walking along at his side, making sure that Ben was doing it right. He placed Syd in her car seat and Emma started to say good night to him, but he insisted on following Emma back to her house to help her with what he knew would be a sleeping child when she got there. So while Emma got Syd strapped into her car seat and put Cole into the back of the vehicle, Ben went inside and thanked Joanie for inviting him over. He came back quickly, got into his Jeep, and motioned for Emma to go ahead. Emma led the way home and when they got there, undid Syd's seatbelt and waited for Ben because Syd was indeed sleeping and would be too heavy for her to carry as dead weight. Ben lifted Syd out while Emma got Cole and they all went into the house.

Ben carried the toddler into her bedroom while Emma directed the way and then undressed her and got her into her pajamas. She had to wake her up so she could go to the bathroom, but Syd was only half awake so Emma decided on skipping both the tooth brushing and the bath and tucked her into bed. They'd make up for it in the morning. Besides, Syd had just been in the pool so she was clean enough for now and after last night, Emma didn't feel like courting disaster. Cole climbed up and snuggled in with Syd, her arm automatically going around his big neck.

"Take care of her, big boy," Emma whispered, backing out of the room, taking Ben with her.

"They make quite a picture, don't they?" Ben asked once they were in the living room.

"Yep, they're devoted to each other, that's for sure." Emma tried valiantly to stifle a yawn. "Sorry, Syd ran me ragged today. Guess I'm not as young as I used to be."

"Thank God, Emma. I'd never be able to keep up with you if you were," Ben laughed as he took her into his arms and gently kissed her on the lips. "I'm going to get going so you can get to bed. I'll call you sometime tomorrow, all right?"

"All right. Sorry I'm so tired."

"Don't give it a second thought. I just wish I could stay and go to bed with you. Good night, Em." Ben gave her one last searing kiss and then went out to his car. As Emma listened to him drive away, she wondered if the happiness she was feeling now could ever last a lifetime, or at least what was left of one.

Chapter Thirty-One

Sydney's Mom and Dad picked her up on Monday morning, Memorial Day, around 11:30. By the time Rob and Mandie arrived, Emma and Syd had already put in almost a full day of activity. Emma had started out the day by actually making pancakes for breakfast, blueberry-walnut ones at that, and surprisingly didn't begrudge the time it took her to do it. It would seem that grandchildren have a funny way of changing a person and Emma was living proof. Anyway, right after breakfast Emma gave Syd the bath she needed, but this time it was done behind a firmly locked door. Cole knew when he was beaten and laid attentively but quietly on the other side. The same couldn't be said for Sydney who voiced her displeasure intermittently throughout the bath. Emma ignored her and got the job done.

Once she was reunited with Cole, Sydney's disposition improved tenfold and they were all soon immersed in various undertakings. They watered the flowers, took a turn on the swing, went for a walk in the woods, stripped the bed, did a load of laundry, read a couple of books, played hide and seek with Cole, packed Syd's things, and had a good old-fashioned pillow fight that Syd had set her grandmother up for perfectly.

319

"Come here, Grammy," Syd had called from her room.

"What, Syd? What do you need, honey?" Emma had asked as she'd rounded the corner and stepped into the room. She'd been immediately hit in the stomach with a pillow as squeals of laughter filled the room. Sydney then had made a mad dash to hide on the other side of the bed. Emma had quickly retaliated with her own pillow, which she threw at Syd before the little imp could find cover. Thus the battle had commenced. By the time they were finished, both had collapsed on the bed, laughing and panting from all their hard work, and pillows were strewn all over the room. Cole had watched the whole thing from a respectable distance, staying safely out of range so he wouldn't take a direct hit and become a war casualty.

While Rob took Syd to pack her gear in the car, and Cole naturally went right along, Emma took Mandie out on the deck and sat her down for a little mother-to- daughter chat.

"Mandie, I have a bit of news to tell you," Emma began. "Umm…I don't know quite how to start, so I guess I'll just plunge in with both feet. Umm, here goes… I've met a man, a very nice man… We've dated a few times. Umm… we've gone out for dinner and dancing. We went hiking at Letchworth and he was at Joanie's party yesterday."

"No kidding? Really, Mom? When did all this happen?"

"Umm…just recently. I met him for the first time when he came into the shop to buy a gift for his niece."

"Really. What's his name? Where does he live?"

"His name is Ben Sievers and he has an apartment in the building next to the shop."

"That's convenient, isn't it?" Mandie asked, giving Emma a sly look and wiggling her eyebrows. "Have you been in it yet?"

"Umm…no. I haven't been in it yet, and what does that have to do with anything? Cut that out. Don't be giving me that look."

"How come you haven't been in it?" Mandie asked, feigning innocence.

"I don't know. I guess we haven't gotten around to it. What difference does it make anyway?" Emma asked, getting a little more flustered than she already had been.

"None. I just wondered. What does he do?" Mandie was grinning from ear to ear, enjoying her mother's discomfort.

"Well, he's a retired FBI Special Agent and umm… now he does a little carpentry work."

"Wow, retired FBI. How long have you been seeing him?"

"Not long, a few weeks, I guess. He was at my party at the Hearthmoor. In fact umm…that was where he asked me out the first time."

"No kidding. How come you didn't say anything before now?"

"Umm…Because I didn't want to tell anybody about it until umm… I knew if it was going to amount to anything or not."

"Sooo, by the fact that you're telling me about it now, does that mean that it has amounted to something?"

"Umm…Yeah, I think you could say that."

"Well, then to borrow one of your favorite phases…holy shit! What does he look like?"

"Oh, God, he's tall, dark and handsome," Emma laughed, "but it's true." She was on a roll now. "He's way over six foot, and he's got black, curly hair that's got just a smidge of gray and the most wonderful mustache that feels…well, never mind, you get the idea. He's got a great body and he's so easy to talk to. He's wonderful to be with

321

and we always have such a good time together. I really like him."

"I can tell. This is just great, Mom. Wait 'til I tell Mack and Tracy."

"Yeah, well…about your brother…."

"Don't worry, I'll give him the word. But then again, it might be fun to let you experience what it was like for Tracy and me."

"No. I can do without that, besides I'm the mother."

"I don't think that'll make any difference to Mack."

"I know; that's what I'm afraid of. Once he hears the news, he'll probably hop the next flight here and start his interrogation."

"I wouldn't be surprised," Mandie laughed.

Rob, carrying Syd and followed by Cole, emerged from the house at that point and Mandie filled him in on her mother's big news. Rob reacted by giving Emma a big hug that lifted her right off the ground and told her how wonderful he thought it was.

It was time for them to get going then and the tearful goodbyes, for Sydney at least, were started. She clung to Emma with tears running down her face not wanting to go. Emma promised that she would see her soon and once she calmed her down, set Syd on her feet so she could say goodbye to Cole. Well, didn't it start all over again with Sydney grabbing onto Cole's neck and crying her little heart out. It took a few minutes before she could be persuaded to let go and when she did Cole gave her face a thorough washing, then walked beside her to the car. He watched as Rob put her in her car seat and gave her a nudge with his nose once she was settled. Emma moved in to give her another kiss and when the door was finally closed, Sydney's face was wet with tears again. The adults did a hurried job of hugging and final goodbyes, and then they were on their way with Sydney waving and crying in the back seat.

Emma was later to learn from Mandie that Syd cried and called for her Grammy and Cole until she finally exhausted herself and fell asleep about halfway home. Emma wondered how long it would be before they let her come back. It couldn't have been too pleasant for them during their ride, more than likely they'd been ready to tear their hair out; they'd need time to recover before they tried it again.

Once they were alone, Emma and Cole went back to normal, routine things. Emma would have dearly loved to lay down for about a four-hour nap because didn't these little kids just totally wear you out, but she wouldn't indulge herself. She had a lot to do to get ready for the dog show and couldn't be wasting any time doing anything so foolish as sleeping in the middle of the day. But that wasn't to say she wouldn't be hitting the sheets earlier than usual that night.

She was just starting to go down to the basement when the phone rang. She picked it up and said hello. She was met with silence. This time, she didn't bother to repeat her greeting and just hung up, jotting down the particulars in her notebook. Outwardly she appeared to be unconcerned, but inside those little nervous butterflies were once again flying around in her stomach.

Emma continued on to the basement and after putting Cole up on the table, began the grooming process for the show. As she brushed out Cole's coat, she pushed the matter of the phone call aside and let her mind wander, thinking about Ben and her kids and wondering when she'd be likely to get Mack's phone call. She decided it would probably be later today if Mandie got on the phone right away, which in all likelihood she would. She chuckled, knowing what to expect from her son. God, she thought, this role reversal thing might end up being a real bother.

After a light dinner of a tuna salad made up of a whole cucumber cut into small wedges, broccoli florets, grape tomatoes, and a can of albacore tuna served with French dressing and buttered, toasted pita bread, Emma went outside with Cole and put him through his paces for the ring. She spent only a few minutes reviewing the procedure since he didn't need much to keep him on his toes and the last thing she wanted to do was bore him to death. They did their special stunt and Cole, looking very pleased with himself, was just as sharp as ever. Emma gave him a big hug and then sent him off to smell the flowers while she weeded and snapped off any flower heads that had gone by.

She was just finishing up when she heard the phone ringing. She dashed in the house and when she picked up and said hello, she was once again met with silence. She held onto the phone for a few seconds and then hung up. Two in one day, that was new. She should probably let Ben know that there had been a change. She decided to call him later, maybe even tomorrow. She noticed that her hand wasn't quite steady when she noted the call in her notebook. At the sound of the door opening she turned, her heart pounding, but it was only Cole. He'd let himself in. She went over quickly and locked the door, searching beyond it for any movement. There was none; everything was as it should be and she relaxed a little. She truly hoped that whoever was behind this would get tired of it really soon; she was getting way too edgy.

She had just finished feeding Cole when the phone rang again. At first, she just stared at it while it continued to ring. Then giving herself a mental kick in the butt, stepped over, and placed her hand on the receiver. Taking a deep breath, she picked it up and brought it to her ear. "Hello?"

"Hey, Mom. How you be?"

"Mack, hi. I'm fine. How are you?" Emma sagged with relief, letting out the breath she hadn't realized she'd been holding and slipped into a chair.

"I'm great. Lindsay's terrific and everything couldn't be better." Lindsay was Mack's wife of three years and the light of his life.

"That's wonderful, hon. What's up?" Emma, still a little shaky, decided it might be to her advantage to play dumb.

"You tell me, Mom."

"Tell you what, sweetie?"

"Okay, Mom, cut the bull. Who's this guy Mandie told me you're dating?"

Mack always had cut right to the chase on important issues and Emma guessed this was one of them. Damn, the dumb ploy hadn't gotten her real far at all. "Oh, him. Well…" Emma gave all the details that were necessary to explain things and waited for her son's reaction. It came quickly and initially as a bit of a surprise.

"This is terrific, Mom. I'm really happy for you."

"You are?" Her amazement was obvious in her voice.

"Well, yeah. Why wouldn't I be?"

"No reason, I'm just surprised you don't want to interrogate him first."

"I didn't say I didn't want to talk to him and find out his intentions. I just said I was happy for you. I'm happy 'cause you're happy, but I'll be up next weekend."

"You will?" God, Emma thought, I knew this had been way too easy.

"Yeah, Lindsay and I'll drive up on Friday and then we can meet him on Saturday if you can arrange it, okay?"

"Do I have a choice?"

"Not really, we're coming up."

"All right. I'll see if Ben can make it. Are you sure this is necessary?"

"Very."

"Mack, you do remember that I am your mother and a grown woman."

"All the more reason to check this guy out. I'll see you next Friday."

"Don't I have *any* say in this?"

"Nope."

"All right, I'm not going to argue with you about it. It won't do me any good anyway, will it?"

"Nope."

"I didn't think so. Bye, Mack."

"Bye, Mom. Oh…Mom?"

"Yeah."

"You will remember to practice safe sex, won't you?"

"Aah, geez."

"Bye, Mom." Mack ended the call laughing and after a second or two, Emma rolled her eyes and burst out laughing too.

Chapter Thirty-Two

By the time Wednesday morning rolled around, Emma felt like half the world knew she'd gotten lucky. She wouldn't have been surprised if there had been a banner flying over the town announcing her sexual success, but thank God for small favors, there wasn't one. She did however, continue to check the skies from time to time just to make sure.

Her daughter, Tracy had called Tuesday morning. She'd been unable to get through Monday evening, probably because her brother had hogged the line and she'd given up after a while. When she finally did connect with her mother, it was a matter of Emma going over the whole thing again from top to bottom and waiting for her reaction. Tracy gave the one she'd expected, she was overjoyed that her mother had found someone. She also gave Emma a dire warning about how Mack was going to react and Emma informed her that their self-appointed "Keeper of the Gate" had already delivered the news that he was coming to check Ben out for himself next Friday. Tracy had started laughing; actually, she'd gotten hysterical. When it was obvious that she was incapable of talking any more, Emma had hung up on her, realizing that in her offspring's mind it was now payback time.

Every woman that had been at the sex ed party called to offer their congratulations and how they found out she didn't know for sure, but had a pretty good idea that Joanie and Sally had had their interfering little hands in it. The women, of course, told other mutual friends and the whole thing had snowballed into a mass communications exercise. She'd been inundated with phone calls both at the house and the shop and had been sorely tempted to pull the plug at each location. She only prayed that the postmaster, Frank Upton didn't get wind of it because if he did, then every man, woman, and child in the town of Glenwood and beyond would know and Emma would simply have to pull up stakes and disappear.

That morning the trip to the park seemed like a godsend to Emma and even Joanie acted like she was looking forward to it. The sun was shining, the temperature was hovering around sixty-seven, and there was a slight breeze when they unloaded the bikes and started on their way. Cole was in great form and the ride was going beautifully, Joanie was even keeping up, until three things happened at the exact same time.

Emma had felt a tingling on the back of her neck just like the other times when she was being watched and had turned her head back toward Joanie to give her a heads-up. Cole had slowed his pace, alerted to the same presence that Emma felt and was starting to growl when the mishap occurred. Emma's front tire hit the gravel that was strewn in the road and threw the bike off balance causing Emma to fall sideways off the bike She landed with her right side on the road and the bike on top of her. She'd had the presence of mind to drop Cole's leash when she had started to go down and Cole was standing free in the shoulder. Just as he started to move toward her, Emma shouted for him to stay where he was.

"Joanie! Grab Cole! Don't let him come over here. I don't trust him to stay where he is. He'll want to try and help me." Emma's attention was fixed on the road. The sun was reflecting off irregular particles in the gravel and as Emma looked closer, she saw that the sparkly bits were shards of glass, some small, but some were quite large.

"Emma! Are you all right? Oh, my God! Look at you! Look at your hands and leg. You're bleeding badly." Joanie had jumped off her bike when her friend had fallen and had grabbed Cole's leash when Emma had shouted her warning. She was now standing next to him in the shoulder of the road. Cole was straining to get to Emma until she again told him to "Stay".

Heeding her command, even though he was unhappy about it, Cole then assumed a posture of pure menace and slowly searched the area for the threat that was nearby. He scented the air and scanned the woods on both sides of the tarmac. He kept shifting his attention from one side to the other and Emma knew that whoever was out there was on both sides of the road. There was definitely more than one person watching them.

"Joanie, don't let Cole get onto the blacktop. There's glass mixed in with this gravel. He'll cut his feet to shreds."

"Glass? Oh, my God! No wonder you're bleeding so much."

Up to this point Emma hadn't taken stock of her injuries, but now she saw that she was indeed bleeding quite a bit. Her hands and leg were cut badly from the glass, and she couldn't help but wince with pain as she pushed herself up.

"Em, can you walk? We've got to get out of here and get you some help."

"I can walk, Joanie, but I think we'd better ride." Emma had reduced her voice to a whisper. "Whoever did this is still out there. Look at Cole. He's watching both sides of the road."

Emma grimaced as she took hold of the handlebars and righted her bike. Joanie quickly picked hers up. "You're going to have to take Cole," Emma said. "I can't hang on to the lead and the bike right now."

"Oh, yeah. Okay." Joanie followed Emma's cue and talked in whispers. "Cole, you're coming with me, boy."

Cole, looking to Emma to make sure she was coming, started to back up and the girls followed suit. Cole was evidently in charge now and backed them up a good fifty feet before he felt it was safe enough to face the other direction. It was only then that the girls hopped on their bikes and started to pedal away. Emma was in the lead, clearly having a hard time hanging on with her injured hands; Joanie and Cole followed closely behind.

When they finally got back to the car, Emma more or less just let her bike drop to the ground, exhausted from the effort it took to hang on. Joanie sat her on the tailgate of the SUV and drenched two towels with bottles of water. She carefully wrapped Emma's hands, then went to work cleaning up her leg with another wet towel. Thank God, Emma's always prepared, Joanie thought as she wiped the blood away. The cuts on her leg kept bleeding so Joanie wrapped the towel around Emma's leg the way she had done her hands.

As Joanie was tending to Emma, a park employee who had been emptying garbage barrels in the parking lot noticed what was going on and came over to offer his assistance. "Are you all right? Do you need any help? Do you need an ambulance?"

"No, no, I think we're all right. I'm going to get her to her own doctor as soon as we leave here," Joanie answered while applying pressure to one of Emma's deeper cuts.

"What happened, if you don't mind my asking?"

"No, we don't mind," Emma said, trying not to wince at Joanie's ministrations. "I took a tumble from my bike when

I hit some gravel in the road. There was glass mixed in with it and that's how I got cut so badly. You probably should get it cleaned up before anyone else gets hurt."

"Glass? That doesn't sound right, but if you're all right here, I'll go clean it up right now. Where about is it?"

After Emma gave him directions, the groundskeeper hopped in his truck and was on his way. Emma gave serious thought to calling the sheriff's department, but knew that by the time they got there, the watchers would be gone. Instead, she leaned back and closed her eyes; she felt a little dizzy. Joanie had grabbed her cell phone and called Sam, who was now on his way up to the park. Cole was pacing nervously in front of the car, frustrated that he was unable to do anything more for Emma than give her a lick on her uninjured leg from time to time.

Within five minutes Sam was there, leaving a trail of dust in his wake. If anyone had seen him drive over, they would have thought he was in hot pursuit of a suspect. He no sooner threw the truck into park than he was out of the vehicle, rushing over to Emma and Joanie.

"Jesus! What happened here? Joanie, are you all right?" At Joanie's nod, he focused his attention on Emma. "Hey, kiddo, looks like you got a little banged up."

"Yeah, just a little."

"Tell me what happened. I didn't get much from Joanie's phone call, just that you'd been hurt."

Emma went through the chain of events and just as she was finishing up, the groundskeeper drove back into the lot, got out of his truck, and ambled over to where the three of them were. "Funny thing, I found where you fell off your bike. There were bloodstains there, but no glass and for that matter, no gravel either. The road looked clean, I mean really clean, almost like it had been swept."

Emma looked at Joanie, Joanie looked at Emma, and then they both looked at Sam. The girls weren't geniuses, but they could figure this one out. They didn't need Sam with all his years of FBI experience behind him to point out what was going on here. They knew the gravel had been put on the road intentionally and whoever had done it hadn't wanted to leave any evidence behind, and so had cleaned it up. Without evidence nothing could be proved and they were back to square one.

Emma slumped and let out a big sigh. "Let's go, we can't do anything more here," she said dejectedly.

"Yeah, and we need to get you to a doctor," Sam said, then turned and thanked the groundskeeper for his help.

Joanie helped Emma down from the tailgate and put her in the passenger seat of her car. Sam loaded Cole and Emma's bike into the back, then threw Joanie's bike into his truck bed. Although it went unspoken, Sam would follow the girls back to Emma's house.

Joanie jumped into the driver's seat of Emma's SUV, put the car into gear, and barreled out of the parking lot. Once they made the turn onto Route 240, Joanie slowed down a little. "I just wanted to get the hell out of there, Em. Sorry if I was going too fast; I guess I was a little spooked… I'm okay now."

"Yeah, you look it. You're hands are shaking." Emma laid her head back on the headrest and closed her eyes.

"I know," Joanie admitted while she tightened her grip on the wheel. "This is getting to be a bit too much, isn't it?"

"You could say that." Emma cracked her eyes open and stole a look at Joanie. What she saw didn't make her feel any better. Joanie was white as a ghost and starting to sweat heavily. "You're not going to be sick, are you?"

"I don't know. I don't feel so good."

"How come you feel sick? I'm the one who got hurt."

"I know; that's what's making me sick."

Although Emma was touched by the sentiment, there was a practical side to consider. "Well, pull over then. I don't want you throwing up in the car. It's hell to clean up."

"Nope, not going to do it. I'm not going to be sick. I absolutely refuse to throw up. I'll be damned if I'll let these assholes, whoever they are, get the better of me."

From what Emma could see, she didn't know if that statement was going to hold up for very long. The least she could do though was give her friend some encouragement. "That's the spirit, Joanie, you tell 'em. How about you start fighting back right now and get control of your stomach for all our sakes, okay? Just calm down, take a few deep breaths…"

"Okay. I'm doing it. I'm better. Just give me a couple minutes to talk myself out of it." Neither of them spoke for several seconds. Emma watched Joanie out of the corner of her eye. She didn't know what Joanie was saying to herself, but it looked like it was working. Joanie's color was definitely better and she'd lost that I'm-going-to-puke-any-second look.

After what Emma hopefully thought was enough time for Joanie to conquer her rebellious stomach, she ventured to ask how she felt. "How you doing? You feel better?"

"Yeah, I'm good. Everything's under control."

"Great! Glad to hear it. I knew you could do it."

"Yeah, well, it was a little close there. But I'm fine now. Whew! That was a close one…But you know what?

"What?"

"I could sure use a drink right about now."

"Somehow that doesn't surprise me…but to be perfectly honest, I'd like one too. In fact, I'd like a really big one… maybe a bloody Mary or a mimosa."

"Screw that. I want a jigger of Jack Daniels. Maybe a couple."

"Yeah? I'm sure your stomach would just love that right about now."

"It would be okay. I gave it the word."

"I'm not even going there. I don't want to know what went on between you and your stomach... What time is it anyway?"

"It's quarter to ten," Joanie replied, checking her watch. She pulled into Emma's driveway and started up the hill.

"Oh, God! What are we going to do about the shop?" Emma's instant agitation was all too apparent. "I'm supposed to be there in fifteen minutes!"

"Don't worry about it. Relax. I'll go down and open up and then see if Tammy can take over."

"What if she can't? How're we going to pack for the show *and* keep the shop open?"

"If she can't, then we'll just close the damn shop. This is an emergency, Em. I'll put a note on the door, people will understand. If they don't, tough shit. Stop worrying. We've got to get you fixed up first and foremost, all right?"

"Yeah, I guess so. Man, what a mess." Emma's whole posture drooped in defeat.

"You're telling me. I think this show is jinxed."

"Jinxed?"

"Yeah, big time."

"Why do you say that?"

"'Cause. First Tank sprains his leg and now you're injured. The gods aren't being kind to us right now."

"I don't think the gods have anything to do with it. Tank's a little off his rocker and somebody's decided they don't like me much. End of story. There's nothing more to it."

"Maybe, maybe not." Joanie parked the car and came around to help Emma out. She was getting stiff now and was moving slowly, her hands and leg still wrapped in blood stained towels. Sam had parked behind Emma's car and was letting Cole out. Cole jumped down and went immediately to Emma's side, brushing his body up against her left leg.

"Cole, it's okay," Emma said as she reached to pet him and then realized she couldn't. "Go take care of business. I know you've got to go." Cole wouldn't budge from her side and it was useless to try and persuade him.

"Em, I think you should get right back in the car. I'll take you to the doctor." Sam said while hauling her bike out of the back of the SUV.

"Okay, but I've got to get Cole into the house first. He can't go with us. Joanie, unlock the door, would you? The key is on the ring. Yeah, that's the one. C'mon Cole."

The three of them entered the house and after Emma had coaxed a very disturbed Cole into his crate and made sure his water dish had several ice cubes in it, the two girls came back outside.

"I'm going down to the shop and do what needs to be done. You let Sam take you to the doctor. And don't worry."

"Okay, thanks, Joanie."

Joanie drove down to the shop in her truck while Sam helped Emma back into his vehicle. They drove into Springville and were in Emma's doctor's office within twenty-five minutes. The receptionist took one look and ushered Emma into an examining room immediately. An hour and a half later, a pale Emma emerged, her hands and leg wrapped in bandages. Total exhaustion was written all over her face. Sam came over to help and after the paperwork was taken care of, got her out to the car.

"Em, do you need to stop and get any prescriptions filled?" Sam asked as he loaded her carefully into the front passenger seat.

"Dr. Wilson gave me a prescription for pain, but she gave me some free samples so I don't have to get it right away. She gave me a couple of shots while I was in there, so I'm all set for a while. To tell you the truth, Sam, I just want to go home and go to bed. Getting these cuts cleaned out and stitched was almost worse than getting hurt in the first place."

Sam closed the door and rounded the vehicle, then got in on the driver's side. "All right. If you're sure, then I'll get you home. You look wiped out. If you need to fill the prescription later, somebody'll go and do it for you."

By the time they reached Emma's house, she had fallen asleep. Sam woke her gently and got her into the house. He sent her right to bed and Emma, for once, complied without a fuss. Sam went back outside taking Cole with him. He put Cole in his kennel and then went out front. Something hadn't looked right when he'd brought Emma home, but he'd been too preoccupied with her to figure out what it was. Now he carefully scanned the area and everything that was in it. His gaze came to rest on Emma's car. It was listing slightly to the left. He went over and looked at the tires. There were two flats on the left-hand side. Son of a bitch! Even Emma didn't have that kind of bad luck. What did this make, four flat tires in two weeks? No way! Examining the damaged tires carefully, Sam found a small puncture in each of the sidewalls. Shit! The holes were almost in the exact same spot on each of the tires. There was little doubt now, at least in Sam's mind, that Emma's tire trouble wasn't as innocent as it had looked. It had to be connected to whatever was going on. He felt it in his gut and his gut had never been wrong. Sam placed his hands on his thighs and slowly stood up. He let his eyes search the adjacent woods. He didn't expect to see anything, but it was an instinctive reaction after years in the field. Whoever they were, they were long gone. But they had been there and that was very unsettling. He figured they must have come while he'd taken Emma to the doctor. Damn! They'd been right there at the house!

And that had to mean that they'd been watched the whole time. Shit! This wasn't good. Not good at all.

Sam had just brought Cole out from the kennel and was walking with the dog in front of the house when Ben arrived. Ben flew out of the Jeep and rushed to where Sam and Cole had come to a stop. Cole was decidedly agitated, his usual calm demeanor nowhere in evidence.

"What the hell happened? Is Emma all right? Where is she? Your wife left a message on my machine saying that Emma had been hurt. I just now got back from a job I was doing over in Holland. What's going on?" Ben was beside himself with worry, repeatedly raking his fingers through his hair.

"Take it easy, Ben. Em's going to be okay. She had an accident and got cut up pretty bad, but she's going to be all right."

"Cut up? How the hell did that happen?"

Sam told Ben what had occurred up at the park and that they had only now gotten back from the doctor's office. "I sent her to bed, Ben; she was really done in."

"Can I see her? I've got to see for myself that she's okay."

"Sure, but she might be asleep already. The doctor doped her up pretty good. Cole needs to get in with her too. He's about ready to explode with frustration. Come on."

Cole led the way to Emma's room and opened the door himself; he wasn't about to wait any longer. Emma was asleep, curled into a ball on her left side, her two hands outstretched on the mattress. Ben sucked in his breath when he saw her bandaged leg and hands. He moved closer and saw that her face was pale even in sleep and that bruises were starting to bloom on her arm and the part of her leg not covered with the sterile dressing.

Cole had very carefully moved onto the bed and was now lying next to Emma's back, facing toward Ben. He watched intently as Ben moved to gently brush back a stray lock of Emma's hair from her face. Even Sam was subject to scrutiny when he covered Emma with a light blanket he'd found in the trunk at the end of her bed. The two men decided not to test Cole's patience any more and retreated to the living room.

"I'd say she's safe for now, Cole won't let anything happen to her. I doubt he'll move from his post for the rest of the day."

"You're probably right, but I'm staying just the same."

"I expected you'd say that," Sam said, not quite successful in hiding a grin. "I'm going to put a call into Deputy Sheriff Tim O'Connor. He's out of the Colden substation and I've known him, oh, maybe fifteen years. He's a good man and I'd like to get his take on this. I think it's time we brought the local authorities in on what's been going on, even if there's nothing we can prove. What happened today changes everything."

"You're damn right it does, now the bastards are going to have to deal with me."

Sam let Ben blow off steam for a few minutes and then made the phone call to the sheriff's department. O'Connor was in and took the call. After listening to Sam's brief account, he said he'd be down within the hour. The two retired FBI men sat down to wait, each wishing at that particular moment that they were still an active part of law enforcement.

* * * *

While the men were waiting for the sheriff's deputy, Joanie was flying around like a bat out of hell. She'd gotten hold of Tammy who was now covering at the store. Joanie had called Sally and told her what had happened; she was due at Joanie's momentarily. Joanie had debated whether or

338

not to call Mandie, but decided to leave that decision up to Emma.

Joanie was rushing around getting her gear together when Sally showed up, her tires screeching when she braked hard and threw the SUV into park.

"All right, tell me everything again." Sally gasped, breathless from her run in from outside.

Joanie went over all that had happened; Sally couldn't stop shaking her head in disbelief as the story unfolded. "This is getting downright scary."

"No shit," Joanie scoffed. "I don't know if Emma will be able to show this weekend. Her hands were pretty badly cut."

"Maybe we should just forget it and do a no-show. Tank can't compete and if Emma can't show, then it's hardly worth the effort to go down there."

"What about Kirby?"

"So we miss this one, it's not a big deal. There'll be other shows."

"Yeah, but you know Emma; if she's at all able, she won't want to ruin it for you."

"Yeah, I know."

"Why don't we do this; let's get me packed and loaded in my truck and take everything down to your barn. I've only got a few more things that have to get shoved into my suitcase and then I'm ready. Once my stuff is down there, we'll get all your gear together and have it ready to load. That way, if Emma still wants to go, we'll pack her up, take her things down, and then load the motor home with everybody's stuff just like we always do."

"Sounds like a plan to me," Sally said, "and we'll have all day tomorrow to do the last minute stuff. All right, let's start humping."

"Okay, but let me call over to Emma's first and see how she's doing. They should be back from the doctor's office by now."

Joanie dialed Emma's number and the phone was picked up on the second ring. Sam answered and gave Joanie an update on Emma and told her that Deputy O'Connor was due at any minute. He informed her that Ben was there and that Cole was guarding Emma even as they spoke. Joanie told him their plans and that they'd be seeing him later on. After she hung up, Joanie and Sally went to work, coordinating their efforts to get the job done.

* * * *

When Deputy Sheriff O'Connor arrived at Emma's, Sam told him in detail about what had happened that day at the park, the two flat tires, and the previous incidents when Emma had thought she was being watched. He included the phone calls and the other flat tires in his report. Emma was still asleep and, not wanting to disturb her, Ben filled in as best he could, showing the sheriff Emma's notations in her notebook about the phone calls. O'Connor took everything down, asking for clarification here and there. When he was finished, he asked Sam to come outside with him while he checked the tires. Then he had Sam accompany him up to the park so he could see where Emma had gotten hurt. After hearing about what appeared to be a cleanup, he doubted there was any evidence left at the scene they could use, but he wanted to give it a look.

Ben stayed behind when they left; wild horses couldn't have dragged him away. He checked on Emma and found her sound asleep, her color a little better now. Cole was exactly where he'd been before, his attention riveted on his sleeping mistress. He was instantly alert when Ben entered the room, watching every move he made. Cole was sure that Ben would never harm Emma; if he'd had the slightest doubt, Ben would never have gotten into the room. But still, he watched and assessed the man whom Emma was starting to care for. Ben tenderly caressed her cheek with his fingertips, then bent and kissed the place where his fingers had just been. As he straightened, he locked gazes with Cole who he swore nodded his head in approval.

Ben had gone back to the living room and was browsing through one of Emma's books when Joanie and Sally arrived. Twenty-five minutes later, they were talking quietly amongst themselves when the bedroom door opened and Emma and Cole stepped out. Ben stood up right away and moved to her side, offering assistance if she needed it. She gave him a warm smile, but declined help as she sat on the couch across from Joanie and Sally. Ben sat next to her; Cole was on her other side.

"How you feeling, Em?" Joanie asked as she took in the bandages and eyes glazed by medication.

"Like I got tackled by a pro football player," Emma laughed. The pills and shots had made her more than a little punchy.

"No offence, Em, but you look like hell," Sally said. "I think you need some R and R." Sally had had to suppress a gasp when she saw the condition that her long-time friend was in. The bandages were bad enough, but the pallor of her skin and the exhaustion etched on her face had shocked her.

"Sounds good, but there's no rest for the weary, Sally… Where the hell did that come from?" Emma asked, looking at Ben.

"I don't know, Em. But it sounded good," Ben answered, playing along.

"I thought so…. I'm a little goofy, aren't I?"

"Just a little."

"Hey…" Emma stopped and didn't say anything else. The three of them looked at her expectantly and waited.

Nothing happened, she didn't say another word, but she did teeter a little bit.

"Em, what were you going to say?" Joanie asked, hoping to refocus Emma's train of thought.

"Say?"

"Yeah, weren't you going to say something just a minute ago?"

"Maybe."

"Well, what was it?" Sally asked, starting to laugh.

"I dunno. Musta not been too important...No, wait. It just came back to me. What are we going to do about the show?" Emma's eyes were beginning to close, her whole body kind of sagging in on itself. It looked like her rejoining the conscious world was going to be very short-lived.

"Do you still want to go?" Joanie asked, watching Emma start to fade.

"Yeah... I think we should go."

"We're pretty much packed with Joanie's and my stuff, Em. But, it doesn't matter to us if you want to cancel this weekend. Whatever you want to do is okay. I personally think we should forget this one."

"No, Sally, let's go."

"Em, think about it. How are you going to show Cole with your hands bandaged like that?"

"I'll be okay... He just about shows himself anyway." Emma was struggling to keep her eyes open. "I'm sure I can manage... Anyway we have to go 'cause Kirby's in too."

"Kirby can wait for another show, Em. It isn't like there won't be another one, you know."

"I know, but she needs to do her thing this weekend."

"Do her thing?"

"Yeah... strut her stuff."

"Strut her stuff?"

"Yeah, take her walk down the runway... shake her bootie... wag her tail."

"Wag her tail?"

"For heaven's sake, that's enough you two." Joanie gave them both an exasperated look. "Cripe! What about the pain you're in, Em? I can tell you're hurting even if you are a little bit wacky right now."

"Joanie, Joanie, Joanie… You worry too much… I'm fine. These little pills are wonderful. You want one? They're really very good… I have more and a prescription I haven't even filled yet…. Hey, we can have a party… Joanie, get the wine, I'll get the pills." Whatever her intentions were, she didn't move a muscle; she made no attempt to get up, just sat there ready to keel over.

"Oh geez, pills and booze. Now I know for sure you're out there in la-la land."

Ben, a smile playing about his mouth, had been sitting quietly while the discussion had gone on around him; he spoke up now. "Em, I think we're going to forget about having a party right now and get you back to bed. You're ready to crash. Let me help you up, okay?"

As Ben pulled Emma to her feet, she turned to him suddenly very serious, almost desperate, and pleaded, "Ben, I have to go. I can't let whoever's doing this win. I just can't. Make the girls go to the show, okay?"

"Shhh, Em. It's okay. The girls, I'm sure, will go to the show. They're just worried about you. I'll even help them get your stuff packed up, all right? Don't worry about anything right now. Just rest."

Cole followed them into the bedroom and took up his position once Ben had laid Emma down and got her comfortable. She was asleep almost before he got out the door.

"Okay, ladies, you know the routine, just tell me what to do," Ben said as he closed the bedroom door and approached Emma's two friends.

"Ben, do you really think it's smart for her to go this weekend?" Joanie asked

"No, but I don't think there's any stopping her. You know her better than I do, what do you think?"

"I think you're right. She'll go no matter what," Sally agreed. "All right, let's get started then 'cause I've got about an hour and fifteen minutes before I've got to be at the restaurant."

* * * *

By the time Glenwood was wrapped in the late hours of the night, everything that could be done had been done and if the parties concerned weren't exactly at peace, they were at least at rest.

All the girls' gear had been loaded into the motor home and there were only a few details that needed to be taken care of the next day. In essence though, they were ready to go. Joanie and Sally were in their respective beds, dead to the world, worn out by work and worry.

Deputy Sheriff O'Connor was just finishing up his shift. The lack of physical evidence at the scene led him to believe that whoever was behind the incident was a professional. He'd put everything into his formal report and Emma Rogers now had a case number. He would be speaking with her tomorrow.

Emma herself, under the influence of pain medication, was sleeping soundly with her faithful Cole keeping watch at her side.

Ben was staying the night, intermittently checking the grounds around the perimeter of the house and dozing lightly on the couch; his firearm, which he'd retrieved from his apartment earlier, was within easy reach.

* * * *

At the beach house on the Connecticut shore, it was a much different story. Though the hour was very late, Cappellini couldn't sleep. He was pacing the floor restlessly, dressed only in a black silk robe; his footsteps were silent on the cream and navy blue Persian carpet. He should have been exhausted; his workday had been frantic with details surrounding his latest takeover of a company, which had made the mistake of not accepting his original, generous offer. Now they would be acquired and totally demolished. Such were the consequences when someone dared to cross Vincent Cappellini.

He had dined out at a posh New York restaurant with the current young woman who tickled his fancy and afterwards they had ridden back to his mansion in his chauffer- driven limousine, which Cappellini referred to as his "work car". He'd taken her to bed almost immediately; the hour had already been late. Although the sex had been hard and rough, almost violent, his pleasure had been tamped down by his preoccupation with the events that were to occur on the morrow.

It was all he could do to contain his excitement as he moved back and forth over the carpet, sipping a drink he had poured in the hopes it would help to relax him. But it wasn't working; he wasn't relaxing. In fact, he was getting more keyed up every minute. He wanted to shout loud enough for the whole world to hear. Tomorrow he would own him! He would have that magnificent animal in his possession and it would be he who felt the thrill of each of his wins. He wouldn't actually have the dog in his own hands until early Friday morning, but tomorrow night Jasper would have him and that was almost as good. He was getting too worked up; my God, he thought as he swirled the scotch in his glass, he was actually salivating, his heart pounding.

He looked over at the huge, four-poster bed where the naked woman was sleeping. Her long blond hair was fanned out on the pillow and her shapely, uncovered body was stretched out as she slept on her stomach.

He had to try and relieve this tension or he'd never get to sleep; he needed to be sharp tomorrow just in case there was a problem. Jasper had assured him that everything was going to go down according to plan; there would be no problems. But Cappellini knew better; there could always be a problem no matter how well something was planned and he wanted to be able to think clearly if there was.

He stopped his pacing and again looked at the woman; she was here and willing, so why not make use of her. Maybe another go-round would take the edge off and he'd finally be relaxed enough to fall asleep. Putting his drink down on the nearest table, he crossed over to the bed, disrobing as he went.

Chapter Thirty-Three

Thursday morning had rolled in bleak and gloomy, the threat of rain hanging heavy in the air. Joanie, for sure, would consider it a bad omen; anything now that wasn't sweet and rosy would be viewed as the devil's own in her estimation. She had declared this dog show jinxed and it would take close to an act of Congress to change her mind.

Nevertheless, when Emma awakened she'd felt energized and registered only a dull ache in her hands and a little stiffness and a slight throbbing in her right leg. True, the reason she felt so much better than yesterday could be explained by the wonderful pain medication she'd taken, but who the hell cared. And she wasn't about to let a few clouds and a little rain deter her either.

Cole's head had been resting on her chest and his big, brown eyes were the first thing she'd seen when she'd opened her own. He hadn't wakened her; he'd just been waiting patiently for her to come to consciousness by herself. And when she had, the look that passed between them spoke of their great love and devotion to one another. She'd stroked him clumsily on the head with her bandaged hands and he'd responded with big sighs of contentment.

Emma had started to get out of bed when she'd heard muted voices coming from the direction of the kitchen. She'd had a moment of panic before she'd realized the two persons involved in conversation were Ben and Joanie. She'd known that Ben had spent the night, but what the heck was Joanie doing there? And since there'd been only one way to find out, she'd gotten dressed as best she could, her bandaged hands making it almost impossible to be anything other than uncoordinated. Looking at her hands and thinking they looked like they were encased in mittens, she'd decided that the yards and yards of gauze wrappings definitely had to go the route of the circular file today.

Upon entering the living room, Emma and Cole were promptly intercepted by Ben who'd heard her stirring in the bedroom. "Morning, Em. I'll take Cole out for you. You go get comfortable in the kitchen. Joanie made breakfast." He gave her a quick kiss on the cheek and before she or Cole could object, scooted the dog out the door.

"How you feeling, Em? You look way better than you did yesterday." Joanie had turned from her position at the stove where she'd been busy making French toast and was now stacking the thick, butter-browned, egg and milk dipped slices on a platter.

"Oh gosh, those smell heavenly, Joan. I can't wait to dig in. I'm starving." Emma licked her lips, imagining the taste treat that awaited her. She was a little unsteady though, Ben had left her feeling a little off kilter with his quick manipulation. "And to answer your question, I'm feeling pretty good. Those little pills work wonders."

"Do your hands hurt?"

"Just a little." Emma was still turned in the direction that Ben had taken, feeling rather like a whirlwind had just gone through.

"What about your leg?"

"It's a little stiff, but doesn't hurt too much." Emma sat down at the table and took a drink of the orange juice that had been placed at her setting; she shook off the effects of Ben and turned her whole attention to Joanie. "Not to sound ungrateful, but why are you here?"

"Isn't it obvious? I came to make breakfast, of course." Joanie rolled her eyes and jiggled her eyebrows. "There is another reason though. Guess what we forgot to do yesterday?"

"I don't know; I was kind of out of it."

"You can say that again...Cole never got his bath."

"Oh crap."

"Yeah, well, I realized that little oversight last night. Sooo, that's the main reason I'm here. Not that I don't enjoy playing cook extradinaire for you."

"I appreciate your efforts." Emma managed to spear two slices of toast, but Joanie grew frustrated watching her and took over, buttering and pouring maple syrup over the two pieces before she cut them into bite size bits.

"There, have at it or should I feed you too?"

"No thanks, I can manage. But when I'm finished you can help me get cleaned up and get these bandages off."

"I don't know if they should come off, Em. They haven't even been on a whole day yet."

"I don't care. I can't do anything with my hands all bound up like this. We'll put Band Aids on. That'll be good enough."

"All right, I'm not going to argue with you, but if your cuts get infected or break open, don't come crying to me."

"Geez, you're all heart. Now stop talking so I can eat." Emma dove into her food and mmm, mmm, mmm'd her delight.

Ben and Cole came back in just as Emma was finishing and while Ben joined the girls at the table, Cole went to his water dish for a long drink. When he'd had his fill, he came over to Emma, dripping water all the way and soaking Emma's pants when he put his head on her leg.

"It's good to know some things never change," Emma laughed as she patted Cole's side.

Ben, sitting next to Emma, was busy forking French toast onto his plate and grinned over at Emma when he saw the result of Cole's affection. "I think you're going to have to change your clothes again, at least your pants."

"I was going to anyway after I got cleaned up so it's no big deal. You learn to live with these little inconveniences when a Newfie's part of the family."

"Must make a lot of laundry."

"It's a small price to pay, believe me."

"You're feeling better this morning?"

"Yes, much."

"Good, I'm glad. I'll help Joanie with Cole's bath after breakfast. The two of us should be able to handle it, don't you think?"

"You'll be fine. Cole loves to take a bath. You might get a little wet though."

"I don't mind; a little water never hurt anybody." Ben made short work of his breakfast and started to clear the table. "Why don't you and Joanie go do what you ladies need to do and I'll clean up the kitchen. Then Joan and I'll give Cole his bath."

After giving Joanie a look that said, "This guy's too good to be real", Emma went and gathered up what she needed and headed for the bathroom. Joanie met her there and when Emma closed the door, she surprised herself and remembered to lock it. The last thing she needed was for Cole to come barging in with Ben in the house. It wouldn't be a good thing to happen. Visions of embarrassing consequences flashed before her eyes and she shuddered. No, it definitely would not be a good thing. Thank God, her brain was working at full capacity.

Between the two of them, they managed to get Emma cleaned up and relieved of her gauzy mittens. She had ten to twelve Band Aids on each hand; they looked ridiculous, but what the hell, she was now somewhat bilaterally dexterous and her hands no longer gave the appearance of being mummified. No, now she just looked like someone who'd been attacked by the Band Aid fairy!

At any rate, they went down to the grooming area and Emma supervised while Ben and Joanie gave Cole his bath. Cole, intelligent dog that he was, thought this was a great opportunity to fool around and shook his body every chance he got until the two washers were completely soaked. Who says dogs don't have a sense of humor? This one sure did and used every advantage he had to have a little fun. Ben was taking it good naturedly, but Joanie knew Cole was being a wise guy and started to fight back, spraying Cole in the face with the hose. He in turn shook his head and drenched her anyway. So who was the smart one? A dog that loved the water or the human who was trying to beat him at his own game? No contest. The dog was the sure winner, but the human was too dumb to know it and besides, Joanie would never say "uncle".

Emma finally broke it up after half the basement was wet and declared the contest a draw. She gave Cole a wink and he knew she knew who'd really won. Joanie and Ben got Cole toweled off and into his crate before putting the two big dryers on him. They probably had an hour or more to kill, so Joanie left to check on the shop. Tammy was covering the morning, but had an appointment that afternoon, so Joanie would have to take over about one o'clock.

While she was gone, Deputy Sheriff O'Connor came by and questioned Emma about what had happened the day before and anything else that was relevant. He assured her that they were looking into the matter in an official capacity and asked her to please notify them if anything else occurred regardless of how trivial it might seem. He was just going out the door when Joanie returned and having known her for a long time through Sam, he made a comment about her wet appearance. She mumbled something about all males being nothing but smart-asses and stalked into the house. O'Connor laughed and went on his way, Emma grinned, and Ben made himself scarce.

* * * *

Once the shop closed that night, Joanie and Tank went down to the Hearthmoor where Emma and Cole were waiting. Ben had driven them, since Emma's hands were still too sore to drive and she had taken one of her pain pills, which put her "under the influence" so to speak.

When Joanie walked in the door, Cole and Kirby welcomed Tank excitedly, but she was greeted by long faces on both Emma and Sally. "What's wrong?" she asked. "You two look like somebody just died."

"Tommy got sick, he left around five o'clock. I'm really sorry, but I have to take over," Sally said. "We can't leave until maybe nine o'clock when it slows down. Then I can close the kitchen except for chicken wings and finger food. Sharon can handle that. What do you think? Do you want to go at nine or should we wait and go early tomorrow morning?"

"I knew we were jinxed this trip. I knew it. Didn't I tell you? Damn!" Joanie looked from Emma to Sally and back again, trying to come to grips with the problem that now faced them while reigning in her disappointment. "Well, crap. It isn't your fault, Sally. We all know this stuff happens when you own your own business. It just always seems to happen at the wrong time. Damn! What do you want to do?"

"Let's go at nine," Emma said. "We're all packed and we're already here. So what if we get there a little later tonight than what we planned. It's still better than doing it in the morning, right?"

"Yeah, it's better to go tonight. It would be too big a hassle in the morning," Joanie agreed. "Okay, Sally, what do you want us to do? How can we help?"

And just like that, the threesome pulled together to get through one more crisis. Emma took the dogs upstairs and supervised their play, making sure Tank didn't overexert with his sprained leg. Sally and Joanie both went to the kitchen where Joanie did whatever Sally needed her to do so that both the bar and the kitchen ran smoothly.

* * * *

Out in the dining room at one of the corner tables, the one nearest the bar, sat Connie who'd come in a little earlier. She'd been trying to listen to the girls' conversation and had heard enough so that she thought she knew what was going on, but she needed to confirm it. Watching for her chance, she almost jumped up from the table when she saw Joanie bring in a tray of cups from the kitchen and start to put them where they belonged in the service area. Instead, she forced herself to remain seated and waited until Joanie was almost finished and then called over to her, "Joanie? Is that you? What are you doing here? Moonlighting?"

Joanie turned and it took her a minute to recognize the woman. "Oh, hi. No, not moonlighting," she laughed. "Just helping out our friend. Her chef got sick and had to leave so Emma and I are pitching in."

"So what? You cook too?"

"No, no. Sally's the cook. Don't worry; she's very good. In fact she used to do all the cooking here. You'll still have a great meal."

"I'm really not worried," Connie said, then looked thoughtful for a minute before she spoke again. "I'm probably getting this all wrong, but weren't you supposed to go to a dog show today?"

"Yeah, in fact we were supposed to leave a little while ago. But then this thing with the chef came up and we've had to delay our departure."

"Are you still going tonight or are you going to wait 'til tomorrow? I'd think you'd be too tired to go tonight if it gets much later."

"Nah, we're kind of used to it. Once it settles down in here, around nine o'clock, we'll take off. We'd rather get there late tonight than have to deal with the ride and the setup in the morning, what with Cole in the ring right at eight-thirty."

"Well, good luck. It sounds like you still have a very full night ahead of you."

"Thanks. We'll get through it, we always do."

"And good luck at the show. Hope everybody takes the win. I'm planning on going, so I'll see you down there."

"Thanks. We'll look forward to seeing you." Joanie went back into the kitchen and Connie, after waiting a few minutes, went into the bathroom and used her cell phone to call Jasper to tell him about the piece of luck that had just fallen into their laps.

* * * *

It was a few minutes after nine when Sally closed the kitchen for dinners and the girls made their getaway. Sally took her position in the driver's seat, Emma was in the front passenger seat, and Joanie again was stationed on the couch behind Sally. The dogs were in their crates, anxious as always to be on their way. It was raining, it was dark, it was late, and there was a tangible excitement in the air. As Sally pulled out of the parking lot, it was official. They were finally on their way to the show and they all gave an enthusiastic hoot, filling the inside of the motor home with enough caterwauling that the dogs joined in and raised the noise level a few more decibels.

They went down Rt.240 and then turned onto Rt.39, which took them through the center of Springville. Once they cleared the town, the girls and the dogs settled in for the hour and a half ride as the road went out into flat farm country for miles. There wasn't much traffic; there never was out in the country, but Sally kept a sharp eye out for deer. It seemed that they were always running no matter what time of the year it was.

When they were on the far side of Gowanda, nearing Forestville and heading toward Fredonia, unbeknownst to the girls, the two cars that had been following at a safe distance started to make their move. They gradually began to close the space between them and the motor home.

Sally noticed their far-off headlights when she checked her side mirror and not thinking anything about it, continued in conversation with Emma and Joanie. After her next mirror check, she noticed that the headlights were drawing closer, but still thought nothing of it, other than the fact that the cars behind her had to be going faster than she was since they were catching up. She wasn't taken totally by surprise then, when the next time she looked they were on her rear bumper. She was pissed, but not surprised.

"Goddamn it! What are these two idiots doing? They're right on my ass," Sally bitched as her eyes again darted to her mirrors. Emma looked to her side mirror to see what was going on and Joanie strained to see from where she was.

"It's probably kids out joyriding. I wonder why they don't just pass? They've got to know the road's clear up ahead; they keep swerving out to check." Joanie was watching their maneuvers in the left-hand mirror.

As if they'd heard, the front car swung out into the other lane and passed the motor home, coming back into the right-hand lane maybe a hundred feet in front of the girls. The second car stayed behind Sally, moving up to ride her bumper.

"What the hell are they doing now?" Sally asked, getting angrier by the minute. If it was one thing she hated, it was people playing games in their cars.

"It looks like they're slowing down," Emma said, watching the front car. It immediately became apparent that was exactly what they were doing, forcing Sally to back off on the gas.

Looking into her side mirror, Sally saw the second car swing out into the left lane and pull alongside the motor home. "Joanie, look out your window and see what that other car is doing. I don't want to take my eyes off this front car right now. I don't know if he's going to slow down again."

Struggling to get a good view out her side window, Joanie spotted the second car and watched it ride alongside, staying to the rear half of their vehicle. It cruised out there for a short time and then dropped back directly behind them. "They're riding out in the other lane and then ducking back behind us."

"Girls, I've got a real bad feeling about this," Sally said, shifting her gaze from the front car to the side mirror and back again, trying to keep tabs on both cars at once. "Time for preventative measures," she mumbled. "Joanie?"

"Yeah."

"That couch you're sitting on, get up and lift the seat."

"Why?"

"Just do it, okay?"

"Okay, hang on." Joanie did as Sally asked and stood there looking into the interior. "Now what?"

"Take everything out and be quick about it, all right?" The second car was again pulling out and coming alongside the motor home, only this time it came to about mid- length before it pulled back in behind them. The front car was reducing its speed a little more and Sally was once again forced to slow down.

"Okay, everything's out. What do you want me to do now?"

"Lift up the bottom and get the gun out."

Joanie froze. "The what?"

"The gun."

"What do you mean, the gun?"

"I mean the gun. The G-U-N. Hurry up."

"Geez, Sally, since when have you had a gun in here? God, I can't believe it! You've got a real gun in here!"

"Since forever. Now, *please*, just get out the fucking gun," Sally pleaded, her voice laced with impatience as the second car came up alongside and stayed there.

"Emma, did you know she's had a gun in here the whole time? Like for how long? Years?"

"No, I didn't know."

"Geez, a gun, Em."

"Joanie?"

"Yeah, Em?"

"Please, for once just shut the hell up and get the fucking gun out. We're in trouble here!" The second car was starting to veer over into Sally's lane, making her swerve onto the shoulder to avoid contact between the two vehicles.

Knocked off balance by Sally's swerve, Joanie fell to her knees and reached in to take the bottom out of the storage area. "I'm doing it! I'm getting it! Holy shit! It's a shotgun! You've got a fucking shotgun in here! Em, she's got a big, fucking shotgun in here!"

"Just take the fucking thing out, Joanie!"

"Yeah, yeah. Okay. I've got it out. Now what?"

"Hold onto it. You've got to load it."

"Load it? I don't want to fucking load it."

"Well, you have to. I can't. I've got to drive for cripes sake and Emma can't because of her hands. So you're elected."

"Son of a bitch! All right, all right. Give me the fucking bullets for the fucking gun."

"Em, they're in the glove compartment. Give 'em to Joanie." Emma got the box of bullets and handed it to Joanie.

"All right, I've got the little fuckers. Now what do I do with 'em?"

The girls' nerves were streaking into the stratosphere. Joanie's whole body had broken out into a sweat and her hands were shaking. Sally's face had a sheen of perspiration on it and her hands were just as bad, but you couldn't tell because she had a death grip on the steering wheel. Emma's heart was pounding so hard she thought the top of her head was going to blow off. The dogs had picked up on the heightened tension (they would have had to have been dead not to) and they were circling in their crates, their ears laid back. Tank was giving his best imitation of a Rottweiler.

"Put the box down for a minute. Hold the gun with two hands and crank open the wagger."

"Jesus Christ! What the hell's a wagger?"

"Sorry, gun lingo. Sorry. It's the locking lever. Do you see it? It's about three inches long just behind the barrels. You need to push on it hard, you've got to move it about an inch."

Joanie found the lever and with some difficulty pushed it over an inch. It didn't help that she felt about as strong as a newborn baby right then. "Okay, it's open. Now what?"

"Let the barrels swing down about thirty degrees. You should be able to see the open ends."

"Got it. I'm looking at two holes."

"Good. Now, put one shell in each hole and hurry it up, okay?"

The second car was staying in the opposite lane, next to the motor home, trying to force it off the road. How Sally was keeping them *on* the road was anybody's guess.

Joanie put a shell into each chamber and with direction from Sally, closed the gun by bringing the barrels back up sharply, and heard the locking lever snap shut. "Okay, the son of a bitch is loaded. What should I do now?"

"Hand it up here to me," Sally instructed as she kept her eyes darting from one car to the other, opening her window as she did so. "Emma, come over here and get on the floor. Slide your foot on the gas pedal as I take mine off."

"Why?"

"Em, don't you start asking questions too, just do it. I can't drive and take aim at the same time. It's been a while since I've shot this thing."

"Oh shit. Okay." Emma got down on the floor and put her foot over Sally's, then made contact with the pedal as Sally's foot moved off.

"Keep that pressure, Em. We're going about the same speed. I'll keep my foot near the brake. If we need to slow down, Joanie'll let you know."

"How?"

"Knowing Joanie, she'll probably scream like a banshee at you."

"Right."

"Joanie, you get over hear and take the wheel. You're going to have to steer. Try to keep us steady."

Joanie moved up to take the steering wheel, the whole time chanting softly to herself, a repeated chorus of words that would make a sailor blush.

Sally flipped the safety off and stuck the shotgun out the window. In a voice that was as loud as she could muster, and hoping the bad guys couldn't hear how shaky it was, Sally called out to the occupants of the car trying to force them off the road.

"All right, you bastards, either get the hell out of here, or I'm going to start shooting!"

The only response she got, other than the wide-eyed look from the ski masked man in the passenger's seat when he saw the gun, was the car moving over so close to the motor home that it very nearly bumped it. That's all it took to goad Sally into action. She aimed down the barrels and pulled first one trigger and then the other as Joanie struggled to keep them from going off the road while avoiding contact with the car. The bullets found their mark; the rear side and back windows of the car were blown to smithereens. The recoil from the discharge brought the barrels up and pushed Sally back in her seat. She recovered quickly and handed the gun back to Joanie to reload while she took over the steering and put her foot back on the gas pedal so Emma could ease herself out.

The car ahead of them accelerated suddenly and before the girls had a chance to resume their battle stations, the second car took off like a shot. Their taillights quickly disappeared in the distance. Sally eased up on the gas while the three of them caught their breaths, which for everybody had been bordering on hyperventilation.

"Everybody okay? Anybody hurt?"

"I'm okay."

"I'm okay. You all right Sally?"

"I'm okay. Christ! We did it! Hot damn, we scared 'em off!"

"Who-hooo! Hallelujah! Save me Jesus!"

"Yahoeeee! We beat the fuckers! Let's have a round of high-fives, guys." As the girls high-fived, there were a lot more "holy shits" and some "Oh, my Gods" thrown around. Damn, they were pumped!

It took a little while, but their adrenaline levels started to run down and they were left feeling like something the cat dragged in. They needed to get their blood sugar back up; they'd about depleted it to zero. That'll happen when unknown persons try to run you off the road and you have to shoot a shotgun at them. It's not something the girls did on an everyday basis and their bodies were telling them they weren't in any shape for this kind of shit. They needed food. Hell, what they really needed, according to how their thought processes worked, was the sugar that came along with booze. But since that wasn't an immediate option, they settled for the candy bars that were stashed in one of the cupboards. Joanie brought out Snickers, Milky Way and Kit Kat. They ploughed right through them, all ten bars. They split the tenth into thirds; nobody was getting short-changed on this go-round, not after what they'd been through.

"Damn, we did good."

"You bet your sweet ass we did."

"They must have had two-way radios in the cars the way the front car took off after I shot at the other one."

"And what a great shot it was. Hot damn! I didn't know you knew how."

"Yeah, I used to hunt with the ex. I haven't done it in a long time."

"Good thing for us you remembered how."

"I wonder what they were trying to do?" Sally asked as she kept a diligent eye on the road up ahead.

"I think it's obvious, they were trying to force us off the road."

"I know *that*. But why, what did they want?"

"Us."

"Us?"

"Yeah, us."

"Joanie, are you all right? Did you hit you head or something? Or are you just freakin' crazy? Why would anybody want us?"

"Why wouldn't they? We're good-looking women."

"Yeah? Well, we're all fifty-something too."

"So what? What does age have to do with it? If you've got it, you've got it. And guys, you know we've got it."

"I don't think I've got it."

"I don't think I want it."

"Too bad, guys, 'cause we've got it big time, whether you want it or not."

"Well, in this case, I'd just as soon not have it. 'Cause if what you think is true, then they wanted what we've got and they weren't going to ask nicely for it."

"Yeah, you've got a point there. Hmm…I never thought about it before, but I guess it could be kind of dangerous when you've got it."

"Joanie, get out of never-never land, will you? On our best day we don't have 'it' on that scale."

"You two are too damn modest. Believe me, I know of what I speak. We're hot stuff."

"You're an ass."

"Yeah, well, that goes without saying, but I'm a hot one."

Sally and Emma gave up. They had to let this conversation die, or Joanie would be on it all night. For a few moments, there was only the sound of the engine and the dogs' agitated movements. Then Joanie was at it again.

"Well, what else could they have wanted? I mean, no offense, Sally, but this motor home doesn't exactly shout 'money'. We don't look like we're rolling in the green stuff."

Determined to divert Joanie's attention to more pressing matters, Sally answered crisply. "I don't know what they wanted, but I think we'd better get this reported. Do you have your cell?"

"Yeah."

"Then do something useful, call 911. Tell 'em what happened."

"All riiight." Joanie punched in the digits, munching the last of her candy and waited for the dispatcher to pick up. When she did, Joanie relayed their harrowing experience. The dispatcher, after getting their vital information and approximate location, told her to have Sally pull into the parking lot of the Twin Lanterns restaurant on Main Street in Forestville and wait for the sheriff.

"Screw that lady," Joanie answered back. "After what we've been through, there's no way in hell we're going to stop 'til we get to the fireman's grounds in Stockton. We've got a dog show to get to, and by God, we're going there now. You tell the sheriffs to meet us there. Over and out." With that, Joanie switched off her cell and sat back.

"Umm, Joanie?" Emma ventured, looking into her friend's set face.

"Yeah?"

"Do you think that was real smart what you just did?"

Shooting Emma a blank look, it was several seconds before Joanie slowly answered. "Maybe... maybe not." Looking a little embarrassed, she crossed her arms over her chest and lowered her head so that when she spoke again, it was directed to the floor. "I guess I got carried away."

"Just a little, don't you think? Are they going to meet us there?"

"I don't know. I hung up before the dispatcher could say anything."

"Geez, Joanie. Well, I guess we have no choice but to wait 'til we get there to find out. Keep driving, Sally."

"Sure, why not? Nothing like a little more tension and worry before we get to bed. Nice job, Joanie." Sarcasm hung heavy in the air, not that Joanie was affected.

"Stuff it, guys. They'll be there, if for no other reason than to bawl me out."

Grinning wickedly, Emma pressed the point. "You could be right. I wonder how they'll take it when they find out you're the wife of a retired FBI agent. I mean, you of all people should know better than to lip off to someone in law enforcement. This could be very interesting, don't you think, Sally?"

"Uh-huh, especially when the sheriffs realize that she's got 'it'."

"I think I should call Sam."

"Good idea, I think you just might want to do that."

While Joanie called Sam and explained what had happened, Sally got the motor home back up to speed and Emma checked on the dogs. They were starting to settle down although they weren't yet laying quietly in their crates. Emma could see that the hair on the back of their necks was still raised and their nostrils were twitching, scenting the air. Emma talked to them in a soothing voice and scratched their sides through the wires of the crates. After a few minutes of coaxing, she got them to lie down and gave them each a biscuit.

Joanie disconnected with Sam and her friends looked at her expectantly. "Sam said, 'Enough of this shit.' He's calling Sheriff O'Connor to tell him what happened and then Richard and Ben. He said the three of them would be coming down to the show grounds tonight. He's getting the camping gear out and they'll stay in the tent. We'll have to make sure there's room for them wherever we set up."

"Really? They're coming down?" Sally asked.

"That's what he said."

"Well, I've got to be honest with you, I don't think I'll mind having them around this weekend."

"Yeah, me neither."

"It's got my vote."

"What'd he say about your little lip-off?" Sally asked, watching Joanie in the rearview mirror.

"Nothing."

"Nothing?"

"Yeah, nothing. I didn't tell him."

"Oh shit. Well, I hope we're through with the sheriff before he gets there."

"Yeah, you and me both." Joanie was definitely down in the mouth now, but Emma and Sally were having a hard time not laughing out loud.

* * * *

When the girls arrived at the fireman's grounds on the south side of Stockton, a Chautauqua County Sheriff's car was already parked near the entrance and waiting for them. Sally turned onto the grounds' dirt road, pulled the motor home up next to the sheriff's car, and shut the camper down. The girls were just emerging, a little nervous about the reception they'd receive, when the officer reached them.

"Ladies. I'm Deputy Sheriff Stone with the Chautauqua County Sheriffs Department. I understand you had a little difficulty tonight."

"Yes, sir," the three friends answered in unison.

"According to your 911 call, two cars were trying to run you off the road. Is that correct?"

"Yes, sir."

"Want to tell me about it?"

"Yes, sir." They were starting to sound like a broken record. They each gave their name and then Sally took over and gave a concise accounting of what had happened, faltering only when she got to the part about the gun.

"What happened next, ladies?" the sheriff asked, looking from one to the next.

Emma looked at Joanie, Joanie looked at Sally and Sally looked at Emma. All three whispered quickly, their words running together, "Wegotoutthefuckinggun."

"Pardon? I didn't quite catch that." The sheriff leaned slightly forward so as to be able to hear them better.

"Wegotoutthefuckinggun," the three girls repeated. A crowd was starting to form; people who'd been out walking their dogs were being drawn up to the entrance by the sheriff's car's flashing lights.

"Ma'ams, if you could repeat that a little slower..."

Taking a deep breath, Joanie just about shouted, "We-got-out-the-fucking-gun."

"Oh, right. I got it that time," the sheriff said, turning his head away to hide a grin that was threatening to burst into, at the very least, a full chuckle. When he had himself back under control and could present his "official" face, he asked the girls to continue. When they had finished, all of them had been participating now, Sheriff Stone asked various questions, hoping to get information that would assist in apprehending the individuals involved. Unfortunately, the girls weren't much help.

"Sorry, Sheriff Stone, but everything was happening so fast; there just wasn't time to get a really good look. I do know they were in SUVs and the cars were a dark color, but I couldn't say if they were black or blue, or what kind they were," Sally offered

"Yeah, and there were four of them, two to a car. But they had ski masks on so we couldn't see their faces. We figured they had to have two-way radios to communicate with each other because of the way the front car took off after Sally shot at the second one. But there just wasn't time to get license plate numbers or anything, " Emma added.

"Well, we do know one thing for sure," Joanie stated.

"What's that, ma'am?"

"One of the cars has no rear side or back window, thanks to the shooting skill of my friend here." Joanie gave Sally a pat on her back while Sally gave her a look that said, "Knock it off."

"Speaking of which, what type of firearm did you use, Ms. Higgins?"

"A double-barrel shotgun, sheriff."

"Been shooting a long time, ma'am?"

"Actually, I haven't shot a gun in close to twenty years. I guess there's some things you never forget, thank God."

"I'd have to say so, ma'am. You did a nice piece of shooting tonight. Might have saved your lives. Where's the weapon now?"

"In the motor home. It's still loaded, but the safety's on. We wanted to be prepared in case they came back."

"I think the danger's past, so why don't you go over and unload the gun and put it away."

Sally left the group to do as the officer had asked and while she was gone, Sheriff Stone asked who had called 911. After giving Emma a look, Joanie confessed and raised her hand, a sense of impending doom descending upon her.

"I understand you gave the 911 dispatcher a hard time."

"No, sir, I didn't. I just told her that there was no way we were going to stop until we got here."

"Even though she directed you to go to a specific location?"

"Well, you see, sir...it was the heat of the moment, sir. This whole trip has been jinxed from the start." And Joanie was off and running. "My dog, Tank, the dumb ass, thought he could friggin' fly and went and sprained his leg when he jumped off the deck after a chipmunk and so he can't compete; and somebody's been bothering Emma for weeks, making her life hell and finally managed to hurt her yesterday; and Sally's chef got sick tonight and we had to stay at the restaurant later than we were supposed to 'cause Sally had to take over the cooking; and then somebody tries to run us off the road and wants to do God knows what to us; and it's raining and it's dark and there was just no way we were going to risk anything else happening by stopping anywhere before we got to where we are right now.

We were on a mission to get to this show and by God, nothing was going to stop us; and besides, I was a little crazy from what had just been going on. I mean, I had to get out that damn gun, and I didn't even know there was a gun; and Emma didn't know there was a gun, Sally had kept it a friggin' secret all these years and we really have to talk to her about that; and I had to load the fucking thing and I didn't know how to load it and Sally had to tell me while she was trying to keep us on the road; and then she had to get ready to shoot the stupid thing so Emma had to get on the floor and put her foot on the gas 'cause her hands are too sore to grab the wheel; and I had to try to steer and Sally had to aim and shoot the gun and try not to kill anybody, 'cause she really didn't want to do that; and the car almost ran into the motor home trying to force us off the road; and I had to keep us steady so Sally could shoot and then when she finally did shoot the fucker, she right away handed the damn thing back to me to reload while she took over the driving; and Emma got off the floor; and the dogs were going crazy; and sir…by the time I talked to the dispatcher I really didn't give a rat's ass about anything except getting here. And that's why I said what I said and we did what we did. So there it is. If you have to take me away, go right ahead 'cause I've had about all I can take right now."

Joanie paused to take a breath and then finished her impassioned speech with, "Did I mention that my husband's a retired FBI agent?"

Emma, whose eyes had gotten as big as saucers during Joanie's monolog, started laughing and couldn't stop. Sally, who has returned at the tail end of Joanie's speech, rolled her eyes and held her breath. Sheriff Stone's mouth was hanging open and he had a dazed look in his eyes. He didn't know quite what to say. Feeling like he'd been run over by a steamroller, he slowly gathered his wits and opened his mouth to speak, but nothing came out. He tried again.

"Umm, it won't be necessary to take you away. You've just explained everything very thoroughly. Actually, you've more than explained it. Whew! You ladies have been through quite an ordeal, haven't you?"

"You could say that," Emma replied, her laughter having died a slow death. "Erie County Deputy Sheriff O'Connor stationed in Colden has been working on what happened to me. You might want to call him. I don't know if what occurred tonight is related, but maybe."

"I'll give the officer a call, Ms. Rogers. Meanwhile, I've got a report to file and we'll put out an APB on the two vehicles. Are you sure you're all alright?"

"We're fine," Joanie said. "After we have a glass or two of wine, we'll be right as rain. And my husband's on his way down with friends, so we won't be on our own for very long."

"Good, glad to hear it, although I think you three could handle just about anything that came your way."

"We're all mothers and business owners, sir. We're experts at crisis management," Joanie explained.

"I guess you would be with those qualifications. I'll need you to come down to the station and file a formal complaint though, and I'd like to go back to where the incident happened, see if there's anything useful at the scene. But that can wait 'til tomorrow. Will that be all right with you?"

"Yeah, we can come in probably, what, around ten? We've got a big break before we have to show the other dog. She doesn't show till around 1:30. We can call when we're on the way. Is that okay with you, Sheriff?"

"That'll be fine. These are directions to the station and the phone number." He handed Sally a card with the information written on it. "Well, I'll be leaving then, ladies, and just so you know," he leaned in closer and said in a whisper, "it's a good thing you had that fucking gun."

"Yes, sir!"

As the patrol car rolled away, the girls were besieged with curious onlookers, many of them friends, and the story of their night's adventure was retold several times. Finally they escaped to the motor home, drove deeper onto the grounds, and found a spot to set up. They went into "hustle mode" and made camp, took care of the dogs, opened not one, but two bottles of wine, and sat down to wait for their men.

*   *   *   *

Cappellini was in a blind rage. When word got to him via Jasper about the bungled job, it was all he could do not to literally shoot someone. But since the only people he had immediate access to vent his wrath upon were his trusted household staff, he unleashed his fury first on several pieces of nearly priceless, antique crystal, hurling them one by one into the huge stone fireplace in his living room and watched them shatter. He then turned his attention to the works of art that hung on his walls and tore them down, breaking the frames and tearing their canvases in the process. He overturned pieces of furniture and threw beautiful rosewood tables against the fireplace, ripping off legs and splintering tops. He picked up Tiffany lamps and threw them against the walls, gauging the plaster and smashing the glass shades. First edition books were ripped apart and custom-made draperies were pulled down and shredded with the pocketknife that he always carried. By the time he was finished, the room was in shambles and he was breathless.

He stood there gulping air and willing his body to stop shaking. He was perspiring heavily, his hair was disheveled, and his eyes, which had narrowed to mere slits during his rampage, were trying to adjust and bring the room back into focus. When they did, he looked around dispassionately, the destruction eliciting no response. His anger spent, he was completely drained of all emotion; his only focal point now - revenge.

He walked out of the room without a backward glance and strode down the hallway to his study. He poured himself three fingers of scotch and picked up the receiver to his secure phone. He punched in the stored number for the farm and gulped from his drink while he waited for the other end to be picked up. When it was, the only words he spoke to the caretaker were, "Get Wilhelm, I have a job for him."

Chapter Thirty-Four

Emma had been quiet all morning, too quiet and Sally and Joanie both knew it. She'd taken Best of Breed with Cole in the Newfoundland judging, but their performance in the ring hadn't been their usual stellar one. Emma had been off her game and it hadn't been because of her injuries. Cole had picked up on it and had lost some of his customary sparkle. If they went into Group that way, they didn't stand a chance of taking a first.

The girls had been trying to get her to open up throughout the morning but so far they hadn't had any success. After Cole had finished showing, they'd left immediately for the sheriff's station, all six of them, and Emma had been quiet as a mouse in Ben's Jeep. Even with all the pushing and shoving to get all of them situated somewhat comfortably in the back seat, Emma had remained strangely removed. Thinking back on it, Joanie decided they should have put Emma in the back with the other three squashed bodies and then seen if she could keep to herself. Not likely. The four of them that had been back there had wavered between complaining and laughing the whole time. Emma, in the front passenger seat, hadn't joined in. She really hadn't even talked to Ben all that much.

After the formal paper work had been completed at the station, the six of them and the sheriff had driven out to the area on Route 39 where the incident had taken place. There was nothing of significance to find and the group had driven back to the show site and regrouped for the afternoon.

One of Nancy Bullis' assistants had stayed with the dogs while they were away from the show grounds, just to make sure nothing untoward happened during the girl's absence. After Nancy had learned about their misadventure the night before, she had volunteered any help she could provide to Emma and her friends. Other exhibitors too, had offered whatever assistance the girls might need; all they had to do was ask. There was a heightened awareness among all the exhibitors and they were closing ranks, alert to anything out of the ordinary.

Knowing the girls were safe on the show grounds, the men went off to do whatever men do together, and the girls began to get Kirby ready for the ring. Emma and Joanie took over the grooming so that Sally was free to change into ring attire. They'd cut it a little tight time-wise. They wanted to get to the ring a bit ahead of the scheduled time for Labrador judging so they could settle into "show mode". All of them needed to redirect their energy and attention to what was going on at the show. As Joanie finished brushing Kirby's short, dense coat, she decided to drop any hint of subtlety and asked Emma outright what the problem was.

"Nothin'."

"No, no. Don't give me that nothin' stuff. What's wrong?"

"Nothin'."

"Emma, I know you almost as well as I know myself, so you can't fool me. I know there's a problem. I'm going to give you one more chance to come clean. After that, I'll beat it out of you if I have to. Now, once again, what's the matter?"

Emma knew better than to press her luck. Joanie might not actually beat her, but she would at the very least put her on the ground and sit on her until she got some answers.

"I guess I feel guilty," Emma confessed, her eyes filling with tears.

"Guilty? Why the hell would you feel guilty?"

"Because last night something awful could have happened and it would have been all my fault."

"Why, in heaven's name, would it have been your fault?"

"Because after I thought about it, I realized that last night had to be tied in with what's been happening to me, and you and Sally are getting caught in the fallout. There's no other explanation. I don't care how much 'it' you think we have."

"Get over here now so I can bitch-slap you! You take the cake; you know that. Like this whole damn thing is your fault. Are you nuts? Stop that crying right now. Come here." Emma gave her a wary look and didn't move. "Come on, I'm not going to slap you, I'm going to hug you. Get your butt over here. And as far as our 'it' goes, Em, we're over the top."

Emma went over to Joanie's side of the table; Joanie grabbed her and hugged her tight. Sally came out of the motor home just then and took in the scene before her.

"Did she give it up?" Sally asked, her gaze fastened on Emma's tear-stained face.

"Yeah, finally. She had this cockeyed notion that she was at fault for putting us in danger last night. I straightened her out."

"I'm sure as only you could, Joanie. Em, are you okay?"

"Yeah," Emma squeaked, nodding her head.

"All right, good. Don't be getting any more stupid ideas like that again, okay?"

"Okay."

"Now that that's settled, get yourself together Emma, old girl, and let's get down to the ring; I've got a dog to show and I need my two best friends down there to cheer me on."

Emma dried her eyes, Joanie snatched up the brush and towel, Sally grabbed Kirby, made sure she had bait and a squeaky toy, and as a unit, they took off for the ring. The guys were already there and Richard held Sally's armband out to her. She put it on, gave Kirby a comforting pat, and settled into wait for her class to be called.

Ben noticed Emma's splotchy face and asked what was wrong. Emma assured him that all was well now and he gave her a quick bolstering hug.

Sam sidled up to Joanie, giving her a look that asked the unspoken question, "Everything okay?" Joanie answered with a big smile that told Sam everything was as right as it could be.

Meanwhile judging in the ring was proceeding and the girls didn't like what they were seeing. The judge, Mr. Dennis Overton from Charleston, West Virginia had been an unknown quantity to the three girls; none of them had ever gone under him before and didn't know his likes and dislikes. From what they were seeing in the ring, he wasn't going to make their "A" list. It was obvious from the dogs that were being put up that the guy was a headhunter, that is, he made his placements based solely on the dog's headpiece; nothing else was being considered, such as movement, ring presence, or conditioning.

When Kirby's class was finally called, Sally went in knowing she was pretty much out of the competition. While Kirby had a really nice head, it wasn't up to what this judge seemed to be looking for. Sure enough, after he'd made his selections, Kirby was in third place, completely out of the running for the win. When Sally came out of the ring, she heard Joanie mumbling.

"What?"

"I told you this whole weekend was jinxed. Look at what just happened here. No way should Kirby have taken a third."

"Joanie, in all fairness, we didn't know this judge. It was a crapshoot. If we'd known he was a headhunter, Kirby would never have been entered. So look at it this way, we took a shot and lost, okay? There is no jinx."

"I'm not buying it, no matter what you say."

"All right, hang on to your jinx theory. You're as stubborn as a mule, for pete's sake."

"Yeah, but I'm cute as a button. Let's watch the rest of this fiasco and then go back."

The final result of the Labrador judging brought no surprises now that the girls knew what the judge was looking for. The Best of Breed winner had a magnificent head, but to say he had adequate movement was being kind. All three made mental notes to put Mr. Overton's name under the heading of "Never to show under again!"

The Working Group judging was scheduled for 3:45. It was the second last group to be judged before Best In Show, the Sporting Group having been given the last slot. So as soon as they returned from the ring, they all gulped down a late lunch and then the girls got to work getting Cole ready. It took about forty-five minutes of primping to get him finished and Emma dressed. When they went down to the Group Ring, Emma was in much better spirits than she had been for the breed judging and Cole, well, he was ready to show his heart out.

* * * *

The number of dogs filling the ring totaled twenty-four. Every breed that was categorized in the Working Group was represented. Emma and Cole filed in with the rest and found their spot. Emma quickly put Cole into his stack, gave him a kiss on the nose, and stood back.

The judge, Mrs. Florence White from St. Louis, Missouri entered the ring and took her first look, her gaze landing on each and every dog presented in front of her. She gave the signal for the go around and the dogs moved out, circling the ring once before going back to their starting positions.

When the individual inspections began, Emma played with Cole and let him relax. She wiped some drool from his mouth with the ever-present towel and gave his coat a few strokes with the brush. When it was their turn, she led Cole out to the center of the ring and set him up. Cole lifted his head and assumed his ring hauteur. Emma dropped the lead and stepped back.

Mrs. White approached and began her hands-on inspection. Most handlers remained at the dog's head, holding the collar to keep the dog's head in position and to keep control. With Cole, there was no need. He stood as solid as a brick wall, never so much as shifting his weight. When the judge was finished, she asked Emma to do the down and back.

Emma gathered up the lead gingerly, basically holding on to it with three fingers. On Emma's signal, the two moved off, their rhythm in perfect synchronization with Cole's powerful reach and drive impeccably showcased. On the way back, when Mrs. White held up her hand for them to stop and go into the free stand, Emma made her move to the right. Cole came down like a cat to place all four feet squarely in position. He looked directly at Emma and gave Mrs. White his version of "the look". The judge smiled and had them go around, then back to their place in line.

While Emma was rewarding Cole with hugs and gentle pats, Joanie was excitedly whispering to Sally, "Hot damn, they're back and I think they're going to take it!"

The individual inspections were finished and the dogs were stacked again, forming a single line just out from under the tent. Mrs. White took her stroll down the line, making her first cut. She pulled out ten dogs to the center of the ring and excused the rest. There, she inspected them once more and pointed for Cole to go to the head of the line. She placed the Rottweiler in second place and the Giant Schnauzer and Doberman Pinscher in third and fourth positions respectively. Satisfied, she gave the signal to take the dogs around and all ten moved out. As they traveled about the ring, Mrs. White pointed to Cole and said, "One," followed quickly by, "Two, three, and four," as she pointed to the dogs she had previously placed in those positions.

Emma moved to the awards area and received the congratulations of the other exhibitors, including those who had taken second, third, and fourth as they went to stand in their appropriate places. The judge handed out the ribbons and prizes, and then moved to the ring across the way for pictures. Emma had Cole's picture taken with Mrs. White, who again congratulated Emma on the win and expressed her pleasure at having had Cole in her ring. Emma thanked the judge and went to join her friends.

To say she was nearly bowled over by Joanie and Sally was no exaggeration. They more or less jumped on top of her when she got within range, shouting and whooping it up as only they could. Thank God, for a rock-solid Cole. He was the only thing that kept her from going down. He gave Emma a look that said, "These two are dangerous!" Hell, didn't she know it!

Sam and Richard pulled the two-pronged wrecking machine off Emma and Ben steadied her on her feet, turning her into his arms for a big, but gentle hug.

"Congratulations, Em. You two were fantastic. I had no idea. I admit I don't know much about showing, but even a complete novice can see that you and Cole are very special in that ring."

"Thanks, Ben. Cole did a really good job; he always does. It was my fault, this morning. I brought him down. Thank God, we still did good enough to get the breed win."

"Hallelujah! You've got another Group One, Em." Joanie was actually doing little spins in the air; Emma was getting dizzy just watching her.

"Geez, Em. Three times out and you've got three Group Ones! This is like, way too much to comprehend." Sally slipped out of Richard's grasp and grabbed Emma in a hug, Emma stiffening a little, bracing for impact.

"Hey, they're judging the Sporting Group already, we've got to get Cole ready for Best In Show. Let's go back." Orders issued, Joanie led the bunch back to the motor home where she unapologetically directed everyone in their appointed task.

* * * *

Thirty-five minutes later, they were back at ringside awaiting the start of Best In Show competition. It was going to be a really tough competition; there were some excellent dogs there that day. Nancy Bullis was there with her top-ranked Afghan Hound, the Toy winner was a beautiful Maltese, Terriers were represented by a Miniature Schnauzer that was ranked number one in his breed, a magnificent, young Irish Setter came from the Sporting Group, the Non-Sporting entry was the number two ranked Lowchen, Bill Thornton's powerful German Shepherd Dog had won in the Herding Group once again, and last but not least, there was Cole.

The ring steward called them into the ring and as Emma slipped inside, her friends wished her good luck. Emma was fourth in, behind the Afghan, German Shepherd, and Irish Setter. Everyone stacked their dogs and awaited the judge, who on this day of blue sky and brilliant sunshine was Mrs. Elizabeth Danforth from Chicago, Illinois. As she walked to the center of the ring, all eyes turned in her direction. She looked down the line of perfectly posed dogs and gave the signal to take them around. The dogs and handlers moved out, the Afghan setting the pace for the bigger dogs; the smaller ones setting their own tempo of motion. After they got back to their place in line and restacked, the individual inspections began.

Emma and Cole did their thing beautifully, but then, they all did. Each team of dog and handler performed flawlessly and it was now a question of which dog, in the judge's opinion, conformed closest to its breed standard and was begging for the win through his showmanship.

After the final go around, Mrs. Danforth went to the table to mark her book, not having given away so much as a crumb as to who the winner was. Once her decision was so noted in the judge's book, she returned to the center of the ring with the ring steward and the Show Chairman of the Conewango Valley Kennel Club. While the others carried the numerous prizes, it was the judge who held the Best In Show ribbon in her hand and after standing silently for a moment, pointed to Nancy Bullis and said, "The Afghan."

Bystanders at ringside shrieked and clapped and the exhibitors inside the ring went over to Nancy and offered congratulations. The Afghan was twirling in the air and jumping on Nancy and it took a few minutes for her to gain control. The judge presented her with the spoils of the win and shook her hand.

Emma and the others left the ring while the photographer was already getting set up to take pictures. Emma was truly happy for Nancy; the Afghan was an exceptional example of the breed and they had performed beautifully.

"Rats," Joanie said when Emma reached her side.

"Oh, Joanie, don't be like that. She deserved the win."

"Yeah, well, so did you."

"Joanie, I can't win all the time. Get serious."

"Well, why not? Cole's the best."

"He may be, but I'm not. Besides, her Afghan is a beautiful animal and Nancy Bullis is a great handler. Give them their due."

"Yeah, I suppose you're right, but I still think you should have won."

"God, you're impossible, but thanks for being such a loyal friend." Emma gave her a hard hug and then released her, her attention shifting to Cole who was waiting patiently for his kiss and hug. Emma gladly bestowed them and then kept her hand on his head, gently rubbing his ears.

"You did a great job, Em, and your handling is right up there with everybody else's. But you're right; it's impossible to win every time. Sure would be nice if you could though." Sally gave Cole's tail a few quick tugs, and then looked over at Joanie. "What, you're not going to spout off some more jinx theories?"

"I don't believe I feel the need. The proof stands before you. If you can't see it, then that's your problem."

"Don't go getting porky, Joanie Davis."

"Pork this." Joanie slipped them the one finger salute, smiling angelically before bursting into laughter. Emma and Sally joined in; the men were kind of at a loss as to what was going on, but Sam and Richard, having been around the three women long enough, told Ben not to even try to figure it out.

"Hey, let's go up and rescue Tank. He's probably ready to climb the walls."

"Yeah, and let's get dinner started. I'm starving."

Two hours later, after having relaxed with cocktails of wine, manhattans, and beer while they did the cooking, the six of them sat down to a scrumptious meal. They had a green salad, crescent rolls, meatloaf, mashed potatoes and gravy, and buttered corn. The men had made it a point to stop at a grocery store on the way back to the show grounds that morning to beef up their food supplies. Sally had brought a Mexican Sundae pie from the restaurant and that along with coffee and tea completed their dining fare.

Tank was exuberant at having been rescued from the confines of his crate where he had been languishing for most of the day and made his presence known to both dogs and people. Sprained leg or not he was going to have some action.

He played with Cole and Kirby, ambushing his big buddy as best he could with the cast on his leg. He mock fought with Kirby and grabbed a ball that Cole had his eye on. He threw squeaky toys in the air and pounced on them before the other two could react.

He jumped on Joanie until she picked him up and then made a royal pain in the ass of himself until she couldn't take anymore and passed him off to Sam. Sam's patience didn't last very long and Tank found himself back on the ground where he utilized what speed he had and jumped Kirby on her blind side. He rolled off her and set his sights on Cole's broad back.

Cole, who had been seeking refuge from the four-legged demon, was trying to hide somewhat ineffectively under the grooming table. He caught the blur of motion just as Tank launched himself and steeled his body for impact. Tank landed with a thud and appeared to have knocked the wind out of himself. He slid down Cole's side and ended up sprawled between his legs.

Cole gave him a look that said he was an idiot and what did he expect? Tank gave him a return stare that conveyed his devil-may-care attitude and then turned his attention to anyone who would dare to reprimand him. He more or less got the message across that this is what they could expect as their just desserts after having abandoned him for almost an entire day.

Joanie blew out her breath and gave him the evil eye. It was shaping up to be another battle of the wills. Sally and Emma started making bets on the outcome; the odds were favoring Tank.

Chapter Thirty-Five

Early the next morning, after a rather large breakfast of grapefruit halves, French toast, bacon, eggs, coffee, and orange juice which the men had taken great pains to prepare without female help, the girls plotted their strategy for getting the dogs and themselves ready for the ring.

The motor home was packed to overflowing with the addition of three men, so while they cleaned up the kitchen, the girls took themselves outside and got the dogs groomed. Cole was in the ring at 9:30 and Kirby at 10:00. They put Cole on the table first and while they worked on him, Kirby and Tank played in the ex-pen. Better to keep Tank in the thick of things as long as possible after yesterday's show of spite.

It was another beautiful day with warm temperatures, bright sunshine, and near cloudless skies. Everybody's spirits were high, including the dogs, the terror of two nights ago pushed out of everyone's mind. Emma's hands were beginning to heal and she'd been able to reduce the number of Band Aids considerably. Her injured leg wasn't giving her any discomfort and although the bruising was still vivid, the cuts and scrapes were scabbed and mending.

She wouldn't win a beauty contest right now, but all her parts were working pretty near to normal.

The girls finished with Cole and let him stay on the table. There'd be no romping in the ex-pen with Tank or they could kiss their grooming job goodbye. With Kirby up on the other table now, Tank had full run of the enclosure and set about to cause as much havoc as possible with the toys that were strewn about. He grabbed hold of one squeaky toy in the shape of a ladybug and with a mischievous glint in his eye, proceeded to gleefully tear it apart. He wasn't content until he held the squeaker in his mouth and bit down on it repeatedly to produce the noise. Joanie barreled her way into the pen and relieved Tank of his prize post haste before he could swallow it. All she got for her effort was another dirty look from you know who.

The men cleared out so the ladies could get ready and an hour and a half later, all three were their usual ravishing selves, their "it" factor polished to a high gloss. They emerged from the motor home primed to kick butt in the ring. Joanie would be doing her butt kicking from the sidelines, ready and willing to assist either friend in the accomplishment of their goal.

The whole troupe went down to the rings, leaving Tank locked in the motor home. Two days of being out of the action was more than he could bear and his usual good manners deserted him; he retaliated the only way he could at the moment, he voiced his displeasure and did it quite loudly. His outraged barking could be heard at some distance as they walked away and everybody knew there'd be hell to pay later in the day.

Emma and Cole were in Ring One and Sally and Kirby were in Ring Five, which was the last ring at the opposite end of the tent. If luck was with them, Emma could be finished by the time Sally had to go in.

The call for Puppy Dogs, age six to nine months, went out and two entries entered the ring. Both handlers were the dogs' owners and one looked to be fairly new to the game. She was having a bit of trouble getting the young dog to stand still and when she reached down to set his back legs, the pup slipped his collar and made a break for it. He stayed within the confines of the ring, but broke into a full-blown game of "keep away". His inexperienced handler was darting around the ring trying to catch her wayward pup and failing miserably. The spectators thought it was great fun, but the judge, Mrs. Evelyn Brown from Terre Haute, Indiana and the ring steward wanted to get the ring back under control and quickly. Someone on the outside of the ring, probably a handler, finally enticed the pup over with a piece of bait and grabbed the lead while the puppy was distracted with the bit of liver it was being offered. The owner came racing over and accepted the lead, thanking her rescuer and scolding the puppy. When they were at last back in line, the judging continued and in spite of all their folly, the misbehaved pup and his owner won their class.

The remainder of the class judging proceeded without incident and it was soon time for Best of Breed judging. Cole was one of only two Specials entered, and he swept to victory with an easy win, far outclassing the other dog.

Despite the delay caused by the errant pup, Sally made it down to Ring Five in plenty of time; Labrador judging had just begun. While they waited for Kirby's class to be called, the group chatted amiably with the other exhibitors; Cole made friends with as many Labs as he could reach. The puppies especially were drawn to him because of his gentle nature.

When their class was finally called, Sally and Kirby strode into the ring ready to put on a show. The judge, Mr. Earnest Mills from Bloomington, Illinois approached the lineup and took his first look. He motioned for the go around and the ten dogs that made up the class were off and strutting their stuff.

Sally and Kirby performed very nicely and were rewarded with a first place win. They remained in the ring while the winners of the other classes entered and took their places. Kirby was first in line, so she led the go around when it was called for. The judge had them all do an individual down and back, and then went down the line laying his hand on a few of the dogs of which Kirby was included.

Mr. Mills stepped back, then pulled out the American Bred bitch and put her at the head of the line in front of Kirby. He gave the signal to take the dogs around the ring and as they were trotting by, called out, "Winners," and pointed to the first place dog.

Sally and the other exhibitors remained in the ring for Reserve Winners and once again Kirby took the honor. Whip-de-do! It still amounted to no points. Sally left the ring with resignation stamped on her face and blew out her breath in defeat as she approached Emma and Joanie. Leave it to Joanie not to let it alone.

"Well, what the hell? What was the guy thinking?"

"Obviously that he liked the other bitch better, Joan." Sally reached down and patted Kirby's side, then gave her a piece of bait as she looked at Sally with eyes that begged for a reward.

"Yeah, well, I think this is just more proof that the weekend is hexed. Geez, what else has to go wrong before you guys are convinced?"

"I don't know about the whole weekend," Sally said, "but I'm starting to be a believer as far as Kirby's last points are concerned. At the rate we're going, it could take another year to get the remaining two."

"Nah, you'll get 'em before winter," Emma said, reaching down to give Kirby's ear a playful tug. "You're always in the running; it's just a matter of time before you sweep to victory."

"Sweep to victory, huh? Before winter? Hell, winter's six months away. That could mean an awful lot of time not sweeping. So let's see, if I'm not sweeping, what am I doing?"

"Swooping!" Emma gave Sally a wink that Joanie missed seeing.

"Swooping?" Sally was ready to play along.

"Yeah, you're getting ready to sweep."

"Which I'll do before winter, right?"

"Right. You have to swoop before you sweep."

"Sooo, I take it I'm swooping now."

"Yeah, and doing it very nicely too."

"Well, thank you so much. You have no idea how much it means to me to know I'm a good swooper. Be still my heart."

"Don't get smart."

"Who me? Never. Though I can't wait to upgrade from a good swooper to a good sweeper."

"What are you two talking about? What's all this swooping sweeping shit?" Joanie gave them both a look that indicated she wasn't buying it.

"Why, whatever do you mean, Joan?"

"Don't give me that, Emma. There's enough bullshit floating around here right now that I'm surprised you two aren't being buzzed by a horde of flies."

"I have no idea what she's talking about, do you, Sally?"

"Not a clue. She must be mistaken."

"Mistake this." Joanie gave them a rather rude gesture. God, but they loved to get her going.

The men went off to watch the German Shepherd judging they'd spied taking place in another ring and the girls went back to the motor home. All was quiet as they approached; Tank must have worn himself out. Joanie didn't know if that was good or bad.

When they opened the door, they found Tank just rising to his feet, his eyes looking a little heavy-lidded. He must have been asleep so just how upset could he be, Joanie wondered. When she made eye contact with him, he gave her an icy stare and then turned his back. Ahh, that upset, she thought.

She opened the door to his crate and called him to come out. He didn't move; he just kept showing her his back end. Well, screw this. She wasn't going to beg. Joanie went over to the fridge and got a Diet Pepsi, asking if anyone else wanted one. Emma took her up on it, but Sally declined, favoring instead a cup of tea.

As they sat around the table talking about this and that, Tank came out of his crate. He put his nose in the air and went back to the bedroom where Cole and Kirby were roughhousing on the bed, not deigning to give Joanie even a sideways glance.

"Boy, he's got your number, Joanie." Emma followed Tank's progress to the bedroom, noting that he had a swagger to his walk even with the cast on his leg.

"That dog could give lessons in arrogance, couldn't he? Geez, he's something. I don't know if I could live with him, though." Sally shuddered at the thought. "He'd probably whip my butt after just one day."

"I think Joanie's the only one who is a match for the little devil."

"Aren't I the lucky one?" Joanie rolled her eyes heavenward, but actually she was pleased. For all his quirks, Tank was a perfect match for her and she loved him dearly, even though at times she was sorely tempted to string him up by his stubby little tail. Of course, if she ever did, he'd only give her attitude on that too.

The men returned and lunch preparations got under way. The girls scooted the male trio out and gave them the job of entertaining the dogs while they went to work creating a standout feast. The girls dished up a meal of barbequed chicken sandwiches on hard rolls, a Waldorf salad, potato chips, and dill pickles; for dessert there was an apple pie. While giving the illusion that they were working really hard, in reality all they had to do was warm up the chicken in the microwave, cut the rolls, assemble the sandwiches, stir the salad, open the potato chip bag, fish the pickles out of the jar and, cut the pie. Thank God for the restaurant!

After lunch, the girls took the dogs over to where there was an open field on the show grounds and let the dogs run around. They didn't take any toys or Frisbees; the temptation to jump would have been far too great for Tank to ignore, and the girls didn't want to risk another injury to his leg. As it was, the speed with which he was able to run, cast and all, was a little frightening.

Afterward the girls went down to the rings to watch the various judging and talk with friends. Sam, Richard, and Ben stayed at the motor home and took charge of the dogs, refereeing any impromptu games of chase that sprang up out of the clear blue.

Eventually the girls moseyed back to get Cole ready for the Group judging. It was over an hour away, so they set to work at a leisurely pace. Emma got back into her show clothes and when it was time they all went down to the ring, minus Kirby and once again, Tank. At least now he had Kirby to keep him company so there shouldn't be any danger of retaliation. The girls still believed in miracles, the silly asses!

* * * *

There was once more a full contingent of twenty-four dogs representing the Working Group. As Emma and Cole took their place, excitement crackled in the air. More than one set of eyes was trained on the young Newfoundland, hoping to see if he could once again win the first place spot.

Emma set Cole up and gave him a kiss on the top of his head. "Here we go, big boy. Let's do our stuff."

Cole struck his perfect pose and Emma stepped back. The judge, Mr. Thomas Rowan from Louisville, Kentucky had entered the ring and was standing in the center, taking his first look. As he looked down the line his eyes rested a trifle longer on Cole before he moved on. Cole had such a commanding presence that it was impossible not to give him more than just a passing glimpse.

The judge signaled for the go around and the dogs moved out with their handlers setting the pace. Mr. Rowan let his gaze fall on every dog as they came within his range of sight and very quickly he formed impressions of each animal's reach and drive. When they were all back under the tent overhang, the individual examinations began.

Emma and Cole moved out to the center of the ring when it was their turn and Emma quickly set Cole up. She stepped back and let Cole show himself. The judge approached; he gave Cole a long look and then laid his hands on the dog. Cole was his usual steady self and became a totally immovable object. Emma smiled as she stood passively, looking on as her dog worked his magic.

Mr. Rowan stood upright and keeping his eyes on Cole, moved back from the dog. He told Emma to do the down and back and once she had gathered up the lead, the two of them took off down the side of the ring flying over the grass so perfectly that they appeared not to even touch it. Coming back to the judge, Emma did her move to the side and Cole hit his stack perfectly. He zeroed in on Emma as only he could and silently shouted to the judge to give him the win.

They circled back to their spot in line after the judge gave them the signal and then relaxed until the remainder of the dogs had presented themselves. When everyone was back in place, the handlers stacked their dogs. Mr. Rowan started down the line to make his first cut. He pulled out ten dogs and placed Cole at the front. Wasting no time, he signaled for the go around and Emma and Cole led them off. As they were charging around the ring, the judge pointed at Cole and shouted, "One." The second, third, and fourth place dogs were quickly pointed out and they all, Cole included, went over to the winner's area.

Outside the ring people were cheering and applauding, while inside congratulations were being given out all around. The judge gave out the ribbons and had a word with each of the four exhibitors who'd placed. He then retired to the ring standing opposite the one they were in for pictures and Emma followed him over.

After the picture taking she went to rejoin her group, taking care to try and stay clear enough of Joanie and Sally so she wouldn't be hit with a full frontal assault. Ben moved in close to cover her back and to provide a sturdy support wall if she should need one. She needed one; they both came flying at her. How did they get that much momentum from a standing start? At least this time she was prepared. They were only able to knock her back into Ben's hard-as-nails chest, a distance of only an inch or two, before she rebounded and met their jubilant squeals and congratulations. God, this winning stuff could get your various body parts severely injured!

As Emma was recovering from the strike force of two's onslaught, she heard someone calling her name. Turning, she saw the woman who'd been in the shop approaching.

"Congratulations! What a wonderful job you did," Connie said, reaching to shake Emma's hand.

"Thank you. I see you made it down," Emma replied as she took her hand, accepting the congratulatory gesture.

"Yes, I got here about 11:00. Sorry I missed the breed judging, but I was held up and couldn't get here any sooner. You'll go in for Best In Show now, right?"

"Yep, that's what we're on to next."

"That's great. I hope you win. You know I'll be watching."

"Thanks. I hate to admit this, but I don't know your name or I'd make the introductions."

"I can't believe I never told you my name. Well, I'll fix that. It's Mary, Mary Cooper."

Supplied with the missing piece of information, Emma made the introductions all around and after a little more chitchat, the group excused themselves and went to prepare for the next round of competition.

Connie watched them for a long time as they walked away. With her eyes hidden behind dark glasses, which she'd donned after they'd said their goodbyes, and with her head tilted toward the ring where another Group was being judged, no one would be able to tell she was still watching them should anyone look back. Now that she had witnessed the dog in action firsthand, she understood what all the fuss was about. Even with her limited knowledge of dogs, she recognized a champion of champions. The Newfoundland was absolutely magnificent and she could appreciate their client's obsession with the dog.

It was going to be over very soon now, in spite of the bungled job on Thursday night. Nobody had anticipated that the women would fight back and with a shotgun no less. Connie couldn't help but admire their spunk. But they were no match for professionals, and now that the client had brought in his own man, well, matters were going to draw to a close rather quickly. This Schmidt guy had begun calling the shots for the team as soon as he'd arrived and he wasn't wasting any time setting things up to end this once and for all. He'd told her to come down here and act out her part and she wasn't about to argue. You did what you were told with a guy like that. There was a calculated coldness in him that came out loud and clear and she didn't want any part of it being directed at her. With Schmidt at the helm, Connie knew Emma and her friends could only lose; the single question remaining was, at what price?

* * * *

They were back at ringside waiting for Best In Show judging to begin. Emma was trying to stay loose; her before-competition nerves were making her jumpy. They shouldn't have come down this early; too much time to wait and think. It was better when they got there with barely enough time to fly into the ring. Ben had tried to distract her, but she'd snapped at him and Joanie had told him it was best to leave her alone. Cole was the only one who could settle her down and from the looks of it, he'd better start doing it pretty darn quickly.

As if on cue, Cole jumped on Emma. He put his huge paws on her shoulders and gave her a big kiss, then nuzzled his great head next to her neck. Emma wrapped her arms around him, turned her face into his, and gave him a kiss back. Next she said words to him that only they were privy to. They stood there like that for a minute or two and then Cole went down on all fours; with one more shared look between them, they were ready.

The ring steward called for the exhibitors to enter the ring and Emma and the six other contestants filed in. Lining up, it was again Nancy Bullis with her Afghan representing the Hound Group, a German Wirehaired Pointer from Sporting, Cole, a surprise winner from the Herding Group, a beautiful Bearded Collie, a Lakeland Terrier from the

Terrier Group, a Lhasa Apso from Non-Sporting, and lastly, a lovely Italian Greyhound from the Toy group.

The judge, Mrs. Lorraine Waterman from Richmond, Indiana entered the ring and took her position in the center. She looked down the line of stacked dogs and signaled for the go around. Nancy Bullis checked to make sure all the handlers were ready and then led them off, circling the big ring once before coming back to everyone's starting positions.

The individual inspections started with the Afghan and while they were going on, handlers kept their dogs stacked and attentive. Cole had stacked himself so perfectly that Emma barely had to touch him. They moved up as each dog went out to the center of the ring and each time the most Emma had to do was make sure Cole didn't have drool hanging off his mouth. When it was their turn, Cole pranced out to center ring and set his feet. Emma checked all four and didn't have to move a one. His head came up and while he stood there in all his glory, Emma dropped the lead and stepped back, giving him center stage. The judge, after giving him a thorough look from a few feet away, moved in and went over him. Coming back to his head and looking into his eyes, she smiled, stroked his muzzle, and asked Emma to do the down and back.

Emma gathered the lead, lightly chucked Cole under his chin, and they were off and moving effortlessly down the sideline. They made the turn and started back, their rhythm unbroken. As they neared the judge, Emma swung to the right, pulled up, and stopped. At the same time, it seemed like Cole was in the air one minute and then down on all four feet simultaneously the next. He was perfectly stacked, his head up, and his eyes daring the judge to find something better than that! Mrs. Waterman had no choice but to chuckle in appreciation for their performance as she signaled for the go around. When Emma and Cole took off, her eyes never left them until they were back in line.

When all the examinations had been completed, the dogs were moved out from under the tent and put into their stacks. The judge moved down the line, looking one more time at each entry. Her face was now devoid of expression, giving nothing away as to who was to be her choice for Best In Show. She had the handlers take the dogs around once more, the bystanders breaking into a round of applause. When they were back in line and being restacked, Mrs. Waterman went to the judge's table and marked her book. She came out to center ring, once again with her ring steward and the Show Chairman of the Conewango Valley Kennel Club, which had sponsored the two-day show. Armed with the Best In Show booty, she lost no time in pointing to Emma and announcing, "The Newfoundland!"

Emma about died on the spot she was so stunned. She'd thought for sure that Nancy was going to take it again. Holy shit! It took her a minute, but she finally moved, even if it was just to turn her head and stare blankly at the handlers coming over to congratulate her. Somewhere in her muddled brain she recognized Joanie and Sally's ear-splitting screams and knew then that it must be for real. If nothing else, they were good for getting a near comatose person to come out of it. Emma blinked and looked at Cole. That's all he was waiting for. He jumped up and wiggled and waggled and about knocked her over. He knew they'd done it and started to bark with exuberant abandon.

The judge came over to present the awards and Emma calmed Cole enough so that Mrs. Waterman wouldn't go flying with a shove from the excited Newf. After the picture taking was completed, the judge told Emma what an impressive dog she had and confided that it was his free stack and the look he gave her that decided her choice. "He was quite bold actually. He just stood there and dared me."

"Yes, I know," Emma said. "He demands his due."

"He most certainly does and, believe me, he deserves every bit of it. Good luck to you both."

"Thank you, Mrs. Waterman."

Emma left the ring and approached her friends with trepidation. God only knew what they'd do, but Ben beat them to it and enfolded her into a very big hug.

"Congratulations, Em. You were great in there."

"Thanks, Ben, but it was all Cole. He's such a showman."

"He was fantastic, but don't try and tell me that you didn't have anything to do with it. I have eyes. I could see how you handled him in there. I certainly couldn't have done it."

The discussion was cut short when Joanie slammed into Emma's back, her arm going around her neck in a tight hug. "Hot damn, Emma, you did it again!"

Emma was laughing now, and between that and Joanie's arm around her neck choking her, she couldn't answer. Sally, who'd been petting Cole up, pulled Joanie's arm away and in the process hit Emma in the nose. The hit was hard enough to make her eyes water and Emma hoped that a bloody nose wasn't to follow. Cripe, these two were a disaster waiting to happen. Both Sam and Richard slipped behind their women, grabbed them around their waists, and pulled them back.

"Hey!" Joanie protested.

"Joanie, give Emma a little breathing room, will you?"

"You too, Sally. You're close to killing the poor woman."

"She needs to be hugged. We've got to hug her." Joanie was struggling to get away from Sam.

"You've already hugged her and just about choked her to death in the process. Ease up."

"This is the last time you're coming to a show, Sam Davis. You don't understand how we do things."

"Yeah, let me go, Richard."

"Not on your life. You about took poor Emma's nose off. You've got to calm down."

"Calm this," Sally said and flipped him the bird. Lord, Joanie was rubbing off on everybody!

Everyone was laughing then and the men eventually released their grips. Sufficiently calmed now, Sally and Joanie hugged Emma without causing injury. But once they started chattering, the excitement level went back up.

"Three Best In Shows! You've got three Best In Shows. Holy shit!" Joanie was waving her arms excitedly and Emma backed up a little. No telling if those arms were going to stay under control.

"I was struck dumb when the judge pointed to me. I couldn't believe it. I thought Nancy was going to take it."

"No. If you could have watched from outside the ring, there was no contest. Cole had it hands down. He blew everybody away. That free stack of his is a killer."

"Em, four times out and you've got three, count them three, Best In Shows. Unbelievable!" Sally was getting worked up; she was starting to pace. The men were getting nervous; they could feel the tension building.

"Yep, it's unbelievable all right. I never in a million years thought this would happen. But I'm…" Emma was cut off when Connie came rushing up.

"Wow! Congratulations again! You two are really something."

"Thanks, Mary."

"This certainly made the trip down here worthwhile. You and Cole were just great."

"I'm glad we were able to put on a good show, but with Cole it's really very easy. He does all the work; I just kind of tag along."

"I don't believe that for a minute. You're both very good at what you do."

"Well, thanks."

"I have to get going now, but I just wanted to congratulate you on your win before I left. I'll see you at the store soon."

"I'm glad you could make it down and we'll look forward to seeing you at the shop. Take care driving back."

"I will and you do the same. Bye everyone."

Amidst a chorus of goodbyes, Connie left and the group walked back to the motor home. The girls let the dogs play long enough to get themselves back into Tank's good graces and then they broke camp and loaded up. With the extra help provided by masculine muscle, it took no time at all before they were cruising down the road on their way home. The motor home took the lead and the men followed close behind in Ben's Jeep.

When they got back to the Hearthmoor, everybody took part in unloading the motor home and Ben's Jeep. Then they reloaded the Jeep with Emma's gear and Joanie's truck with her and Sam's stuff. Richard's car was also there, so they helped put his things into it and then they all brought Sally's paraphernalia in. When all that was done, they washed up in their respective bathrooms and got a table in the barroom; the dogs came right along with them.

Sitting around the table, the dogs at their feet, Emma and Joanie relaxed while the men went to the bar and ordered their drinks. Sally slipped into the kitchen to make sure all was running smoothly there. At about the same time as the drinks were being brought to the table, Sally reemerged from the kitchen and joined them.

"Everything okay?" Emma asked as Sally sat down.

"Looks like it. Sharon said everything ran like clockwork while we were at the show."

"Is Tom okay?"

"Yep, by Friday morning he was fine. Must have been something he ate didn't agree with him."

"That's good. I hope the shop ran well," Joan
already back to thinking about the kiss of dea
gave inventory. That thought prompted her next requ
"Can I have another glass of wine?"

"You're not through with the one in front of you."

"It'll be gone in a minute. I'm in dire need of fortifying.
I just remembered I've got a rough day in front of me
tomorrow. Right, Em?"

"More than likely. Thankfully Tammy only worked on
Friday."

"That's more than enough and you know it."

"You're right. If she was busy, it'll take us all day to
figure everything out."

"Sam? You're driving home, right?"

"Looks that way."

"All right, bring on the wine then." Sally motioned to
Hank at the bar and he brought over the bottle, placing it in
front of Joanie.

"Ahh, Hank. What would I do without you? You are
truly a prince among men."

The entire table rolled their eyes, but Hank only smiled
as he went back behind the bar. Hank knew the girls well
enough to appreciate their wackiness and got a kick out
of their sometimes-offbeat humor. They made the job fun
whenever they were around, that was for damn sure.

The group put in their dinner order and when it came
shortly thereafter, they dug in with gusto. Everyone
started with crisp, green salads and various dressings, and
then went on to mouth-watering, juicy, grilled burgers,
smothered in thick slices of melted provolone cheese,
sautéed mushrooms, lettuce, tomato and mayo, all layered
on lightly toasted sourdough rolls. Accompanying these
quarter pound delights were French fries made fresh from
real potatoes, which half the group drenched in ketchup and
the other half sprinkled with vinegar. Both halves agreed

on the salt- lots of it. They finished off with chocolate chip pie and ice cream for dessert and for those who wanted it, coffee and tea.

Conversation came to a gradual standstill; fatigue was catching up with everybody, dogs included. In fact they'd already been snoozing while their people talked and ate. Even the smell of food wasn't enough to rouse them out of their restful slumber. It had been a full two days and it was time to bring it to a close. Good nights were said and everyone left except for Sally, who still had to put her restaurant to bed before she could get into hers.

Out in the parking lot Richard left first and then the Davises pulled out with Ben and Emma the last to leave. The ride home was blessedly short and when Ben and Emma reached her house, they wasted no time unloading her things. Once Cole's bathroom needs had been met and he was in for the night and the house was deemed secure, Ben gave Emma a long kiss goodnight and said he'd see her on Sunday at the shop. Reminding her to lock the door after he left, he went out to the Jeep and drove the short distance to his apartment.

Emma didn't bother to unpack a thing; she simply moved everything to the side and out of her way. She fed Cole, got done in the bathroom, changed into her jammies, and slipped into bed. It took only minutes for her to fall into a deep sleep, untroubled by worries or disturbing thoughts. For the moment, she was at peace, blissfully unaware of what tomorrow would bring.

* * * *

Cappellini was on his lower deck enjoying the early summer night; his excitement was palpable, but controlled. He had just gotten off the phone with Bill Thornton and knew that Cole had taken two Group One's and one Best In Show at the Stockton shows. God, the dog was simply amazing, he thought, and by this time tomorrow, he'd be his!

Everything was in place; there'd be no screw-ups this time, not with Wilhelm directing the operation. On this end, he'd taken his own precautions to make sure everything went according to plan. He'd had Dr. Morgan put more or less under house arrest at the farm; he'd had to make sure that the good doctor had absolutely no opportunity to indulge in drink before he was needed to do his part. Morgan had to be completely sober and steady to do his job effectively and Cappellini certainly wasn't going to leave that to chance.

The farm personnel were always at the ready to do his bidding, so no problem there. All the arrangements that had needed to be made were taken care of and the only thing that had to happen now was the arrival of their special guest.

Cappellini was going to the farm immediately after he received a phone call from Wilhelm confirming that he had the dog. He wanted to be the first to welcome Cole to his new home, even though the dog would more than likely be unconscious. It didn't matter; he would still savor the victorious moment of taking possession of that exquisite animal. God, he could almost taste it. He was going to win again!

He reached for his glass and raised it in salute. "To the loser, Mrs. Rogers. You never really stood a chance." He broke into a hearty laugh before he raised the glass to his lips and took a healthy drink, his eyes gleaming maliciously.

Chapter Thirty-Six

It was raining and cold, only about fifty degrees. The skies were a leaden gray, the rain was coming down in sheets and to top it off the wind was gusting to near twenty miles an hour. A perfect Sunday it wasn't.

It would have been nice if the rain was one of those delightful, warm, gentle sprinkles that make you want to don your rain gear and get out there and enjoy it, especially since Emma was kind of in the mood for a walk in the woods. But no, this was a steady, heavy downpour that would swell the creeks and streams with amazing speed, and transform them from trickling brooks to raging white-water rapids.

It was a good thing that Emma and Cole were taking the day off from roading. It was one of the perks they deserved for taking another Best In Show. It would have been a miserable day to be out there and God knows Joanie would have been a complete bitch about it. Emma's ears burned just thinking about what would have come out of her friend's mouth had they been out in this deluge.

So instead of braving the elements, Emma was going to enjoy a languid morning within the confines of her house until it was time to go to the shop. She'd already exercised, eaten her breakfast, and indulged in a long, soaking, relaxing bath, an added treat since it wasn't even Monday. Afterward, she'd leisurely unpacked her things from the show and started some laundry. There wasn't much to straighten in the house, so now she'd slipped some country music CDs into the player and had taken a seat in her favorite wing-backed chair, ready to start a new mystery novel.

Cole was content to follow Emma's lead and other than to go outside to relieve himself, which he did rather quickly in the inclement weather, he was most agreeable to laying around and being lazy. He'd give "Froggy" a few tosses every so often, but for the most part he was satisfied to stretch out and doze, happily chasing balls only in his dreams. In other words, they were both being slugs and enjoying every minute of it.

* * * *

The four men were in place; they had been since four o'clock that morning. They'd come in from the back of the property, leaving the two-man ATV's at the boundary of the state land that bordered Emma's woods. They'd come the rest of the way on foot, quietly and stealthily, managing not to snap so much as a twig as they took up positions in the copse across from Emma's front door. They wore camouflage clothing and were all but invisible nestled in as they were among the trees and low bushes. They were waiting now for the right opportunity, which they knew would come at some point that morning. The rain was a bit of a bother, but they'd been trained to stoically endure all conditions when on an assignment. Besides, three of the men knew that the big German in charge wouldn't take kindly to complaints.

And so, they waited in silence; their clothing offering them their only protection against the elements. Occasionally, one of them would become bored with watching the house and would instead let his attention drift idly to the rain running off the waterproof tarp at their feet, the one that concealed the two rifles that lay beneath it.

* * * *

Of course, their lackadaisical respite had to end, so about 11:00 Emma got ready to go to work. She thought it just might help if she got there a little earlier than Joanie so she could look over Tammy's receipts and possibly decipher at least a few of them. Plus, she had to make sure that the staple gun and other small tools that could be a danger to herself, Joanie, or the customers were hidden. She'd asked Jackie to do it on Saturday, and although she was sure that Jackie had, she'd feel safer if she checked for herself before the maniac got there. The woman went a little crazy when she got into Tammy's receipts and Emma didn't want anybody accidentally injured when Joanie morphed into her dark side. She'd better take down a bottle of wine too; she wasn't sure how much was at the shop, and Lord help them all if they ran out.

So after bundling herself up in a rain jacket, a baseball-style cap, and lightweight hiking boots, Emma was ready to face the elements. Armed with a bottle of the god's favorite nectar, well, Joanie's anyway, Emma and Cole left the cozy, dry interior of their house and ventured out into the wet and windy weather that would be their habitat as they walked down to the shop.

* * * *

Wilhelm was the first to see the front door open; his attention had never faltered, not even once since four o'clock that morning. The men with him had thought that he was almost in a trance, so complete was his concentration. He hand signaled to the others and the rifles were brought out. They gave him the twenty-two-caliber gun first and he

407

eased it into position, aiming the rifle in the direction that Emma would be walking.

*   *   *   *

They were about seventy-five feet from the house when Cole stopped dead in his tracks. Emma, distracted by thoughts of inventory and placating Joanie, went on for a few more feet before she realized that Cole wasn't with her. She stopped and looked back; ready to tell him to catch up when she froze, a cold shiver going down her spine. She knew in that instant that they were there. The watchers were in *her* woods!

Cole's hair down the center of his back was standing on end and a low, but steady growl was coming from his throat. Suddenly, he moved very quickly and got in front of Emma as if to block her. He pushed against her legs to move her back toward the house and turned her slightly. It was at that moment that she heard the shot and in what seemed like a second later felt the searing pain. It brought her to her knees as she clutched the left side of her chest, the bottle of wine she had held in her right hand falling to the ground. Emma brought her hand away and as if she were outside of her body looking on, stared at her bloody palm as rain mixed with the bright red, vital fluid.

She felt herself falling, the wet ground coming up to meet her back; her vision blurring, she was only half aware that Cole was straddling her body trying to protect her. She thought she heard him cry out and tried to call his name, but her voice sounded like it was coming from a great distance away. Cole hovered over her, his head resting lightly on her right shoulder; his tongue licked her face once. Emma couldn't move, not even to lift her hand to pat Cole's side to reassure him; the pain in her shoulder and the loss of blood had left her in an almost paralyzed state. She knew she was drifting in and out, unsure of what was real and what wasn't. It seemed like hours had passed before she felt a crushing weight drop onto her body and she fell into total blackness.

* * * *

As soon as Emma had gone down and Cole had moved over her to protect her with his body, Wilhelm had switched rifles and shot a tranquilizing dart into the stationary dog. In what Emma thought was hours, but was really only a matter of minutes, the drug took effect and Cole collapsed on top of her.

The instant Cole dropped, as unconscious now as Emma, the four men acted quickly. Three of them sprang from the spot where they had hidden all morning and rushed toward the inert pair. Wilhelm and one of the other men dragged Cole off Emma and rolled him onto a sling that the third man had layed out on the ground. At Wilhelm's signal, they picked him up and, on the run, started carrying him to the back of the property where the ATVs were waiting. The man that had stayed behind in the area where they had taken up their surveillance, packed up the rifles, picked up the spent shell, and erased all evidence of them ever having been there. Joining the man who had layed out the sling, they sanitized the area around Emma and obliterated their tracks as they followed the same path that Wilhelm had taken.

Once the men reached the ATVs, they secured Cole to the back of one of the vehicles where gear would normally be carried. The rifles were secured on the other machine and the four men hopped into their seats and took off, going through the state land to the road where they had left their SUVs and attached trailers. Upon arriving there, they first put Cole and the rifles into the back of one of the SUVs and then loaded the vehicles onto the trailers.

The cars pulled out; the entire operation, from the time Wilhelm had shot the twenty-two to now, had taken only twenty-three minutes. Cole was on his way to Connecticut.

Chapter Thirty-Seven

Joanie had been busy since she'd put the key in the lock to open up. Cripes, there'd been customers waiting in the parking lot when she'd arrived and she'd barely gotten the lights on when they'd started coming through the door. In a way it was a blessing; she hadn't had time to even think about the receipts from hell.

But now that the first onslaught of customers had petered out, she realized as she looked at the clock, registering that it said 12:42, that Emma wasn't there yet. Where the hell was she and why hadn't she called if she was going to be late? This wasn't at all her usual modus operandi; Joanie wondered if something had happened or if she'd just gotten involved in something and had lost track of time. Well, whatever it was, it was time to find out where she was and get her butt down there.

Joanie picked up the phone and dialed Emma's number just as Mrs. Foster came in. She listened to the phone ring repeatedly while greeting one of their favorite customers. "Hey, Mrs. Foster, good to see you."

"It's nice to see you too, Joanie. How are you?"

"Oh, I'm good. And you?" Joanie replaced the receiver after the answering machine picked up; the concern she felt obviously showing on her face.

"I'm feeling very well, thank you. Is something wrong, Joan? You look worried and where's Emma and Cole today?"

"That's what I'm worried about. They should be here by now and I just called up to the house and there's no answer. The machine picked up. Emma always lets me know if she's going to be late and I haven't heard a word."

"Maybe she's on her way down right this minute."

"Yeah, maybe, but she still should have called."

"It's possible she just forgot, isn't it?"

"Yeah, but to tell you the truth, Emma doesn't forget things like that. I don't know, maybe I'd better go up and check, just to make sure everything's okay. I've got a funny feeling; too much crazy stuff's been going on. Remind me to tell you the latest, but right now could you do me a big favor and watch the shop 'til I get back?"

"Why certainly, dear. You go right ahead and check on Emma. I'll just come behind the counter and watch things for you. I think I even remember how to use a cash register."

"Thanks, Mrs. Foster, you're a doll. I'll be gone probably no longer than ten minutes, okay?"

"That'll be fine, Joanie. Don't worry about me; I'll keep things under control. You go on now."

"Okay, if you're sure."

"I'm sure. Go. I'll be fine."

Shifting her gaze over to where Tank was standing, Joanie directed her next remarks to him. "Tank, you behave yourself and stay here with Mrs. Foster. Be good and don't be a wise guy." Tank gave her an innocent look that asked, "Who me?" and Joanie gave him a look right back that said, "You bet your sweet ass, you."

With one more meaningful look delivered to emphasize she was on to him, Joanie hurried to get her jacket and hat.

Putting them on, she gave Tank one last "be good" before she walked out the door.

The rain smacked her square in the face once she stepped off the porch and turned to go through the parking lot and up Emma's road; Joanie lowered the brim of her hat and hunched her shoulders up reflexively. Eyes downcast to watch for puddles and hopefully alert enough to avoid the biggest ones, she trudged up the hill.

Joanie had just reached the top of the incline and rounded the bend when she saw Emma lying in the road. "Emma! Oh, my God! Emma!" She screamed, running now to close the distance between them. Going down on her knees when she reached her, she tried desperately to get some response from her friend. There was none; Emma lay unconscious; the only sound the rain continuing to fall as it had been all morning.

"Emma! Oh, God! What happened? Emma? Can you hear me? Emma! Oh, Jesus!" Joanie had been concentrating so hard on Emma's face while she tried to elicit some kind of response that she hadn't looked any further, but now her eyes drifted downward and she saw the blood staining Emma's red jacket.

"Oh shit! Oh shit! Emma! Oh, my God!" Joanie looked closer and gently probed the fabric, shrieking when she saw the hole the bullet had made.

"Oh, my God! You've been shot! Holy shit! Somebody shot you! Oh, Jesus! What do I do? What do I do? Oh, God! Oh, God! I've got to get help. Em, I've got to get some help. Don't worry; everything's going to be all right. Don't worry; you're going to be fine. You hear me? Listen to me, Em. You're going to be fine."

Joanie choked out the last words between sobs and pulled off her raincoat, gently placing it over Emma. "Em, I've got to go and get help, but I'll be back. I'll be back in a few minutes. Oh, Jesus, Em! I have to go, but I'll be back, I promise, I'll be back."

Joanie got to her feet, reluctant to leave her friend. But knowing she had to get help, she turned away. She took a few steps, then hurriedly came back and gave Emma a quick kiss on her cheek. With her vision blurred from the tears pouring from her eyes she took off down the road, her feet flying over the gravel.

*   *   *   *

When Ben entered the shop he was surprised to find the elderly, well-dressed woman behind the counter. As he approached her, he wondered where the girls were.

"Hi, I'm Ben Sievers. I was looking for Emma. Would you know where she is?"

"Oh, Ben. Hello. I'm Mrs. Foster, a friend of the girls. I'm watching the shop while Joanie went to check on Emma."

"Check on Emma?"

"Yes, she didn't come down to the shop and didn't call to let Joanie know that she'd be late, which I guess is very unlike her. So Joanie went up to the house to see if everything was all right."

A small prickle of fear stabbed Ben's heart as all kinds of possibilities ran through his mind. He was just about to pose another question to Mrs. Foster when the front door banged open with such force that it hit the wall. Joanie, soaking wet, water streaming off her clothes, ran in shouting, "Call 911! Call 911! Hurry!" By then she was at the counter and grabbed the phone, Ben and Mrs. Foster temporarily frozen in place by her wild appearance.

Joanie punched in the numbers and at the same time, said to no one in particular, "It's Emma. She's been hurt. I think she's been…" She broke off as the dispatcher came on the line and Joanie told her that she needed the police and an ambulance, her friend had been shot.

414

Freed from his momentary paralysis by those words, Ben grabbed Joanie by the arms and shook her to get her attention. "Where is she?"

"On the road at the top of the hill. Ben, she…"

Ben didn't wait to hear anymore; he tore out of the shop and up the road with speed that he didn't know he possessed anymore. He saw Emma as soon as he made the turn. He rushed to her side and kneeling, felt for a pulse. It was there, but weak. He lifted Joanie's raincoat and saw the bullet hole and blood. He lifted Emma slightly off the ground and felt her back. There was no exit wound; the bullet was still in her body. He quickly took off his jacket and then his shirt. Clad only in his tee shirt now, he rolled up his jacket and put it under Emma's head. Then he pressed his balled-up shirt over the wound, hoping to staunch the flow of blood. God, she was pale. How long had she been out there?

Joanie was ninety seconds behind Ben. After finishing with the 911 dispatcher, she'd asked Mrs. Foster to call Sam and Sally, and then fled out the door running back to where Emma was. When she got close to Emma and Ben, she slid on her knees like she was coming into home plate to reach Emma's side. She took Emma's hand in her own. She wasn't letting go, no matter what! If Emma reached any level of consciousness, she wanted her to know right away that she was there.

"Emma, can you hear me? It's Ben. It's going to be all right. Help is on the way." He could hear the sirens in the distance; they'd be there in a matter of minutes. Please God, he prayed, let them come in time. Ben touched Emma's cheek and her eyelids fluttered. "Emma, I'm here, Joanie's here. It's going to be okay."

"Cole…" She whispered before sinking back into darkness.

*   *   *   *

415

Two sheriff's cars arrived stopping in the driveway just a few feet from where Emma lay. Deputy Sheriff O'Connor was in one of the vehicles. The two policemen exited their cars and first checked with Ben and Joanie on Emma's condition. Then they quickly searched the area. Finding nothing in the form of armed intruders, they radioed the volunteer firemen, who'd been instructed to wait in the parking lot until the scene was secured, to send the ambulance and EMTs up. The rescue truck and its crew would stay below and help to keep traffic flowing.

While the EMTs administered to Emma, Joanie and Ben were forced to stand off to the side. Joanie was none too happy, having been loath to give up her hold on her friend. Ben assured her that Emma was in good hands, but that didn't prevent him from watching their every move. One of the EMTs used his radio to call down to the firemen stationed at the shop and Joanie heard them call for Mercy Flight, the medical helicopter that would take Emma to the hospital.

"Oh, my God! They have to Mercy Flight her?" Joanie was hovering on the edge of panic.

"Joanie, calm down. They'll take her to ECMC because of the gunshot. You know that's the best hospital for her to go to. They just want to get her there quickly. It's going to be all right." Deputy O'Connor put his arm around her shoulders and gave her a little squeeze. ECMC was short for Erie County Medical Center and it had the best trauma center in Western New York.

"I know, I know. It's just that this is all so unbelievable. I can't believe she's been shot."

"I know. It's a shock, but you've got to believe that everything's going to be all right. Come on, I've known you a long time and you're made of sterner stuff than this. You can handle it."

"I guess."

"None of this 'I guess' stuff. I know you can. Besides, Emma is going to need you to be strong."

"Okay, okay, you're right. I can do this."

"Did she say anything, anything at all?" Deputy O'Connor looked from Ben to Joanie, his eyes full of questions that he didn't have any answers to.

"The only thing she said was... 'Cole'," Ben looked at Joanie, the realization of the missing dog finally breaking through their shock and scrambled thoughts. "Where the hell is he?"

"Oh, God, I don't know." Joanie looked like she'd been poleaxed. "He wasn't here when I found her, but...but... it didn't sink in. I was so worried about Emma, that he never entered my head. Oh, my God! He would never leave her! Never!"

The medical personnel had Emma on a collapsible gurney now and were putting her into the ambulance. The firemen had called for Mercy Flight and then had gone over to the ski resort about a mile down the road and made sure everything was set for the helicopter to land in it's large parking lot. With lights flashing and siren going, the ambulance backed down Emma's driveway, turning around in the shop parking lot, and then raced down the road to Kissing Bridge. It seemed like they had no sooner arrived than the sound of rotor blades slicing the air could be heard overhead. When the helicopter landed, they quickly transferred Emma to the care of the chopper's EMTs; within minutes Mercy Flight was back in the air and headed for ECMC.

Chapter Thirty-Eight

The helicopter, after the short trip from Glenwood, landed on the roof of ECMC and was met by two nurses and a security officer from the hospital. When the hospital is very busy with incoming flights, the helicopters also land in a cordoned-off area of the institution's parking lot and are met there by an ambulance under contract to the medical center, which takes the patient to the emergency room. It looked like today was a slow day.

The Mercy Flight EMTs brought Emma over to where the hospitals personnel were waiting and they all took the service elevator down to the emergency room where the EMTs handed her care over to the ER medical team. She was quickly transferred to the trauma unit where the doctors soon hustled her off to an operating room where surgery would be performed to remove the bullet and repair the damage it had caused.

One of the reasons this unit was so good, other than the fact that the doctors who staffed the teams were each highly proficient in their field, was that the trauma center was self-contained. The examination, x-ray, surgical, recovery rooms and labs were within feet of each other. No time was lost transferring patients to other areas of the hospital for necessary services; precious minutes and seconds were saved and therefore many lives. It was known to be the best in trauma care and lived up to its reputation every day. Emma couldn't have been in a better place.

* * * *

The four friends were on their way to ECMC; it was going to take them a little longer to get there than it had Mercy Flight since the hospital was located on the east side of Buffalo. Ben was driving; Joanie, Sam and Sally were his passengers.

Sally had called Emma's daughter from the shop and she and her husband were on their way to the medical facility, too. Mandie had said that she would call her siblings, Mack and Tracy, and Sally was certain the out-of-towners would be there as soon as they could get a flight out of Bradley International Airport in Connecticut.

Once Joanie had informed Sally that Cole was missing, she'd made a call to dog people in Springville, explained what had happened and asked for a search to be organized to look for the Newfoundland. She was assured that it would be coordinated and set in motion within a few hours.

Mrs. Foster had taken care of closing the shop and locking up. After that, she'd driven Tank home and left him in the care of Joanie's two sons. Upon arriving at her own house she was going to man the phones and call up every one she knew who frequented the shop and get volunteers lined up to help out in any way that was needed in the days ahead.

Meanwhile, the sheriff's department was treating the whole of Emma's property as a crime scene and yellow police tape had been strung from tree to tree. The crime scene investigators had been called in and the grounds were being thoroughly searched for evidence even as the four sped down the highway.

* * * *

When the friends arrived at the hospital, Mandie and Rob were already there, pacing in one of the private waiting rooms provided in the trauma center for members of the family. Emma was still in surgery and would be for a while yet according to the latest report.

Mandie and Rob were, of course, full of questions and Joanie and Ben tried their best to answer them. This was, for any of Emma's family, their first contact with Ben and introductions were made somewhat belatedly, what with the more pressing issues at hand. Nevertheless, there was instant rapport amongst them and Ben was accepted unconditionally. Of course, he was still going to have to pass the "Mack" test.

While they waited, all the recent events were rehashed and speculation arose as to how everything was connected. Mandie and Rob knew nothing of the previous threats or injuries and were dumbfounded that they'd been kept in the dark.

"I can't believe Mom kept all of this from us." Mandie was more than a little upset. "Why'd she do that, Joanie? And for that matter, why didn't you or Sally let me know what was going on? I can't believe this."

Sally jumped in, willing to take the brunt of Mandie's anger. "Mandie, she obviously didn't want to worry you and it was her call. After your mom got hurt at the park, Joanie thought about letting you know, but felt it was Emma's decision and she apparently decided to keep it from you. In retrospect, maybe we all should have done some things differently, although I honestly don't know what more we could have done."

"Geez…sorry guys. I didn't mean to jump all over you; I'm just so upset. I know how Mom can be. She's always tried to protect us. But does anybody have any idea who's behind this or why?"

Nobody said anything for a minute or two and then Ben, hesitating only a little, spoke up. "Maybe because I'm somewhat removed from the dog scene, I can see things a little clearer, but I think the whole thing has to do with Cole. I don't know who the person or persons are, but I think somebody wanted him, Emma got in the way, and they had to get rid of her to get him. I mean look at everything that's happened. If you think about it, you'll see the connection and like Joanie said, Cole would never leave Emma, especially if she was hurt. Somebody took him and unless he managed to break away, I doubt that we're going to find him."

When the truth of what Ben suggested had sunk in, there was very little left to talk about. An oppressive silence filled the room, each one of them knowing how the loss of Cole was going to affect Emma. She was going to be, in one word, devastated.

There was the sound of rustling footsteps in the hallway and they all turned expectantly toward the doorway. The doctor, garbed in his surgical scrubs, entered the room and sought out Mandie. With a smile brightening his haggard face, he told her that Emma had made it through the operation in fine shape; the bullet had been removed and they'd repaired the damage. Nothing vital had been struck, but she had lost a lot of blood and was very weak. He emphasized that a full recovery was expected and barring any complications, she'd be able to go home in four or five days. She was in the recovery room right now and still sedated, but members of the family would be permitted to go in for five minutes.

Everyone breathed a sigh of relief and rose from their chairs, a lot of quick hugging going on. Then they turned as one to go and see Emma.

"These are all family members?" the doctor asked.

"Yep," Mandie smiled as she looked at each of her mother's friends, "every last one of them."

"Okay, but only five minutes, all right? The nurse will take you down."

"Thank you, doctor. Thanks so much for everything."

The doctor directed them to where a nurse was waiting, and she took them into the recovery room. Emma was the only patient in there and she looked very small in the white, sterile bed. Her face was almost as white as the sheet and blanket that covered her and her left arm had been put into a sling, its bright blue color in sharp contrast to the achromaticity of the surrounding environment.

Mandie and Rob stepped forward first to give Emma's cheek a kiss and murmur words of love and support while tears flowed down Mandie's face. When they moved back from the bed, each of Emma's friends took their turn and all came away if not with actual tears trickling, then at least with eyes that were overly bright and water-filled. The five minutes ticked away at astonishing speed and they had to leave. The nurse told them that Emma would likely be there another hour or two before she'd be in her own room on the seventh floor, so why didn't they go and get something to eat while they waited. They all realized they were starving now that the danger had passed, and so they went down to the cafeteria, each of them feeling like the weight of the world had been lifted from their shoulders.

* * * *

Wilhelm was making good time. He was on the New York State Thruway passing Syracuse, headed toward Connecticut. Cole was sleeping in a crate in the back of the van and except for the hassle of getting the unconscious dog into the crate, he hadn't been any trouble. Even with help from Jasper's men, lifting and maneuvering the dead weight of a 150-pound dog hadn't been an easy task.

After they'd snatched Cole and driven to a secluded area near Springville, Cole had been transferred into the crate, which was inside a waiting custom Chevy van. With his few personal effects and the injections he might need already in the vehicle, Wilhelm had immediately taken off.

Jasper's crew, including Connie, had been left to return the trailers and ATVs that they'd rented under assumed names. The two rifles had been smashed into pieces and the barrels cut into thirds. Their parts were divided and wrapped in fast food bags to be dumped in garbage receptacles at numerous rest stops along the way. They'd checked out of the hotel and packed their belongings in the cars the night before, so after making a switch in license plates on the SUVs, they were ready to hop on the 219 Expressway that would merge with the Thruway and make good their getaway. They were only an hour and twenty minutes behind Wilhelm.

* * * *

Emma woke up in recovery feeling like she'd been run over by a truck. Nevertheless, she was very thankful to be waking up at all. She remembered little, but the agonizing pain when the bullet had struck had not diminished in memory. She was still terribly groggy, but aware enough to know that the nurse was checking her vital signs and giving the okay to move her to a regular room.

It seemed like only five minutes had passed after she was settled into her new bed when Mandie, Rob, Joanie, Sam, Sally and Ben descended upon her. God, she was happy to see them! "Hey," she whispered weakly to no one in particular but encompassing every last one of them.

"Hey, yourself, Mom. You gave us all quite a scare. How you feeling?" Mandie had moved to the side of the bed and was holding Emma's right hand, giving it a little squeeze.

"I'm...fine." Emma's eyes were at half-mast, her speech sluggish. "They've...got me...on...some pretty good…stuff…for pain… Joanie…you'd like it." Everybody snickered at that.

"Do you need anything, Mom?"

"No…going…to sleep…now." Emma's eyes closed and they thought she was sinking into slumber, but her eyes partially opened for a second and she softly breathed one word before she drifted off, "Cole".

"Oh, God. It's going to be bad when she finds out," Joanie whispered.

"Let's not even go there right now," Sally suggested. "Let's just get her well and we'll deal with the Cole thing after that."

Three of her friends gave Emma a kiss somewhere on her face, be it forehead or cheek with Ben choosing to leave his gentle caress on her lips. As he lifted his head and started to move away, he watched Emma's mouth curve into a little smile and he was helpless to prevent his own mouth from doing the same. When he left her bedside, his eyes were sparkling with an inner glow.

They went out to the waiting room then, leaving Mandie and Rob with Emma. The six of them had decided during lunch that they'd take turns sitting with Emma through this first night. Nobody was leaving and Lord help anybody who thought differently.

* * * *

At about the same time that Mack and Tracy were arriving at the hospital, coming directly there from the Buffalo airport, Wilhelm was pulling into the driveway at the farm. He'd had to stop once for gas and after checking on Cole and seeing that he was beginning to stir, had given him an injection to keep him lightly sedated.

Now as he came to a stop in front of the barn, Cappellini stepped out and stood waiting for Wilhelm to get out of the vehicle. The two men shook hands briefly and Wilhelm led Cappellini to the back of the van and opened the doors. There, sleeping peacefully, was the object of his obsession. His face broke into one of his rare, sincere smiles and he clapped Wilhelm on the back.

"Congratulations, Wilhelm. I knew I could count on you to get the job done."

"It was again my pleasure, Mr. Cappellini. All went well and according to plan."

"Good, very good." His eyes hadn't strayed from Cole since the doors had been opened, and now he reached out a hand to stroke his coat through the wires of the crate. "He's magnificent, don't you think?"

"Yes, sir. He's a gorgeous animal. You will achieve great things with him, yes?"

"Oh, yes, Wilhelm, great things." Cappellini continued to admire the dog for several more moments before he motioned over the two groundskeepers who'd been waiting silently near the entrance of the barn. "Take him into the kennel. We'll let him sleep it off in the crate."

The two men moved forward and pulled the crate out of the van. Then carrying it awkwardly between them, because of its cumbersome size, they brought it into the barn. When Cappellini was sure they were beyond hearing distance, he asked one more question of Wilhelm. "The woman, Mrs. Rogers?"

"I assure you, she's no longer a problem."

"Did she know she lost? It's important to me that she knew."

Wilhelm remembered the look in Emma's eyes as she went down. "I think it's safe to say that she knew."

"Excellent. As usual you have served me well; let me express my gratitude for a job well done." Cappellini reached into the inside pocket of his jacket and withdrew a sealed envelope, handing it to Wilhelm.

"Thank you, Mr. Cappellini. I appreciate your generosity. Now I'm going to go up to the house, if you don't mind. I have an early flight in the morning and it's been a very long day."

"Of course, and since there's nothing more to be done here at the moment, I'll come up with you. A drink to celebrate?"

"Certainly, sir, if that is your wish."

"Wonderful! I've been saving a very special bottle of thirty-year-old Macallan for just such an occasion. I guarantee you're going to enjoy it. I know I will."

The two men walked toward the restored colonial in silence; the one savoring his satisfaction in the successful completion of his assignment with its just rewards held in his large hand and the other reveling in the win of yet another contest and the glory that the spoils of that conquest would bring him.

Chapter Thirty-Nine

Cole woke the next morning when the first rays of sunlight were coming through the high windows. He was disoriented; he didn't know where he was, but he was cognizant of the fact that he wasn't at home. Where was Emma? He knew she'd been hurt and that he'd tried to protect her, but what had happened then? Why wasn't he with her and how did he get to wherever he was?

Peering through the wires of the metal crate, he looked around and saw only the reflective stainless steel walls that made up the kennel run. He slowly moved his line of vision to the chain link gate at the front of the kennel and beyond that saw only an empty corridor and across the way, a vacant kennel run the same as he was in.

He heard some movement, the low throaty sound that dogs will make when they're stretching, and a few short barks. He smelled bleach, urine, feces; he smelled other dogs. He wasn't alone; more of his own kind were here, but where was here?

Footsteps were approaching and he instinctively lowered his head to rest on his paws, his eyes closed to mere slits, his body still, feigning sleep. The footsteps stopped outside his gate and then the gate was opened. A man came inside and closed the gate, looking at Cole. Cole had never seen him before and didn't know who he was. The man knelt and opened the crate. Talking in a low, soothing voice, the man slowly extended his hand and petted Cole's head. Cole opened his eyes.

"So, you're awake, are you? Would you like to get out of there? You must be a little stiff. You've been in that crate a long time. Come on, you can do it." The man rose and backed away and Cole, giving him a wary look, slowly got to his feet, his legs a little unsteady. He walked out of the crate and stood looking at the man.

"Kind of confused, huh? Well, don't worry about it; we all are sometimes. You are a beauty, that's for sure. Would you like some water? You must be hungry too. I'll be back in a minute. Stretch your legs."

The man left and closed the gate. Cole looked after him for a minute and then walked around the kennel run, once, twice, checking the perimeter. The man came back with a raised feeding platform, the dishes holding kibble and water. He put it down while he opened the gate, drew it inside, and then closed the gate. He took it to the back corner and set it down while Cole watched him guardedly, keeping a safe distance between them at all times.

"Don't blame you, boy. I wouldn't trust anybody right now either."

The man moved away from the food and went back to the gate. Cole, with one eye on the man, moved over to the water and took a long drink. Checking again on the man's position, he sniffed the kibble, but didn't eat any. He turned his head back once more to make sure the man was still at the gate and then, satisfied the man posed no immediate danger to him, he drank some more.

"Feel a little better now that you've had some water? Wish you'd eat some of that food, but I guess you're not ready for that yet, huh? I'll tell you what, boy, while you're hanging around back there, I'll just get this crate out of your way, okay? You don't have to be afraid of me, I'm not going to hurt you."

Cole, who'd been keeping an eye on the man as he spoke, continued to do so as the man pulled the crate out of the run. The man closed the gate quietly, watching Cole watch him.

"Don't worry about me, boy. We're going to be great friends. I'm Dr. Morgan and we're going to get on just fine. I've got to make a few little changes in you, but other than that, it's going to be clear sailing. You eat some of that food now. I'll be back later."

The man left and Cole prowled the run, up one side and down the other. The man hadn't made him feel any better; in fact he was more unsettled now than he had been before the man showed up.

* * * *

Emma had awakened at almost the same time Cole had. Actually she'd been dreaming about him winning another Best In Show, when the nurse came in to check her vitals and sent the dream hightailing it out of there with the abrupt, no-nonsense business of taking temperatures and blood pressure. Emma had to smile; it kind of reminded her of when Cole gave her the full body slam to wake her up. The result was the same, instant awake. The smile was short-lived though; all she had to do was look around and reality came crashing in. She was in the hospital; somebody had shot her.

She had to talk to somebody, find out what was going on, and make sure Cole was all right. There wasn't anybody in the room right now, but she'd been somewhat aware throughout the night that somebody had always been with her. One time when she had partially risen to the surface of consciousness, she thought it had been Joanie who was

431

sitting in the chair next to the bed, and then later it had been Ben; the next time, it was Mack. If she knew anything about her kids and friends, then all of them had taken a turn, even if she could only nebulously remember the three.

The door to the room opened and Joanie walked in, smiling broadly when she saw that Emma's eyes were open. "Hey, you're awake." She crossed over to the bed and gave Emma a kiss on the cheek.

"Yeah, they don't believe in letting you sleep in around here."

"Leave it to you to wake up the one and only time nobody was in here with you. I'd just stepped out for a minute to tell Sam to get me some coffee and boom, I miss the big wake-up."

"You've always had rotten luck, Joanie."

"Don't I know it? How you feeling?" Joanie moved to the chair beside the bed and sat down.

"Oh, like I've been shot."

"No shit, really feels like that, huh?"

"Joanie, you ass."

"I know, but I'm such a good one, aren't I? I come by it naturally. I mean you're going to be a good ass if you've got a really great ass, and I've got a great ass, don't I? Look, tell me that's not a great ass." Joanie was up and out of the chair, had turned around and was showing her backside to Emma, who was laughing now and that had been Joanie's goal all along. "If you were a guy, Emma, you'd be ready to jump this sweet little ass. I don't know how Sam manages to keep his hands off me for any length of time. I mean, come on, with this ass? I've been told I've got a world class ass here."

"You *are* a world class ass, Joanie."

"All the better to entertain you, my dear." Joanie sat back down on that prize winning ass, still trying to keep the conversation light. "You sound better though; I mean you're talking in regular, non-stop sentences today. Big improvement from yesterday."

"Joanie?"

"Hmm?"

"How's Cole?"

Joanie had been the obvious choice to tell Emma about Cole. She'd only hoped that she'd have more time to prepare for it, but then her partner never had been one to be very patient. Joanie knew she wasn't going to be put off any longer. Joanie inched forward on the chair, reached out and took Emma's hand, holding it tightly. "Can you tell me what you remember? Is it any clearer this morning?"

"Well, I...remember locking up the house and starting to walk with Cole down the driveway. I...I had a bottle of wine 'cause I wanted to make sure you had plenty to get you through those damn receipts." Emma laughed a little and Joanie smiled back. "I heard...a gunshot and then I felt an awful pain in my chest. I vaguely remember falling to my knees and looking at my hand. It had something on it. I guess it was...blood. Then I was on the ground and I think Cole was straddling me. The last thing I remember was a heavy weight falling on my chest."

"That must have been Cole falling on you."

"Why would he fall on me, Joanie?"

"I don't know, Em." Joanie looked away, avoiding Emma's questioning eyes.

"Joanie, look at me. What aren't you telling me? What do you know?"

There was no way to step around it now; she had to tell her. "Cole's missing, Emma."

"Missing? What do you mean, missing? He's gone?"

"Yeah, he's gone."

"But...but where?"

"We don't know. We've got search teams out looking."

Emma just stared at her, tears spilling over, rolling down her cheeks. She blinked several times trying to focus on Joanie's face, but the tears kept coming, obscuring her vision. "Do you ...do you think he was ...shot too?"

"I don't know, Em."

"Maybe... that's why... he fell on me."

"That would explain it."

Emma stared steadily at her friend, waiting for Joanie to give her something more, but there was nothing additional for Joanie to offer in way of explanation. The two locked gazes for several seconds and then in a voice firm with conviction, Emma said, "He's not dead."

"Em..."

"Don't go there, Joanie. I would know if he was dead. I would. I would feel it in here." Emma shook loose Joanie's hand and touched her heart. "He's alive, I know he is. He may be hurt, but he's alive."

"I want to believe that for your sake, Em."

"Then believe it, Joan, 'cause I know he's not dead and I'm going to find him."

"Well, you'll have lots of help there. The search parties were organized and out looking two hours after Sally called in the troops." She hesitated before adding, "They haven't found any sign of him yet though."

Emma felt her brave front beginning to crumble and asked Joanie if she could be alone for a while. Joanie understood that Emma needed some private time and got up to leave the room, telling her friend that somebody would be back with her in about half an hour. Was that enough time? Emma nodded "yes" and Joanie was out the door.

When the door swooshed shut, Emma felt a desolation that was so complete, it took her breath away. Only one other time in her life had such a feeling reached out to paralyze her with such despair and that had been when her husband had left her. As it turned out, losing him had been a blessing, the cheating bastard. But to lose Cole, well, there was no comparison. He wasn't just a great show dog; he was her friend and companion. He was somebody that Emma could always count on, no matter what. He was somebody she could tell her most private thoughts to and he wouldn't pass judgment no matter how whacked out they were. He was somebody that could make her feel better if she'd had a bad day just by licking her face. He was somebody that could make her laugh just by being who he was. He was somebody that Emma could love and trust completely without fear of betrayal.

She had to hang on to the belief that he wasn't dead, she had to. She wasn't just spouting off with Joanie about him being alive. She knew deep down that if he was dead, she'd know. She'd feel the strong connection that bound them together severed with a gut-wrenching pain. She knew she would. But, where was he? Was he hurt? If he was, was it bad? Had he been taken somewhere and if so, why? Was he wondering where she was? Why she didn't come for him?

Emma was tortured by the questions that were buzzing around in her head. She had to get some answers and find her friend, bring him home. But first, she had to get out of the hospital and to do that, she had to get strong. So with the quiet resolve that had seen her through other rough times in her life, she set her mind to do exactly that.

* * * *

By mid morning the flower arrangements and bouquets were arriving in droves. There was a steady stream of hospital aides making deliveries well into late afternoon. The room was filled to overflowing with flowers sent by relatives, friends, customers from the shop, and dog show people. It was an amazing outpouring of love and affection for Emma and she was overcome by the show of sympathy and concern.

435

She couldn't help but think how Cole would have loved this; his nose would have been doing double-time trying to take in all the different fragrances. She could picture him, looking up from the latest bud that had warranted his attention, his nose covered in pollen. He would have been happier than a pig in shit! Her eyes misted over, thinking about it and she quickly put the thought aside. She had to focus all her energies on getting well because she had a treasure hunt to go on, the treasure being her most precious friend.

Emma's phone was rarely silent what with people calling to see how she was and during visiting hours, Emma was inundated with well-wishers. There was a constant stream of visitors with people having to limit their visit to ten minutes so that everybody who'd come could get in to see her. The waiting room down the hall was serving as an on-deck staging area with Mack in charge. Leave it to him to bring order to chaos. In the room, one of Emma's children or one of her long-standing friends was always close at hand and if they saw that she was tiring, they politely but firmly scooted the visitors out the door.

* * * *

Sometime during the morning hours, when they'd been off shift from Emma's room, Mack had pulled Ben aside and put him through the wringer. Once Mack was convinced that his mother was going to be all right with no lasting impairments, his focus had switched over to the man who had entered his mother's life, at least long enough for him to conduct his inquisition. He'd been relentless with his questions, examining the older man's motives. Former FBI or not, Mack wanted to make sure Ben's intentions were on the up and up, and he'd finally been won over after an hour of interrogation that Ben thought law enforcement could take a lesson from.

Ben had assured him that he had deep feelings for Emma and only wanted to make her happy. It was at that point that Mack had given his blessing to the relationship, but along with it a veiled threat that bad things would happen if Ben hurt his mother. Ben thought they could use a man like him in the Bureau, or maybe even the Mafia.

When Ben confided to Emma what had transpired in their little tête-à-tête, she was both mortified and shocked. Who knew she'd raised such a holy terror? Now she knew how the girls must have felt when they'd introduced their intended boyfriends to the brother from hell. Heaven help us, it was a miracle they'd ever made it to the altar! What guy wanted a maniac for a brother-in-law? One of these days she was going to have to sit him down for a very long talk, not that it would change anything she was sure, but at least she could say she'd tried.

Both Mandie and Tracy attempted to commiserate with their mother when they found out how their brother had cornered Ben, but they couldn't keep a straight face and soon were laughing outright.

"Payback's a bitch, isn't it, Mom?"

"Boy, you can say that again. Who knew?"

"Just think, you have the pleasure of knowing that your son is going to be watching every move Ben makes."

"Well, he can hardly do that. Mack lives in another state, for pete's sake."

"Mom, you're such an innocent when it comes to our brother. You've got a lot to learn."

"What do you mean?"

"You'll find out."

"What do you mean by that?"

"Uh-uh. Nope, we're not saying another word. This is going to be so much fun 'cause you don't know what's coming."

"Enlighten me."

"Can't do it, Mom."

"Why not? Let's not forget I'm your mother."

"Doesn't make any difference. It's the code."

"What code?"

"The code of once you've lived through Mack's portrayal of 'Keeper of the Gate', then you're honor bound not to divulge his methods of protection. Don't worry, you'll find out all on your own."

"I can hardly wait." Emma was quickly learning of a new facet to her girls' personalities she hadn't glimpsed before; they both had a sadistic streak!

* * * *

Deputy Sheriff O'Connor stopped by in the early afternoon and questioned Emma about what she could remember. He suggested that Cole might have been scared off, but Emma told him no, Cole would never have left her. She'd said it so convincingly that the sheriff didn't doubt her when she said that she thought he'd been taken. As for a motive, nobody could come up with one.

He reported that they'd finished with the search of her property and had come up with nothing. Whoever had shot her had been extremely meticulous in not leaving any compromising evidence behind. They were however expanding the search into the state land, hoping that something would turn up there.

For what it was worth, O'Connor said that Deputy Sheriff Stone had called and reported that they'd found one of the SUVs that had been involved in the incident on Route 39. It had been located in a remote section of the county by a couple of young teenage boys out for a daylong hike. The right side and back windows were blown out, so there was no doubt that it was the right vehicle. But it had been wiped clean, the license plates gone, the VIN number destroyed, and any other type of identification removed. Even if they could somehow trace the SUV, the sheriff was convinced the trail wouldn't lead to the guilty party. These guys were professionals through and through and wouldn't have left anything to chance. But now with the escalation of this latest crime, the two sheriff's departments were working in cooperation with one another on the investigation and sharing information. Hopefully they'd see some positive results.

Chapter Forty

They'd left Cole pretty much alone for the rest of the previous day, letting him acclimate to his new surroundings. Cappellini had wanted to go and inspect his new possession up close, but Dr. Morgan had convinced him that it would be better for the dog in his agitated state to have contact with as few people as possible right now. So Dr. Morgan had been the only one to approach him with food and water, although Cole still hadn't touched a single piece of food. He had no appetite; the urge to eat was gone. He'd sniff the food and then turn away, his stomach rolling. He was much too upset to eat, trying to figure out what had happened and where his friend was. He missed Emma and wanted to be home.

That morning however, a different man came to the gate and opened it. He was taller and heavier than the other man. He had loose clothes on and he smelled like medicine. He had a kennel lead in his hand and while talking softly, approached Cole and slipped it over his head; the man let it settle around his neck. With a little tug, the lead tightened and the man led Cole out of the kennel and into another room.

Cole became instantly more guarded, his nose twitching. He knew that smell. It was the same as the veterinarian's office where Emma took him sometimes. Cole looked around. The only thing that looked familiar though was the table in the center of the room. He hadn't been in a room like this before, even though it smelled the same. Everything was shiny like the kennel run, the lights were very bright and there were a lot of machines. There were shiny instruments sitting on tray covered with a blue cloth and on another tray was some kind of a tool that had a lot of needles and a jar with something black in it.

He was still looking around when a door opened and Cole's eyes immediately focused there. Another man came in, the one who called himself Dr. Morgan. He was dressed in the same loose clothes as the other man and he motioned for the man with Cole to bring him to the table. The two men, working in unison, lifted Cole to the top of the table and laid him on its shiny, cold surface.

"It's okay, boy. You're just going to take a little nap. Remember those changes I told you I was going to make? Well, we're going to do them now, but you won't feel a thing. I am going to have to give you a little poke, but then you'll just drift off to sleep. Okay? All right, hold still now." With the other man immobilizing Cole, Dr. Morgan found a vein in Cole's front leg and injected the sedative.

As soon as Cole's eyes closed and he slumped on the table, Dr. Morgan finished preparing him for surgery and the tattooing. He'd do the surgery first while he was fresh, he didn't want to make a mistake there; Cappellini would probably kill him himself if he did.

Through the use of the state-of-the-art radiograph equipment provided by his demanding boss he located Cole's identifying microchip. The replacement chip, the one from the imported dog, was sitting in a sterile petri dish waiting to be switched with Cole's.

These microchips, no bigger than a grain of rice, were implanted with a syringe, much like getting a shot. No two chips had the same number and therefore each animal had its own unique code; they were unalterable and supposedly irretrievable. The animals and their corresponding chips were registered with a worldwide tracking system.

As far as irretrievable went, well, Morgan was proving that wrong. Between his near genius skill and Cappellini's advanced equipment, the doctor had already done it once and was about to do it a second time. He loved to perform the impossible and briefly regretted that he wouldn't be able to tell anyone about it. But compensated with the large fee that Cappellini was paying him, he could forego a little bragging.

Because of his surgical skills, Cole would be up and about with nothing more than a dull ache between his shoulder blades in about a week. He'd be a little sore on his inner leg where the tattoo was going, but that was inconsequential. Hell, he wasn't even going to shave the surgical site; he would part the hair and although it wouldn't be quite as sterile a procedure, the dog would be able to be shown in the ring within a month. The scar would be miniscule and an untrained eye would probably never notice it. So now, with everything ready, he began; his hands were steady, his mind clear of alcohol and intently focused on doing what was, to most of his so-called colleagues, impossible.

* * * *

On the same day that Cole was undergoing surgery, Emma was gaining strength and improving rapidly. She was going to have to wear the sling for a couple of weeks and have physical therapy two to three times a week for about a month to get her soft tissue stretched and loosened up, get her arm strengthened. But she was doing well enough, despite a slight rise in her temperature the night before, for her doctors to hint that she might be able to be released in two days. That was provided there were no other complications and her temperature remained normal.

There were now so many floral arrangements in Emma's hospital room that it looked like a greenhouse and they were still arriving every few minutes. There was nowhere left to put them other than the floor and on top of the bed. So when it looked like Emma would have to share her bed with a bouquet of a dozen roses and an arrangement of iris, carnations and what have you, she decided that some of them had to go. She had Joanie and Sally load many of the creations that had arrived yesterday into their cars to be taken to the shop and her house. She asked them to put one at the nurse's station and to give several to other patients who might not have anything to brighten their rooms.

Although she still tired easily, Emma was eager to catch up on all the news from her children and grandchildren. Tracy and her husband, David had two children, Brandon and Megan, and even though Emma didn't get to see them as often as she'd like, she was thrilled to learn about all they'd been up to.

Brandon, on the brink of being a teenager, was quite the athlete, excelling in baseball and basketball and doing very well in his scholastic studies. During the past year, he'd been on two basketball teams, one for his middle school and the other, a travel team. According to his mother, he was the cleanest player on both teams; he'd never fouled. Well, they were trying to fix that, coaching him to be more aggressive. Emma was quite sure that when Brandon committed his first infraction, Tracy'd be cheering from the sidelines just as much as when he scored a basket.

Megan, age nine, was quite the talented dancer, especially in tap and jazz and was somewhat of a whiz in the classroom. Whether she'd been influenced by her brother or not, she'd just found a new love in basketball herself this year. In her first game, she'd almost scored four times and had stolen the ball once. Her mother, proud as a peacock, had gone ballistic. There hadn't been any doubt in anyone's mind who Megan's mother was. It was also crystal clear that the kids hadn't inherited their talent from their maternal grandmother. Basketball was one sport that Emma couldn't make head or tail out of; in fact, she hadn't been exposed to playing it until she was in college and then she'd been forever fouling and hadn't had any idea why. So more power to Megan if she could figure it out because it was way beyond her grandmother.

Sydney, of course, wanted to come to see her Grammy. However since it wasn't allowed, she had to make do with a phone call, which can be in itself an experience not soon forgotten. Two and a half year olds are notoriously bad conversationalists, especially on the phone. The conversation is usually punctuated with a lot of dead air while trying to get a response from the little urchin who has since decided that she's done talking and simply walks away from the phone. *Hello?*

Syd's phone call went predictably along those lines, but still it did Emma good to hear her voice. The only stumbling block had come when Syd, quite naturally, asked about her furry friend, Cole. Emma had to fight back tears before she could answer her granddaughter and then said only that Cole had taken a vacation and would be gone for a little while. Syd seemed satisfied with that and went on to other things before ending her side of the conversation by dropping the phone on the floor and going off to play with her princess dolls.

* * * *

Meanwhile, outside of what was happening at the hospital, two significant things were taking place. First of all the search for Cole was in full swing. It seemed as though the entire dog community of Western New York had responded to the call for help in locating him. Volunteer upon volunteer had turned out to not only scour the immediate vicinity, but the all-breed clubs as well as the local Newfoundland clubs, and the obedience and agility clubs had organized searches in their respective locales on the off-chance that Cole might have wandered into their communities. The local clubs were even offering a reward of $2,000.00 for the safe return of the dog.

Flyers had been made up and distributed; some dog fanciers had grabbed handfuls to take with them to various upcoming shows, regardless of whether they were in state or out. Flyers were being mailed to dog clubs throughout the state and even into northern Pennsylvania. Nearby Canadian clubs were being contacted and the flyer sent over the Internet.

All animal control, humane societies and animal shelters within the state of New York and northern Pennsylvania had been notified as well as all rescue groups within these areas.

Cole was a rising star in the dog world, a point of pride for Western New York, and Emma was well-known and liked; everyone was getting involved and word of his disappearance soon spread far beyond the local region.

Secondly, the shop was open and running smoothly with Mrs. Foster at the helm. She'd recruited the help of Aunt Agnes and a dozen or so volunteers and between them they were keeping the place open and functioning.

Mrs. Foster and Aunt Agnes had taken over the majority of the workload and they were enjoying every minute of it. The two most unlikely women to form a friendship had done exactly that and acted like they'd been close confidants for years. The moneyed woman of class and the lovable, but fashion-impaired aunt of Emma's (and that was saying it nicely) were polar opposites who had found a common thread and were having one hell of a good time running the shop.

Business was good; in fact, it was great. Could be that Aunt Agnes was the draw once word got out that she was there; people came to see if what they'd heard was the truth. They were never disappointed.

Similarly with what was happening at the Whistling Thistle, Sally's staff at the Hearthmoor had taken over in her absence and was keeping everything going there. Her crew was working a lot of extra hours, but there wasn't a complaint to be heard. They all personally knew Emma and Cole and would do anything to help out. The restaurant was actually being used as the base of operations for the search teams and Sally was providing free lunches for the volunteers. A lot of people were staying for dinner when their shift was over and the restaurant was flourishing.

Chapter Forty-One

Two days later, an impatient but thankful Emma was released from the hospital. Her recovery was progressing wonderfully, in large part due to the great physical shape she was in. Perhaps also because she was determined to get well quickly so she could find Cole. At any rate she was discharged on Thursday, armed with pain medication and instructions for physical therapy. Her children were there to collect her personal items, take care of the final paperwork, and drive her out to Glenwood. Joanie and Sally had driven in to the medical center to help distribute the remaining flowers to other patients and help in any way they could. When their tasks were completed, they were ready to head out.

Mack led the way in his rental car; Emma was in the front passenger seat and Mandie and Tracy in the rear. Joanie and Sally were following in Joanie's big Silverado truck. Naturally, they had to go through the shop's parking lot to get to Emma's driveway. As they approached the store, Emma saw the big, red banner with white lettering fluttering in the breeze on the outside of the building welcoming her home. As if that wasn't enough to bring tears to her eyes, she about lost it completely when she saw the reception committee that was waiting for her as they turned into the lot. There, lining both sides of the driveway, as far up as Emma could see, were friends, customers, dog people and relatives, waving, clapping and cheering as the car drove up the road toward her house. There was another huge "Welcome Home" banner attached to her house and there, waiting on the porch were Ben, Sam, Richard, Rob and Sydney.

The car had no sooner come to a stop, in fact, Mack hadn't even put it into park yet, and Ben was there at Emma's door opening it and helping her out. Catching a look from Mack that Ben didn't bother to interpret, he kissed Emma and hugged her carefully. In the next instant, Sydney was there and demanding attention from her grandmother. It was obvious that Rob and Mandie must have warned her not to touch her Grammy's arm, because she took a long look at the sling (you could almost see her thought process) before she grabbed Emma's leg and attached herself like a little leech. Sam, Richard, and Rob took their turns at welcoming Emma home while the people that had lined the driveway were congregating in her front yard.

The first to step forward was none other than Aunt Agnes in all her gold and silver glory. If Emma wasn't mistaken she appeared to have upwards of a pound or more additional jewelry on than she'd had the last time Emma had seen her. Yep, that was definitely a new silver-plated watch up near her right elbow, and there was a new gold bracelet with a silver design clanging on her left wrist. She didn't remember seeing that gold pin near her right shoulder either; it was shaped like a…what was that? Oh, a lobster… a lobster? Emma couldn't begin to imagine what significance a lobster held for her dear aunt. What? A good meal? And what was that glint of gold on her nose? Oh my God, she'd had her nose pierced! There in all its dazzling splendor was a little gold ball sitting right above her left nostril.

The woman was out of control! Emma knew right then and there she was going to have to have a serious talk with Uncle Lou; see if he could rein her in a bit. Cripe, next thing you know, she'd be getting her eyebrow pierced, or heaven forbid, her tongue! Then there were other possibilities that made Emma shudder to even think about. She'd have to make it a top priority.

"Emma, dear, welcome home," Aunt Agnes prattled as she air-kissed Emma's cheek. Her hair had a decidedly purplish tint to it, maybe to compliment her outrageously bright deep purple muumuu that enveloped her overly plump body from head to toe. "We're all so happy to have you back, sweetie. But you take your time now; don't feel the least bit pressured to come back to work 'cause Grace, Mrs. Foster, and I are doing just great. Business is booming and all your customers are so very nice and friendly. Why, they just love to come in and talk and talk. But don't you worry; we make sure they buy something too. So you just concentrate on getting well and we'll take care of business."

"Thanks, Aunt Agnes, you're a peach. Having fun, are you?"

"Oh Emma, you don't know the half of it. We're having a blast."

Emma laughed and gave her aunt a loving look. Aunt Agnes gave her hand a squeeze and moved off to the side, making room for other people to come up and express their good wishes. No one stayed too long, knowing Emma was still weak and would tire quickly. Ben, her children, and her oldest friends hovered protectively.

One of the last people to approach was Stuart Berger from Springville, the person who had organized the search for Cole.

"Hi, Stu, thanks for coming. This has been quite the homecoming."

"Glad to be here, Emma. You're looking pretty good. How you feeling?"

"Better. I'm getting stronger everyday. It's kind of a pain having this arm out of commission, but thank God it isn't my right one. I'd really be sunk then. Don't tell anybody but I'm a complete klutz with my left hand."

"Your secret is safe with me, Em, but I'm sure you'll be back good as new before you know it."

"Thanks, Stu, I hope you're right."

"Listen, Emma. We're going to keep searching. We're not giving up. Everybody's spreading the word. We'll find Cole; it just might take a while. If he's gone from the area, then the search will just get bigger, that's all. You know how the dog world works; everybody gets into the act when one of our own needs help. Don't give up hope."

"I won't, Stu. I know he's still alive and he's out there somewhere. I'll find him with some help from my friends."

"We'll do all we can, Em."

"I know you will, Stu. Thanks."

"You take care now, get some rest and I'll keep you updated everyday on how we're progressing." Stuart gave her right arm a gentle squeeze as he turned and left; the few remaining people talked with Emma for only a short while before they too took their leave.

It was finally time for Emma to go into the house. It was something she would have rather put off indefinitely, knowing she'd be assaulted with memories of Cole as soon as she stepped over the threshold. But she had no choice; she had to go in. So she squared her shoulders and went in amidst her family and friends. But when she entered the living room, her newfound resolve seemed to evaporate and she thought she'd fall apart as her eyes zeroed in on "Froggy", which was lying on the floor next to her favorite chair. Syd was quick to spot the toy and snatched it up, bringing it over to Emma.

"Look Grammy, Cole forgot his 'Froggy'. He's going to miss him."

"Oh. Syd..." Emma couldn't get anything else out; her throat had closed up, choked with tears. Her eyes filled and she turned away so Sydney couldn't see.

Mandie stepped in so fast it was like she'd been shot out of a cannon and in one swift move scooped Syd up into her arms. "Let's go see what kind of cookies Grammy's got," she said as she made for the kitchen, deftly taking "Froggy" out of Syd's hand and stuffing him into the first cupboard she passed.

Emma sank into her chair and tried to compose herself. Damn, this was going to be hard! Everywhere she looked there were going to be reminders of Cole, and why shouldn't there be, she reasoned, he lived there. It was that snippet of insight, that light bulb going on, that made her sit up, straighten her spine, and sniff the last of her tears away. He lived *there*, with her, in that house, and by God, she was going to get him back where he belonged.

* * * *

While Emma had been well enough to go home, Cole was still recovering from his surgery in a large crate in the same room where Dr. Morgan had operated. The doctor wanted to monitor his progress and at the same time, keep him confined so that his movement would be restricted and he couldn't accidentally injure himself.

Cole wasn't groggy any more like he had been the day of and the day after the surgery. He was aware of a pain between his shoulders and some soreness on the inside of his right rear leg. He was also aware of another man who had come into the room and was talking to the doctor. When the man had finished speaking to Morgan, he came over to the crate and stood looking down at Cole.

Cole knew intuitively that this man, the doctor had called him Mr.Cappellini, was his enemy. The stench of his malevolence was rolling off of him in waves and Cole recoiled in response. Cappellini extended his hand toward the crate, his fingers barely touching the wires; Cole curled his lip and growled deep in his throat.

"A bit touchy, are we," Cappellini smirked, his voice holding a note of disdain. "You don't have to like me, boy, all you have to do is keep winning and know who your new master is."

"Mr. Cappellini, it would be better if you don't upset the dog right now. He's making good progress." Morgan had advanced toward his patient when he'd heard the growl.

"Morgan, are you presuming to tell me what to do?" Cappellini turned to face the doctor, his eyes having gone cold and deadly.

"No, sir, I wouldn't dream of telling you what to do. I just don't want the dog to get upset and injure himself. I mean, it would be a shame to suffer a setback now when everything is going so well."

Cappellini studied the doctor intently, noting his nervousness and subservience. He owned this poor excuse for a man, but he decided to concede the point. "All right, I'll leave him alone for now, but the time will come very soon for him to learn who is in control."

"Yes, sir."

"And by the way, the dog's name is going to be Remy. Start calling him by it. I want him to learn to respond to it."

"Yes, Mr. Cappellini. Will there be anything else?"

"Just make sure you stay sober, at least for a while longer."

"You don't have to worry about that."

Cappellini gave him a disbelieving look. "Don't try to bullshit me, Morgan. Remember I know you. I'm the one who keeps pulling you out of the gutter."

"Yes, sir."

Seeing that Morgan was sufficiently cowed, Cappellini left the room. The doctor edged closer to Cole and went down on his haunches. Speaking very softly, he addressed the dog. "Didn't take you long to figure out what a bastard he is, did it? Honestly, it took me quite a bit longer, but then I don't have the natural instincts you have. Even if I did, I'd probably have ignored them. See, he can't buy you off. Money means nothing to you, where with me, well... Let's just say I'm weak *and* a drunk, and the combination is insurmountable, at least for me. But let me give you some sound advice, okay? Don't fight the man; don't cross him. You've got to play along; you've got to do what he says. I don't want to see you get hurt or worse."

Cole listened to the man, not understanding all the words, but comprehending the tone and sincerity with which they were delivered. He just wasn't sure for whose benefit the man was speaking.

Chapter Forty-Two

Late Saturday morning, Mack and Tracy had to leave to go back to their respective homes in Connecticut. After a tearful goodbye, they were on their way to the airport in the rental car. Mandie, Rob, and Syd were going to see them off, and Joanie and Sally moved in for the day to take over as Emma's caretakers. However, how accurate a statement that was, was anybody's guess.

They helped her, if you could call it that, with her bath and washing her hair. Getting her makeup on and styling her hair was a comedy of errors and getting Emma dressed was something right out of the Three Stooges. Somehow, everything took twice as long and was twice as hard as it had been when Tracy was helping her. Maybe it was because there were two of them and they had to divvy up the work equally. God forbid one of them should be shortchanged. Most likely, it was because they were both idiots. That was probably it; Emma would wager money on it.

The two nurse wannabes put Emma through her physical therapy exercises, or at least attempted to, before she got pissed off and told them to go to hell in a hand basket. It seems they were exerting a little too much pressure stretching out her left arm and Emma took exception to it. Besides, they were arguing over everything; one of them thinking her way was better than the other person's, regardless of the way it was supposed to be done. So Emma told them to can it and just sit and talk to her or else she was going to send them packing.

"Cripe, you're getting a little cranky, aren't you, Em?" Joanie gave her an injured look that Emma ignored.

"Maybe, what's it to you?"

"Not a damn thing, just trying to gauge your mood."

"Well, my mood is, to put it in one word, frustrated."

"Would that be sexually or...?"

"Oh geez, Joanie, don't you ever think of anything else?"

"Not if I can help it. Besides, it would be natural to be frustrated that way. You'd only just gotten it on with Ben when all hell broke loose. You haven't had sex with him again, have you?"

"No, only that once. But that's not the way I'm frustrated, at the moment anyway. I'm tired of not being my normal self. First it was my hands and leg which, thank God, are pretty much back to normal now. All the stitches are out, compliments of the doctors at ECMC and the bruising is just about gone, but now I've got to deal with this gunshot wound. I guess I just want things to be the way they usually are...I want Cole here."

Emma's last statement was the real crux of the problem and the girls knew it. Emma didn't give a damn about a physical problem; she'd fight her way through it like she did everything else. It was her missing dog that Emma couldn't handle.

"Listen, Em, we're going to find him," Sally said. "I know there hasn't been anything positive to report yet, but everybody's still out there working hard to find him. Stuart said they just had more flyers printed up and they're being mailed to every show chairman whose club's got a show coming up in the next few months. They'll be tacked up at shows from Ohio to the east coast."

"I know, it's just that I feel so useless. I'm not doing anything and it's driving me crazy."

"Look here, you dope. You are doing something. You're getting better. You're getting your strength back and, whether you know it or not, you're what's keeping us going."

"Me?"

"Yes, you and your unshakable belief that Cole's alive."

"He is, Joanie. There's no question."

"Well, there you go. You're our inspiration not to give up. Believe me, you're going to be at full strength real soon. Then all I can say is, whoever has Cole had better watch the hell out, 'cause I know you're going to go after him like one totally bad-ass bitch woman."

"You've got that right"

"All right. So for now, just concentrate on getting well. Let your friends do the legwork 'til you can step in and lead the charge."

"I know you're right. It's just so damn hard not to be out there looking."

"We know, Em. But believe me, everything that could be done is being done."

"Okay, I know you're right. I'll try to cool it. Sorry if I'm being ornery."

"Oh, no more than usual."

"Joanie…"

"Yeah, yeah. Hey, do you have any wine?"

"Well, yeah, but what time is it?"

"Who the hell cares? As long as we can't do anything around here, we might as well have a cocktail."

"None for me, thanks; but you two go ahead. I don't think it would be too smart to mix alcohol and the pain killers I'm on."

"Bummer."

"Joanie, at least you're still normal. I don't think I could cope if that ever changed."

"No worries there, you can count on me. Come on, Sally, let's get the glasses and wine and have ourselves a little libation. Emma's counting on us to stay normal and we don't want to disappoint her."

*　*　*　*

The girls stayed until dinnertime, and then Ben took over bringing food from the Hearthmoor for their meal. There were dinner salads with crumbled blue cheese and a citrus/cranberry dressing, Tom's super mashed potatoes, barbequed ribs and delicious, homemade baked beans. Dessert was peanut butter pie. If she kept eating like this, Emma was sure she was going to gain ten or twenty pounds, what with not being able to exercise. But damn, it was just too good to turn down.

After dinner, they went out on the deck and enjoyed the gentle breezes and warm temperatures of the June evening. The flowers' fragrance drifted by and the air carried the occasional squeak of the hummingbirds. They could hear the buzz of insects and the croaking of frogs in the nearby stream. It was peaceful, so much so that neither one of them felt the need to talk.

Once the sun went down, it got a bit chilly so they went inside and watched a movie. Emma's eyes were starting to droop; it was time to get her settled for the night. With only a little help from Ben she managed to get out of her clothes and into a nightgown. When she was ready for bed, she expected Ben to kiss her goodbye and leave. It didn't happen.

He carefully tucked her into bed, went around the house making sure all the doors and windows were closed and locked, took a turn in the bathroom, turned off all the lights, and came into Emma's bedroom. He lay down on the bed next to her on top of the covers. He was still fully clothed except for his shoes, and he lay on his back, one arm up and wedged under his head as he stared at the ceiling.

"What are you doing?" Emma asked, the corners of her mouth lifting into a smile, even as her eyes opened wide with puzzlement.

"I'm staying the night."

"You are?"

"Yep."

"How come? The danger's past; they got what they wanted."

"Doesn't matter, I'm not leaving."

"Really?"

"Really."

"Okay."

"Okay? You're not going to try to talk me out of staying?"

"No."

"Good."

"Are you going to get undressed?"

"Nope."

"Why not?"

"It's safer this way."

"Safer?"

"Yep."

"How come?"

"Do you really have to ask, Em?"

"Oh."

"This is going to be hard enough with clothes on."

"Really?"

"Yes, really. You're a damn attractive woman, Emma. Being this close to you and not doing something about it is hard, very hard. But I'm not here to ravish you, although I confess I would love to. Right now, at this moment in time, I'm here as a friend, albeit a very close one. I just want you to know that I'm here for you; I want to help you get through a hard time, okay? You can lean on me, Em."

"Ben, that's so sweet, but…"

"But what?"

"You have to promise me something."

"Sure, anything."

"You have to promise me, that at some later date, you will ravish me."

"You have my solemn word on it, sweetheart." Ben smiled in the dark and leaned over and kissed Emma on the cheek.

"Ben?"

"Hmm?"

"Thank you."

"Your welcome, Em. Now go to sleep. I'll be right here."

Emma drifted off almost immediately, glad she wasn't alone. It would have been her first night by herself since Cole had been taken and she'd been dreading it. Ben had somehow known that and how hard it would be on her. He hadn't been about to let her go through anything else on her own, even if it meant sleeping like this until Cole was found. He couldn't think of a more pleasant way to spend his sleeping hours. Well, all right, he could, but that would come. This was more than enough for now.

* * * *

The next several weeks' activities fell into pretty much the same pattern. Emma went to physical therapy three times a week and was getting her arm and shoulder back to their former strength. She totally immersed herself in the search for Cole and was on the phone and Internet a great deal of the time spreading the word. The actual physical search of the Glenwood/ East Concord region by the many people who had volunteered had been terminated after the second week. The general consensus was that Cole had to be out of the area by that time; so the search continued, but on a much larger scale, via phone, mail, and the Internet.

Emma went down to the shop for a brief period each day, where she found that Joanie had been forced to stage a coup to wrest control away from Aunt Agnes and Mrs. Foster. For two old ladies, they were pretty damn tough. The only way Joanie had gotten them to relinquish their command was to promise that they could come in and work occasionally when she and Emma needed some time off. Who knew those two sweet little old ladies would get power hungry?

Joanie had even managed to get through Tammy's receipts from the Friday she'd worked when they'd gone to the Stockton show. It was a first that she had done it without Emma's help and she was pretty darn proud of it. Nobody needed to know that it had taken her three days, three bottles of wine, and so much swearing that Tank, who'd hidden under the table in the back room the first day, had flatly refused to go back to the shop ever since. It was, in all likelihood, going to take Emma's cajoling to get him back; he wasn't having anything to do with Joanie. She could sweet talk him 'til the cows came home and it wasn't going to make any impression on him. Besides, without his buddy there, the shop wasn't half as much fun as it used to be. Maybe he'd just stay at home and sulk until Cole came back.

As far as Ben was concerned, well, he continued to spend the night a few times each week and had graduated to undressing and sliding under the covers. While Emma's wound was still healing, they'd contented themselves with just holding each other close. But once Emma gave the word, Ben had fulfilled his promise to ravish her and had done so with gentle lovemaking that brought them both fulfillment and a growing attachment to one another.

The actual criminal investigation, however, was going nowhere fast. Any hope for a lead when the sheriffs had searched the state land had dried up. There'd been evidence in the grass on the shoulder of the road that some kind of vehicles had been parked there, but that was all. There weren't any tire treads left at the scene to make casts of, just crushed grass.

They'd seen signs of possibly one or more ATVs going through in one of the wetter areas. But the heavy rain had washed out everything except the fact that the earth was churned up, indicating the vehicles had gotten bogged down at that point.

The sheriffs had canvassed the few places where ATVs could be rented in the area and did turn up the rental of two during the relevant time period. A check into the identity of the two men who had rented the machines found that the names and all other forms of identification, including pertinent vehicle information were false. The descriptions given by the shop employee proved to be worthless.

The case was quickly going cold. Finding the dog could well be the only means of breaking the investigation open.

* * * *

That same period of time was, for Cole, one of adjustment, supposed acceptance and continued post-surgical healing. His superb physical conditioning was as instrumental in his speedy recovery as Emma's was to hers. It wasn't long at all before the doctor had him swimming lengths in the lap pool and then exercising on the treadmill.

In a short time he'd be back in show trim and able to be exhibited.

Cappellini had called Bill Thornton off the show circuit and he was starting to work with Cole. All the other dogs in his care were to take a back seat to this project and since Cappellini was paying the bills, Thornton didn't argue. His other clients might not be happy about it, but they were all acquaintances of Cappellini and had learned long ago that the powerful businessman's interests came first. While they were aptly compensated for any down time from the show ring their animals experienced, it still stuck in their craws that it took longer for them to win their championships and that their interests were of secondary importance. None however, were about to complain or challenge the wishes of the ruthless tycoon. It was smarter to suffer in silence and much more profitable to keep taking his money.

As far as Bill knew, the dog was from a kennel in the Netherlands and was called Remy. He had noticed the remarkable physical resemblance to Cole and although the word had spread to him that Cole was missing, he had no reason to believe that this was Emma's dog. The dog was beautiful, but lacked the attitude that had set Cole apart from other dogs when put through his paces for the show ring. This dog, in fact, was wooden in his response and Thornton had to work really hard to get any kind of expression from him. And when he did? Well, the look in the dog's eye was a clear declaration of "Go to hell". Cole had picked up more than one useful thing by hanging around with Tank.

However, his attitude had earned him not only harsh words but also a few well-placed punches to the head from Thornton. They weren't hard enough to injure him, but they were meant to get his attention and they had certainly succeeded in that regard, only not in the way that Thornton had intended. Cole tuned into him all right, but with a

465

growing dislike that was second only to what he felt for Cappellini.

Cappellini, meanwhile, was unlikely to get within six feet of the dog before he bared his teeth and snapped. Their so-called relationship had deteriorated to this point after Cappellini had taken exception to Cole's growling every time he got near him, and had whipped him repeatedly with the leash to bring him into line. It hadn't worked.

If that wasn't enough, Cole knew now that this man was responsible for Emma getting hurt; he could see it in his eyes and hear it in his voice when he talked about her. Their private conversations at first had been suffused with Cappellini's self-glorification and demand for complete capitulation. Once Cappellini discovered that Emma was still alive however, his taunting had become malicious and riddled with evil intent. If given the chance now, this usually gentle, friendly, happy-go-lucky dog would gladly tear him apart.

Chapter Forty-Three

In the beginning of July, on the first weekend after the Fourth, the girls attended two dog shows. The first show was at the Hamlin Fireman's Field in Hamlin, New York hosted by the Genesee Valley Kennel Club. The second one was at the International Agriculture Center located on the Erie County Fairgrounds in Hamburg, New York, which was just a short ride from Glenwood, sponsored by the Kennel Club of Buffalo.

Neither Joanie nor Sally entered their dogs; this was strictly a mission to spread the word, get feedback if there was any, and to eyeball in person any Newfie that was being shown. Tank and Kirby did ride along though and went with the girls as they made their way around the show grounds; the girls aware that the dogs might detect something they would miss.

At both shows, it took Emma only minutes to eliminate any of the dogs that were in the ring. But that wasn't the end of it. The girls went through the grooming tent at each location first, and then they stopped at every exhibitors setup. They were not only searching, but also handing out flyers with Cole's picture and pertinent information. At every stop they made, they let the dogs sniff around. For all outward appearances, they looked like they were just being dogs. Well, they were, but they were searching in their own way for their buddy. It took them all day at each show, and the girls were mentally exhausted and the dogs physically worn out by the time they finished speaking to the last handler at the end of the weekend.

They continued to direct the search from home after that and chased down any lead that came their way. There were only a few and they turned out to be false. Mack and Tracy were even blanketing any show they could find in the New England area with flyers and going to as many as their schedules would allow. So far, they hadn't turned up anything either.

In August, the three friends traveled to a cluster of shows that were being held in Ballston Spa and Saratoga, New York. It was close to a six-hour trip and the girls decided that this time, it would be better if Kirby and Tank stayed home, even though they'd come along in July. It was going to be too hot to have them along for the whole day and the girls knew they wouldn't have time for rest breaks. The shows had started on Wednesday, the fourth, and continued through Sunday, the eighth. The girls were only able to go for the weekend, but they reasoned that anybody who had entered on Wednesday, Thursday, and Friday would more than likely be there on the weekend when entries were generally higher in number and the chance for a major win greater.

The Saturday show was being held under the auspices of the Southern Adirondack Kennel Club at the Ballston Spa Fairgrounds and the Sunday show was being presented by the Bennington County Kennel Club whose show site was a few miles away at the Saratoga County Fairgrounds. The threesome had reserved a hotel room about halfway between the two venues.

They followed the same procedure as they had at the July shows, minus the dogs, and had just about as much luck. They didn't find Cole but by chance did pick up an interesting bit of information. It seemed that one of the professional handlers they'd spoken to mentioned in passing a rumor he'd heard. According to the handler Bill Thornton had just picked up a new dog, a Newfoundland from the Netherlands. Thornton was supposedly going to bring him out this weekend at the Harrisburg Kennel Club show in Pennsylvania. He didn't know any other details, but that little scrap of gossip he'd just handed them was enough for Emma's instincts to come to full alert. Each one of the girls remembered that Thornton's unknown client had at one time wanted Cole and wanted him badly. It was a long shot, but maybe, just maybe they had something to go on; at the very least, they had to check it out.

* * * *

Information was hard to come by. The girls didn't know anybody offhand who had gone to the Harrisburg show and they could hardly call Thornton, not that he was likely to divulge much anyway. He'd always been rather secretive and trying to get the lowdown from him was an exercise in futility. Besides, Emma doubted that he would be the least bit receptive to any inquiry from her because of her refusal to sell Cole.

So with lack of a better plan, the girls wrote down the name of every person they could think of who might have been at that show and then supplemented it with names they picked out from catalogs of past shows that year. The catalogs listed addresses but no phone numbers, so if the girls didn't already know the numbers, they had to call information to get them. It took a lot of time and a lot of effort, but they stuck with it. The entire daylight hours of that Monday were spent on the phone, getting numbers, leaving messages, and if they did get through to the party they called, asking questions. It was going on nine o'clock that night and they were tired and discouraged, ready to call it a day, when Emma's phone suddenly rang, surprising them all. It was Nancy Bullis returning their earlier call.

"I got your message just a few minutes ago, Emma. I've been outside cleaning the motor home all day and then I had to take care of the dogs or I would have returned your call sooner."

"That's all right, Nancy. I'm glad you got back to me this fast."

"In answer to your question, yes, I was at Harrisburg this past weekend."

"You were? Great! Did you happen to see the Newfies?"

"Just briefly. I was in with my Afghan when the Newfs were being shown."

"Was Bill Thornton there?"

"Yeah, in fact he had a Newf in. First time I ever saw him with one. The dog must be new."

"Did you happen to get a look at the dog?"

"Not really. Like I said, I was busy with Cleo."

"Did you happen to catch if it was a dog or a bitch?"

"A dog, I think. It was good size, too big for a bitch. I doubt Thornton would show an oversize bitch."

"Was it a black?"

"Yeah, but that's all I can tell you. I saw the dog from the side; I don't know if he had any white markings on his chest or feet. I just didn't pay that much attention; I kind of had my hands full at the time."

"No, no, that's okay. Anything you noticed could be helpful."

"Em, what's this about? Has it got something to do with Cole?"

"Maybe. I don't know. It's just I've got a funny feeling about this dog. Could be wishful thinking too. I can't help but remember how Thornton was with me about Cole though."

"What do you mean?"

Emma went on to tell Nancy how Thornton had repeatedly approached her on behalf of his mystery client about buying Cole and the large sums of money she'd been offered. She also told her how unhappy Thornton had been with her after her final refusal and all the things that had happened previous to her being shot, including the motor home incident which Nancy had already known about.

"Geez, Em, I didn't know all that had been going on."

"Yeah, things have been screwed up for awhile now."

"I guess so."

"Would you happen to know where Thornton's next show is?"

"No, I don't. Sorry."

"That's okay. Where are you showing next?"

"This upcoming weekend I'll be at the Tioga County Kennel Club shows in Owego, New York."

"Will you do me a favor?"

"Sure, if I can."

"While you're at the show, if you have time, will you look around for Thornton? If he's there, will you check out his Newfie?"

"Absolutely, and I'll try to find out where he'll be next. Okay?"

"Oh, God, that would be great, Nancy. Thanks so much."

"Don't mention it. I'll call you after the show. All right?"

"Fine, thanks again."

"I'll be talking to you. Bye."

After Emma hung up, she turned to her two friends with a big smile on her face. "You got the drift of the conversation?"

"Yep, hopefully we'll know more after this weekend, huh?"

"Yeah, if he's there, we'll know who he's showing."

"We can count on Nancy, she'll do a good job."

"I know she will, I just hope he's there."

"I guess we've got no choice but to wait and see what happens. But like you said, Joanie, if he's there, Nancy'll get the job done." Sally gave Emma a reassuring smile, hoping for her sake they'd get a break.

"Yeah, she will, but in the meantime we can certainly make the waiting easier, starting right now," Joanie said, walking out to the kitchen. She grabbed the wine out of the refrigerator and the glasses from the cupboard. She poured them each a glass and proposed a toast. "Here's to Cole, wherever you are. Hang in there, big boy, 'cause we're hot on the trail."

The girls clinked their glasses together in salute and Joanie and Sally drank deeply. Emma, too choked up to swallow, merely rested her glass against her lower lip and watched her friends, thankful for their very presence, but afraid to hope that Cole could be coming home soon.

* * * *

While the girls were having their mini celebration, Cole was in his kennel run thinking about Emma and wondering if he was ever going to see her again. He missed her terribly and he missed their house. He missed her bed where she let him sleep even though he was too big, and he missed waking her up in the morning. He missed his "Froggy" and he missed smelling all the flowers in the yard. He missed going to the shop and carrying bags for customers out to their cars. He missed Joanie and Sally, he missed Kirby and he really missed Tank. He sure could use him for backup right now.

He thought about Sydney and how little she was and how she needed him to keep her safe when she came to visit. He thought about the time when she was in the bathtub and he opened the door and jumped in with her. Boy, that had been fun. He missed her arms around his neck, giving him a big hug. He thought about chasing Tank around the shop and he couldn't help but smile in his own doggy way. He thought about swimming with Kirby and Tank in Joanie's pool and about the time Tank stole that cellophane package and he'd acted as the diversion at the party Joanie had had with all those women. They'd sure pulled off a good one that time.

He wondered what Emma was doing; was she looking for him? He knew she was, that is, if she was able to. He didn't know how badly she'd been hurt, but he did know one thing. She was alive. He'd know if she wasn't because he'd have a big pain in his chest that would never go away. He'd looked for her this past weekend when they'd gone to the show. It had only been for one day; that Thornton guy had said he wanted to start him out slow because he wasn't performing as well as he'd hoped he would be by this time. Well, he could keep right on hoping as far as Cole was concerned. And they were calling him another name now too, Remy. That wasn't his name and it never would be. He didn't care though; they could call him anything they wanted. He was and always would be Cole, Emma's Cole.

When they'd arrived at the show and he'd recognized it for what it was, Cole had searched for Emma relentlessly, hoping to see her among the hundreds of people there. He was even looking when he was in the ring and supposed to be still. He'd kept turning his head, scanning the crowd and had received a slap or two to the head from Thornton when the judge wasn't looking. Cole didn't care; he was going to look for Emma. Only he hadn't found her that day and he'd been so disappointed that he'd been depressed and listless ever since. He wasn't eating again either.

Cappellini had come to the show, thinking he was going to witness the dog's first win with himself as owner, but it hadn't happened. Cole had placed third in his class and it was largely due to his poor attitude and behavior. Cappellini had been fit to be tied and had taken his anger out on the dog as soon as they were back at the motor home. They'd gone inside and with Thornton hanging him with the choke collar, Cappellini had punched and kicked the defenseless animal. Cole had only known kindness and gentle handling from Emma, so this physical assault was a shock not only to his body but also to his mind.

It wasn't until they got back to the farm that Cole was shown any kindness and then it was Dr. Morgan who had taken charge and administered to his bruises and sore muscles. Even though the doctor had tended him with gentle hands and soft words, the beating, combined with Cole's disappointment at not finding Emma, had plunged him into deep despair, any hope of rescue shattered.

But now, after mentally getting past his current predicament and centering his thoughts on everybody and everything he missed, especially Emma, he wasn't going to be dissuaded. He was going to find her. If she was too hurt to be looking for him, well, then he'd do all the searching and somehow, someway he'd get back to her. He wouldn't allow himself to give up; he had to stay strong. He had to keep eating and always, he had to watch, he had to be on guard. His chance would come at some point and he had to be ready because then he could go home.

Chapter Forty-Four

The phone call from Nancy Bullis came at 10:30 Sunday night. Emma hadn't expected to hear from her until Monday at the earliest.

"Hi, Emma. I hope I'm not calling too late."

"No, not at all. I usually don't go to bed until 11:30, after I watch the local news."

"I wanted to call you right away with what I found out."

"No problem. You have news then?" Emma's heart was thumping so hard in her chest she thought it might come right through.

"Yeah, that's why I didn't want to wait to call. You ready? Thornton calls the dog Remy. He showed me his papers, and the dog is from a kennel in the town of Marken in the Netherlands, championship lines on both sides. It's…"

"That doesn't mean much, anybody can false paper a dog."

"That's true enough."

"Go ahead, I didn't mean to interrupt."

"Okay. It's a male like we thought and, according to the papers, he's only a few months younger than Cole. He's solid black, no white markings at all. Thornton put him up on the table for me and I'm telling you, Em, he could pass for Cole's twin. I went over him and it was like Cole was standing in front of me. It was weird."

"He looks that much like Cole?" Emma's hopes were sky high now.

"Yeah, you wouldn't believe it. The only difference I could see was that this dog was a little light, he needed to put on a few pounds to bring him up to good show weight."

"Well, that could be from the trauma he's been through, if it's Cole. Right? He was probably not eating for a while. How did he show?"

"Not like Cole. He had no animation and he kept turning his head, looking around even when he was moving. I mean, some dogs will turn their head a little to either side when they're moving, but this dog was almost doing a 180. Thornton's showing him from the Open class and from what I saw, the dog's not giving him much. He placed fourth out of five in the class. He doesn't look like he enjoys it at all. His eyes are kind of dead, you know what I mean?"

"Yeah, I do. There's no light in his eyes, no sparkle. That doesn't sound like Cole. He loves to show. Anything else?" Emma was telling herself that it could still be Cole. He could be showing badly because he was severely depressed or in pain. Who knew what had been done to him. But her common sense was kicking in and she could feel herself deflating like a balloon, her hopes sputtering away.

"Yeah, when he was on the table, I noticed that he had some pigmentation on the inside of his right rear leg. It was kind of neat 'cause it looked like a cloud. Did Cole have that?"

"No." This was like a death knell. "He didn't have any pigmentation on his legs or belly, much less anything that looked like a cloud." Emma was quiet as she crashed and burned; there was no way this dog could be Cole.

"Em, are you there?"

"Yeah, sorry."

"No, I'm sorry. I really thought you were on to something."

"Yeah, me too. I wanted this dog to be Cole so badly, but the pigmentation thing clinches it. It's not Cole."

"Em, I'm really so sorry. I wish I wasn't the one to have to dash your hopes."

"No, no. Don't feel that way. I'm very thankful that you went out of your way to help me. I can't thank you enough."

"It's not that big a deal. You'd do the same for me."

"Yeah, I would."

"I guess it doesn't matter now, but I wasn't able to find out where Thornton's going to show next. He was as closed-mouthed as ever, but then with the dog performing like he is maybe he doesn't know where he'll be next. He might have to pull him off the circuit 'til he gets his act together."

"Sounds like he should if the dog is doing so poorly."

"I should think he'd know the dog's not ready to be in the ring."

"Maybe there's pressure from the owner."

"Yeah, that could be, probably is. Some of them are extremely impatient. They just want to see results, regardless if the dog is ready or not. Hey, you know, there was one funny thing."

"What was that?"

"For as squirrelly as the dog was in the ring, he was real friendly to me. It was almost like he knew me."

"Really? That's odd. From what you've said I wouldn't expect him to be outgoing at all."

"I know, me either, but he was wagging his tail and he kept butting his head into my hand to get petted. He was way more interested in me than in Thornton. Bill, he just kind of ignored him, didn't really want anything to do with him."

"Could be he dislikes the ring and anything connected with it so much that he takes it out on Bill."

"You might be right. A lot of dogs hate to show."

"By the way, did you look up who owns the dog in the catalog?"

"Yeah, it's a Vincent Cappellini from Southport, Connecticut."

"Whew, rich, rich."

"Very."

"Well, that figures in with what he was offering me for Cole."

"Guess he found somebody who couldn't resist his money."

"Looks like it."

"Doesn't look like he got what he paid for though."

"No, not at all. Listen, I'll let you go. Again, thanks for all your trouble."

"Don't mention it. I'll keep in touch and hopefully I'll see you at some of the shows. Take care, Emma"

"I will and you do the same. Good luck at the shows."

"Thanks. Bye."

Emma hung up the phone, thinking she was back to square one again. God, she'd thought this time the lead was going to pan out, but there was no denying that pigmentation. That sealed it up tight, case closed. Well, she'd just have to look elsewhere then. There were still more shows to go to and more people to inform and question. One thing was for sure though she wasn't giving up.

* * * *

At the end of the month, the girls, Tank and Kirby traveled up to Albion, New York where the Tonawanda Kennel Club was hosting a two-day show at Bullard Park. Neither dog was again entered in competition, but their presence helped to keep the girls spirits buoyed throughout the long days. The three friends paid close attention to the Newfoundland judging both days, but there was nothing there that even remotely resembled Cole. They made the rounds of as many of the exhibitors as they could and they had to have passed out a couple of hundred flyers and asked just as many questions, but to no avail. By the end of the weekend, they'd come up with nothing new and went home more than a little discouraged; even the dogs were down in the mouth.

* * * *

September rolled in and with it, the busiest time of the year for the shop. From now through Christmas, the store was a hub of constant activity. Joanie and Emma were already woefully behind schedule with what they needed to make for the shop and the craft shows they attended. Additionally, the fall classes were supposed to start the next week and not one piece of wood was ready yet. They were going to have to work overtime to make up for the lost time they'd spent searching for Cole and reduce the amount of time they were away from the store.

The girls had plans to go to only one show that month and it was a big one. It was the Wine Country Cluster held at Sampson State Park in Romulus, New York and was being held from September 23rd-26th. They had originally planned on going for all four days, but now because of the increased pressures of the shop they were only going to go for the weekend.

But before that happened, they had to work long hours to get the shop up to speed. Everyday was spent selecting projects, making patterns, tracing patterns on wood, cutting wood, sanding, painting, staining, gluing, screwing, stapling, and embellishing. Lunch was fit in when and if they thought of it, and at day's end they were tired and usually had sore fingers from twisting the wire they used. The next day they'd be right back at it again.

On one such day, Emma and Joanie were busy waiting on customers. Many of them had come out to the region to see the changing leaf colors, although it was still pretty early for that. In between ringing up sales and helping people, they were assembling some twenty-five or thirty garden stakes, some decorated with jack-o-lantern faces and others with snowman heads. The phone rang in the midst of everything and Joanie grabbed it and shoved the receiver between her shoulder and ear while she continued to use the rechargeable power hand drill.

"Good afternoon, The Whistling Thistle," she said absently, her mind on what she was doing for a change.

Emma couldn't hear what was said on the other end, but the next thing she heard was Joanie, saying in an exasperated voice, "I'll can't deal with this now, I'm busy screwing. You'll have to call back some other time." Then she disconnected, threw the receiver on the table and continued to drill start holes into the piece she was working on.

Emma just looked at her and burst out laughing. "Do you realize what you just said?"

"What?"

"Tell me this, who was on the line? A man or a woman?"

"A man."

"Well, you just told him you were busy screwing."

"Yeah? Well, I was."

"But Joanie, he probably thinks you were, you know, *screwing* screwing."

"Yeah, you think so. Cool."

"Oh, God, we'll be known as the shop where you can screw."

"Or the shop where you get screwed. I like the sound of both of 'em, if you know what I mean." Joanie waggled her eyebrows and struck a provocative pose.

"Oh, Lord, help us."

"Honey, we don't need His help. We can do it all by ourselves."

"Joanie, go back to work and do me a favor, don't answer the phone."

"Spoilsport."

"Somebody has to be or the vice squad will be pulling up to the door."

And that was how it went for the three weeks before the show. Between the long hours, the heavy workload, the increased number of customers, the classes held two nights a week, the two-day craft show they did the week before the dog show, and the ever present thoughts and worry about Cole, the girls got overtired, strung-out, and a little punch-drunk.

Chapter Forty-Five

Emma, Joanie, and Sally had left late Friday night for the show in Romulus. They'd had to wait until the rush at the restaurant was over before they could make their getaway. Kirby and Tank had been safely tucked into their crates and the motor home had sped down the highway with the night sky clear and sparkling with stars. Traffic had been light and the roads dry enabling them to make good time. The girls had arrived at their destination in a little over two hours.

They'd found their assigned campsite and quickly set up, opting to do just the necessary. They'd finish in the morning when it was light. The girls had been tired and ready to go to bed immediately, but the dogs had been fired up so they'd taken them for a long walk around the grounds before they'd finally called it a night around one o'clock in the morning.

The wakeup call had come early, way too early for people who didn't have to get dogs ready for the show ring. It was only going on six o'clock when a chorus of barking, in stereo no less, broke the stillness of the morning air. Emma sleepily looked out her window and saw six or seven Lakeland Terriers in an ex-pen at the camper next door

483

barking for all they were worth. Joanie, a natural grump first thing in the morning, looked out the window on the other side and saw four Basset Hounds similarly ensconced in their ex-pen with their heads tipped back howling in unison.

"What the hell are they doing? Trying to harmonize or just outdo each other?"

"Doesn't much matter. We aren't going to get any more sleep now. Might as well get up and get going."

Joanie turned away from the window and honed in on Tank who was lying between Emma and herself on the bed. His eyes were still closed and he was snuggling deeper into the blankets. "Oh, no you don't. I know you're awake, you little faker. Time to get up. If I've got to get moving, so do you. Come on, move your butt."

Tank slit one eye, but that was about it. Kirby, who'd been lying on the floor next to Sally who was on the couch, walked into the bedroom and promptly jumped on the bed and settled in next to Tank. She gave a big sigh and closed her eyes, her body curling around Tank's.

"From the looks of things, I don't thing they're going to be moving for a while, Joanie."

"Oh, the hell with it. Let him stay there. We might as well get cleaned up and dressed 'cause I don't think the serenade is going to be over any time soon. You think these people really like to hear that?"

"It must not bother them, or they'd shut 'em up."

"Maybe I'll go shut 'em up."

"Knowing you, that's a bad idea."

"What?" Joanie gave her a look of pure innocence that didn't fool Emma in the least.

"Never mind, devil woman. Let's get ready and start handing out flyers and asking questions."

"Emma, it's too early."

"By the time we get cleaned up and eat breakfast it'll be close to eight o'clock. Everybody's up by then."

"All right, but first we've got to get Sally's ass in gear. She's still on the couch." She wouldn't be for long. Joanie flew out of the bedroom and pounced on her.

"Hot damn! What are you trying to do? Kill me?"

"No, just get your ass moving."

"It's moving, it's moving, it's just slow. I was awake. I heard you. I was just taking my time."

"Time's up, come on."

"All right, I'm up. See, I'm vertical." Sally had moved off the couch and stood before Joanie could muster another attack. "Jesus, sometimes you're like a madwoman."

"Gotcha moving, didn't I?"

"Yeah, yeah."

"Okay, let's roll. Who's in the bathroom, first?"

Emma went first and the others followed. While breakfast was cooking, the dogs decided now was the time to get up and Joanie put them out in the ex-pen to take care of business. As soon as they were finished Tank let out his personal vocal rendition of, "I'm done, let me in, I want to eat." Joanie brought them both inside before Kirby could add her voice to the mix.

Breakfast was orange juice, bacon and egg sandwiches on flaky homemade biscuits, home fries, and coffee, tea, milk or Diet Pepsi. Sally chose coffee whereas Emma and Joanie opted for the Diet Pepsi. Caffeine was caffeine no matter how you got it. Tank and Kirby weren't to be denied, so they got some egg and bacon sprinkled on their dry dog food.

The girls were out the door at ten minutes to eight and began their quest with anybody they saw out and about. Newfoundlands were in the ring at 9:30, so they had an hour and a half to question and inform. They passed out flyers and tacked them on trees, although they found that someone had already put up quite a few.

The day was proving to be one of those perfect fall days that you could look back on in the middle of winter with fond memories. The sky was a stunning blue with wispy, white clouds here and there, and there was a gentle breeze that brought that wonderful fall smell to anyone who was outside. The leaves were turning colors and red, yellow, and orange dotted the landscape. The sun was bright and radiated a warming glow that was quickly heating the crisp morning air.

The show was being held in Sampson State Park and it was one of the nicest venues on the circuit. The park itself was wonderful, located as it was on beautiful Seneca Lake. Events were planned for the exhibitors each evening and even included a dinner cruise on the lake. The bathroom facilities available to the campers were excellent. The buildings were very clean and the showers, well, they were to die for. It was no wonder that this cluster of shows was one of the most popular, reflected by the large entry it attracted year after year.

* * * *

The threesome, plus their two four-legged friends, found themselves at the outside corner of Ring Four at 9:25. Technically Kirby and Tank weren't supposed to be there because they weren't entered in the show, but it would suffice to say that everybody brought tag-along dogs around the ring from time to time. The ring was at the end of the line and it had two sides open. The outside corner was the best spot to be if you wanted to watch how a dog moved; you could see how a dog looked from the side and coming and going. Emma wanted to see it all.

The Newfoundlands were assembled under the tent, waiting to go in and Emma couldn't really distinguish one from the other. The small, shaded space behind the ring was crowded with dogs and people and she couldn't get a good look at any one dog. She did however, spot Bill Thornton, but another exhibitor blocked his Newfie. She'd have to wait until they came into the ring.

* * * *

Cole was indeed under the tent and he was searching for Emma. He couldn't see much since it was so crowded, but he kept scanning the area. He lifted his head so he could see above the other dogs and twitched his nose to pull in any scent that was drifting his way on the slight breeze. Thornton kept trying to keep him close, but Cole pulled on the lead repeatedly to gain a better view and fresher air than that which was stagnating under the tent. He endured a fist to his side and a vicious tug on the lead that tightened his choke collar painfully, but nothing Thornton could do would make him stop.

He faced toward the ring and scented the air. He did it again and then once more. There, he smelled it; he was sure. It was Emma; it was her scent. She was here! But where was she? He couldn't see; there were too many people and dogs in the way. Cole leaned forward eagerly, trying to get closer to the ring. Thornton pulled him back so hard he put Cole on his back. Cole got to his feet and shook; Thornton immediately started to brush out his coat while maintaining a death grip on Cole's collar. Cole, excitement building under the calm demeanor he presented to Thornton, couldn't wait to get in the ring.

* * * *

Judging began and Emma scrutinized each dog as they entered the ring. She'd dismissed the puppies outright, but with the American Bred and the Bred by Exhibitor dogs, her eyes had been glued to each one as they performed. Now it was time for the Open class and Emma watched the six entries file into the ring. Three were of the Landseer variety, so Emma didn't even look at them. One of the other entries had a white blaze on his chest, and another was too short, so they were out. That left Thornton's dog and he was doing exactly what Nancy had said he did. While Thornton was stacking him, he was swiveling his head like he was looking for something or somebody. In fact, he'd struggled to look around when he'd been brought into the ring, but Thornton had kept him choked up tight and he hadn't been able to move his head more than a fraction of an inch.

He sure did look like Cole, Emma thought as she looked him over top to bottom, head to tail. She watched him turn his head slowly until finally he was looking in her direction; she could see him scenting the air. His head stopped moving, his body visibly snapped to attention, and his gaze bore into hers. Emma watched his eyes as recognition registered and he just lit up. For a moment she was transfixed, afraid to believe what she knew she was seeing.

"Oh, my God…it's…it's Cole! It's him!" Emma said in a whisper so soft nobody heard her. Rather Joanie and Sally were reacting to Kirby and Tank who were straining at their leashes and barking, causing a bit of a disturbance.

"What's wrong with them?" Sally asked, trying to hush Kirby.

"It's Cole."

"What?"

"Thornton's dog, it's Cole!"

"Cole? Are you sure?"

"Yes!" Not realizing she was moving, and without thinking what she was doing, Emma called out in a loud, clear voice, "Cole!"

What happened next would be remembered for a long time in dog show circles. Upon hearing Emma call his name, Cole came alive and broke free from Thornton, snapping viciously at his hand as he did so. Then he ran toward Emma. Emma hopped over the ring fencing and ran toward Cole. They met somewhere in the middle, Cole's momentum taking Emma down when he crashed into her. It didn't matter; he was all over her, licking her face, his tail wagging a mile a minute, excited whines of pure happiness coming not from his throat, but his elated heart. Emma was crying and laughing at the same time, running her hands over him, and hugging him like she'd never let him go.

While Cole and Emma were having their jubilant reunion, Thornton had started to come forward to take his dog back. Kirby and Tank, whose attention had been on their long-lost friend, reacted automatically when they saw Thornton move. They took advantage of Joanie and Sally's inattention and slipped their collars by backing out of them. This was all done in the blink of an eye and once free, they lunged for Thornton. They stopped him long before he could get to Cole. Tank strategically positioned himself between Thornton's legs, snarling and snapping, and Kirby stood right in front of him about a foot away, baring her teeth and growling.

Joanie noticed the standoff once she took her eyes off Emma and Cole and realized there wasn't a dog on the end of her lead. Poking Sally in the ribs to get her attention, she pointed to where Thornton was being held at bay. With a shit-eating grin on her face, she slowly sauntered over. "Well, well, well. Looks like you've got some explaining to do, Thornton."

"What do you mean?"

"That dog is Cole and you know it."

"No, it isn't."

"Are you blind? Look at him. That's Emma's dog."

"You're wrong. Now call off these two mutts so I can get him."

"I don't think so, and if you don't want to be one nut short of a load, you won't move." Joanie gave the dogs a big smile. "Watch him, guys." Joanie turned her back and started to walk back toward Emma. She heard two ungodly, deep growls and turned around to see that Thornton had moved one foot forward.

"I'm warning you Bill, unless you want to sing soprano, you'd better not move. Tank might be small, but he's deadly, and Kirby, well, we don't know the extent of her talents yet. So it would behoove you to do exactly what I'm telling you." Joanie turned away and then back again, a sadistic grin on her face. "On second thought, asshole, make Tank's day. He's just dying to bite somebody. Go ahead and move."

Thornton's face blanched a sickly white, sweat breaking out on his forehead; he stayed motionless right where he was.

Needless to say, all activity in this ring and the rings adjacent to it had come to a complete halt. Soon the rings on the opposite side were at a standstill as word spread that something very unusual was happening in Ring Four. The amount of people on the outside of the ring had swelled to several hundred and was still growing. The judge in Ring Four had sent her steward to get the Show Chairman and the AKC representative.

Emma had since regained her feet. Cole was standing on his hind legs, his front legs on her shoulders, his paws encircling her neck with his head next to hers. Emma had her arms around his body, holding him close. They were just standing there, Emma murmuring soft words and Cole absorbing her nearness. Nobody approached them. It was obvious the boundless love they shared and the tremendous joy they were feeling at being reunited. Everyone, even the Show Chairman and AKC rep once they got to the ring, let them have their moment. There would be time enough to hash everything out and get to the truth.

Chapter Forty-Six

They were all in the superintendent's tent: Emma, Cole, Joanie, Tank, Sally, Kirby, Bill Thornton, the AKC rep, the Show Chairman, and the Superintendent. Outside the tent there were about a hundred people, mostly friends and acquaintances of the girls who wanted to know what was happening. It had been about thirty-five minutes since the reunion in the ring and the interested parties were verbally duking it out.

"This is not Emma's dog, Cole. It's Balanceran's Black Knight from the Balanceran Kennel in the Netherlands. His call name is Remy and Mr. Vincent Cappellini of Southport, Connecticut owns him."

"Yeah, and I'm the freakin' Queen of England, you jerk. Can't you see my jeweled crown?" Joanie interrupted.

"Ma'am, please," cautioned the rep.

"Look at his papers, the bill of sale. It's all right here." Thornton continued as he handed over the documents, which he'd retrieved from his motor home.

The rep, Mr. Thomas Alexander studied the papers and announced that they did seem to be in order.

"Now I'd appreciate it if I could have my dog back." Thornton took a step toward Cole, who had been glued to Emma's side since they'd left the ring. Cole, Tank, and Kirby reacted as a single unit, issuing a warning growl that made the hair on the back of the rep's neck stand up.

"Mr. Thornton, hold up there. Step back, please."

"This is ridiculous," Thornton complained, but he did step back. "All right, look, let's end this. Get the vet out here and have him scan the dog's microchip. That'll prove whose dog it is once and for all."

"Mrs. Rogers?" The rep turned to Emma for her input.

Emma, whose hand had never left Cole's head since they'd entered the tent, contemplated exactly what she was going to say before she spoke. When she did speak, it was in a tone filled with absolute resolution and finality.

"Mr. Alexander, let me tell you this. No matter what the results of reading that chip are, this is my dog. There is positively no doubt in my mind, or in the minds of my two friends and their dogs that this animal sitting beside me is multiple Best In Show winner, Ch. Scarlet Morning Midnite Star. He is known to everyone as Cole and he was stolen from me almost three months ago; I have been searching for him ever since. As a matter of fact, hundreds of people have been involved in the search and you may have noticed that there are flyers posted at this very show detailing the facts.

Earlier this year Mr. Thornton, on behalf of his client who I now know is this Mr. Cappellini, approached me in regards to buying Cole. Mr. Thornton offered me a great deal of money, which I turned down. He then offered me a blank check and I again refused the offer. When I informed Thornton that Cole was not for sale at any price, he became very angry. I believe his client did also and took steps to intimidate and harass me. I won't go into detail about what happened, but the sheriff's department is investigating. The trouble ended with me getting shot and Cole stolen.

Now I'm not sure how they did it, but they put a patch of pigmentation on his inner right rear leg in the shape of a cloud, which I'll bet matches the same in the dog that he's supposed to be. As far as the chip goes, I wouldn't be surprised if it's been switched. I don't know how difficult that would be, but I'm sure it's possible. Be that as it may, I know unequivocally that this is my dog and I can prove it."

"But how can you do that Mrs. Rogers? All the physical evidence, especially if the chip is matched to the imported dog, points to the fact that this is not your dog."

"Mr. Alexander, where is this dog sitting? Whose side is he not leaving? He's on lead, sir, but I'm not holding it." Emma held up her empty hands. "He could get up and leave any time he wishes. And not to rub it in, but whose head is he ready to take off?" Emma gave a cock-sure nod in Thornton's direction.

"Umm, yes, I see what you mean. All right, how do you mean to prove that this is indeed your dog?"

"In the ring."

"Excuse me, but did you say, in the ring?"

"Yes, sir, and to make sure there's no doubt, the Group Ring."

"The Group Ring. And what do you propose to do?"

"Why show him, of course, but in a very special way."

"How?"

"If I tell you, it'll spoil the surprise, Mr. Alexander."

"I don't know, Mrs. Rogers. It would be highly irregular to allow this."

"I know that, Mr. Alexander, and I wouldn't ask if I didn't feel that there will be absolutely no doubt as to who owns this dog after we're through in the ring."

The rep looked pensive for a few moments; he had never had to deal with a situation like this before and had no precedents to guide him. Finally he came to a decision. "This is extremely unusual, but I'm going to go along with it. I'm willing to try anything to clear this matter up."

"Now wait just a minute here," Thornton objected in a loud voice and again stepped forward.

He was once more put quickly back in place by the intimidating growls of three watchful canines who had themselves taken a step forward to insure Thornton's compliance.

"Mr. Thornton, it might be wise to be a bit more careful and I don't think I'd raise my voice if I were you. You seem to have made enemies of these three dogs," cautioned Mr. Alexander.

"Yes, sir. Are we through here? I need to make some phone calls."

"We need to discuss a few details, Mr. Thornton, and then you can leave, but I would do it very slowly."

It was agreed that Emma could have her chance in the Working Group Ring. They'd do a mock run-through of ring procedure, complete with a judge for Emma's benefit before the actual show judging. But it would be strictly up to the exhibitors if they wished to participate. Until that time, Cole was to stay there, in the tent. The vet on call would be contacted to see when they could bring Cole in to scan the microchip and to have the spot of pigmentation on his leg examined. Mr. Alexander wanted Cole to have no other contact with either party until the Group showing. Emma was extremely reluctant to leave him, but the rep guaranteed that he would be well taken care of.

So having no other choice in the matter, Emma and crew left the tent, but not before she'd reassured Cole. Dropping to her knees, she'd cuddled him close. "Listen, big boy, I have to leave now for a little while, but I'll be back. I promise, okay? These people will take good care of you; you don't have to worry about Thornton, all right? You be good and I'll be back before you know it. I promise, Cole. I'll be back."

Cole was pressing so close that Emma was in danger of tipping over. Emma was choking back tears and then Cole gave *her* a reassuring lick on the face. He moved back a bit, letting her know he'd be all right until she came back. As Emma got up to leave, Cole gave her a small woof and then lay down to wait until she returned.

Of course, nobody had counted on the tenacity of the other two canines once they'd found their friend; they absolutely refused to leave. No amount of pleading or tugging would get Kirby and Tank to give up their position on either side of Cole. If he was staying, so were they! The girls knew they weren't going to win this battle, so they convinced the rep to let the two dogs stay with Cole. Astute man that he was, he knew when he was beaten; he knew when they were all beaten. The two guardians remained where they were.

* * * *

The girls had no sooner cleared the front flap of the tent than Joanie started her inquisition. "What are you going to do? God, I can't believe we found him. What did you teach him? Is it the drool-flinging thing? 'Cause if it is, I don't think that's going to cut it."

"No, it's not the drool thing."

"Then what is it? What's he going to do? What trick did you teach him and how come we don't know about it?"

"Like I told Alexander, he's going to show himself."

"Well, what's so special about that? He shows himself every time he walks into the ring."

"Not like this."

"Meaning what? What's going to be different?"

"He'll be solo."

"Solo? Like what?"

"Like alone."

"You mean, all alone? Without you?"

"Yep."

"Honest to God."

"Yep."

"Solo. By himself. You're not with him."

"Exactly."

"Holy shit."

*   *   *   *

It seemed to take forever, but finally 3:00 arrived and the Working dogs assembled at ringside. The girls had gone over to the superintendent's tent and picked up the dogs and along with Mr. Alexander walked over to the ring. Thornton was already there and the rep informed both of them that the vet would see them in his office at 9:00 the following morning.

Word had spread rapidly throughout the show grounds of what was to take place and people were crowded three deep around the ring. When Mr. Alexander explained in detail what was needed to the Working Group exhibitors, every last one of them filed into the ring, anxious to help. The judge as it turned out was Mr. William Adamsley from Pittsburgh, Pennsylvania who had given Cole his second Best In Show. He was therefore familiar with the dog and knew how he performed.

Cole got a kiss from both Kirby and Tank and then from Sally and Joanie before they moved off a short distance so Emma could have a few minutes alone with him. She knelt down and took his big head in her hands and looked into his eyes.

"Cole, my boy, this is it. We're going to show 'em just who you are, okay? I know it's been a few months since we did this, but I know you'll remember and you'll do just fine. I love you Cole; no matter what happens, I love you and you're staying with me even if I have to steal you back. So don't worry; nobody's going to separate us again. Besides,

496

we've got crazy Joanie and Sally on our side and Sally knows how to use a gun. So come on, big boy, let's show 'em just who you belong to."

Emma gave him a kiss on the nose and Cole gave her a lick back. Then Emma stood up, adjusted the lead in her hand and together they walked into the ring like they owned it.

The judge directed Emma to the third spot in line and then waited for Emma to stack Cole. With a minimum of handling, Cole went into the stack and raised his mighty head and looked straight ahead, not moving a muscle. Emma stepped back, dropping the lead and let Cole take the spotlight.

At the judge's signal, the Group then moved around the ring with Emma and Cole moving together the way they always had, in perfect rhythm. Once everyone was back in place, the individual judging began. While the first two dogs were examined, Emma kept Cole in a perfect stance.

Now it was Cole's turn, and Emma and Cole knew that this was where the real show would start. Everyone's eyes had been glued to the two of them from the moment they'd entered the ring and now everybody was holding their breaths, waiting for what was going to happen next. Joanie and Sally had crossed their fingers, arms, legs and eyes, hoping that everything would go well. Tank and Kirby were sitting at attention, their eyes trained on their friend. At the same time they were acutely aware of where Thornton was, just in case he decided to make an unwise move.

Emma brought Cole out and set him up in the center of the ring. She stepped back and Mr. Adamsley came forward and examined Cole. Cole, once again, never moved and kept his head up at an almost arrogant angle. The judge stepped back and called for the down and back. Emma calmly walked up to Cole and took off the lead. The judge, along with the people both in and outside of the ring, looked and blinked, not quite believing what they'd just seen. Emma brought Cole around to the position he needed to be in and then with a hand signal, sent him out. Cole, trotting in his perfect gait, went down the side of the ring and when he got to the end, turned and came back in a perfectly straight line to where Emma and the judge were waiting, never once breaking stride. When he was about eight feet away, Emma gave him another hand signal to stop and stand. Cole did his thing and came down on all four feet at the same time. He stood like a rock, looking right at Emma.

Once Emma had taken the lead off, the ring had been bathed in silence. But now it erupted in cheers and applause that were deafening. Cole held his stack until Emma released him and then he was all over her. She calmed him down and then spoke to the judge. Mr. Adamsley nodded and Emma positioned Cole again in the correct position. The crowd quieted immediately, not knowing what more to expect. Emma gave Cole a different hand signal and he went out as before, but this time he executed a perfect triangular formation while keeping in correct gait. On returning to the judge, he did his now patented free stand and the crowd went absolutely wild.

Emma lined him up again and gave him another hand signal. Cole moved out and executed an "L" formation, which was rarely used anymore, and the most difficult of the four directives to perform. The crowd watched in stunned silence as Cole moved through it perfectly. After he completed the free stand the applause was thunderous.

But Emma and Cole weren't finished yet; they were going to give everything they had. Emma gave Cole the signal for the go around and he took off, circling the entire perimeter of the ring. Emma had moved to center ring and on signal, Cole joined her. He stopped perfectly, facing Emma. She waited a moment and then gave him a signal. He bowed low and she reciprocated. Then, they turned to the crowd and together, Emma and Cole bowed again. The crowd went ballistic; exhibitors inside the ring broke rank and surged forward to congratulate them and show their support. Mr. Adamsley conferred with Mr. Alexander and let him know that there was no doubt in his mind as to who the dog was and to whom he belonged. After that demonstration, there could be nobody who doubted who Cole was or that Emma owned him, and that included Mr. Thornton.

Joanie and Sally were doing one of their embarrassingly bad dances and whooping it up. In fact, this was the worst one that Emma had ever seen. Tank and Kirby were barking like mad and running in circles around their two crazy owners. Emma looked over at her two friends and their dogs and started laughing, knowing it was going to be another night of celebrating with wine and manhattans.

Only Bill Thornton stood alone, apart from the jubilant crowd. Mr. Alexander made his way over to him and simply asked, "Can you match that performance, Mr. Thornton?"

"No, sir, I can't. To be perfectly honest, the dog won't perform for me. He barely tolerates me."

"I see, and how is the dog with Mr. Cappellini? Will he work for him?"

"No, sir, he won't. In fact the dog hates him. Mr. Cappellini can't get near the dog without him growling and snapping."

"I think it's apparent then that Mrs. Rogers claim is accurate. The dog was stolen from her."

"Yes, sir, it looks that way."

"Mr. Thornton, appropriate measures will have to be taken."

"Yes, sir, I understand. But I have to say in my own defense, I didn't know, Mr. Alexander. I really didn't."

"Mr. Thornton…I believe you. Now as a gesture of good faith, I think it would serve us all well if you were to apologize to Mrs. Rogers. This must have been an extremely painful time for both her and the dog, not withstanding the fact that she was shot in the process of having her dog stolen."

"Yes, sir, I'll do it right away."

Emma was just emerging from the ring with Cole when Thornton approached her. She was still surrounded by well-wishers and Joanie and Sally had joined her. As Thornton drew nearer, Cole, Tank, and Kirby set up a protective barrier in front of Emma. When they were within three feet of each other, Thornton stopped with the AKC rep hovering in the background.

"Emma, I want to apologize to you. I had no idea that the dog was Cole. I really didn't. I had no reason to doubt he was anything other than what he was presented to me as. He certainly didn't act like Cole when he was with me."

"No, I don't imagine he did."

"So you believe me?"

"Yes, I believe you didn't know it was Cole, but you mistreated him, didn't you?"

"What? Mistreat him? Why would you think that?"

"Because I know how you treat the dogs you show and all I have to see is how Cole reacts to you and I know."

"Well, you can't…"

"Listen to me and listen very carefully," Emma interrupted. "If you ever so much as touch this dog again, I'll come after you with everything I've got and believe me it'll be more than you can possibly handle. Do I make myself perfectly clear, Mr. Thornton?"

"Yes, Mrs. Rogers, you do. Now if you'll excuse me." Eying all three dogs nervously, Thornton backed away to a safe distance and then turned and strode swiftly toward his motor home.

Crisis over, Mr. Alexander withdrew and went about what he had to do. The Group judging commenced, the crowd around Emma gradually dispersed, and the three friends were left alone to enjoy their moment of victory as they had many times before. Only this time, the win meant a great deal more than points or ranking.

As they walked back to their motor home, their arms linked and the dogs happily frolicking in front of them, any passerby would have heard Joanie announce as only she could, "Hell, it's after 4:00, you guys. We're behind schedule. Let's hurry and break out the booze, we've got a lot of damn celebrating to do!"

And son of a gun, that's exactly what they did.

Epilogue

Two weeks later

While everyday life in Glenwood had returned pretty much to normal, all hell was breaking loose in Connecticut.

When Connecticut authorities had been contacted by New York Sate law enforcement concerning Cappellini's involvement in the case, they had been only too willing to cooperate. It seems that the state of Connecticut, in conjunction with the federal government, had been involved with an investigation of their own into Cappellini's activities for years. His illegal business practices had been the target of their probing, but up to this point he had managed to avoid prosecution. Now, the charges of conspiracy to commit murder, attempted murder, and grand theft leveled by the State of New York might be able to accomplish that which had so far eluded Connecticut and the federal government, namely putting Cappellini behind bars.

A search of Cappellini's cell phone records and the subsequent investigation brought Jasper and his crew into the indictment. The muscle-for-hire outfit was well known to the Connecticut authorities and already had an established link to Cappellini. Emma and her friends were shocked to find out that Connie Stark a.k.a. Mary Cooper had been deeply involved in the plot to steal Cole.

Dr. Morgan, whether he had an attack of conscience or simply knew the gravy train was about to end, turned state's evidence to avoid prosecution and more or less put the nail in the coffin when he confessed his part in it and led investigators to the slain dog's burial spot.

The veterinarian from the show, Dr. Randolf White had already confirmed that the spot of pigmentation had been tattooed on Cole's leg. After he had scanned the microchip and found that the number did indeed match the one registered to the imported dog belonging to Cappellini, he had meticulously examined Cole's skin between his shoulders blades. After painstakingly parting small sections of hair repeatedly, he'd found the tiny scar that Morgan had left.

Bill Thornton was having problems of his own. Prompted by Emma's accusations of mistreatment, Mr. Alexander on behalf of the AKC, launched a probe in connection with the Professional Handlers Association of which Thornton was a member. Complaints and testimony were still being compiled, but it looked like Thornton would be facing disciplinary action from both the AKC and the PHA.

The only one who avoided being caught in this legal housecleaning was Wilhelm Schmidt. True, he was safely ensconced in his villa in the south of France and extradition from that country would be a legal nightmare, but that wasn't the reason he wasn't indicted with the rest. No one, including Cappellini, brought his name into the mix as the shooter. The embattled multi-millionaire knew from the first time he'd used Wilhelm, that should anything go wrong, he was on his own. To bring Wilhelm's name into it would be signing his own death warrant. The dangerously well-connected mercenary had a very long reach when it came to vengeance and Cappellini, along with his accomplices, weren't about to temp fate.

* * * *

Back in Glenwood, the girls were setting up for the last run of Tank's favorite game. The day had been really busy with large deliveries coming in the morning and a deluge of customers all day. People were still coming in to talk about "the ordeal", the tag that Angie Newmann had christened the whole affair. She'd been an almost daily fixture in the shop for over a week now, and Emma was once again on the verge of doing Angie grievous bodily harm or vacating the shop herself for an extended period of time. Since she'd just gotten back into the swing of things herself at the store, she'd opt for getting Angie drunk and pushing her out into traffic. Joanie thought it sounded like a great plan and if Joanie approved, how could you go wrong!

The deliveries had brought in a fresh supply of white Styrofoam peanuts and Tank had demanded his due. Well, why not? They hadn't done it in a while. So after they closed for the day, the girls had set up for *the game*.

Tank had taken eleven runs and was now on his last one. Cole had looked to Emma with an expression that said, "Enough, already." With Tank's last flying dive into the peanuts, Cole bolted out into the main store area, taking adhering peanuts with him. The back room was, by this time, a complete mess with peanuts scattered all over the floor and many more clinging to the boxes the girls had stacked in the corners of the room. They were on top of the big table, they were attached to the walls by static electricity, and now with Cole's help, they were moving out the door.

"Well, we'd better contain this mess and get it cleaned up," Emma said as she surveyed the shambles that had once been their very neat back room.

"No, let's leave it."

"Leave it? Joanie, we've got class in little less than an hour."

"Yeah, I know. That's the whole idea."

"What is?"

"This." And she lifted her arms to encompass the entire room.

"You're going to have to explain. I'm not following."

"God, Emma, I'm going to have to whip you back into shape, girl. You're not thinking deviously enough any more."

"Forgive me, I've been traumatized. Now explain to me why we're leaving this mess."

"Okay, look. When the ladies show up for class, we explain that we put the peanuts down for atmosphere. You know, to get them in the mood. Some of them are working on snowmen so voila, snow. Get it."

"Yeah, but I'd hate to tell you where."

"Cute, Em."

"When do we get to the part about getting this mess cleaned up?"

"Well, at the end of class, you dope. We ply 'em with liquid refreshment all night and by the time class is over, they'll be a little tipsy and they'll do anything we ask. So we put 'em to work cleaning up all the 'snow'."

"Tell me, do you stay awake at night thinking these things up?"

"Yeah, as a matter of fact, I do."

"A lot?"

"Yeah."

"Oh, Lord, help us."

"No, no, we don't need Him. We've got you and me."

"Maybe you don't need Him, but as long as I hang around with you, I certainly do."

"Right, Em. Tell me another one."

"I don't think I should."

"Come on, let's set up for class. This is going to be fun. You'll see."

"I can hardly wait."

"Me either."

Emma's sarcasm wasn't getting through, no surprise there. Joanie was oblivious to everything but hatching her own plan. It was going to be an interesting night that was for sure and strange as it may sound, a completely normal one.

About the Author

Diane Bridenbaker has had a life-long love affair with dogs and has been involved with her canine friends in one way or another for the past thirty-five years. She's experienced in both conformation showing and obedience training and was fortunate enough to successfully assist in the delivery of several healthy litters.

She currently resides in Glenwood, New York, where she owns and operates a country gift shop. She also works part-time as an orthodontic assistant.

Ms. Bridenbaker is the proud mother of three grown children and loving grandmother to their three offspring.

This is her first novel.

Printed in the United States
35017LVS00001B/31-510